CRY

OF THE FLYING RHINO

Ivy Ngeow

**Winner of the International Proverse Prize
2016**

Proverse Hong Kong

Cry of the Flying Rhino
by Ivy Ngeow.
First edition published in paperback in Hong Kong
by Proverse Hong Kong, under sole and exclusive licence,
November 2017.
ISBN: 978-988-8228-97-3
Copyright © Ivy Ngeow November 2017.

Distribution (Hong Kong and worldwide):
The Chinese University Press of Hong Kong,
The Chinese University of Hong Kong,
Shatin, New Territories, Hong Kong SAR.
Email: cup-bus@cuhk.edu.hk; Web: https://www.chineseupress.com
Distribution (United Kingdom):
Christine Penney, Stratford-upon-Avon, Warwickshire CV37 6DN, UK.
Email: chrisp@proversepublishing.com

Alternate edition available from: https://www.createspace.com/7328621

Enquiries to:
Proverse Hong Kong, P.O. Box 259, Tung Chung Post Office,
Tung Chung, Lantau Island, NT, Hong Kong SAR, China.
Email: proverse@netvigator.com; Web: www.proversepublishing.com
-

The right of Ivy Ngeow to be identified as the author
of this work has been asserted by her
in accordance with the Copyright, Designs and Patents Act 1988.

Printed in Hong Kong by Artist Hong Kong Company,
Unit D3, G/F, Phase 3, Kwun Tong Industrial Center,
448-458 Kwun Tong Road, Kowloon, Hong Kong SAR, China.

Cover image, 'Green Jungle', by George Hodan, is a free stock photo from Public
Domain Pictures: (publicdomainpictures.net). License: CC0 1.0 Universal.
Cover design by Ivy Ngeow.
Map of Malaysia and Borneo by Ivy Ngeow.

British Library Cataloguing in Publication Data.
A catalogue record for this book is available
from the British Library.

Cry Of The Flying Rhino

Ivy Ngeow

Proverse Hong Kong

2017

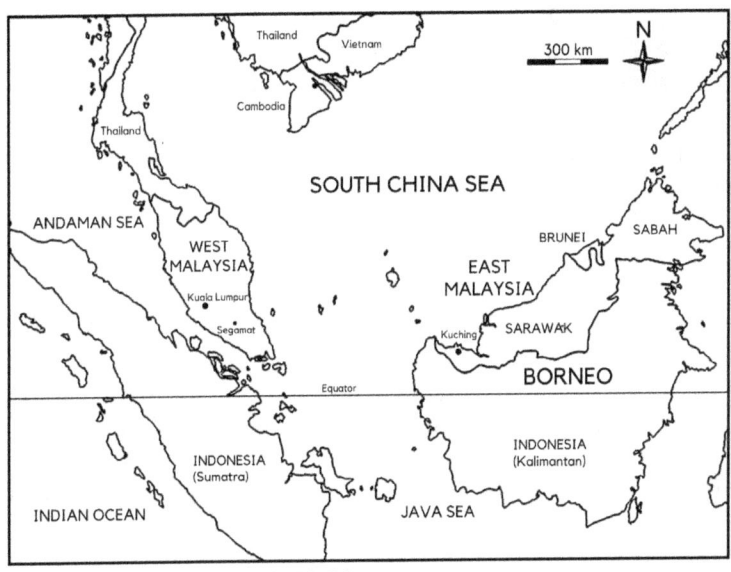

MAP OF MALAYSIA AND BORNEO

CRY OF THE FLYING RHINO is set in 1996 Malaysia and Borneo, told from multiple viewpoints and in multiple voices. Malaysian Chinese family doctor Benjie Lee has had a careless one night stand with his new employee – mysterious, teenage Talisa, the adopted daughter of a wealthy, crass Scottish plantation owner, Ian, in the provincial Malaysian town of Segamat. Talisa's arms are covered in elaborate tattoos, symbolic of great personal achievements among the Iban tribe in her native Borneo. Talisa has fallen pregnant and Ian forces Benjie to marry her. Benjie, who relished his previous life as a carefree, cosmopolitan bachelor, struggles to adapt to life as a husband and father. Meanwhile, Minos – an Iban who has languished ten years in a Borneo prison for a murder he didn't commit – is released into English missionary Bernard's care. One day, Minos and his sidekick and fellow ex-convict Watan appear in Segamat, forcing Benjie to confront his wife's true identity and ultimately his own fears. Are the tattoos the key to her secrets?

IVY NGEOW was born and raised in Johor Bahru, Malaysia. A graduate of the Middlesex University Writing MA programme, Ivy won the 2005 Middlesex University Press Literary Prize out of almost 1500 entrants worldwide. She has written non-fiction for *Marie Claire*, *The Star*, *The New Straits Times*, South London Society of Architects' Newsletter and *Wimbledon* magazine. Her fiction has appeared in *Silverfish New Writing* anthologies twice, *The New Writer* and on the BBC World Service. Her story 'Funny Mountain' was published by Fixi Novo in an anthology *Hungry in Ipoh*.

Ivy won first prize in the Commonwealth Essay Writing Competition 1994, first prize in the Barnes and Noble Career Essay Writing competition 1998 and was shortlisted for the David T K Wong Fellowship 1998 and the Ian St James Award 1999. Her debut novel, *Cry of the Flying Rhino*, won the Proverse Prize 2016.

Ivy has been a highly-accomplished multi-instrumental musician since childhood and won fifth prize (out of 850 entrants) in the 2006 1-MIC (Music Industry Charts) UK Award for her original song, 'Celebrity'. Her second novel, *Heart of Glass,* is published by Unbound (UK).

To my family

Author's acknowledgements

Thanks to my lecturers Sue Gee, Josie Barnard and Ferdinand Dennis from Middlesex University for being the first readers of this book, Jason S Polley for the preface, Lawrence Gray, Robert Raymer and Vaughan Rapatahana for the advance commentaries, Isabel White, my former literary agent who has always had complete faith in me and my writing, the organisers and judges of the Proverse Prize, Professor Gillian Bickley and everyone in the Proverse Publishing team for their tireless devotion and efforts in making this book not just a reality but a work of art. To my family and friends and those I have not been able to individually mention, special thanks for your love, support, chats, hugs, food and beverage through all the highs and lows of my writing life.

Preface

"My shoes felt like sinking boats"

My first visit to the legendary Borneo was in February 1999. I landed in Brunei Darussalam's Bandar Seri Begawan after a 48-hour trip. It had begun in Ottawa, with stops in Dulles, Dubai, and Kuala Lumpur, where a one-night hotel was provided before the final three-hour leg to "Bandar," as anyone who was anyone referred to the "Brunei" capital.

Brunei: that quarter-million strong sultanate, British until the mid-80s (so two decades longer than its Eastern/Borneo Malaysia neighbours Sarawak and Sabah) and recently renowned for its free amusement park Jerudong, which the profligate Prince Jefri reputedly had built in a bid to make Brunei the Bahamas of South-east Asia.

Sundowners – which I learned meant "drinks at sunset" to the Shell Oil helicopter pilots and EOs, Canuck & Brit English teachers, and the bevy of welcoming socialite wives who meticulously planned all the entertainment for this alarmingly male cast of breadwinners – were, as in the Bahamas (I had no reason not to surmise), in serious demand.

Alcohol in a sultanate? In a place where police maintained Sharia law? In a nation-state where religious police enforced Islamic moral order? A country where you left one-Brunei-dollar coins on your car's windscreen when you parked, so the meter-maid or -man could exact the precise half-hourly fee. Downtown Kuala Belait: an urban zone where there were always coins left on the windscreen when you returned to the vehicle. There was a comfort to that, but also a sense of Old Testament "fear," as in the archaic denotation "dread and reverence."

Borneo.

A few days after arriving in Brunei, and this in preparation for an after-sundowner cocktail pre-party to a Valentine's Day Ball to be held on the estate of Shell Asia's British CEO (whose wife crazily hailed from the capital of Canada's smallest province – Charlottetown, PEI – and who agonizingly missed "the wonders of Damascus terribly since relocating to this humid, jungly hellfire outpost"), it was time for my first "booze run."

Cross the border from KB into nearby Miri, Sarawak. Buy a flat of this. A case of that. Two bottles of this. Tiger. Bombay. Jack. Diligently complete and have validated hairsplitting=customs forms.

Muslims need not apply. Not exactly the Bahamas that movies and travel brochures advertised. Also, not exactly the Brunei that the West and the East advertised either.

*

Ivy Ngeow's *Cry of the Flying Rhino* summoned my near photographic memory – *memotret memori* in my elementary yet lyrical *bahasa* – of the above details with an almost divine clarity, the type of revelation that can only ever be conjured through the ineffable forces of spiritual *and* literary epiphany. Not unlike Nikita Lalwani's *The Village* (2012), Arundhati Roy's *The God of Small Things* (1997), Upamanyu Chatterjee's *English, August* (1988), Anthony Burgess' *The Long Day Wanes* (1956-9), Malcolm Lowry's *Under the Volcano* (1947), and George Orwell's *Burmese Days* (1934), Ngeow transports her readers to another time and place, to another world we know is ours; albeit, a world we can only ever truly visit in parallel, only ever really grasp figuratively, only hear, see, smell, touch, taste via the *machina* of fiction. A key difference, however, is that Ngeow's *Cry of the Flying Rhino* is not, for present-day readers, "another time." It is certainly another place. It is Borneo, but it is *now* (well, it's the mid-1990s). Like Lalwani's Ashwer, Roy's Ayemenem, Chatterjee's Madna, Burgess' Perak, Lowry's

Quauhnahuac, and Orwell's Kyauktada, Ngeow's Segamat in the Peninsula's southcentral *and* Kuching in Borneo's northwest are places we come to know intimately through the dogged doings of vastly unique characters – personages from a large scope of social and ethnic spectrums, individuals whose stories we increasingly crave as we speed toward the at once incredible and inevitable intersection of the novel's five main arcs.

There's the jeep-driving Ian MacF, the rubber plantation owner, a man's man who drinks Tiger beer pretty much exclusively. Unafraid to wield, and fire, a gun, he's a self-made chief whose Scottish accent deepens by the day despite his decades-long full-time investment to Segamat and his supervisorial familiarity with Malay and Tamil. There's BMW man Benjie Lee, returned to open his GP clinic in his hometown at his generous parents' behest after carousing London's pubs (and coeds) for the duration of his studies. There's chauffeured Talisa, his indeterminately-aged yet young, tattooed, *orang asli* Iban wife, who's by force of will and cunning, escaped her longhouse life in the jungles of Sarawak. There's the character Minos, newly christened as Luke, the erstwhile national park pillager turned CD and DVD bootlegger, a likeable *indigenous* Iban ex-convict carefully co-plotting his deserved retribution for his wrongful, and officially pardoned, decade-long prison sentence. There's Bernard the English missionary, who (so his letters to his former home, his personal diary entries, and his courageous connections with convicts and complaints attest) has long cultivated, and acquired the understanding to empathize with, "the arcane world of spirits and secrets" – spirits and secrets that only a writer of Ngeow's talent and compassion can expose and make such a virtue of.

*

Since that 1999 arrival in Borneo as Chinese New Year and Valentine's Day almost overlapped (they had last literally coincided in 1953 and did not do so again until 2010), I've returned to Borneo many times: Bangar, Miri, Mulu, Kuala Belait, Kota Kinabalu, Tawau, Semporna, Sipadan, as well as tens of scuba diving sites in the Celebes and Sulu seas. One of my best friends, with whom I dive for a week every six months, is an instructor of not small renown, originally from KK. He's spent the bulk of his fifteen-year career in and around Semporna and Sipadan. Like Benjie in *Cry of the Flying Rhino*, his surname is Lee. Yet, unlike Ngeow's Dr Lee, who favours English, professional diver Lee is conversant – and quite comfortable – in more than a handful of languages, including Hakka, English, Mandarin, Malay, Cantonese, and several local and state dialects. He's forever lighthearted. Whenever trouble arises (as it can do when a jumble of holidaying strangers of diverse underwater skills and unique mother tongues converge in hopes of sighting Hammerheads and Hawksbills), he reflexively responds with "I'm from Borneo, man!" followed by an insouciant and reassuring smile.

I can't wait to send my best Borneo friend this book. It's helped me to know him better, to understand better the aplomb and bounteousness that he and his kindred-spirit cousin, who's an admired young politician, forever happily offer. This is what the best people do. This is what the best literature does. This is what *Cry of the Flying Rhino* does: it just keeps on giving. Then it gives a little more – and this not only to Borneo residents, Peninsular inhabitants, and Old Malaysian Hands. Anyone impressed, anyone imprinted upon and inspired by Lalwani, Roy, Chatterjee, Burgess, Lowry, or Orwell, will be correspondingly affected by Ngeow. She gifts a serious slice of the world to her readers, to a worldwide audience of particular World Englishes; in this case, a skillful sampling of Malaysian Englishes, their select speakers, and their unique sociocultural mixes and milieus.

Jason S Polley,
Associate Professor, Hong Kong Baptist Univesity

1

Benjie

2005

Until I crashed my BMW into a rubber tree, I had not woken up.

My gripped fingers tingled on the steering wheel. Thoughts crawled in my head like awakening insects. I shook them off abruptly. The sensation, like worn-off anæsthesia, made my skin burn with realisation and rage. I had made my mind up. I didn't want to be like my forefathers, living their shadowy deferential lives fearing authority, quietly banking their fistful sums so that their children could go to Uni abroad. I wasn't an immigrant. I was second generation Chinese. I took orders from no one, least of all Talisa, the employee pregnant with my *child*, and Ian, her father. *They* were the immigrants. I had to make that call. I had to get my message across tonight.

The headlights dazzled the tree and the windscreen wipers still danced madly, unaware of the car having stalled. This was not just any tree in Segamat, but a rubber tree on one of the many plantations owned by Ian MacFarlane, the town's richest, most dreaded man. I was on my way to the Gagak Country Club to meet him, but nature took hold of the steering. The evening was blood black and the monsoon rain came down heavily. I skidded....

It was no accident. It started with a seedling called the *Hevea brasiliensis*, brought by the British from the Amazon. Since that day a hundred and twenty-eight years ago, acres and acres of plantations had replaced wilderness to bring money in, which now was taken out to bring in sophisticated German cars instead. Nature just smashed mine up. The rubber ball had bounced back to me. Vorsprung....

I looked out of the car, my heart pounding from the collision, my ears whistling from the impact noise. *Traum* was dream, in

German. I was in my own trauma, but I came to my senses. The cruelty of my own random misgivings astonished me. I was in pain. Uninjured, but nevertheless in pain.

My car would not start. I tried a few times but the engine would not turn over. I'd have to abandon it. The bonnet looked crushed but I couldn't tell the full extent of the damage from sitting inside. There was no signal on my phone, so I would have to run to the timber shack bus-stop and try again there.

Earlier today, at lunchtime when there were no patients, Talisa urinated on a stick. When two blue lines came up, I was speechless. I had shares in rubber. How could Ian, who tapped our natural resources, who represented the infallibility of condoms, have let me down? The Year of the Rooster, supposedly the most romantic of the twelve Chinese zodiac animals, was beginning horribly wrong for me.

'I don't understand,' I said finally, shaking my head, still staring at the two blue lines.

She made a cursory shoulder movement. Not even bothering to say, 'nor I', she completed her shoulder movement and just shrugged. She *shrugged*. She yawned like a cat and scratched her neck, as though she'd had enough of this boredom. Then she pouted and smiled.

I resisted climbing out of the wreckage of my car when I remembered that face. I stared at the steamed up windscreen and allowed myself the full memory of our exchange today, the biting pleasure of my misery.

'You'll just have to tell me Dah,' she said, at which I crumpled. Not only him, I thought, but Ming Jen, my girlfriend who was safely 200 miles away in the city of Johor Baru.

Talisa's Scottish accent and temperament distressed me each time she spoke because she was of the Iban race of Borneo, formerly known as the Sea Dayaks. She left ten years ago, but provincial life in Segamat had not changed her. She was adopted by Ian eight years ago when her mother, Ian's housekeeper, died. Living in Ian's eccentric household only made Talisa more alien. She had a primordial strangeness about her, a freedom, that made her a predator, and I, her prey.

I mentioned that with a little assistance from the patient herself, I could perform a termination. Visions of Johnny Depp in *From Hell* sprang to mind, except I would do a better job than

14

the Ripper. At my suggestion, she threw her lunch at me. I asked if she perhaps wanted another doctor to carry out the task rather than myself?

"No!" she screamed.

There were rice and chicken bits everywhere, even in the paper clip tray. I had to remind her who the boss was. She then told Shue Ling the doctor had made a total mess of his lunch. Shue Ling, being full-time staff, should pick up the pieces. Part-time staff like herself didn't do 'heavy cleaning'. I knew it was too late. I had glimpsed the real Talisa only today.

What I didn't see was the real me – how could I, a twenty-six-year-old GP, a pillar of the community, have made this crazy mistake? Pillock of the community, more like. Ming Jen, a fellow doctor, my long-distance girlfriend whom I met in Uni, would ask the same question.

It would crush me to tell her because I knew she would not blame me but herself, and that was so much worse. She had already forgiven me over another indiscretion during a medical conference in Bali two years ago. She must have known then it was the beginning of the end. Now Ming Jen would be totally broken.

But already she had faded. It had happened well before the two blue lines. It had happened five weeks ago in fact.

Once the vision of Ming Jen's expression was completely replaced from my wet windscreen with the post-tantrum image of Talisa calling Ian from my surgery telephone, I got out of the car.

I was drenched as soon as the car door opened. I ran to the bus stop. Under the tin roof, I checked my phone. There was no signal. My shoes felt like sinking boats. It was not far, perhaps a fifteen minute sprint, if I cut through the banana groves rather than take the route through the rubber estate. I could not walk along the highway when visibility was this low.

I ran past the tapioca shrubs. I skidded on the mud. Banana trees which looked like fans, their flowers dangling like red genitalia, appeared leering and mocking. Underneath me, the ground slithered from moss, dead leaves, fallen trees, reptiles and amphibians. The earth sank from the weight of the monsoon.

A monkey shrieked.

WHEN I GOT TO the familiar tiled verandahs of the GCC, I hoped no one would see me. I looked like an asylum escapee, the living dead or a complete and utter mug.

'I... had... a... car... accident,' I said to the doorman, who of course, let me in once he saw who I was. I'd been a member since I graduated three years ago. I sneezed twice. I went straight into the Bar where Ian was, naturally, perched. I burst in sodden in mud and leaves. I shivered in the air-conditioning, my clothes sticking to me like cling film. My shoes squelched great torrents of floodwater even as I advanced towards the Bar, a monster.

'You look terrible,' said Ian.

'Thanks,' I said. I didn't just *luke* it.

'Get yourself a fucken drink for chrissakes. You deserve it.'

'Why do I de...' I sneezed again, 'deserve it?'

'You're getting married! Wa-hey! Talisa's told me the good news. You're in the family now.'

Oh, the good *noose*. In the family way now.

'I don't want the child and we're not getting married,' I said. That was the one phone call I had to make, the one message I had to deliver, and now I had delivered it.

'What? Why not?'

'Because we're not. I'm too young to be tied down. Besides, I have a girlfriend, and she's...'

'Let me put it to you clearly. And this is like man to man, you hear.' He leant closer like he was my dad or something, trying to share a homegrown piece of heartwarming advice.

'Uh. Huh.' I listened, convulsing, confused and shivering.

'There is no such thing as the right person.' He delivered each word with such emphasis that their collective weight alternated between my eyes like flashing lights. 'Every person could be the right person. But there is such a thing as the right thing. You need to do the right thing, young man.'

What *pairson pairson*? I was seething. The berk was only a landowner because he came here decades ago and beat some poor old Ceylonese farmer to a pulp before the toddy-soaked chap signed over the land. Being white here meant being a figure of authority. He addressed me the same way as he spoke to his employees whom he had to rise above. If he was civil, they could revolt. He would not be able to run his plantations with order and strict discipline. 'Don't be too soft on them,' I overheard him

16

saying to another white man once in the bar. I didn't need to be told who "them" meant.

Ian was only in the little railway town of Segamat, the Swindon of Malaysia, so that he could continue to lord it over everyone. I was London-educated, I knew all my pastas and all my Chardonnays; Ian subsisted on boiled offal and he was telling me what to do? In London he would not be sipping Tiger and practising his golf swing. He would be some jobbing builder picking re-usable radiators out of other people's skips.

'I'm not getting married,' I replayed my message to him and turned around. I walked out of the bar.

The next thing I knew I was on the floor of the verandah. I pictured myself as the Ceylonese farmer signing away life and land on some literally bloody dotted line, carefully avoiding one or two knocked-out incisors on the piece of paper.

Thankfully, it was a quiet night because of the bad weather. Even the doorman had stepped inside his cabin to watch telly. No one could see that Dr Lee was sprawled on the floor, gasping, groaning, wet as a flapping bleeding carp. Another punch flew out at my stomach. I could see Ian's shadow above me, his beery breath stank like a bin. Bastard. He dared to lay his cartoon uncouthness on me. This was what he and his ancestors had done to my people for over a hundred years: here, have a school, have a hospital and a main road, have a slap.

I was not some piece of junk like him. I was not going to hit back. But as soon as I was on my legs, my right fist sailed towards his mandibles. Pointless, all that energy which had gone into it. Ian dodged and I missed his jawline completely.

'Listen to me, you scum,' he hissed while he grabbed my shoulders, tearing my Ben Sherman shirt. 'This is not London, OK mate? You do not fuck up and fuck off. And don't even think for a minute that you're going to fight a Scotsman.'

I thought he spat at me. Perhaps it was the rain spitting. It hurt me to stand up for myself but I did. I growled with pain, less with pride.

'I got married. Best thing I ever did. Loved it so much I did it twice,' he chuckled. 'Do the right thing, for fuck's sake. Have a fucken family. You're bloody old enough. What you waiting for? You weren't going to marry that lass either, were you?'

I saw and felt his shadow but everything was out of focus. The man was hideous and insane, and his rubber plantations which covered Segamat, would be a constant reminder of my idiocy.

'Were you?' He shouted, reminding me that in fact he had asked a question. He nagged me and now he was hugging me, welcoming me into the family. 'We're going back to the bar, aye, we're going to make sure you understand everything about family life.'

I was still groaning and panting. I sneezed again, and my snot was bloody. Seeing my speechlessness seemed to excite him even more.

'If you do not do the right thing, I'll make sure everyone in this town knows what kind of doctor you are. Don't you forget I've been in rubber long before you were born. I know everybody and everybody knows me. You won't escape. If you do, I'll break your legs, I swear.'

He laughed at the breaking ye legs bit. Was my...my *child*...going to swear like this man? The question throbbed in my mind as I trudged back to the bar. I saw my reflection in the bar mirror – I had panda eyes and a goatee of blood, my nose swollen like a giant strawberry.

'Quick,' barked Ian to the barman. 'Large scotch please for the gentleman, he's had a car accident, ain't you, poor lad, and I think he's in shock.' He propped me on the stool like I was a puppet. He shook me by the shoulders every few seconds to make sure I was *compos mentis*, that I wasn't going to conk out and that I understood every word he said.

My drink poured, the barman went off to the pool bar and retrieved a large white towel. Ian covered my head like a tent and rubbed his puppet's head and shoulders all over with the towel. I was relieved at the warm, dry, darkness. Ian was more than one person's father. Even the evil were kind to their own. Ian must have already considered me family. Something about the intimacy of being thoroughly dried weakened me yet made me trust him. After swimming, my dad used to do the same to me when I was a boy.

I peeped through my towel tent. In the corner of my panda eye, I could see Talisa sitting calmly in the sofa area of the bar, in her dreamy way, sucking a bile-yellow drink from a straw, probably pineapple juice. She was reading a fashion magazine, I could not care to notice which. The memory of us having sex, with our clothes on, pierced my mind momentarily. I thought of her slim muscular body, her slight legs, her round, high breasts that you'd see on ancient tomb carvings. I felt sick. She looked over at me. Her eyes shone with the urban innocence of a child mugger.

'Don't worry, I'm going to drive you home tonight,' Ian slurred, 'Make sure you get some rest! You're not going to get much sleep when the baby comes.' Now I had to trust this man's drunk driving too. The rollercoaster ride had just begun. *Wa-hey.*

2

Minos

5.47am Kuching Prison, Sarawak, BORNEO

I already make friend real quick. Cos I know everybuddy born good. Like I. Tho they lock-up in here. Cos why they is called 'everybuddy'? Cos everybuddy is a buddy. And why they is called 'inmate'? Cos everybuddy 'in' is a mate! They make some mistake that they don't mean to, and the mistake become big problem and even God cannot save them.

That's what happen to people.

When I look in bathroom mirror like everybuddy in the morning when we shave, I look how skinny I is now. I look like some dead man. Even slightly greeny-yellow skin, though digging in the sun all day. The veins show but they also greeny. I look like I already part of plants. Long time ago I make wrong turning and now I never find way back. And I ain'ts done nobuddy wrong.

That is what is eating I. I got blunt hair cut, like girl's. If new inmate, they have very short hair like army. But I now been in here long time. I can have TV in room. I is like friend of the taxpayer.

I got TV. Cos they not scared I electrocute myself, cos I already in many many years, why electrocute myself with TV when I can watch TV? TV is world beyond. Is the good world I already forget about. Thank God for colour TV. For Amerika, for Inglan, especially God bless Amerika. If guard know I think all this, I surely get beat up. Guard is behind, like tiger prowling.

I carry on have shower. Watan is beside I, also shower. I look down, on wet floor. Is like big landscape, all water soapy running off somewhere, but where? Some drain. Is so filthy, it make I sick. Water is grey, full of pubes, soap, grease, all the thing I so hate about everybuddy. And floor is like up and down landscape made of sheet rubber cos there be no tiles. If got tiles, when tiles break, they become weapon.

'I hear you gwan out soon. Three months?'

That is Watan. Yeah, it sounds like Satan. But is just opposite. I only see Watan once or twice before. But I know Watan is good bloke. But fat. He always fat, eat or no eat.

'Yeah, I been here already ten years, Watan. Actually in for fifteen.'

''Snough.'

And then guard coming, so we shut up short while. And we speak to each other in Inglish. We from different tribe, Watan is Bidayuh, a Land Dayak, and if we speak in Malay the guard will understand what we sayin. So we speak a kind of like island Inglish, like we learn from mishnaries like Pastor Bernard. Who give we Inglish and love of God. And that is GOOD.

Guard go 'way.

'What about you, Watan?'

'I been here ten months. And I got only another month to go. But other block go for renovation. So they put me here. Actually I only spose to be here five months. But lawyer *buruk*! Useless!'

There is actually another block? A world that is beyond mine. I been here so long and I don't even know that! There sure is lots of concrete in this place, man, and it surrounded by miles and miles of thick jungle. No wonder for long time I not see hornbill go past my barred window, or even hear laugh of small monkey.

'What you gwan do, Minos? You gwan miss this place?'

'I get my own TV. Then I not miss so much!'

3

Benjie

I had seen her once, months ago at the Club. I had never given her a second thought or glance. She was just a girl. She was cute, but cute girls were everywhere. Girls in miniskirts, whose dads were company directors, played pool at the Club and said things which could make a bloke raise an eyebrow.

I wasn't a company director. I was a young upstart. The only reason I came back from the UK was because my dad shelled out for me to open my own practice. I was bribed into leaving the pubs of Old Street, where I'd downed many a tiddly-wink with the lads. I abandoned inclusive European circles for Asian social exclusivity. My family handed me a means-tested elitist Club membership. Through the Club, I met Ian and others of his standing, from whom I received a database of patients who worked on the estates and plantations. I left the world of provincial B&Bs and hostels while working as a student in NHS hospitals. Instead I was now invited to world-famous five-star resorts in the name of medical and pharmaceutical conferences. Bali. Phuket. Maldives. The world looked upon me in my gilt cage in which I was still gnawing on my silver spoon like it was a lolly.

Within four hours of Ian casually asking me if there was a position going, the girl was in touch. Her Scottish accent set her apart. She was taken into Ian's house as a child and was taught by a private tutor, a Scottish woman, wife of one of the planters hired by Ian. My London-trained ears could understand any accent but no one else could. She would not be able to get a job in Carrefour or any of the rollerblading hypermarkets.

She had no CV as she had only just left school. The only job she ever had was helping Ian with the administration and payroll at the estate on Sundays. Her real skill was languages. She was fluent in more than five: English, Mandarin Chinese, Malay,

Iban, Tamil and three other Borneo dialects – Kayan, Penan and Melanau.

'Even Tamil?' I asked, perhaps a too excitedly. She shrugged. It was the first time I had seen her shrug. It confused me when applicants shrugged at interviews. What did it mean? Was I too easy on them? Anyway, she said yes, she had learnt Tamil on the estate. The tappers were all Indian, I remembered.

'Once you know more than two languages,' she said, 'it's easy, the others all fall into place.'

'Fall into place,' I repeated, like I was under hypnosis. But *Iban*. Yes. I knew a little about Iban, from my schoolboy's knowledge of South East Asia. Iban and the other Borneo dialects were Austronesian languages related to Malay.

What did I remember? She asked. It seemed I was now the interviewee, not the interviewer. I scratched my chin like a cat. Then it came back, and I was glad my brain hadn't been pickled in medical school formaldehyde during my wild days.

'Iban is the largest of twenty-five Borneo tribes,' I announced in a leonine manner. She smiled, perhaps thinking that I was not that ignorant. Ian had filled me in already. When she was eight years old, she left the island of Borneo with her mother. She referred to her mother as *Ebu*, which is Iban for 'mum'. Ian said her mother worked as a cleaner and housekeeper in his household for two years. She passed away from TB, which was why Talisa came to be adopted by Ian at age ten.

'All these years since Ebu passed away, and still I am an immigrant to Segamat,' said Talisa. 'In fact, in the Kayan language, *Iban* means *immigrant*, and that is how I will always see myself.'

I agreed that no matter how long one had been in a small town, one didn't really become a part of it, whereas you would be a part of a big city the day you moved into it. I was only here because I was born and brought up here.

She said I had a nice watch. My immediate reaction was to look at my wrist. Oh that, I said.

'It's Etienne Aigner, she said. 'The black strap tank watch. Such a classic.'

She said it as *Aniay*: correctly French-pronounced, but what a horrible word.

'It might be. I don't actually know. My mum gave it to me when I opened this practice.'

'I can tell,' she said.

I didn't know what she could tell: that my mum gave it to me or that I didn't actually know? What the hell was a tank watch anyway?

'I like the the little logo of the brand – you see the arch with the line through it?'

I nodded, not quite believing I was having this surreal conversation about a bloody watch, like the mesmeric chats you were given by conmen before they conned you, to put you in a trance.

'The Ibans love nice things,' she sighed and sat back in the patient's chair, crossing her legs, so relaxed we could have been in a restaurant, satiated and waiting for the bill. 'Who says we are uncivilised?'

Not me, I said, though it did cross my mind that she did come from the jungle and lived in a hut at some point or other, or in a tree. I was suddenly flooded with the imagery of Borneo, the jungle, the rivers, the dug-out canoes. Still I hadn't a clue about the tribes. I knew more about the queue of tribes outside clubs in Elephant and Castle in the freezing cold trying to get in.

After the interview of sorts, I decided not to give the girl the job. She chatted too much. How was she going to do any work? But within a few weeks, after interviewing six girls, I had to take her on. I had to take the pressure off Shue Ling, the other receptionist.

Talisa seemed beyond her eighteen years. I took her on because there was no one like her. Within days of starting work here, she turned the waiting area into a kind of clean calm space. She always wore long-sleeved tops, and in fact looked like a saint. She made sure everything was in its place. The curtains were laundered and had new tasselled tiebacks 'to make them appear new'.

There were fresh flowers in a gigantic glass vase every Monday which she said was the 'most important thing in this room.' I was momentarily moved when she said that it was the infirmed and ugly who needed beauty, not the fit and lovely. Shue Ling demurred by informing me that the money actually came from the till. 'Don't worry,' Talisa was quick to reply, 'I got the receipts and it is a tax expense. Dah does things like that all the time.' The marked change in the décor and general tidiness included magazines and toys being put away immediately. Even the backs of the sofas were spotless. She probably got this no-nonsense approach from her late housekeeper mother.

In the corner of the reception, next to the water dispenser, Talisa had made all the Chinese New Year decorations, little red and gold ang pao envelopes dangling on red threads on a kumquat tree in a glazed terracotta pot, a Chinese version of a Christmas tree. Plum blossom sprigs in a blue and white porcelain jar stood in the corner. Talisa was not even Chinese. Shue Ling had her own family to decorate for. The most she would do for last year's decorations was to put up a few cards which patients and pharmaceutical suppliers had sent.

NIGHTS HAD BLURRED INTO each other, like smells. It was a Friday night four or five weeks later, a February night that looked like dawn. I remembered it so clearly! Wonderful thing hindsight.

Storm clouds had gathered. There had been no patients for an hour, just cancellations. I was dying to get off, away, whatever, and have a drink. Ming Jen never called once, even though she was supposed to be coming for the weekend. I wasn't good at calling. Her mobile phone was switched off when I tried it once about a week ago. Like most men, I thought about it, and then didn't, or forgot, or both. Thinking equalled done.

Business was poor. No one was ill in February. It was considered very bad luck since the year of the Rooster had just begun. Everyone was cocky. I rang my mates to see what they were up to. Ringing mates was not the same as ringing one's girlfriend. Ringing mates had no consequences except the possiblity of a night out involving alcohol, dancing, sports- or female-watching and in other words, complete and utter joy. Ringing one's girlfriend could end up in a row.

It was very irritating that I had to leave messages for a couple of my friends, and those that I could actually get hold of could not meet up with me at Little T's Sports Bar, which I suggested because it was a properly respectable establishment with two large sports screens, waitresses in shorts and fishnets, Irish

25

knickknacks on the walls and of course, good beer on tap. Damn, I was stuffed...Friday night and I had nothing planned.

I was born in the year of the Sheep. Sheep, goat, ram: all the same word in Chinese. Yang. 1979. Earth Sheep. Intuitive and sure-footed. Technically, I could bear great pressure while remaining stable. I could drive myself to the cliff edge at great speed, and still cling on and amuse myself with wistful mutterings and musings without the need to even whisper so much as a 'help!'

IN THE LITTLE MALAYSIAN railway town of Segamat, 122 miles from Kuala Lumpur, the stormy weekend was about to begin. Segamat was surrounded by mountains, hot springs and golf courses. Thunder rumbled, and the green of mountains faraway was obscured by dark clouds. Segamat River, which ran through the Old Town, would no doubt be flooded. The bloated bodies of drowned chickens and cats would soon float downstream like they were asleep, dreaming of food.

I stared out of the window. I wished the girls would hurry up and do the tills. Oh good. I heard the clink of keys. Shue Ling was inside, locking all the glass medicine cabinets and putting the afternoon's patient files away. There were now complicated combination locks to deter drug-seeking burglars. I supposed they could just smash up all the cupboards if they really wanted to get the drugs.

I pretended to tidy my desk in my surgery. Talisa was outside pulling the shutters down. I whipped open the till and counted a few fifty ringgit notes for her wages. Talisa was part-time so she got paid less but more often. She was here Wednesdays, Thursdays and Fridays. I left the rest of the money in the till for Shue Ling to tot up. The notes, under artificial light, looked artificial. I lifted the till, used it as a paperweight and shoved the brown envelope under it.

I waited around for my mates to text me or ring me back. The Sheep could not be but patient. Every now and then, I looked up from my phone. Even the streetlights had not come on. A night that looked like dawn. Only the luminous milky appearance of the clouds gave away that it was the monsoon season.

Talisa was sweeping the area near the files with a coconut broom. When the rain did not subside, I popped my head back in

26

to the reception area and noticed that she had found the brown envelope and was smiling. She thanked me, waving the envelope at me and then stuffing it into her concealed money belt. Her cheesecloth top had elegant long bell sleeves which slightly folded over as she inserted her money, but she quickly pulled the sleeves down again, as though they too were a kind of secret purse, hiding something.

'When we first arrived here,' she suddenly spoke as she zipped her money belt up, 'my mother and I had nothing but a few packets of instant noodles.'

'Well I've done the cups in the sink and I've done the bins.' Shue Ling said, panting as she came in. 'I'm going to make a run.'

Thunder resounded in the Pulai mountains, crunchy and bassy. I grabbed my white Adidas golf umbrella from under my desk. The clinic was plunged in a silvery darkness. I saw Talisa's silhouette outside, sitting on the painted timber bench. A deep verandah was essential in tropical architecture. Sometimes patients sat on this bench when they were checking on their cars, looking out for the parking attendants.

The palm trees shivered in the gusts of the powerful wind.

'Do you want a lift?' I could see that my voice had interrupted her thoughts.

'OK.' she said.

'Wait here,' I said. I opened my white Adidas golf umbrella and went through the back door, locking it after me. I drove my car round to the front of the building. I pulled the brake, leaned over and flung the passenger car door open.

She got in without being asked.

'BMW,' she said, like some kind of greeting.

She put on her seatbelt straightaway, expecting to be driven off. But I didn't drive off straightaway. I felt like I was a teenager again, driving my first car.

She smiled enigmatically, and smoothed down her pre-washed denim skirt darkened in spots by the rain.

'How's your mum's hypertension?' I asked.

'Oh you mean Marmy. She's not my mum.'

Baffled, I didn't reply.

'She's your patient,' she said, 'you probably know better.'

'You live with her.'

'But I don't treat her high blood-pressure.' She half-smiled.

'No,' I added. 'You probably caused her high blood-pressure.'

She sniggered. She ran her fingers over the leather seats, the dashboard. She had a heart-shaped red glass ring on the third finger of her right hand. She was already part of the upholstery, smooth and warm. When she moved in her seat, the leather groaned and sighed, like the whole machine was alive, breathing and throbbing with German technique and design. The knobs and dials sparkled, the dashboard was wood, so highly polished her ring shone from it. My blood shot up like a river on edge. My head became light in the airless car.

She reached out for the gearstick with her right hand, imagining, I supposed, what it would be like to drive. Ian MacFarlane had two crap cars, an ancient beige Toyota and a mud-covered Land Rover for going around on his estates. It was his way of making a point, that being Scottish, he damned well did as he pleased with his money.

'I've only seen nice cars in the movies,' she said, too revealingly. 'Thrillers, chases, Harvey Keitel. I can see myse...'

She stopped before she said too much. I started the car and we were on our way. People were running in flip-flops, with newspapers on their heads, their trousers rolled up to their knees.

Then I blurted like some crazy English guy, 'You like this weather?'

'I love this weather,' she said, looking out. 'The Ibans believe that everything has, and is, a spirit. The rain and the wind, and even every plant.'

'What's a spirit?' I said, aware that I was on the brink of yawning but from my schoolboy days I knew how to hide a yawn by making a frowning grimace. I was humouring her.

'A spirit is simply an energy, a force, with more semangat than you or I.' The word *semangat*, gusto, must have been the same in Iban or Malay, as I knew the word.

We were silent for a while until we got to a set of traffic lights. She was looking at my hands on the wheel. I'd been told by Ming Jen that I had well-proportioned hands, with clean neat finger nails, as though the hands themselves had an intelligence of their own, hands which had never done a day's manual labour, a rich man's hands. Ming Jen's voice sounded as distant as the hills now.

I looked in the rear view mirror and I could see my eyes. I had good eyesight. I was fit and tall. My hair was cut short, leaving only a cowlick on my forehead that was continuously unruly. Ming Jen said it made me look like a baby. She only said that because she wanted one. The unpleasant thought of having children made me jerk my steering wheel temporarily.

'Ebu could read hands, both the back and the palm,' said Talisa, as though replying to my thoughts. Her voice became child-like when she said: 'Shue Ling is probably already home and watching her favourite Cantonese soap on telly.'

We passed the timber mills and a few car workshop garages, some restaurants – three Chinese and one Indian-Muslim – and a mobile phone sales office. You could hardly see them in the storm, but I knew this place, this town. I knew every road even if it was pitch black. A banana tree had been uprooted by the side of the road. Four children between the ages of three and twelve, the older ones boys and the younger ones girls, were all bare-chested and in shorts. The first thing that crossed my mind was that I hoped they didn't catch pneumonia. I glimpsed Talisa looking at them with undisguised contempt. These were slummy, scruffy children, urchins from the squats. Under the dim streetlights, they picked out the smashed from the salvageable bananas from the bunch.

The pasar malam night-market stalls had shut. Street hawkers and vendors selling mangoes, noodles, clams, watermelons, mobile phone cases, satay, haberdashery, pirate CDs and DVDs, all had long disappeared. It was a ghost town.

I turned into a small lane, one lined by heavy shrub growth and a few little attap huts.

I pushed the CD into the player to take my mind off things. A learning Chinese CD: Lesson Two, *At the Post Office*. I needed it for my job. I was so embarrassed that I was Chinese and I was learning Chinese. I had been English educated all this life, even before I went to University in London.

Talisa showed no expression, looking just a little sombre. Perhaps she knew that I was a banana. Yellow on the outside, white on the inside. My impoverished Guangzhou-born grandparents immigrated in the thirties to seek their fortunes here. They travelled barefoot, with only the clothes on their back. I had never been to China. I learnt nothing from their frugality. Little by little and decade by decade, my grandparents and parents put away so much just to hand it over to me in a lump sum. They loved me, spoilt me and saved me from eternal hardship. Now the second generation, mine, only knew how to spend and where to spend it.

In contrast Talisa's tough life was handed down from several generations of Ibans. She went to a state Chinese school after she arrived in Segamat, even though she was not Chinese. She wouldn't have spoken any Iban since her Ebu died. It must only exist in her mind now, just like London only existed in mine. I fiddled around with the eject button. The CD came out and the radio came on instead. The DJ rambled on. Mis-Teeq, Timberlake, Sugababes.

'This is where I live,' she said.

'In the coffee plantation.' Ah, coffee. Another accursed import from Brazil.

'Er, no, not quite.' She laughed. 'There are a few houses just behind.'

I turned right suddenly, so as not to miss the turning. Narrowly we missed colliding with a huge timber-laden lorry coming in the opposite direction. My heart raced from the near-miss. The excitement made me laugh my horrible clunky laugh. As we turned there was a strong whiff of coffee, being ground all night in the planters' cabins. The sound of the lorry's horn echoed like distant gongs.

On the right side of the road, there were neat rows upon rows of silver-barked rubber trees with tiny cups tied to the trunks to catch latex when it was tapped. The burning stench of latex, nauseating, impudent, wafted into the BMW from the rubber plantations, where all condoms and tyres began their lives.

We parked in the car porch. The house was dark. I took my seatbelt off and it snapped back with a ferocity that alarmed me. Was it alive? I supposed I'd better go in and say hello to Ian. I saw both the beige Toyota and the mud-covered Land Rover. Wayward climbing bougainvilleas tumbled over the porch columns, their thorny limbs arched, their papery orange flowers were see-through in the glare of the headlights. High above, a pungent musky scent floated down, of tree moss, and wet orchid roots, clinging onto the banyan tree.

I got out, took the umbrella, opened it, went to the other side and opened the passenger side door in a well-rehearsed routine. She got out and we went into the house together. I looked down warily so as not to tread on any baby cobras which might have wandered in. Ian's house was on the edge of the vast rubber plantations. A variety of serpents often came to the house searching for food and to escape the heavy rain. They were silent except for the whiskery sound of their scales on the polished floor. Looking out for them was not enough, one had to listen hard too.

The terrazzo floors felt cool and damp, and all I could hear was the loud ticking from the grandfather's clock, an antique that must have been picked up by Ian in Malacca on one of his trips. A gecko clucked. In Asian households you were supposed to remove your shoes, but as I was in Ian's household, I wasn't sure whether or not the rule applied, but evidently so. She switched on one of the hall lamps, took off her wet shoes and asked me to do the same. I kept expecting to see Ian and Mrs MacF, and their two biological children, Greg and Melissa.

'Where's everyone?' I said

'They're in Scotland.'

'What?!'

'Dah had a Burns Night do that his old bunch of mates had organised and Marmy and the kids decided to go too. They're away for a couple of weeks.'

'I don't believe it! Where?'

'Scotland. It's north of England.'

'I know where the bloody hell it is. Why didn't you say anything?'

'What's there to say?'

She put her arms round my neck, and kissed me hard. There was a stale odour of rain on her, but her breath was sweet. Her lips parted and I put my tongue on hers. I was compelled to shut my eyes, but I sensed that hers were open. She pressed herself against me like a piece of paper, and I could feel the protuberance of her money belt contents, which I had seen her zipping up so carefully hours ago – my money once, and now hers.

'I need a drink, please...' I said. I needed assurance that I was indeed under the influence. How else could I justify what I was about to do?

'You're in a Scots household and you're worried there's no drink?' she teased. 'I think we've got some Balvenie!' She turned and went into what I thought was the kitchen.

I had never been here before. It was a mansion. Chandeliers, teak floors, animal heads, the works. I followed her. The kitchen was gloomy and seemed to go on forever. So this was how the expat landowners and planters lived. She brought a full bottle of whisky and just one cut glass tumbler. As she poured she was hummed a tune I did not recognise.

I grabbed the tumbler and gulped the whisky back. She took the glass from me and slugged it too. I snarled and drew my teeth back, waiting for the poison to seep into my gums. We passed the tumbler back and forth. She kept refilling it when it was empty. I was hard. I needed fuel to get me going. We kissed again. I felt the biting heat of the Balvenie on her tongue. I needed a bit of tooth strength to tear open the condom wrapper. I thought I might still have one safe and warm in my wallet in preparation for Ming Jen's imminent arrival. Talisa headed for the stairs. I followed her.

She stood halfway up the stairs and lifted her denim skirt. I stood on the step below her and reached out for the thighs below the bunched up skirt. She put her arms around me, which I never realised were so strong. She imprinted herself deep into me, in an embrace so tight I could smell the sea.

A CRACK OF LIGHTNING, then thunder. And after that, no more.

The cave had opened with the touch of my hand and the tide flooded in.

Lightning had made everything appear momentarily bright as midday. It put me off when I was reminded of where I was. I didn't want to go into her bedroom. The clock chimed once. 1am. My head buzzed lightly from whisky, terror and fatigue. I staggered into Greg's bedroom. I fell asleep on his bed surrounded by toys and posters of sharks, so eerily lit by lightning. Even the child's bed was teak and had a one-foot-thick mattress that sighed as you sunk into it. Still in my light sleep I could hear the distant dogs that barked and cried in succession from fear. It was bright, sticky and humid when I awoke. As I descended the staircase, the grandfather's clock chimed nine times. Beyond the bamboo thickets which protected the farms, came the faint howls of siamangs, the tailless, arboreal, black-furred gibbons. It was the magical call of morning, so resonating it travelled miles to my ears. How my head suffered.

'Coffee,' she said. Talisa was already up and wearing a different long-sleeved top and white jeans. She had kept her top on when we made love. Again I felt I really didn't want to see this house by daylight. I wanted to be in my own bed. I didn't get to slip away because she was up before me. I felt for my mobile phone in my pocket. It was off. I didn't switch it off at all yesterday. How long was it off and was the battery down? Already?

'Coffee,' she said again. I kept demurring. More poison. The bottle of Balvenie was on the worktop, a third left. No wonder my head was banging. When finally I drank my coffee, it was cold. I ate a boiled egg as there was nothing else in their fridge. There was only one egg, so she let me have it. There wasn't even any bread to go with it. She must be living on takeaway while the others were in Scotland. Only later on did it sink in that her culinary skills were non-existent.

'I've got to go,' I said.

'OK,' she said, undecided. 'Your BMW is waiting for you.'

Why did she have to say BMW? Why not just car?

'You will have to call me Dr Lee at work and at the Club,' I said. 'And besides, I have a girlfriend.'

She said nothing.

I did not touch her as I fled via the wayward climbing bougainvilleas and inhaled their strong morning perfume. I jumped into my 'BMW'. The radio was still on the same station as before. I left the heart of rubber country, Ian MacFarlane's baby. Haha. Ian will be so not amused to know that his adopted daughter had just test-driven rubber.

I drove ten miles to get home. I wanted to drink my own coffee, using my own Made in Italy stove-top espresso maker, something I'd brought back from my student flat in London. A battered and stained little souvenir, but all mine.

I wanted to get back my life as soon as I could. When I got in, I straightaway switched on the mobile phone and checked for messages.

I couldn't believe it. Ming Jen had left two messages. She had been trying to call me. She tried the clinic landline twice too but I was always busy or had stepped out. The girls never gave me the messages. She sent a text message instead. Had I known I would have definitely called Ming Jen back. It had to be turned off during working hours. I couldn't let it go off while I was treating patients. I used the mobile phone to call those bastard mates of mine just before six. It was on then.

How long would it take to get my life back in order? The espresso maker spurted away on the stove, bubbling with fury. I switched off the stove, and as I poured the coffee into my favourite Fulham Football Club chipped mug, the landline phone rang and rang. Oh shit. I picked it up after five.

'Ming Jen!' I said, swallowing my black sugarless coffee. Gulp.

4

Bernard

Revd Bernard Strong,
Eternal Light Ministry Ltd,
'Orchid Villa',
83-85 Jalan Buluh,
Kuching, Sarawak, BORNEO.
Tel. +60 9 207 207 (Registered in England 44898733)

Hi Margaret, well you must be surprised to hear from your dear brother! We have just got broadband. Seems strange that we are so many thousands of miles apart, and you are reading this seconds after I have sent it. You may remember when Wendy and I first came here all those years ago to work on the jungle ministry. With email, it is easy to forget time and space. When Wendy and I first arrived here all those years ago, after twelve hours of flying, and changing planes in Kuala Lumpur, we had to endure another two hours to get here to Kuching International Airport, followed by a three-hour four-wheel drive. We then trekked for five hours or more through dense jungle, up and down very tough terrain, just on foot, with Caterpillar boots and Berghaus outdoor clothes, bottled mineral water and New International Bible that we always carry, and at the end of all that, when we were dead tired, we'd go very fast, like mud-splattered bearded pigs, downhill to the riverbank where there is a tiny jetty. Still this was not the end. From the jetty, we travelled three hours by longboat on snaky rivers: forks, currents, rivers with as much force as electricity itself, rivers the colour of coffee, filled with leeches, crocodiles and winged serpents. The rivers are the seedbed for stories. Legend says that in ancient times there was a large serpent called Nabau. One day, the mystical serpent Nabau turned into a human form who tried to make love to a warrior's wife. The warrior caught and sliced the serpent into seven pieces which he threw into the great Batang Rajang river. They formed seven rocks, the site of the seven Pelagus rapids. Margaret, these are not just rocks from a garden centre to make an alpine garden. They are magnificent boulders the size of ships, which, in low tide, prevent large boats from passing, and in high tide, rage with whirlpools.

Each year the rapids claim a few lives, and each year the locals make offerings to appease Nabau. Pre-tourism, the eight-mile long rapids prevented Ibans from migrating upriver and trespassing on previously settled tribes. Nowadays, the Pelagus Rapids is just another tourist resort. If I am not mistaken, it's the Hyatt Regency whose terrace café, overlooking the treacherous waterways, serves American breakfasts of blueberry pancakes. Margaret, you asked what modern life is like here!

That's why we can only get to most villages by longboat unless we are already inland. When you next break down somewhere and call the RAC who arrive in an hour, try imagining our thirty hour journeys into the heart of darkness.

Wendy and I are both fine. How is mum? She's asked if I am coming back to Brighton, and I've said to her not yet. Home is where God has work for me. Please ask her not to keep the spare bedroom ready for me! Wendy may go back without me this time. She misses M&S Food Hall.

There is too much to be done here at the Ministry, especially since that additional work in Kuching Prison now, which I find simply enjoyable and fascinating. God has given me this privilege and gift to be able to work with and communicate with the convicts, and I thank Him for that. In Borneo, third largest island in the world, Kuching Prison is the most hi-tech in Malaysia and is situated in capital city of Sarawak state. It has electric cell lock control and monitoring, lock interlocking system, card access control system, badging system, duress alarm system, integration to CCTV, Intercom, Call Button, Metal Detection System, and Supervisory Management System. The inmates know that escape is out of the question.

Boy-boy has just brought me my tea. We have had very heavy thunderstorms in the last couple of days. The water came up to the centre of our van wheels, which means we didn't get anywhere far. It's intolerably hot and humid, which makes dust and grease gather like moss on every surface: tables, shelves, floors. Fortunately, Boy-boy keeps the bungalow spotless.

We are surrounded by well-tended gardens within half-a-mile of the Church itself. In the evenings we look forward to visits by our local friends – the Striped Tit-Babbler and the Yellow-bellied Flowerpecker to give us a song or two.

There is an abundance of orchids, both wild and grown by hand, from seed, by Boy-boy. Of course we don't need glass houses here. When I think back on Kew, I think how much we have tried to imitate what is wild, free and truly beautiful about nature and life. How can you tame an orchid? It wants to be here, in Borneo. I just remembered: please let mum know that I have seen that uPVC conservatory on the Wickes website, that she was interested in. They are having their sale – it's forty percent off. If she likes, I thought you and I can both chip in.

Boy-boy doesn't say much, if at all. He is as silent, and part of the family, as the church cat. Of course he's not really a boy anymore. He's a young middle-aged old man! Without people like Boy-boy, the Ministry would not be able to function. Certainly I think that these boys who are left at the steps of St Joseph's as babies have views very different to us, with regards to serving God when they grow up: they have a duty to the church. Without the kindness and the generosity of the church, they would have not survived. And how fortunate we are to be able to provide them the chance to live.

The heavy rain has impeded our work here somewhat, but it gives us time to reflect and to pray. It also means that I cannot go to the prisons for a while. But the moment the weather is better, I am going back. It breaks my heart when I see some of our old boys from St Josephs in there. One of them in particular that I can think of seems not capable of hurting a fly. He's only in for a short time. His friend is a new convert, and needs plenty of prayer and TLC. He's been in there for a decade. I am guided my prayer. We need to pray for more donations for the volunteers here to go off and treat the tsunami victims. And we also need a basketball court.

We have a prayer meeting in about an hour, so I must go and type up some notes now.

Your loving brother,

B.

5

Benjie

The Monday after, I felt nervous and I decided to give Talisa the sack.

I didn't like complications. I wrote the letter out offering two weeks' severance wages. (Loved that word *severance*! Cutting off all ties!) Ian would never forgive me. Firstly, he made the call on the pretext of making a job enquiry but in actual fact, he made me take her on. Secondly, I was a shareholder in rubber and thirdly he would stop sending all his tappers and coolies to me and I would lose my patients. With great reticence, I tore up the letter and put the money back in the till.

I called her into my surgery and asked her quite directly if she a) received any calls from Ming Jen and b) turned off my mobile phone after 6pm, after I called my useless mates.

To my surprise, her corresponding answers were a) she did receive calls and she did leave messages and b) she did turn off my mobile phone for my safety because of the risk of electrocution. 'Eight people so far had died from being electrocuted, Dr Lee,' she said. 'One minute they were on the phone, the next minute they were floored, charred and very dead.' I was impressed by her honesty and her concern about me, but I did wonder why I didn't see the messages that she left. I simply took her word for it.

Talisa continued to call me Dr Lee as per my instructions and I was cordial and insincere to her. I'd decided: no more lifts. I acted normally and continued to string Ming Jen along. I wasn't going to make the same error of confessing, not after the episode at the Bali conference. She went to pieces then. This time she would deteriorate so much people would think she was my grandmother.

For five weeks, I went back to my cocksure self and lived up to my notoriety as a ladykiller. There were plenty of girls, foreign-educated, from which I could take my pick, if they didn't pick me first. I bought rounds, raised glasses, shouted and hooted at teams on screens, reeled into bed, staggered to work. I resumed my hectic nightlife in the bars and at the Club with the lads, not realising they were a series of stag nights. Mine.

ONCE I HAD RECOVERED from Ian's beating at the Club, my mum said, 'this girl is bad luck'. In Chinese, it actually translated as 'this girl no good luck', which was not only more accurate, somehow it sounded worse than bad luck.

My mum, being Chinese-educated only spoke to me in Mandarin, which was technically my mother tongue but I always replied in English. I'd lived for so long in London and I'd gone to English schools all my life. When I spoke or tried to speak Mandarin, it came out wrong.

My mum insisted that we needed a fortune-teller when Talisa was about seven weeks gone. I was sceptical, being a man of science, but I went along with it. When women had an idea in mind, it was hard to talk them out of it.

Some astrological expert called Mr Lim, with a great big mole with a long strand of hair sticking out of it, was called in straightaway. The mole was probably there for luck. He had a book of diagrams which looked like lines and triangles, a pair of mirror balls and a blue and white porcelain container that looked like a toothbrush holder containing sticks.

On the table was a wedding menu from the Mayflower Restaurant, the choices for which we were studying with my mum. Talisa came round to my house for the first time. Her eyes couldn't stop looking around at my mother's gold and jade bracelets, my mother's own wedding presents from when she married my dad. How could Talisa be so blatant?

Mr Lim spoke in Mandarin and asked Talisa her date of birth. She hesitated. She said that her animal sign was the Dog. 'But what is your date of birth?' he repeated impatiently. Talisa said 5th May 1987. I never knew her birthday but I wasn't going to remember it anyway. 'Well then, young lady,' he said, 'you are not an Earth Dog, are you! You are a Fire Rabbit!'

Maybe she got the animal wrong because she wasn't Chinese, but even Malays and Indians knew what Chinese signs they were.

The fortune-teller did a quick calculation of the date and hour of birth. He consulted the books and used the mirror balls as well. 'Those born under this sign,' he said in Mandarin, 'are talented, obliging, always pleasant, valuing security and tranquillity. The Fire Rabbit has more strength of character than the other Rabbits – Wood, Water, Metal and so on. In spite of Fire, making her more temperamental, she can mask her emotions with charm and diplomacy. Fire Rabbits have a high level of intuition and even psychic ability. Being cautious and conservative, they will make good lawyers, diplomats, or actors. Their best life partners are Sheep or Pigs. So you see, Fire goes with Fire, you and your prospective husband are a perfect match!'

'Hang on, I just noticed something,' I said in English. Mr Lim looked questioningly at my mum for a translation but she was too interested in what I was saying.

Talisa seemed to turn white.

'Technically you are only seventeen,' I said. 'Eighteen is the legal age... we can't... not until...'

She sighed with relief, cutting me short. I was put off by her impatience for me to finish. 'We can wait until May the...' Talisa struggled, 'Fifth.'

My mum translated to the fortune-teller. 'It's fine,' Mr Lim chuckled. 'You're nervous, young man!' I burned with irritation. I was trapped by my circumstances. I was powerless to fight them.

'Now we'll pick a date,' he said, shaking the sticks in the porcelain container. I studied the menu card out of boredom, and noted on the back, at the bottom, the very smallprint: **First printed 5th May 1987 by Suntech Lithographers, Singapore**.

'Um, I have never known my actual date of birth,' Talisa confessed to the fortune-teller, suddenly observing that *I* had noticed the card. 'Not when you... not in the jungle. What's a date anyway? I could... say any date... and my luck would change.'

'You've completely wasted my time,' said the fortune-teller, 'young lady.'

Mine too. Her sneakiness had caught me off-guard and I didn't appreciate it.

'I'm so sorry,' My mum stepped in immediately, not wanting the man to lose face. 'I believe we can still choose an auspicious date, if your calculations are correct, er, the year of birth is still correct?'

Mr Lim grimaced. He proceeded with the sticks thrown about randomly three times, and came up with Saturday 21st May.

'Can I give you the invoice now, Mrs Lee?' he said to my mum.

I saw him out to the street. 'Plants doing well!' He said as he passed the papaya trees.

He frowned and smiled at the same time, a face that only a businessman could make, and then he got into his Toyota and gave me a wave.

The next day I took the morning off work. I sensed that Shue Ling had not been the same since the wedding announcement. Talisa and I went to Old Town for a fitting of our wedding outfits, or fancy dress according to my dad. Since Ian laid his hand on me, I woke up every day asking myself if it was a bad dream. But it was real. I was marrying someone I didn't *know* at all. I pinched my ear lobe and cringed from the ache. The rings sat in their velvet box next to my alarm clock so that every day I woke up and remembered what I had done.

We would have a traditional Chinese wedding, for the more conservative relatives, as well as a modern Western-style wedding to please everyone else. The Western wedding dress was cream, in a Duchess Satin, I was told by Talisa, and long-sleeved. Of course. But it was not the most expensive in the range, she assured me. Everything about this was a crime. The spending. The sham marriage.

After the fitting, we went for lunch at The Nanyang Kopi Tiam, a very famous corner coffee shop dating back to the early twentieth century, near Old Town's wet market. People usually came here for morning coffee, which you could smell from a street away. I loved the strong Javanese kopi here, a brew sweetened with condensed milk. It was mandatory to drink the coffee with the traditional Malaysian breakfast of roti bakar. Introduced by the Arab traders in the sixteenth century, the roti

41

was freshly baked bread toasted over a charcoal fire, spread with margarine and kaya, coconut jam.

My uncle came here as a child, and when he grew up, he brought me here when *I* was a child. I looked at Talisa with contempt, imagining her kaya-deprived childhood.

'Why do you always wear long sleeves?' I asked, sipping my kopi, served in the old-fashioned Chinese blue and white chunky ceramic cup and saucer.

She put her roti down and picked up her cup. 'I don't like the sun,' she said. She slurped her kopi.

TONIGHT WAS MY LAST night as a bachelor. I drove slowly.

Thunderstorms had never stopped me from driving fast. The fast lane was my only lane in this little town. It seemed that I had been travelling during thunderstorms forever. The sun had set. The blue-orange sky was crackled like fine pottery, but clear as glaze. The full moon would make it a bright night. With some body work, the car looked as though it never crashed. I could do with a bit of panel beating and new parts myself.

Even on a Friday evening, there was very little traffic. In Segamat, there was no such thing as traffic jams, unless there was an accident. I liked to do my thinking in the car because it saved time. Deplorably, I didn't *think* the rest of the time.

I drove past the Padang, the cricket ground, bordered by colonial two-storey buildings such as my old school, the Sekolah Tinggi, formerly the English High School, and the District Offices. The brick and timber balconies jutting from the first floor, wide verandahs framed by sturdy brick piers; everything had a pleasant symmetry. The easy rhythm bounced off on the palm tree-lined boulevards, frames within frames of colonial viewports. The clock on the clocktower said it was 6.10pm. It had never been late.

I crossed the little iron bridge. How many times had I driven this route with Ming Jen? I once looked forward to her visits every alternate weekend because they kept me in check, even though I started to think that the back and forth arrangement had become tedious. She'd never have moved to Segamat anyway. She had her own successful practice in Johor Baru, a city with a million people and I was only some small town oik.

I hummed along to Kanye West's *Diamonds from Sierra Leone* on the radio. Before the song had ended, I pushed the learning Chinese CD into the slot. Meaninglessly I mouthed words along to the CD, marvelling at my own voice making the strange sounds.

I was heading to the Gagak Country Club (established 1890) for a pre-wedding family dinner, a seafood barbeque buffet. If I dared to walk out, I'd have to eat Ian's fist sandwich.

I turned up the air-conditioning in my white BMW 5-series. Some people say it was a doctor's car, like a Mercedes was a builder's car and a Volvo was an architect's car. All rubbish. I only drove it because I drove it. Talisa called it the BMW, cautioning me of her status-consciousness. The wedding had given her the excuse to go crazy on the shopping. A price that I would have to bear for the sake of my child. Our child. If I knew anyone who wanted to marry an Iban girl, I would give him a good talking to and save him from financial hæmorrhage.

Once I'd left the town centre, there was a lonely stretch of uphill road which cut through the thickest of estates, the very same hill I climbed after I crashed the car and was rewarded with a black eye. 'Estates' meant oil palm or rubber plantations, not real estate. On one side of this road was rubber and on the other, oil palm. The road divided them like a parting on a head of hair.

In the darkened evening light, you could see the oil palm fruits gleaming, reddish-purple, ripe, ready, like jewellery in a store. These were the treasures of the growers. The oil palm was monoic, having both male and female flowers on the same tree.

I liked peering into the depths of these plantations at dusk. It was an eerily accurate glimpse of the other world, the well-tended world that the planters left behind when the day ended. The thorny leaves appeared more menacing, more irregular when in the day they were like benign tines of a feather. Each tree was a grand, stately Corinthian column of capitalism, at a perfectly still and regular distance apart, making a prickly canopy where all the T-junctions of the leaves met.

Deeper and deeper still, into the plantation, it was eternally night.

If oil palm were squat barbed bankers on a trading floor, by contrast, the rubber trees were girls on a catwalk. Smooth

43

stemmed, straight, slim and light-skinned, the elegance of tall rubber trees were accentuated by the little cups they wore, like a hipster belt. It was hard to connect the banality of latex gloves with these refined trees carrying very understated green or cream flowers. Each rubber trunk was unbranched up a long way and then much-branched in its leafy canopy, like a girl's blow-dried hair.

Each tapper could complete a hundred trees per hour, a rate Ian MacFarlane boasted about with utter joy. Trees were tapped early in the morning when the flow of latex was highest; flow decreased with temperature and usually ceased in about three hours. Many of my patients were chain-smoking tappers. Smoke was a mosquito repellant. If you were tapping between 4am and 7am, which was the norm, lighting up stopped yourself from being savaged to death by mosquitoes. You could tell tappers by the way they looked. Their teeth were stained or rotting from nicotine and terrible dental health. They wore long sleeves, headscarves, hats, long trousers, rubber boots, like they were in camouflage ready for combat. Mosquito armour. In fact, Ian was totally guilty of encouraging smoking since he gave them 'free' cigarettes as a perk of the job, without mentioning the rather common side effect of lung and throat cancer.

Bushcrickets singing from either side of the road parting made an intermittent chirping sound, shrill, like faulty office equipment. On the top of the hill was the GCC, from where you could have a splendid view of the Segamat River, the bridge and the town centre, while you practised your swing and impressed your colleagues, friends, family, in-laws, rivals.

At dusk, one had to drive slowly on this hill road anyway to avoid snakes crossing the road. If they were little and they whizzed across, you'd miss them. But if they were pythons... if they were pythons! You'd have to switch off your engine and simply wait. You waited and you waited. Until they had crossed. You could not run them over without offending some folks, for these slitherers belonged to the estate owners. (Some people call them snakes too!) The snakes were bred to eat the rats which ate the oil palm dates. It was said that these snakes were higher on the food chain than country club members.

Segamat's evening breeze carried with it the easy acrid scent of woodsmoke. Over some roads, streetlights were non-existent.

Tonight the full moon lit the roads but only by driving slowly could you stop in time. Many of the reptiles were slim and quick, like sequinned women in nightclubs. You didn't necessarily see them, but you knew them by their movement.

The road was clear. No snakes about. I stepped up the gears until the BMW crunched the gravel in the GCC's grand sweeping driveway. Everything was polished and neat, even the bollard lights lining the driveway were wiped clean of dead moths on the hour. I parked and got out. The car door shut with a soft thud and, with satisfaction, I listened for the two beeps of the electronic car locking.

The GCC was the nearest I'd ever get to experiencing ye oldey worldey pub ambience. Three years. Three years since I left London. I didn't know what I'd been doing all this time, but I *did* know what I was going to do from now: I was going to be a father. I was going to stop buying things just for the hell of it, things I didn't even look at, unwrap or even *like*. I was going to stop going out, spending money, meeting girls, eating junk food, getting drunk. I was going to stop having fun. Yeah.

The entrance portico was all white, with classical proportions: Roman columns, black and white Carrara marble floor from Italy. There was a verandah all around the building, like a skirt, also with the chequerboard flooring. The verandahs were so wide and clean, you could live on them.

At the entrance steps, there was a black pinboard with white letters that were assembled to show what was on, like on a menu. There was also a permanent sign: *No pets except guidedogs. Restaurant Dress Code: For men, no jean, open coller t-shirt and selipars. For woman, no selipars. Please keep clean! Thank you!*

This place still had old-fashioned standards. The night air was burdened with the scent of jasmine and tree orchids. Fairy lights dangled like necklaces from the tree canopies.

In each arched bay of the verandah was suspended a glass lantern on a fish hook fitting, like an earring. Each lantern was identical, yet cast a pure, exacting English light, from a single light bulb. This place felt right for our wedding celebrations, as it was where I had first glimpsed Talisa. Yet it felt wrong, because of the circumstances which caused this wedding to take place.

Poor Ming Jen whom I'd more than pissed off forever. A mutual acquaintance, a surgeon, had said to me she was clinically depressed. I was not surprised, after the way I'd dumped her.

The date so carefully picked with sticks had indeed crept up. At twenty-six, I was quite old to be just getting married in this small town, where nothing happened. I'd avoided getting married to Ming Jen for so long that most people assumed I was gay. In a small town, if you couldn't marry the girl you'd knocked up, you might as well kill yourself.

The Members' Bar had tartan carpet. It looked like it was in Scotland or the Barnard Marcus estate agent's in Hammersmith. It had crystal chandeliers, wall candelabras and stuffed animals' heads hanging on the walls. In glass cabinets there were stuffed civet cats with marble eyes, and some stuffed monitor lizards, caught on the premises. The Victorians had a fondness for stuffing. Above me, ceiling fans rotated slowly. You could get anything you wanted at the bar. A Cuban mojito. Long Island Iced Tea. Singapore Sling. The sign on the bar said: *Anything from anywhere in the world. That is available in Segamat.*

The pre-wedding buffet dinner at the Club felt surreal: that all this was in honour of me having a casual shag. My only sibling was my brother, Ray, now thirty, a computer programmer who spent his spare time playing with his Playstation. Typical geek. Like me, he was a banana. He had stopped using his Chinese name long ago, claiming it was uncool. Now he lived in Dubai, like a third of the world's programmers, so I hardly saw him. He said very clearly that he was only coming to give my parents face, unlike my mostly absent relatives. None of those mates, who had caused the entire night of foolishness, were here. They let me down. It occurred to me that they were not friends after all. I need impress no one now. Songs on the radio. Books on the shelves. Wine on the racks. *Those* were my friends.

The smell of grilled seafood floated above the warm air. I heard laughter. Music. I passed people I had sort of seen before and could not remember if I recognised them or not. They could have been patients of mine or simply members I'd seen on the tennis courts.

I caught sight of two little second cousins, six-year-old twins who were going to be bridesmaids, tearing down the swimming pool terrace. I could not remember their names.

'Benjie!' a heavy Scottish voice called. I turn around.

'Mr MacFarlane!' I said.

'Oh, please, just call me Ian. How many times must I tell you that?' said Ian. 'Just do not call me dad or I'll kill ya!'

I thought I laughed, surprising myself at the ugly sound of it. Everyone else called him Mr MacF. I didn't know if I should shake his hand, but I didn't anyway.

'Talisa's waiting in the bar,' said Ian, grinning. 'We were wondering where you were.'

'SD,' I said vaguely.

Which meant snake delay.

Ian gave me a *goodboy!* or *welldone!* pat on the back, still grinning. He'd been here forty years, married his Chinese housekeeper twelve years ago, and he still sounded like he came from Ibrox, Glasgow yesterday. No flying punches, as long as I agreed with him.

'I wonder if your parents are here yet?' said Ian.

Talisa wore red lipstick. Her hair looked glossy. I could appreciate her allure, although my disgust was just as strong. Attraction and repulsion, worn together, like a pair of cufflinks. She'd like me to notice that she'd been shopping, probably at that trendy new boutique in Jalan Genuang. She wore a long-sleeved green blouse, with sequins. Loose, to disguise the bulging mound of her pregnancy.

My dad came round. 'You should eat something,' he said. 'You've lost tons of weight in the last few weeks.'

'Wow, no kidding,' I said. 'I wonder why!'

'Don't be so hard on yourself,' he said.

I said nothing.

'Do you know, your Third, Fourth and Fifth Uncles haven't turned up?'

'And Third, Fourth and Fifth Aunties, and all my cousins, may I add,' I said.

'What can we do, Son? Don't worry about them.'

'Thanks,' I said, 'I think they're ashamed of me. Us. I made them lose face.'

'No, that's nonsense. Don't be silly, Benj. I didn't bring you up to say such a stupid thing. You've never let me down. You've been to England. You've got your own practice, and now you are about to have a beautiful wife. What have you to be sorry about?'

I was quite touched. 'Let's eat, Dad,' I said. 'I'll get you some prawns.'

'No, thank you,' said my Dad. 'You help yourself. I'm watching my cholesterol, heh heh.'

Ray appeared. 'Not having anything?' he sneered. 'You going to toast your new father-in-law?'

At the pool, there was satay, pasta salads and grilled fish. Guests had helped themselves to the serviettes, cutlery and plates from the buffet table. The full moon was reflected in the pool like a ship's light. Ian made sure that no one's glass was empty.

People clustered around the buffet table like shrimps near a rock. There were noodles for long life and good luck, cooked in the proper Johor way, lots of king prawns, mussels, la-las. The pool was beautifully lit with underwater lights and you could see the intricate mosaic fish pattern on the floor of the pool. It was just renovated last year. I looked at all these beautiful things, people, food, drinks, lights – with sheer sadness. Could they be celebrating my loveless life? My worthless marriage?

'Are you going to change your surname when you get married?' asked Mrs MacF's sister in English.

'Auntie, I've already changed it once when I got adopted,' answered Talisa with a sweet knowing smile.

'Och! If it's good enough for me, it's good enough for me lass!' Ian butted in, laughing with his mouth open, having returned with a bottle to top up people's white wine. There were quite a few Scottish voices cutting through. Yes, I could see some of the other shareholders, planters and landlord types and others who were Ian's family and friends.

'Well, in that case I may change it again,' replied Talisa. 'What do you think, Benjie? Should I change my surname?' She looked at me. I found my tongue tied and my jaw clenched. I would have been the bad guy whether I said 'yes' or 'no'. People were tittering along with the banter. Oh! The pain! The pain of listening to her quiet confidence in front of all these people, making light of marriage, exercising her *right*, as though she was already a doctor's wife, my wife, while I, the groom, stood in the wings, a mug! There were people I never wanted to see again, well, most people here. Everyone was sitting at the pool terrace now, on delicate metal chairs, enraptured by her charm, drinking up and soaking up the glow from us, the wedding couple. Was it not enough to be humiliated, but had I to be humiliated *in style*? I detested myself for allowing this to happen. 'Here's to Benjie, Ian raised his glass at me, 'without whom half of Segamat would be skiving off work!'

The MacF's had two children, Melita, who was twelve and Greg, who was eight. Ian had another two, from his previous marriage, all grown-up, one in East Dulwich and the other in Crouch End.

I'd wondered if they bore any resemblance to Greg and Melita, whether they were recognisable in public as Ian's progeny, since I had never laid eyes on them and there were no photos. They would not be coming to the wedding, said Ian earlier. He looked disappointed yet proud, an expression that only a parent's face could make. His eyes glinted, addressing me as though I was his son. 'Children are an investment, you know,' he said. 'You wait and see.'

I'd often imagined the exotic and mysterious lives of these two grown-up children of Ian, perhaps inserting pound coins and pushing trolleys in Sainsbury's or something, doing the things that you did if you lived in London. I forgot their names.

'Are you worried about Ian?' My dad asked quietly later on. I looked away, giving away nothing. 'You have to forgive him for... being the way he is,' said my dad. 'His first wife, whom he was thoroughly devoted to, died of throat cancer. And now his current wife won't allow any photographs of her or of his first two children. You see, everyone loses face....'

As the Gagak oil palm and rubber estate owner manager, Ian was respected by the community, because, yes, he owned those snakes. Like Talisa, he'd never read a book in his life, yet he could speak passable Malay and Tamil, which was quite essential for a hands-on capitalist. Most oil palm labourers and rubber tappers were Indian. Ian's business was all about using cheap labour to acquire obscene wealth, *à la* his colonialist predecessors.

Everyone knew that the Chinese were the most racist race on earth. Rumour had it that the first white man ever seen in these parts was Scottish, which was why the Hokkiens still called the generic white man angmoh gwee, Red-haired Demon. The Cantonese left the colour out completely. They called him gwailo. Demon Bloke. Ian was neither. He wasn't even the stereotype of the safari-suited, pith-helmet-toting, Protestant colonialist. He loathed gin and tonic and all those silly drinks, preferring Tiger beer. Cricket, as far as he was concerned, was a singing insect.

Ian might not be Bible-bashing but he certainly didn't mind ear-bashing or doctor-bashing. Londoners were safe from this sort of pairson. He didn't exist in a metropolis. He wouldn't last two minnets in a civilised society. He had been here so long that he had become a caricature of himself. It was not just him. The Aussies became more Aussie and only wore flip-flops all the time, which they insisted on calling thongs, and the Germans became more German. They even had their own supermarket called Danke Schön near the port. The foreigners, expats, consultants, whatever they called themselves these days, each made their own 'wine region', a valley of their own identity haven. Since they came a hundred years ago, it was their way of protecting themselves from the loss of themselves. The climate was harsh and the lifestyle competitive. There had been only one other Scottish person, and that was Talisa's tutor, who'd gone back to the UK. There was no other point of reference or cultural reality for Ian. His Scottishness over the years became more distilled and hard, like whisky.

'You cannot beat the weather here,' Ian said. 'Aye, I've putted in Gleneagles but somehow it's always a wee bit too wet for me in Auchterarder!' He was more familiar with playing golf in the Australian Perth (four hours' flight away) than the Scottish.

His face and visible portions of his entire body were so darkened by the sun, sometimes people thought he was Indian or Malay. He was balding but dark haired, and of a small slim stature. His thick moustache, big as a paintbrush, just added to the confusion. He might look like a benevolent little Terry Thomas but he was no comedian. When it came down to

50

business, he certainly knew which bones to break better than a plastic surgeon.

His Teochew wife had been made stout by decades of washing clothes and lifting heavy laundry. Only a few people knew her by her real name, Teo Bee Lian. The others didn't know and didn't care. They called her Pam, or Mrs MacF. She had been in service for so long, she was cut off from society. No amount of gentrification or gratification could remove the hard-grafted fat, inflated further by an even richer diet of haggis and fried dumplings. Now she suffered from high blood-pressure too.

I had warned her of her diet many times. It was my duty not only as her GP but now, so extremely recently, as a future son-in-law. No doubt, as she had moved up in life, it was hard to eat fruits and vegetables. Those were for poor people and pets. As the wife of an estate owner manager, she knew that a rich diet meant you were rich. In fact she was quite pleased she couldn't buy her clothes off-the-shelf. They were tailored by some poor Hokkien seamstress. If you could get your clothes made, it meant you could afford to.

Melita MacFarlane took after her dad, minus moustache, while Greg was a Eurasian version of his mum, a mini marshmallow man. Talisa was talking and laughing with Melita. Something was obviously making her hysterical with happiness. There were so many people to talk to, and who wanted to talk to Talisa. She was the real star. Being a doctor's wife was a role well-suited to her.

They always said weddings were for other people, not the couple, and in my case, not for me either. I was like the uninvited guest to a party where I also happened to be the groom. We were in this together, *ad infinitum*. Marriage. *Ad hoc. Ad nauseum.* I had learnt something at medical school after all – a bit of Latin, ten milligrammes, instructions: apply liberally when required.

I would have to leave my car behind tonight and rely on the minivan that my dad had chartered to take everyone home. There was no tube. I reminded myself that I was not in London, but in Segamat, population: one hundred and sixty thousand.

All big cities were big in the same ways, and all small towns were small in different ways. Chinese, Italian and Jewish weddings had so many similarities: they were all about not offending anyone. If no one was offended, it was a brilliant success. The protocol for me to squeeze into was like an outfit in your cupboard which you hadn't worn for some time, but still sort of fitted. Ignoring a scowling ex-girlfriend, whom I spotted in the bar earlier on, was the right thing to do.

Shue Ling was here too. Of course. I forgot she'd been invited. She'd been witness to it all. Did she think that she could have been the one getting married to me? I hoped not. They all knew that I was not the marrying kind. She smiled and waved at me from across the poolside bar where Ian was refuelling the tanks of her alcohol consumption. Ray sauntered towards her. He looked like he was going to chat her up, and good luck to him. I bared my teeth like an animal, and waved back.

Mr Kumar, the too-handsome, too-cool high priest of cosmetic surgery was here too. Who invited him? Why was he giving me that pathetic sympathetic smile? Did he feel sorry for me or was he just drunk? Luckily Mr Kumar is not Chinese, and therefore unrepressed. Binge drinking, falling over, ranting and railing – not now. I was saving all the sports for my wedding night.

I was not ready to be impounded, incarcerated, married. I had to pay for my actions, just as Ming Jen was paying, just as Ian was paying (but then he was doing most of the consuming so it was only fair). People had to bear their own bling, carry their own 22 carat jewel-encrusted crosses. Just as each and every perfectly spherical glittery oil palm fruit belonged to someone, someone who had to ultimately take care of it, Talisa was going to bring up my child. For him or her, I was paying. The tab was already open.

6

Minos

Seems like waste to have shower in morning. Cos after that must work in the vegetable fields before sun get too high and too hot. All morning, digging and watering, shovelling shit. Lots nice veg like long beans, brinjal, lady fingers, we end up eating. Must not think that is our own shit have been use as manure. Is how is done in village too! Nothing wrong. But that's another thing that I hate about this place. It's shit.

After lunch in canteen, we must sort and pack all kind disposable things, into exact plastic container or fitted plastic sheet back, and stick label on. Takeaway boxes, drinking straws, even disposable sandals for hotel, paper plate, cup, fork, knife, spoon. Count exactly then put away. Label to say how many and what is.

Paper cuts. I get, hate, paper cuts. Watan say he know trick how to avoid. Cos he say he use to working with plenty paper, before he come in here. He wink.

'So Watan. Why you in here for five months, then eleven months?'

'Well Minos, is strange story…'

'Is related to the paper cut story?'

'Yah. It long story, you wan hear?'

'Hey Watan, I got time. Three months in fac.'

'OK. I actually got high hopes. I was from proper mishnary Inglish school, you know? St Josephs? You know St Josephs? No. OK nevermind. I wan go into air force. Cos I like travel. I like go around, see places, you know?'

'OK, get to point, Watan!'

'Shaddap. Go places, do new things. I still wan. If somebuddy say, lehwe go tomorrow, I go. I still young. But,' say Watan, with suck his breath sharp, then sigh big, 'a girl got me in big trouble.'

'Yeah, always is a girl.'

'Yeah, always a girl, why is it, dammit?'

'Them smarter than man, you know, that is why man eat the forbidden fruit. Is what Pastor Bernard say. He come in later. You can ask him.'

'Oh yeah? So what forbidden fruit you eat of the girl then?' say Watan, blinking and grinning.

'Fuck, don't make me laff, man.'

Count one sugar, one salt, one pepper, one dairy creamer sashay, one stirring stick, one toothpick, one folded serviette, one refresher towel, then put in machine to seal up. All this stuff pack so nicely only to be throw away.

'Anyway. The story, Minos. Very stupid story. I mean, I very stupid. Not the story very stupid. A girl got all my money I save up for airforce. I have think she love me too. I give her things. I take her everywhere she wan go. She make me buy nice Honda Civic and drive her everywhere. Cos I say no to buying Merck. And she got many many friend in filem industry. And I love filem. I can watch two a day. Mebbe three, if kungfu filem. And she also love filem. And one day she say, you wan make filem, Watan? You wan make filem? I have friend provide all the technology. Camera, filem, software, computer do edit, everything. Of course I say OK. That be the forbidden fruit now I think back.'

'But then?'

'But then she never tell me in return for all this technology, I must make filems for her friend. And I say what filem? And she say, everything organise already. Just go to the cinema and friend will tell you what to filem. And of course, is to filem actual filems at cinema to make fake DVD.'

'So you actually pirate?'

'No I just filem filems to make more filems. Is sound good, but I tell you is not easy, Minos. We make tons, I have tons of papercuts until I know the trick I just show you. We make the boxes, we print the covers professional, everything, and it look real, and we sell to our distributor boys and girls for three ringgit each and they have to sell for six ringgit each throughout Borneo in retail malls. You see?'

'Uh. So you get the money first. Already upfront.'

'Yeah. I make only a bit of money. Is not enough. Because the mega boss he take it all. You know? He is called snakehead.

Cannot just start DVD bizness. Cos whole thing is run by snakehead. Every few weeks they come round and get money from you so that they shut up about you bizness. And if you no pay the money, you gwan get beat up big time.'

'He take all the money?'

'He take most. And still I won't have be in trouble if I not greedy and wan my money back that my girlfriend take from me. And I so desperate, and have no money and she get me into doing these crazy thing of fileming filems. Cos I love her. And I don't even love bloddy filems that much as I love her! And one day, three robbers come into cinema where I do fileming. And they got guns. Robbers like cinema cos dark. Cannot identify. Maybe they even friend of the projectionist. And they have pillowcases to take people's wallet and jewellery. And people who try run, they got shot. Cos all the exits already lock up. If they not friend of the projection man, that man also tie up already.'

'And then?'

'Minos, take it easy. I'm getting there. If I just take my camera and go, everything OK, I not talking to you in here today. But no. I stupid. I see robbers they drop just one pillowcase. I go back and pick up one bag and that is why I got thirteen months at first. I even say, judge, judge, I didn't know the pillowcase got money in it, or something stupid like that. And judge, I went to mishn school, y'know, St Josephs? But all useless. Then I plead I guilty. When I plead guilty, it go down from thirteen months to eleven. I blame the girl for everything but what can I do, she already gone.'

Watan sigh, and for first time, he look so down. He eyes, become dark as the cinema, with only slight flickering that come from the screen. As if he in a sad movie, and he not hero, but baddie. And then Watan say:

'At least nobuddy can say I kill or rob anybuddy. I only got done for pirate DVD. Is nothing really. No big type deal.'

'You gwan find this girl?'

'No, Minos, she dead.'

'She dead?'

'She dead. Cos she one of the people the robber shoot.'

IS **LATE AFTERNOON**. IS so hot, the cell is going crazy. Every afternoon, always somebuddy burst into tear, cos so hot, it make them think of sad thing. And when I look at Watan, he in tears, no matter how he wipe, he eyes still wet. He keep his eyes open, he never blink once, and is cos he love this girl. And this hot afternoon hour is time for the visiting hours. One of the visitors, three times a week, is Pastor. He don't have to speak to everybuddy, just whoever wan him to pray for them.

'But uh. Your girlfriend, Watan. Why she in the cinema?'

'Cos she gwan out with somebuddy else. And they watching filem together. And he also dead by robber. Mebbe God sayin something there, y'know?'

'Then why He do this to you?'

'Dunno. Is good question. Mebbe I ask Pastor Bernard later on.'

'You gwan tell Pastor you story, Watan?'

'He know story already, from when I in the other block. And you know, Minos, I think the mishnary, how many hundred year they travel to Borneo, and so many of they get taken by headhunters, so many get blowpipe in their neck, and yet they still come. They still come to see us.'

'I know. They come to my village too. Everybuddy now Christian. And is cos, the mishnaries, they fly all the way from Shivering Cold Places, like Inglan.'

Pastor have arrive. He sit down with I first. He come here to pray for everybuddy. Not just I. And everybuddy never tire of lisnin to Pastor.

He make everybuddy feel that nobuddy is alone. We as inmates also have make such a journey, maybe a thousand more times than Pastor. And we need human from outside to remember them what life use to be, should to be. Life where only plant and animal important. In jail, is opposite. Only life of human is important.

Pastor speak slow, clear, and make everybuddy feel calm, though he talking about crocodiles, and sweat is pouring and the room is so hot is like being inside a kettle. I look down, as though to pray, but really checking out if Pastor wearing Caterpillar boots. But no, he not wearing them.

And they not scare of anything. That they maybe lose their head! They not scare. Even if you chop their head, another

56

mishnary come months later. Cos they like it here. All this to give the villages the word of God. And all this cos they love God, and not for the love of some stupid girl. And that's the story that I and everybuddy know.

I many time look at Pastor from head to toe, toe to head. I some time try to guess how old is Pastor. But I can never tell with white people. Cos could be anything from twenty to fifty. Is what I think. He got so many lines on face cos of sun, and it make him look older. And his shoes is like young person shoes. So who can tell.

And the Pastor take the signal when I looking down at his shoes, and he say, why don't we pray for you Minos, and he pray for I, with his eyes shut. But I keep my eyes open. Today the Pastor wearing clean white shoes and socks, like he come from playing tennis. And he wear shorts and t-shirt, like he always wear, and the t-shirt say something, with Chinese words and the sign of a fish, but I cannot read Chinese. Pastor Bernard pray that God will find a way, for I, to find meaning in life as I approach my day of freedom. He pray that I will be strong and loyal to God, to listen to God's will and to believe in the power of prayer.

And some other things as well, which I don't understand.

7

Benjie

Days before the astrological encounter, I had met the future in-laws. Of course, I'd met them before, but this was to *meet* in a formal way, as in glower at them. My Dad and mum, Ian and Mrs MacF, Greg, Melita and an aunt and uncle from my side were all there too. We went to the Mayflower Restaurant at the club. Going to Chinese restaurants, especially those with chandeliers, fountains and painted wooden dragons, would have been an incredible treat for people like Talisa and her Ebu.

My family presented Talisa with presents of gold jewellery, a centuries-old tradition. Betrothal gifts include tea (cha-li, tea presents) and phoenix (bride) and dragon (groom) bridal cakes. These gifts were purely symbolic, I could not see Ian being enraptured by the sweetmeats or tea presents. The bridal cakes were for Talisa to distribute amongst her friends and family as an announcement of the wedding feast. Did she even have any friends? Her Ebu would be so proud of her. Here was her daughter having the time of her life.

In return, the MacFarlanes gave my family gifts of food and clothing. I was sure my mother, who was always dressed in the *smart casual* so dignified for women her age, would be dismayed by Mrs MacF's taste in tailor-made clothes shoddily made by half-blind pre-pubescent Hokkien seamstresses.

'You like your bling,' I smiled at Talisa. The sarcasm was lost. She grinned back, radiant with gold. I did not know the first thing about her, only that she wasn't like everyone else. For the sake of my unborn child, I wanted what I knew she wasn't.

A ROOSTER CROWED AND crowed in the distance. It was partly light, a yellowish grey day on the equator. Outside the window, Segamat was waking up too. I could hear the articulated lorries purring their engines as they set off to wherever they were supposed to go from the many sawmills that surrounded me on their mysterious silent dusty journeys at dawn, carrying planks of laminate timber flooring. Open top lorries carried woven baskets of heaped pineapples and bananas like tusks, next to which, Indian coolies sat glumly, bored, hands interlaced, and their day, like mine, had barely begun.

The Seiko clock at my bedside was ticking. I felt a little queasy, and my head was damp and cold. I was hungover. I checked that the rings were next to the bed. They were. Everything was true. It was my wedding day.

I'd ruptured the traditional process. In the old days, marriages were arranged so it was quite normal for the parents to dominate the bride-seeking process. Girls from rich family would be sought out by other rich families and poor girls married poor boys. Hence the Chinese saying: bamboo door is to bamboo door as wooden door is to wooden door. My mother would be disappointed at my bamboo door, but for my sake and not because she was Chinese, she would not show it.

We would be having a traditional Chinese wedding as well as the registrar office kind in suits. Ray was my best man, worst man. Today, both the bride and the groom's houses had red decorations. The make-up lady and the good luck woman would have turned up early to get Talisa ready. A good luck woman was a friend or relative who had many, many children or living family. The make-up lady had to perform the hair-dressing ritual for the bride, which would be centre-parted first, and then combed into three conspicuous chignons, Star Wars-style. The overall effect is Queen Amidala.

Bathwater infused with pomelo was to cleanse her of evil influences (too late for that). The bath was in Ian's en suite bathroom. Nobody else in this tropical heat would have a bathtub, only a Scotsman. This bath tradition was a hangover from the days in China three generations ago, where it was cold and there were baths. The good luck woman lit dragon-and-phoenix candles and chanted words of blessing while dressing Talisa's hair in the style of a married woman. Ian probably tut-tutted at the traditional ceremony, but sometimes it was hard to tell what he really approved of or not.

A long time ago, before cars, the groom's family would have had to send out a procession of servants, musicians and a carriage which was carried by four servants to the bride's family to bring the bride back. As we lived in modern times, we were minus the four servants, and we would be using my Dad's trusty old green Volvo (c. 1985, older than Talisa, which was saying something) which would serve as the wedding limo, decorated with red ribbons. Ray had already compiled a tape of classical music he'd like to play in the car as there was no CD player. My Dad was happy to be chauffeur. He was not letting anyone else touch his Volvo, and sure as hell not going to use Ian's mud-covered Land Rover.

The good luck woman actually had to be very strong. She had to carry Talisa on her back to the 'main hall', which was really the MacFarlane family's TV room. In fact, Mrs MacF had turned the TV on, as a filler of space, energy, or maybe just to relax everyone. My heart was beating fast, and imagining the pregnant Talisa ride piggy-back, in her underwear, on the good luck woman's sweaty back was so awful, I prayed she would not vomit onto the woman's neck. Another hangover from the past – when the piggy rider would be a chaste virgin, not an eight-stone mother-to-be! Talisa almost hit the floor – it was a very low ride on a roller-coaster. I should not have permitted it, being her GP, but I enjoyed the torturous spectacle so much that I forgot the risk.

In the main hall, where the TV was blathering at low volume, Talisa had to put on her bridal outfit, which I imagined was red, red and more red: a silk embroidered jacket and matching slippers, and a full length skirt, slightly quilted for puffiness. The puffy skirt was the third hangover from the old cold days in China where thin skirts were never in season.

The spokeswoman who would oversee the whole process was my Tua Ee, oldest aunt on my mother's side. She invited us to enter Ian's main hall. I was in my black and red silk gown, with matching skull cap. My entourage and I arrived at last in the green Volvo, to bring Talisa back to the Lee house to perform the marriage ceremony witnessed by all the relatives and friends.

Ray seemed to be charmed by Shue Ling's eyeliner before he turned around and told me I look stunned by the sight of my bride. I denied it. I believed Talisa had tricked me previously and this was all still part of the illusion. She wore a Phoenix crown, a Chinese tiara decorated with fur, beads and tiny mirrors. A red silk veil, which hung from the crown, covered her face. Even with her face uncovered, she was a complete mystery, let alone covered. It was like she had always worn an imaginary veil, one that held her together, without which she would fall apart.

On the white terrazzo floor, the sight of her slippers, like a pair of red boats covered in flowers, sent a shudder through me, a warning of the tantalising journey ahead.

We shuffled into my Dad's green Volvo, which seemed to calm my senses, because it was so familiar. The number of times I'd gotten in and out of this Volvo, inhaled its fabulous vinyl seat smell, throughout my childhood and youth brought me a sense of comfort. The bride and groom would worship the heavens and the earth, meaning: we'd kowtow to the Lee ancestral altar. A4-sized framed black and white stern photographs of my Grandma and Grandpa gazed down at us. I could almost swear Grandpa disapproved of me even from his photo. Benjie, you stupid bloody fool, he seemed to be saying, just with his eyes alone. There was a good reason why kowtow was a Chinese word – it means 'to bow one's head down', implying slavish obeisance.

We served tea to all of our superiors in the family, meaning anyone senior to us, or in the generation above, who sat on a pair of thrones (my gran's antique pearl inlay rosewood chairs) and in turn gifted us with the ang pao filled with cash and wished us well. Most of these packets would contain some form of 22-carat gold jewellery. For security, Ray would take them away to be put in my mother's safe until we could retrieve the gifts ourselves anytime after the wedding. Luckily Talisa wore a veil, or everyone would see her eyes popping out on stalks. I   was mistaken to assume before, with her language skills and part-time work at Ian's estate office, that she liked her independence and money. She was only doing that to escape. She liked *my* independence and money. She was now free of Ian.

The roles were then reversed when bride and groom sat on the 'thrones'. We were served tea by the kids, cousins, younger relatives in the generation below us, and anyone who were our inferiors. Good word inferior: medical yet derogatory.

The huge feast (lucky Ian) was thrown by the groom's family for the friends and relatives. Since it was not fair that my dad paid for all of my Crazy Mistake, I'd got my credit card out, ready to foot half the bill. Before the bridal entourage piled into the green Volvo, Talisa changed into the Duchess satin 'Western' wedding outfit. Anyone who had been to a Malaysian Chinese wedding would have seen that the bride went through several outfit changes, the best of East and West.

The feast took place at the Mayflower, where the in-laws first formally met one another all those weeks ago, for the ten-course wedding meal. It was a typical Chinese restaurant, with red table cloths, chandeliers and an aquarium full of swimming fish. Tua Pek, my uncle acting as emcee, would be toasting us, the wedding couple, every so often.

After the meal, Talisa and I travelled to Hot Springs Resort, which Talisa had chosen and booked of course. It was at Air Panas (the name of the village itself literally means Hot Water). A better name for it would have been Hot Potato.

Once we'd checked into the bridal suite, I was beyond words and smiles. Tua Ee, my auntie married to Tua Pek, offered sweets and fruits to us to wish us a long life and lots of kids. Oh please, Tua Ee, I said. She disappeared. I slammed the door. My brain was pickled with brandy and Tiger beer and all sorts of cold beverages. Then, finally, after the world left us alone and I am supposed to take off the red veil that covers my bride's face, I just gave up. She sat at the dressing table while I collapsed on the emperor-sized honeymoon bridal suite bed, decorated in single stem roses, which I facetiously brushed off onto the floor.

CHIT CHAT WAS THE blood that pumped a small town's heart.

In the clear morning light, as I examined my wife's body, I began to understand why she longed to be protected by me. Someone of status and authority, she must have thought.

I traced the patterns so carefully imprinted into her skin. The tattoo started above her right knuckles and finished under the elbow in a delicate floral pattern, so delicate and so fine, it was like a Beaux Arts glove. From far her arm looked greyish green, like river moss in the sun. If you looked carefully, the pattern changed with the light, because it had a spiralling central branch of the floral which kept the design dynamic, flowing with the natural curve of the arm. It deceived the eye, as patterns did.

Tattoo Girl, I whispered, with a mixture of disdain and awe. I kissed her harshly, her fingers, hands, arms. I could imagine the kids in school making fun of her. I kissed her again hard on the lips, then I retracted myself and shudder. I was full of hungover bitterness, and I did not want to touch her at all. I pushed her away lightly. She didn't look hurt. She looked down at her hands, as if already thinking of something else.

Dotted black spikes connected from wrist to knuckle, like a series of 'A's, truss-like, as though these lines were articulating and controlling her fingers. The tattoo, made of dotted lines, was faint and light as each dot was only a pin prick in size. I had never even noticed it before. I originally thought she stained dots left by henna hand decorations, which was common. She had tricked me.

We ordered room service. I felt rough and I needed some fried food fast.

'Has it got a name?' I asked as I pour champagne into my flute for my hair of dog hangover treatment. I sat as far away from her as possible, at the little table next to the French windows, while she reclined in bed.

'It?' she said. 'It's not a pet.'

'OK, whatever you call it, skin art, body art, whatever the politically-correct word for it is.'

'Politic-what?' She pouted with her full lips. There were bags under her eyes and she was pissed off that she couldn't have champagne. Served her right.

'What is the design?' I said slowly.

'It's a… well, a knuckle spike design. The Iban name for this artwork is the song irang.'

'What does song irang mean?' I questioned, genuinely interested.

'Iono,' she said, her lazy way of saying *I don't know*. Probably feeling embarrassed by her sheer utter laziness and supposed ignorance, she added, 'Ummmm, I think it's bamboo shoots, which represent plant life and fertility.'

So she did know. 'Oh, I see. It's anthropomorphic,' I said.

'What?' she said.

I burst out laughing. I had nothing in common with this common woman.

'They used to make fun of me,' she said, 'the kids in school.'

'What, here in Segamat?'

'Here in Segamat.'

'What did they say?'

'*Tattoo Girl, Tattoo Girl, wicked grin, lizard thin, let's pinch... her... SKIN!*'

'How did you get it anyway?' I asked, changing the subject, feeling slightly bad.

'They gave it to me. Because the villagers thought that I am a spirit catcher. A manang, or shaman. But I'm not really.'

'No, I wouldn't have said you were spiritual.'

She gave a snorty sarcastic laugh. 'Thanks!' she said.

'My mother is from Borneo,' I said.

'Fuck,' she whispered.

'What? Why did you say fuck?'

'No reason. Just surprised that's all.'

'I don't want my child swearing like...'

'OK, OK, sorry,' she said. 'Where in Borneo?'

'You know Bau? It's the gold mining town,' I clarified.

'My ancestors came from China in the 1840s to work on the mines. What about you? Do you have anyone left in Borneo?'

8

Minos

So. The Pastor go.

And I is left with feeling mess up again, like the other day last week Watan tell his story. Pastor Bernard give I a book to read. But I already say, I don't read much. I just like to read signs, menu, ads on TV. I never have read book in my life but the Holy Bible, New International Version, which I keep under my pillow, to keep it firm. The pillow, not the Bible.

Pastor Bernard say, after praying, 'Do you like reading?' and I shake my head.

'We...e...ell, I think you'll find that you'll enjoy this book.' And the book is called Ten Steps to Please God. 'It's written in very easy English, look, and there are pictures to help you understand,' say the Pastor.

What it means? Is Please God a place? And I put my hands together, like I is shaking hands with myself, and I pray to understand. Somebuddy to please explain please.

Then guard open door to cell. I got my own cell, but Watan still sharing cell. Because he small-timer, and just transfer from other block. Watan come into room, and then guard lock door and stand outside, with face looking in from the bars on window. He see and hear everything. But long as nobuddy talk about the guard, guard don't tell nobuddy nothing. And everything OK. And he hear everything every day anyway, and it's all not so interesting to he. Everybuddy got the same old same old bad luck sad story. Nothing new.

Watan say, 'Put that damn book down. Lehwe watch TV, only for haff hour then dinner-time.' I put the book under my bed. Then I find some TV channel to watch. Reception poor. Only two channel. But at least in colour. I adjust aerial.

'So other day, I tell you that I in here by accident,' say Watan, not looking at I, but at TV.

'Becos one stupid girl.'

'Right. Becos one stupid girl. But Minos, let me ask you, why you in here.'

'I gwan to xplain soon. But,' and I sigh, 'I dunno how to xplain.'

'Xplain from the start.'

'Is also becos of one girl. But is not what you think. Ten years, Watan! Fuck! Long time! In the jungle village of Kelewang, only two mile from Bau, I get this job, uh, and I about eighteen years old. At first I think real job, is so good, because both ma and pa old. And money so good. For two years I work like this, all we do is cut down tree, we have uniform, landrover, everything. Tons of free time. I just a gofer. I gofer the border. Every day I travel one and half hour by lorry with the others to the border with Indonesia. You know?'

'No.'

'Uh. Is a very small border town, near the National Park. We get into speedboat, have equipment, all kind railway tracks and rope, and generator, to cut down hundreds of trees, we got all documents; who knows, maybe all fake. And in broad daylight! Trees one by one go down, all kind of tree, hardwood, for people all over the world they garden furniture and they flooring. Chengai, meranti, keruing, jati.'

'Then?'

'Watan, now your turn to just listen OK? Uh. Lots of other things we do as well. When tree go down, we get the animals.'

'What animals?'

'You know, animal you are not spose to take away, turtle, deer, et cetera. We kill them sell for meat, can get tens of thousands of ringgit. All kind of animals. Labi-labi! River turtle! Awww taste so good, man. They swim up all time. We use river to transport all the logs. Park rangers don't know a thing: them only got two speedboats. We see them like once or twice a year. We got like twenty speedboat. Uh. We got lights so bright, is like morning even if at night. Cos you know how dark jungle is all time. We got lights that people in filem studio use, you know?'

'Yeah, yeah, I'm in filem industry, Minos.'

'Many, many other animal, yeah, they go running when all this trees come down. Cos they live in them trees. Orang utan, marmoset, flying snake, lemur, macaw.'

'But they just animals.'

'Yeah. So anyway, Watan, there is loophole in export law. I love that word loophole. Everybuddy got a loophole, but how come I ain't got none? What hole I ever got in my life? If tree got no bark on, it not counted as logging. Just wood far as they concern. And so is OK for export. Can get certificate at the port, before it even go on ship to rest of world.'

'Wow, I didn't know that.'

''Strue. So we chop all this tree down even more. Until it just wood. And no tree left with bark. And the bark not wasted. Uh. No. We sell on in bags, plenty of garden people wan bark chip. Fac is, we even sell back to the National Park for making the walk path! Is so funny! And all the tourists got something nice to walk on. Soft, local, brown skin which will never go overseas. Like the girls.'

'Ha. Minos. You funny. You funny!'

'And all this time, mebbe two year I work with this syndicate, I never know all is illegal. Cos we so much more organise and so much bigger than the park ranger. When I in court, somebuddy say to judge: 'Your Honour, seventy to ninety percent of logging is illegal.''

'How you spose to know that Minos?'

'That's what I say! How I spose to know? But by then already too late. I already standing in this wooden box in front of judge!'

'You is Iban, Dayak from the Sea, good at making boats, and me is Bidayuh, Dayak from the Land, good at making buildings. Iban biggest group in Borneo, Bidayuh second biggest. We different but we believe the same. Every tree got spirit, Minos! Even rice got a soul. That's why you chop people's heads. Cos then you get they soul. So you cannot pis on the tree without sayin 'Spirit, is it OK if I pis on you'. So how you feel chopping they tree down?'

'Yeah quite good question is that.'

'You so full of shit.'

'You ask me my story, Watan.'

'And for that you got fifteen years? You don't think that a bit too much? Your lawyer mus be drunk.'

'No. Is cos something else, Watan. Is to do with a girl. And by now she be a young woman. With a tattoo. Today I got no

time to tell you. But continue story another day. Now TV finish.
Lehwe go have something to eat fus.'

9

Benjie

The tattoo was her curse.

If she didn't like the question, she didn't answer. There was no possibility of a straightforward conversation between us. My wife and I would wake up each morning, chatted a little about what we each dreamt about, and she would interpret my dreams, just like she and her Ebu did. The Ibans only knew how to live through their dreams. You unloaded your night's nightmares on someone else, and therefore cleansed yourself of the evil that the nightmare had foisted upon you.

Talisa went through the entire pregnancy silently and calculatingly, as if it was a secret illness. She didn't read baby books or ask me questions. I was at the very least medically qualified to offer her free antenatal advice. In addition, was I not the baby's father?

The second daily conversation we had was at night – on the most riveting topic of home furnishing and design. My humble bachelor squat behind the coffee plantation was not good enough for her. She wanted a new house, one that we had to move into before Wendall arrived, and should be as far away as possible from the smell of coffee and rubber. I should have smelt a rat then, never mind coffee and rubber. I ended up negotiating a land deal with Ian, about eight miles from Old Town. I made Ian even richer.

Talisa appointed an architect. The next thing I knew I was looking over A1-sized plans and construction was underway. While she paced with my son in her belly, dreaming of chandeliers and gold taps, I found it hard to see the wood from the trees. The Ibans were skilled makers of the longboat, a canoe dug out from the meranti tree. The meranti tree would now be lucky to be laid in some wealthy household somewhere in Europe or America, where it would be preserved for centuries, from longboat to Long Island. She would only have a hardwood floor.

Thousands of ringgits left my account to fund some stupid gold taps from Italy. She saw them on Desperate Housewives. She watched it on pirate DVD and freezed the frame so as to get a closer look. Swan-neck – to run the water, you broke their necks. Everytime I turned the taps on, I turned inside.

She didn't know who the Prime Minister was, where Australia was, or what a carcinogen was. She knew every fashion designer's name and collection, the name of every celebrity and every brand of beauty product, shoes, handbags, clothes and eyewear (the term for sunglasses, according to our friend). The only song she knew was Angel, by Robbie Williams. It was her favourite song, apparently, which was not a tough decision, if it was the only song you knew.

I discovered that Talisa could only cook one dish, if you could even call it cooking. It was an intolerable jungle chicken stew she learnt from her Ebu but I wish she could unlearn it. Within days of moving into my peasant cottage, she hired a housemaid, a Filipina, from the agency. Talisa had not consulted me, but perhaps I would have said 'fine', albeit with reticence. Being pregnant, she couldn't do any labour-intensive housework anyway.

Naturally, Asuncion's job included preparing dinner. I missed my mushroom risottos and spaghetti vongole, with a wonderful rocket and parmesan salad on the side. Living in Asia had made me crave standard Italian meals, even the Waitrose ones would do, with perhaps the 3 for 2 Chablis deal from Thresher's. These were the simple pleasures I once took for granted.

I BROUGHT JAPANESE ORANGE chrysanthemums home for my heavily pregnant wife. 'Kek wa!' Talisa called them by their Sino-Malay name. 'Lovely,' she said, grabbing the orange bunch. There was even a street in Segamat named after chrysanthemums, so popular were they in this town. 'When our ancestors die, their spirits become or live in flowers,' she said, tossing the bunch at Asuncion, who put them in water.

'Uh-huh,' I said, opening the fridge and pondering over whether I should have a Carlsberg or Tiger.

'In Iban, we live and dream flowers. They're a good sign, because your ancestors are there to protect you.'

Carlsberg. 'They're just flowers, darling,' I said, pulling the ring on the can.

'Not long to go now,' she said, rubbing her beach ball belly like it was a magic lamp.

After yet another inexorable episode of CSI, it was time for bed. Once it was my 'humble peasant cottage' bedroom, filled with CDs and books, but now it was ours and cluttered with clothes, DVDs, lingerie and cosmetics which Asuncion had not been able to tidy in time. Over the bedhead, hung Ebu's wrap-ikat weave cloth called Pua Kumbu. Handwoven in Talisa's family longhouse, it was a heavy blanket-like fabric, with rich and fine red, gold and black threads.

'Ebu said it's supposed to be magic. It will save me one day.'

'Oh yes? What does Pua Kumbu mean?'

'Pua means blanket and kumbu means sacred. Ebu said it's believed that those who have a pua kumbu can fly. In Iban stories, the word for blanket is the same as wings.'

'That's fascinating,' I said. 'Can you fly?'

She thought about it. 'I can't,' she said, shaking her head seriously. She did not intend it as a joke but I burst out laughing. She looked hurt and said no more.

IN THE MORNING, WHEN I was putting on my one pair of Kenneth Cole work shoes, I noticed something I had not noticed before. Since our wedding, the cabinet in the carport downstairs had become filled with trainers, stilettos and sandals. However, next to the said cabinet, another cupboard had appeared, whose sole purpose would seem to be for housing pointy shoes. It was stuffed to the proverbial gills.

Talisa shrieked with laughter, like a bad child. It was her revenge on me. She found it terribly amusing when I pointed to the cupboard, slack-jawed and speechless. She said I was really funny, that I was the funniest guy in the world, that I made her laugh, that it was like being in a sitcom. She took her 'sense of style' (her words, not mine) from *Sex and the City*, the full three series of which we had on DVD, for her to educate and entertain herself while she painted her toe nails. Why didn't I watch them with her, she pouted. They were *fan-dabi-dozi*!

'Well, I've got to go now, darling.' I said, a little robot-like. She was my little pirate. No wonder the colonialists called them Sea Dayaks. They tore down the torrential waterways, rivers with the force of electricity itself. They grabbed what they liked and made themselves at home.

10

Minos

The old-old Ibans say: a man without tattoos is invisible to the gods. Myself and Watan have no tattoos at all. That mean we have achief absolutely nothing in life. That's right. Cos every year MAN should be getting more tattoo. Old man, if he worth anythin at all, if he good brave bloke all his life, if he good at carving, playing ruding, taken many heads, is covered in tattoos, so no more skin can be see. Is good for cammo-flage too.

If you in lock-up, as we in lock-up, is like being teenager. Is like there is no memory cept for your childhood. Everything they say you do, you do. And when they say read quietly, you read quietly. Very boring. And you get to watch TV at set times. Usually when is cartoons. And you feel shit about everything. But myself and Watan not teenagers. Myself almost thirty and Watan three years more old than myself. And we have achief absolutely nothing.

But if I understand correctly from Pastor Bernard, all this is OF NO MATTER. God still love we no matter what. Each and every one inmate. Everybuddy is call brudder. And brudder is better than buddy. There are three Gods. There is the father and son team: God the one who gives instruction, and God's son who takes the instruction and die on cross for we all. And the third God is the spirit. And so we be given the gift of eternal life. Et cetera.

And that's GOOD.

But there ain't no sound good as a hornbill flapping in the garing tree, the immortal tree.

Before shower this morning, I take out the New International Version Bible from under my pillow. I now got two book. The other is the Ten Steps to Please God book. That one is clearly cheaper. I prefer New International Version Bible. I like to touch the red leather cover, is the most expensif thing I ever hold. Is red leather! With gold lettering. And the lettering not just print on top, but eat *into* the leather, like the cow with marking. And I let my finger touch each letter. I open and touch inside pages and make them fan out to get the smell. Is a clean sharp smell, like midnight.

The paper is so thin, is like cloud. You can see words from the other side from the front side. And to touch very, very thin paper is like being learned. Cos if your finger very coarse, torn, blister from diggin up road in sun all day, you ain't gonna turn the page. I don't always wan turn the page. Cos I don't wan spoil it. Snough for me to just open and close it every now and then.

But I cannot read anymore. Cos that is the siren going off for the day beginning. And everybuddy got to get going.

TODAY MYSELF AND WATAN in the field. Half of everybuddy dragging giant hoe which look like the comb of a crazy woman. And half of everybuddy is clearing new site and break up pieces of concrete that sit on the ground. There are only two tree in this whole field. Nobuddy can go nowhere or climb tree.

The ground next to some old British air-field and the British they love they old cement panel huts with concrete floor (all broken). They put them everywhere before war, during war, after war. They look like rough grey cube, and all they same. Pastor say that they are pre-fab. Means ready-made. In fac Pastor himseff born in one of these, he tell I with smile.

The heat rise from the concrete like it is the concrete's spirit. The heat make everything not clear at all, but slightly wavy, like old mirror. So of course, Watan already acting like he gwan faint. Cos he so fat, and he never get thin even if smashing concrete up all day. Wheelbarrow up and down thick plank, into a giant metal box, but he look like he should be wheeling himseff around.

'Hey Minos!'

'What?'

The guard prowling like tiger.

'So you gwan tell me more? More of the serious shit you been doing? How come you een for fifteen years?'

'Uh.'

I look around. Guard gon. Somebuddy in trouble with guard cos he dump rubbish in wrong place. And guard talking to him

74

real loud, like machine gun. Myself and Watan go about to back of the giant metal box.

'So, Minos! Tell your story.'

'So OK. Where I stop? Where I start? Oh yes. So after two year with this logging syndicate I lose my job. Cos somebuddy tell the govment. What this syndicate have been doing. So I think I gwan to city, I gwan leave all this shit, rainforest, turtles, speedboats, all this shit behind. And first I go to National Park office nearby my own village. I wan get new job. Maybe like driver or whatever. Even guide. I speak Inglish. Simple words I learn from logging. From mishnaries that have come and go. Plus all the other tribe languages. Plus Malay. I know the jungle like I know my own body. Every plant, every animal, I know the name. I know what to do when accident or snakebite or ill or whatever. I can guide people, I myself have walk in jungle, five hour, eight hour a day, no problem. In total darkness sometimes. And still they say no job. No.'

'They say no?'

'They say no. And you know why Watan? Because they say they already know what I doing before. I bring shame to whole village. And I say who say all this? Cos I can't believe it. And they say the man name is Peliris....'

The guard he is back. Shouting. Watan make face, but is lost cos his face so round. And again, I run out of time, and never got to say what actually happen to I and how come I een yah for FIFTEEN YEAR, reduce to TEN.

REST OF THE DAY, we got split up. Guard order half of everybuddy go elsewhere. Watan got to do something else and myself, don't know what. Sometime we get easy time somewhere else to package even bigger thing. And that evening, I can see nothing from my window. I have not see sky at night for long time. Because my room look into courtyard. The window is as small as a bowl. I only know it raining from the sound. TV is better. Is like a window with more than one view.

I need to lie down to think. Cos I don't dream no more.

Peliris. The name is come back to me now. He the reason why I een here. Big chief. He father have even eat Japanese soldier brains. Cos they say if you eat Japanese brains, you get smart. Ancestors of Peliris have collect loads and loads of heads.

Heads of enemy tribes, mishnary, heads from battles. And they hang in his ruai over the fireplace, every day smoking and drying out, until they become little black skulls with yellow hair and teeth. And everybuddy scare of him. He cover in tattoos.

Everybuddy know he is nasty drunk. He manage to cheat the rice from the people. Rice counting in Iban is like accounting. Is better than money, which you cannot eat. Peliris work in another logging syndicate. This mean he just wan to close down my syndicate. And that is why he report it. He make me lose my job, even though his syndicate look real, but is fake with fake documents and all. And they also take not-allowed animals.

The day I go to see him I remember real clear, is bright as eyes of turtles. Is late afternoon. I come back from the National Park office after I lose my job. When I walk through all these paths I know so well, the rope bridge I cross and pounding of a waterfall nearby, my head full of bees. Nibong fence is growing around Peliris longhouse to keep wild animals out. Is very sharp blade plant, use for making knife and spear tip.

I climb the log ladder of Peliris longhouse. Is one great tree trunk, with notches cut out of it for feet to step onto, also to keep out wild animals. Actually, no wild animals will want to bother Peliris. And to further keep out animals, the longhouse is fifteen feet above ground! The tanju is wide, maybe ten foots. Is like a verandah, a timber deck, no hand rail. So when you look up you don't know if anyone in or not. You must call out to whoever is in the house to see if they in or not. But I dwan to call out. Cos Peliris is only gonna tell I to fuck off. So I climb.

I see on the great tanju, a long piece of skin of python, covered with the beeswax, salt and gum of tree. Whoooaaa! Great big snake, ten or twelve feet long! Is pin all around onto the wooden deck, cover in flies. Shheeeeeez! Almost diamond shape, cos the tail end it taper to nothing. Python skin worth lot of money. Is for selling to travelling musician, to make the drum skin and to make shoes. Peliris family must have already eat all the meat. That day I nothing to eat, and the hope I have for this job with the National Park is all eat up. My stomach is singing with hunger.

What make me not think straight is strong smell of cooking. The whole thing happen becos of this smell, and cos of the python skin. Up this high, the longhouse tanju is well in the tree canopy. And sun is going further down, sun actually lower than the longhouse already. The smell of something frying – is it smell of tapioca fritters? I just wanna die. I don't think Peliris gonna offer I any. Inside a longhouse is always very dark, humid. Eyes cannot see straightaway. The teak floor is creaking from the attap matting, and I call out before I go any further. Mebbe they not in.

Then my eyes get more strong. Peliris come out at far end of deck. He stagger like bull, and there is strong smell of tuak on him. Mebbe he is drunk. His clothes half on, his eyes red. What he been doing?

'Who are you?' He shout.

'I'm Minos. You got my syndicate shut down. I have no job now. Can I have a job?'

He laugh so hard, it make me mad. 'Why you laugh?' I say.

'What syndicate?'

He is lying of course. He cheat rice money all the time from the village. 'Give me a job,' I plead. He laugh again real hard. I get so angry I fly at he and push him. He push me back twice as hard. I feel my shoulders explode. 'You better fuck off before I cut your throat,' he say. 'How dare you come here?'

I must admit, I should have go at this point, but I do not. My blood is cooking inside me. Every muscle in me make me push him back, harder than he push me. He get very angry. He start to grab me up like a just a bunch of flowers, so easy for him!

I see a girl come out from the bilek behind him. Mebbe twelve or thirteen years old? Must be Peliris daughter. She move silent as a snake. She come out so quick and with a long lesong, the stick to beat rice. Before he can lift I, she use a small tap of the lesong on his back, and she push Peliris over the edge. He go flying. And then a SNAP, sound of Peliris hitting ground fifteen feet below. Akh!

At first I think, why this little girl want to save me from Peliris? The next second I feel a sharp push from my back, mebbe with another lesong. I fall over. I get up. I am a quick young monkey, I'm not Peliris. I turn around and see her close. It is a woman. She is holding a lesong. Her beautiful face cover in bruises and tears. And her clothes only half on. She must be Peliris wife, the one who is famous for weaving, the one with Pua Kumbu skills that won the heart of many men.

I jump on the serpent skin, so sticky with tree gum and beeswax. I kick, step up and down, I dance the ngajat. Her face break like a jar. She looking down at my foots. She cry out: 'The skin!' I look down. She drop the lesong with a heavy plop. The more I dance, the more I ruin the skin. She and the daughter trying to save it. For she knows is worth small fortune, come to think of it now, maybe even a thousand ringgit. My standing on it is gwan cost her. They pulling this way and that, I dance like Nabau the serpent himself, when he meet Naga the dragon from the world underneath. The skin is tearing into big pieces first and then tiny pieces. They cry millions tears. They both yelling. I kick off my sandals and run for it. I don't care I leave my sandals behind. Sun already sink to the ground, like Peliris.

I run until I reach the log ladder and I go down quick as monkey. When I going down halfway, I think the woman must following me, but no. I hear woman and girl both are crying and they still on the deck above. They speaking in Iban.

The woman weeping, 'I'm sorry I married that man,'

'He's gone now, Ebu,' the girl say.

'Thank you, daughter,' she say, so softly that I go up one notch on the log ladder to hear better. They think I am already gone.

'Why did you try to kill the thief?' the girl ask.

'Because he… saw,' the woman reply, 'He saw you…'

There is no reply. 'He got away,' the girl then say, 'but the skin cannot be saved, Ebu.'

'No one must ever know what really happened,' the woman say.

'No, Ebu,' say the girl.

I gently slide to the bottom of the log ladder. Peliris land on the nibong fence, which go through him in so many places, I vomit when I see his body.

I think of that GIRL. Big black holes for eyes. Eyes fill with worms.

A gereja bird is singing its high, sad song, as I run home, barefoot. Tree sparrow, fly away. Don't sing. I ain't lisnin to you now.

'**NOW THEN WATAN**, I remember everything, yet so little.'

'So what the woman say in court?'

'She say that I push the man because I have come to rob the place. But I haven't push the man. I have kill no one. In my pocket is only twelve ringgit and forty-three sen. Is nothin, but I cannot prove that is my own money and not rob from Peliris. Truth is, only time I rob somebuddy is when I in the syndicate, is not counted! I rob somebuddy who rob me first! All this I say in the court room. What is the use? No use! When the judge ask me, why did you go to the longhouse to see this Peliris? I say, your heightness, I go to see this man to... to get my job back.'

'Why do you think you can get your job back from this man?'

'Becos I think he the one that make the logging syndicate shut down.'

'What make you say that?'

'Er, somebuddy say so.'

'Somebody said to you that Peliris is responsible for your job?'

'Somebuddy say that Peliris tell the govmen that the logging we dwan is illegal. I say to judge, 'I need the money, your heightness. Peliris is man of great power. He can get me job.' I cannot say more than that to the judge becos then he will know that everything I make from the logging is also illegal.'

'Why you plead guilty?'

'Cos my lawyer say to do that, cos of my petty crimes and like I just tell you, all the logging I do is illegal. They are strong. I am weak. And of course, stupid.'

'No, don't be stupid. You not stupid.'

'All I know is: I have see the girl kill her father. The woman try to push me over the edge because they don't want me to tell anyone. The serpent spirit knows what I saying is true! But Watan, remember? Nabau save me. They bring my sandals to court to prove everything. The thief's sandals, they call them. After the court case, I wonder of my sandals, all cover in the beeswax, salt and gum of tree: what they do with my sandals? Watan, are you even listnin?'

'I'm thinking.'

11

Bernard

October

Margaret,
 Sorry I haven't got back to you. I have been in the jungle for four days. Some photos for you to look at (see attached). I have been to the funeral of a grand old Iban lady, Talina Menduk. She was only seventy-four. She accepted Christ as her Saviour two months ago. Now she is returned to the Lord.

You wanted to see what a longhouse looks like. This is it! Have only just mastered the art of downloading photos. Not too *au fait* yet. A longhouse is basically a village in the air. The central communal highway is a kind of gallery called the ruai. There is a photo of the hearth (that thing which looks like a campfire in the centre of the ruai) where trophy heads taken by the village chief and his ancestors are hung. A view of one of the eight bilek, or apartments.

The moment you visit a longhouse, your hosts will give you a cup of tuak. It is rude to refuse, even if you don't drink, but after you have had it you will be feeling completely incoherent. The old lady was Peliris' mother-in-law. He has been dead about ten years, and she continued to live in his longhouse, since her daughter and granddaughter left Borneo. Woman and daughter fled in the middle of the night, the day after the trial. They had to flee because if they waited too long, the evil spirit of Peliris would be back.

No one knows where they have gone. They simply vanished. Even the boatman does not know. He stands next to the river all day and night, the river which gleams like a brown beetle. He, like Charon on the River Styx, waits for passengers on the airless riverbank, intoxicated by tuak and by the smell of smoke from his torches which provided the only illumination. Now Margaret,

I would not like to use the digital camera on the river, because it will only show how crass flash photography will turn out, so you will just have to believe me, it is like a fairy-tale.

I hope you are not revulsed by the shrunken heads. Margaret, when we were children, you were the adventurous one. I stayed home and read and you climbed the trees. You concocted poison from some crazy recipe you found. And you hid it under the house. You hoped to give it to someone who annoyed you. Like that girl, what's her name, Kimberley Cushionface. Do you remember?

Anyway, coming back to Peliris' longhouse. It is made of the ubah katak ('frog-changing') tree, *Rhodamnia mulleri*. Very excellent hardwood. The tree itself has berries munched on by birds, monkeys and squirrels. Now, this is an interesting story. Do you remember the new convert I mentioned in my previous email whom I believe is innocent? Let us just say his name is Luke. (That is the name I will give him when he is released, to protect his identity so he may return to the community. So I may as well start practising calling him by his new name.)

Luke is in prison for the murder of this man Peliris. On the day of the murder, Luke went to Peliris' longhouse. Luke says that he is innocent. However, he was a petty thief and all the work he had ever done was illegal. Luke is what they would call a tau tepang. (How can I explain this? It roughly translates as 'person with the evil eye who ruins everything and anything he looks at'). Tau tepangs are from the poorer strata of Iban society, who project loss and failure onto the successful. Because they are poor and lack success, they hunger after padi. They break in to steal the proverbial rice. No one would take his word over that of Peliris and his family of established Ibans who weave textiles and skin reptiles for good money. He pleaded guilty as advised by his lawyer, who described the murder as an accident, and got his fifteen years instead of life.

Talina Menduk, like her son-in-law Peliris, had a gigantic send-off, which I witnessed yesterday. The burial ceremony is called the Gawai Antu which means Festival of the Departed Souls. She really wanted the traditional ceremony even though she has converted to Christianity. I demurred of course. We had to compromise, the church and the village chief. I would carry out the normal service and prayers, and the burial ceremony had to go ahead as planned by the villagers.

Death is not so important as treatment of the dead, sending away of the spirit. The rituals are complicated and they puzzle me even after so many years of living in Borneo. You will be pleased to hear, it is just as well since many cosmological rituals are going to be extinct soon due to conversion of the Bornean peoples to Islam or Christianity.

Talina's traditional coffin is made from the meranti (Shorea) wood, the largest and most valuable genus of dipterocarp. The *Meranti pitis* is a tall, straight tree whose seeds species are eaten by various jungle animals. Margaret, I am so glad I trained as a botanist before going into missionary work. I never realised it would come in handy. You know what it makes you realise? Something profound: if you consider the molecular make-up of every species, we are related to everything that has a life. Even scoundrels get the best wood for their coffin, so that their spirits do not come back and bother anyone.

The coffin should be shaped like a boat and modelled on the kenyalang or rhinoceros hornbill, since it is a woman who has died. The hornbill is a sacred bird and is associated with the creation of the world. If you hear a hornbill's characteristic ha-honk call and its flapping wings, it's a good omen, because it symbolises the female gender, from whom, and in which, man is created.

The hornbill is symbolic of motherhood because of their unusual 'maternity leave'. To protect their young, the mother bird is sealed in a hollow tree, such as the benuah, for three months using bird droppings, mud and grass but leaving a small orifice through which the father bird is able to feed his Missus. When the chick has hatched the mother bird chips her way out. There are festivals just to celebrate and feed hornbills *en masse* at a gigantic bird table the size of your local Homebase.

Burial men dance around the coffin, wearing animal masks and grass cloaks. It is curtained off in an A-frame tent called a sungkup, whose headboard is painted and carved with foliate scrolls and arabesques of nabau (serpent) and naga (dragon) representing the beasts of the underworld. Woven by Talina's own daughter and kept all this time for this purpose, the sacred blanket, Pua Kumbu, forms the curtain of this tent. The dead woman is given a painted hat to wear for her journey into the afterworld.

The coffin is put into the burial canoe. It is to drift down the river, taking three days to reach heaven, to which the Dayaks have maps. At a burial ceremony, I have often wondered if I can also take a look at these maps. If heaven is only three days away, why doesn't everyone go there? But only the burial officials, or mediums with messages from the spirits, could look at the maps.

Psychopomps or spirit guides direct the deceased to the underworld, making sure the dead would not get stuck on fallen trees. For three days, the dead has to move continuously. As I write you this long email, Talina's body should still be sailing. The journey may be hit by storms and the energy of the river would still be needed, be stronger, be braver, than any obstacles in the way, the energy which comes from the psychopomps.

The burial men jump up and down outside the canoe. With as much gusto and as little splash as they can drum up without disturbing the crocodiles, broadcasting to any spirits listening that the three-day journey has begun. They half-run, half-swim alongside, they push, they shove, give instructions and directions to the spirit guides. The canoe bobs heavily with all that force, revving, ready. It is like a river taxi, without a driver. The burial men's neck muscles bulge and pulse like a row of reptilian throats. They remind the villagers (and I, of course) that we are alive. Talina had sailed away.

Yes, of course, I do feel that I am in conflict, Margaret, especially as you seem to think that I am holiday. A) I am not on holiday and B) Christianity still co-exists with animism, because your concept of God is different to theirs. C) Eternal Light's expansion is of paramount importance.

After the funeral comes the party. Tuak flows freely and there is also ngajat dancing. Why did I spend 4 days partying with them, then, you may wonder. Margaret, this is our big break. Since the party, the headman has already given us the green light. The longhouse is ours now, Margaret. Otherwise this place will just go to seed, deserted and abandoned. The old lady was living here all alone. With her contagious illness, she was avoided by the villagers. She had no descendants save for Talisa, whose whereabouts are unknown and whose intention to return is unlikely. To think you once doubted my PR skills.

Young people are leaving the longhouses for the city. They generally do not return. They don't want to do any carving or weaving. How many times have I seen in downtown Kuching, tribal folk sitting on the roadside, on the actual kerbs, just waiting, waiting. Waiting for what? They think that work will come to them. Somehow a spirit will descend and give them a job. They don't understand, Margaret. They don't connect CVs, job applications, employment agencies, reading, speaking and writing English to opening and shutting car doors outside hotels.

Please cobble something for the Newsletter. If not, the church may think nothing is going on and I may as well be sent back to the UK. I pray that the Ministry is shining its Eternal Light on us out here. Sometimes I feel that we are all waiting on kerbs all our lives.

Yours,

B.

P.S. Maybe I should start a blog.

12

Benjie

Builders. They said tomorrow and they meant next week, and next week meant next month. Although the decorations were not quite finished, I was glad we moved in three weeks before Wendall's ETA. Asuncion at least had the chance to clean the place thoroughly. The house made up for the mind-numbing wait. My London mates still stuck at Tooting NHS St George's Hospital would probably laugh their heads off at my absurd middle middle-class taste involving classical mimicry and pastiche. They would call me a *parvenu*. Marble tiles with the cabochon detail, half-price leather sofas, Astro TV and broadband. The newly-landscaped garden had young trees still in their braces, hoops and props. They were babies themselves, learning how to stand.

The master bedroom bed which Talisa had chosen was Italian-designed, according to the sticker, but probably made in China. We had giant mirrored built-in wardrobes made by the best carpenter in town who was booked up three months in advance. The sliding tracking system for the mirrored doors came from Germany. Talisa was very fond of the 'hotel style' as she called it. For a non-reader, she seemed to have acquired a library of books on interior design. 'We're going to slowly finish off all the other rooms,' she announced jubilantly, 'if and when we get any visitors at all.'

For someone not Scottish, Talisa seemed to favour tartan. Ian's influence must be far more pervasive than I would have liked. Wendall's room was all tartan. I hoped he would not grow up with a preference for haggis. Fortunately, it was not on sale in the supermarkets here.

IT WAS NOVEMBER WHEN Talisa was full term plus 2 days overdue when she had her SROM: spontaneous rupture of membranes. Her waters had to break when she was shopping, of course. When her contractions were two minutes apart, Talisa checked herself into Lim's Specialist Maternity Home to have Wendall. She had not attended a single antenatal class but she said she had seen enough births in communal longhouses. She knew her breathing techniques, and just like a good Sea Dayak, she was fearless and in control. If there was anyone at all to be her 'birth partner', Talisa would have had her Ebu, not me. Helplessly, I wanted to capture my little Wood Rooster's first yawn on my new Canon Ixus digital camera. I had wanted to hold not her hand but his, which I imagined would fit into mine like a small warm pebble. Instead I was at Little T's Sports Bar. A part of me died when he was born.

Wendall's only skills were lying down, kicking and looking around without really looking. Very young babies could only focus on the human face, yet I found it disconcerting to face him. Medical school did not prepare me physically or mentally for fatherhood. It made me a doctor, not a father. I did not know what this person was doing lying in a cot in my house, yet this house had been designed around him, for him. I thought rather cruelly, that perhaps he would go away or something, and I could divorce Talisa. I suffered a stabbing pain on the side of my head every time I thought of the woman whom I had to marry and the child I had to father. I never whispered his name even to myself. He was simply a blob who yelled.

Within a month of Wendall's birth, Talisa had hired a driver with his own car, a silver Toyota Altis. I thought: maid, yes, but driver? She had been harping for a two-door sexy little Mercedes C-Class Sports Coupe or some such 'practical' car for her and baby, so naturally I demurred when she asked if she could have a car and driving lessons (in that order). She thought I was being gallant and protective of her, so she promptly hired a driver, Ibrahim.

My mother, being a typical frugal Malaysian mum, baulked at the very idea of it, but I explained that it was more like a chartered taxi. 'Driver' somehow always made it sound costly and frivolous. I regretted giving her a lift that stormy night. I should have just driven away, just like my instinct told me to do.

Talisa found the name Wendall from the internet. The name meant *traveller* or *wanderer*, which Talisa immediately liked. The Chinese were keen on names that could be translated easily into Chinese, so Wendall fulfilled that requirement for my parents. In Iban tradition, babies were supposed to be named after their grandparents but Talisa was against it. She was named after her Nenek, Talina, but was re-named by her mother with a name not too dissimilar to Nenek's the moment they arrived in Segamat. They were indigenous people who had 'no identity', and therefore they both needed to apply for identity cards anyway. 'To have the same name would have been a curse,' Ebu had said. 'Might as well change it now.' Talisa agreed, using her Nenek's name would be a regression to her uncouth past.

In severing her past, Talisa refused to breastfeed because she thought it was uncivilised and regressive, thereby marring my reputation as a GP. She did not even try. She proudly bought tins of formula *at trade price* by the boxful from my clinic's pharmaceutical supplier, as if to humiliate me further.

A young baby, whose stomach was the size of a walnut, had to feed every two hours over a twenty-four hour period or twelve times a day in the first few weeks of their life if he were breastfed, and every three hours, or eight times a day, if he were formula-fed. Talisa already knew what was coming and was not interested in losing beauty sleep over it. She started him on formula straightaway. To avoid his night awakenings, she wanted him fed by Asuncion. Talisa would never consider using a breast pump to express milk for Wendall, who actually slept in Asuncion's bedroom.

I knew what Talisa thought: formula cost money. It was bound to be better than breastmilk, which was free. If you bought formula, it meant you could afford to. As a doctor, how could I then preach to patients the benefits of breastfeeding for both mother and child when in fact my own wife refused to be 'primitive' and breastfeed 'like a savage'? She was not a mammal, but a cold-blooded being.

I made myself cuddle the baby but I was deeply uncomfortable. And just like my wife, I left nappy changing to Asuncion. Little wonder then, that I was terrified of my own son, the stranger in the cot. Maids and drivers were how we subcontracted parenthood. Talisa and I were united – we both shunned our child. Asuncion fed and changed Wendall and Ibrahim drove everyone around, except me, leaving Talisa and I plenty of time to scowl in silence. The number of people in my house seemed to have quintupled, and all on my tab. I spent my evenings at the Club.

Then a miracle happened. When Wendall was six weeks old, he started to smile, not at objects or pictures, but only at Asuncion. I scratched my head. Why was he smiling at Asuncion? Never did it occur to me it was because he saw her all the time. For the next couple of weeks, I made sure that Talisa and I smiled at him all the time, even if we never smiled at each other. It worked. For months after, he was so generous with his smiles every time he saw me. Ian called children an investment. What I put in I got back a million times over. Wendall was my world and I was his. He was totally in love with me. Someone loved me. That was when I knew my heart could melt, that I was no longer a bachelor.

IT WAS CHRISTMAS DAY, which also happened to be a Sunday. I believed Malaysia had one of the world's most number of public holidays, about eighteen days in total per year. There were holidays for royal dignitaries as well as festivals to celebrate every religion.

Both sets of grandparents had stopped by my house to see Wendall and drop his presents off. There was no expectation for Asuncion to prepare a meal for so many people so I thought we could go to the Banana Leaf to give Ibrahim and Asuncion a break. This place was famous for fish head curry, a traditional Sunday favourite of Ian's, and he always got his way. Luckily, everyone was fond of fish head curry too.

'If only these hammocks had been around when I had my first two!' Ian said. He was referring to the 'sarong on a spring' in which Wendall had just woken from his mid-morning nap.

'Dah,' said Talisa, 'They've been around for centuries.' She rolled her eyes as she picked up Wendall from the baby hammock. 'What did you think!' she asked him. Her eyelashes were long and black, like spiders. She'd made herself up before the relatives arrived. That was her main priority. Talisa had eye creams which cost over four hundred ringgit a pot. She moaned that Wendall still woke up at least twice a night even though it was Asuncion who woke to feed Wendall, not his mother.

Once Wendall had been lifted out, the hammock deflated like a balloon. My mother had her turn at cuddling him. Although

Wendall had a cot, he preferred the sarong. It made him feel safe and secure, because he was held firmly by the calico sides and soothed by the two-way movement. Since he could not turn around, he would always be on his back. It was snug, warm and like being in a uterus, but he would have to transfer to his cot sooner or later. He would be too heavy for it by the time he was a year old.

Wendall smiled as we talked about him. I held a colourful rattle in his face and he squealed with delight, kicking his legs furiously.

'If he woke up in the night,' I said to Ian, 'Asuncion can just jiggle it using this string tied from her toe to the hammock,' I pointed to the red raffia string so carefully constructed to the perfect tension and compression. 'As the hammock is spring loaded, the movement sets off the swaying and baby is rocked to sleep again.' I gave a slight tug to demonstrate. 'Of course there is no baby in it at the moment, so the effect is somewhat lost.'

'No, you're not in it now, are you, wee man,' he said. It was Ian's turn to cuddle Wendall. I remembered being in a hammock myself, pulsing and swaying, like being at sea. I felt slightly seasick when I remembered it but nobody complained of seasickness in a womb when you were really floating in a bag of saltwater. Some people liked to mimic this pre-birth feeling in alternative healing, such as going into a flotation tank. Having a child brought you back to your own childhood: I kept buying various modes of toy transportation: cars, planes and trains for Wendall, not sure if I was actually buying them for myself. He was far too young. The toys would stay in their boxes for a good couple of years, on my study shelves where I could admire them and play with them every now and then. I called it downgrading. Shrinks would call it regressing.

'Yesterday I was out shopping… in Star Plaza,' said Talisa.

'Yesterday she went shopping,' I said in Mandarin for the benefit of my mum, carefully leaving out the Star Plaza bit as my mum would have said it was too expensive to shop there.

'Don't you think he's just so cute?' Talisa continued, in English, slyly ignoring my edited translation. 'There was this elderly lady who could not stop smiling at him, and when she asked how old he was, she couldn't believe that he's nine weeks old – he's big for his age.'

On the rare occasion when we spoke, Talisa and I spoke English. Although I could speak basic Chinese, as I did to my mum, I was otherwise illiterate.

I was not motivated to learn Iban since Talisa was in the process of gradually erasing her entire past, culture, self, identity. She was deliberately de-culturising herself. Whereas I was de-cultured not by choice, but by my parent's decision to put me through an English school, deemed more posh than a Chinese school. I blamed my parents and my parents blamed the colonialists, who in turn blamed the natives, all in triangular fashion. I blamed them all!

Talisa knew much more about Chinese culture than I ever would. This was all fairly irritating to me, more so as I was playing the learning Chinese CD in the car on the night of the Crazy Mistake.

Talisa's Ebu came here in order to make a living. She was a survivor, but not enough to see Wendall. She was not the right 'pairson'. A hard life was a short life. Surya had instilled in Talisa that her tattoo was the only indication of her achievements, but I think a far greater achievement was that she entangled me in her net. I wondered if Ian loved Surya, Talisa's mother. Perhaps she didn't manage to ensnare him as I had been ensnared by her daughter.

The tattoo was not for every Iban woman, because tattooing was much more unpleasant for girls than for boys. When asked why it was more unpleasant, Talisa's answer was: 'cos it just *is*?' She wasn't a shaman or a manang and she wasn't in the community who believed she was a heroine.

As Talisa was not one to explain, I looked into it myself. I learnt that she could endure great pain, unimaginable pain, which was probably why she found childbirth bearable. She had raised her pain threshold so high she gave birth without the epidural, the Pethidine injection or Entonox gas and air. To me this was staggering when one imagined the size of a human infant head, yet that was how it was done for millenia, and at fatal risk to both mother and child.

I found out about Iban tattoo art from a biker himself, a patient of mine, who was a tattoo artist to bikers. For men or women, he said, tattoos were the ultimate symbols of achievement, rewards for acts of heroism. Girls tattooed girls, he said, to make sure that the art never died but grew with each generation, with children being trained as 'tattoo artists'. Although there were machines nowadays, the tools used by these juvenile 'tattoo artists' were primitive, simply consisting of two or three prickers and an iron striker kept in a wooden case. The prickers were wooden rods with a short pointed head projecting at right angles at one end. Three or four short needles protruded, attached by a lump of resin to the point of the head. The striker was merely a short iron clad, half of which was covered with a string lashing. The pigment was a mixture of soot, water and sugar cane juice, kept in a shallow wooden cup. The best soot was believed to be obtained from the bottom of the metal cooking pot.

Quite candidly, after I took his blood-pressure, he told me that the tattoo designs were provided by the more senior tattooists, who were young women themselves. The designs were carved in high relief on blocks of wood that were smeared with the ink and then stamped onto the part of the body to be tattooed. The designs tattooed on girls were in longitudinal rows or transverse bands, with zigzag lines marking the divisions between the rows or bands. I was too engrossed to mention that my wife said her design was called the song irang.

My biker patient said that the subject to be tattooed had to lie on the floor, with the teenage tattoo artist and her assistant, also a similar-aged girl, squatting either side. The tattoo artist or her assistant stretched the skin to be tattooed with their feet, and dipping a pricker into the pigment, tapped its handle with the striker as she worked along a line, driving the needle points into the skin. The operation was painful and slow – it could take a day. There was no antiseptic and often a new tattoo ulcerated. Hearing about the process pricked my eyes with needle-like tears, but I kept it to myself – my wife need not know of my newfound knowledge.

Well! I had never blowpiped an animal, taken a head or rowed my way through a thunderstorm in a tiny boat filled with hunted birds. I had no tattoo. How tedious then, that this heroic, deceitful woman, was now my wife. Indeed I was jealous of her, fearful of her. My fatuous realisation was that she was the mother of my child. Pity my serendipity.

TONIGHT, MY WIFE AND I were sitting up in our Italian-designed bed. I was reading the latest 'overseas' edition of the British Medical Journal in nice airmail see-through paper, for which I paid heavily in subscription fees.

I looked over Talisa's shoulder. I asked her what she was reading, since she didn't usually read. It was a Chinese paperback. There were no pictures or diagrams, just columns and columns of Chinese script, fine as eyebrow hair, read top to bottom, and right to left of page. 'It's my only book,' she said nonchalantly, 'Christmas present from your mum.'

She read out a love poem, *The Song of Eternal Sorrow* by the Tang poet Bai Juyi.

'Darling, that's beautiful!' I said in English, sounding like a Londoner who found everything interesting. 'What does it mean?'

She explained the poem line by line, in English, technically and without charm:

> In sky we are birds inseparable by wings aligned
> On ground we are trees with twigs intertwined
> And though heaven and earth may one day come
>   to an end
> There is no end to this sorrow in my mind

After we turned out the lights, I couldn't sleep. I faced away from Talisa and I realised something: her eyes didn't move once when she read. You could always tell when someone was reading silently in Chinese, because they had to move their head in a nodding action due to the top to bottom direction of text. I was looking for that nodding motion but there was none.

The joke was that the Chinese always agreed with what they read. You read from top to bottom and back to front by starting at the 'back' of the book in order to progress to the 'front' which was really the end of the book. When my mum read romantic short stories in the car while waiting for me to come out of school, she nodded away until she nodded off. She liked short stories because she could finish one per school run.

Those beautiful eyes, with their spidery lashes, stayed on the same spot on the page, somewhere a third the width of the page, a page that might as well have been covered in dirty, streaky rain. When she blinked every now and then, she looked up at me and smiled. I thought it was like Wendall's smile, innocently crooked. We were all a family now.

The feeling gnawed at me under the duvet, with its Habitat cover, and I felt cold. I could see the glow of the nightlight from the corridor. I got up to switch the air-conditioner off and the ceiling fan on instead. The sound of the electronic beep stirred her. Above us, the ceiling fan's motor started grinding, and the fan rotated and sped up, until you couldn't see the individual blades. I got back into bed. I thought she was sound asleep but in the semi-darkness, I saw her reflection in the mirrored wardrobe doors.

Her gigantic hole-like eyes glimmered like a record deck playing in the dark.

13

Bernard

The internet was down. So much for boasting about our new broadband status. God must be admonishing me for such conceit and ribaldry. For censorious reasons, I had bashfully omitted from my email correspondence to Margaret that at Orchid Villas, we grew both the orchid and the clitoria. The orchid with its lewd appearance, was supposed to resemble a man's organs and the honestly-named clitoria was the climbing plant whose light purplish pink flowers resembled the open female labia. The Garden of Eden was here.

More vigilance on my part. When I last wrote to Margaret, I wanted to add something else, something about the old lady, but I didn't. It was not time yet.

Before she died, I was called to her bedside. She was covered by a pua. A flying doctor was in attendance. He didn't say it but his look said, 'A horrible way to go.' They called him Lang, a term of reverence. Margaret would not understand the Iban significance of the flying doctor. All Iban gods were birds and all birds were ominous. The greatest of the bird gods was the god of war and headhunting, Lang Singalang Burong, a Brahminy kite, but he was represented by a rhinoceros hornbill at the Gawai Burong bird festivals. In the past, birds had to be consulted before headhunting raids. Nowadays they were prayed to for guidance in agricultural activities. The flying doctor was seen as a bird too, because he or she could fly, hence he was called Lang.

Talina Menduk had TB and had gone untreated for a long time. It pained me to see her suffering so badly. Her face blackened from last breaths. The whole bilek was rank with a sickly sweet rotten smell. The smell of expiration. Still she spoke, gasping. Talina told me in Iban that she was at the longhouse the day Peliris fell. The old lady knew in her heart all along that Peliris was an evil man who beat up her poor daughter, Surya. When she tried to stop them, she was also abused. He threatened to evict her from the longhouse if she tried to meddle and the shame would have been too much.

Now that she had converted to Christianity, she felt she had to 'come clean' to me. I said what did she mean. She said that no one knew she was watching, they all thought she was taking a nap that afternoon.

There was an argument. And there were many in their household. But this time there was a stranger. Someone she had never seen before, a young man, probably a teenager.

I knew the man was Luke, from knowing his case, but I said nothing.

Talina said that the young man did not do anything wrong. He did not even rob them, or at least, he did not get to rob them. Next to the rice jars, there was a pair of carved *agom* figurines, a male and a female, to protect the store of harvested padi in the loft from the lowly and envious tau tepang. The man had asked Peliris about some job or other. But Surya wanted him to take the blame. Somebody had to. Talina said that she saw her grand-daughter push the violent man to his own death. She knew that the girl did it in order to save her mother and herself from further abuse. Surya tried to push the young man too, because he too had seen what the girl had done. But he managed to get away.

Talina was afraid of her own granddaughter's wilfulness. The girl was even rewarded with a tattoo in an elaborate ceremony lasting eleven hours. After the trial, Talina convinced her daughter 'and grand-daughter to run away, somewhere far, somewhere where Peliris' evil spirit would not haunt them. And she said to them never to come back.

I wrote all this down. The old lady signed the testimonial where I pointed, and it was witnessed by Lang the flying doctor. I asked the old lady in Iban, 'what was the name of your grand-daughter?' And she said with a croaky sigh, 'She had the same name as me, but her mother changed it. I was quite upset. How can we trick the spirits this way? The night before they left, my daughter told me my granddaughter's new name – Talisa.'

14

Minos

'So what you gwan to do when contract finish?' say Watan.

Cos Watan he see the sentence as 'contract'. It's more like a job that way. If he don't see it as job, he just get real mad about why he's een yah. Same with me.

'I gwan look for job,' I say.

'Only three week to go.'

'Yeah. I'm scared.'

'Don't be, Minos.'

'You gwan call me my new name. So I get use to it.'

'Yes. LUKE. I don't like the name.'

'Is only a name. Is the new Minos.'

'I have say already: 'Yes, LUKE.' Happy?'

We doing exercise every day. Cos I gwan soon, I exercise a bit harder, cos who know what my new job may be? Cos for sure it ain't gwan be logging! Maybe some easy job. That's my aim. To get easy job. Forget all about this 'contract'.

And today, we doing weight training. Is only good for the non-violent crims. Cos everybuddy must get fit. Fitness of body and mind they go hand with hand. Is already enough punishment to be inside. Violent crims not allow to touch weights. Them do sit-ups or push-ups. Violent crims not even allow to use skippin rope. Cos rope is also weapon: can strangle somebuddy, or can use to hang themself. But who is afraid of who? Is them who do weights, who not violent, afraid of them violent ones, or other way round? Nobuddy talk that much when exercising. Is between your mind and your body, like machine with no on-off switch.

Well I got this good news already, cept I don't see it as good news: I got accepted into some place, train people to lay brick, pour concrete, put door up. *Laybring*. Is what the prison set up for me already. But I know I have learn much Inglish from

Pastor. So why I wan do such hard work? You don't talk to nobuddy all day. Is like doing weights all day, and all that Inglish that I learn is wasted. I gwan try out mebbe for a short while to make them parole fellars happy. Then I wan get easy job. Something to do with TV or filem. That is what Watan and I like very much.

Watan got another couple of months of his 'contract'. The word sentence don't seem right. Cos sentence is not a sentence, is a word. Also it seem a sad way of lookin at things, now that everybuddy have made friends real quick in here. If you spend that much time with people, is called a 'contract', like when you make work-friends. Cos everybuddy know everybuddy's sad story. The same different sad story. Made more same and more different each time is told, and less sad. That is what Pastor say.

'You know where the girl is?' say Watan.

'Girl?' I say. 'Ain't no girls in here, buddy, what is you talkin bout?'

'Girl. You know what I sayin. The one cause you come een yah. For fifteen year minus five. Ten year.' He do lunges quietly. Or as quiet as he be when lunging at far away objects and thoughts. 'I think you crazy from be een yah long time,' he continue. I walk away, he throw towel over his shoulder.

Guard is coming near. Diam! Which is shaddap in Malay, and I whack Watan on shoulder and I sigh softly to myself at the lift-up bars.

15

Bernard

December

Dear Margaret,
Internet is down. The router has been struck by lightning during the thunderstorm. This is quite a common occurrence. Boy-boy said that before broadband, modems and telephone junction boxes used to get damaged too. Someone is supposed to go up to the roof and install some electrical point to deflect the lightning, plus a separate cable indoors, with a surge protection device. Boy-boy has refused. I guess we will have to eat into the funds and get somebody else, like an electrician who does not suffer from acrophobia.

Thus I'm writing to you in this old-fashioned way. Thank you for your kind prayers and thoughts this Christmas. Tonight there is a lovely cool breeze, one that you can only get in the tropics, one that smells like heaven, like rain, fruits and flowers. Wendy and I are sipping a chilled glass each of Riesling on the verandah before the sun goes down.

We listen to the three 'live gigs' for our entertainment every evening. First act: the cicadas. They warm up and practise all day from about noon. Their songs which are triggered off by temperature changes, are loudest by about 6 o'clock. They make their characteristic clicking, ticking, factory machinery sound from the vibration of a hollow sac of air in their stiff shell. Next act: the frogs take over at sundown, which is about 7pm here. This is a bassy, resonating and rhythmic performance. The headlining act comes in the late evening: the grasshoppers. Usually this is from about 9pm onwards, the chill-out hour. Grasshoppers make a kind of woody brittle sound, like scratching the teeth on a comb, or scraping a wash board. The noise is made by a row of pegs on their back legs, which they rub against their forewings which act as their amplifiers.

Borneo is a very strange place, Margaret. It is home to barking deer, flying squirrels, bearded pigs and stick and leaf insects. It has the world's smallest bird and the world's largest flower. It is like being in a recurrent dream. The bird is the white-fronted falconet (*Microhierax latifrons*) and the flower is the Rafflesia (*Rafflesiaceae*), which is one of the strangest plants I have ever seen. It is red and yellow, a parasite one metre in diameter which opens at midnight, like some exclusive members' club, only that it doesn't carry the perfume of cash and credit cards – it smells like a rotting buffalo carcass! The plant has no stems, leaves or true roots. It is named after Sir Stamford Raffles, who led an expedition in 1818 to Borneo and founded Singapore a few years later. He was also an amateur botanist, you may be pleased to hear, Margaret!

The weather has improved. Wendy, myself and Boy-boy have been tending to some new orchid seeds. Amazes me that you can see the power of God in such minutiæ. (Is that the correct spelling?) Orchid seeds completely lack any food reserves of their own. They seem to be ill-prepared for life's journey ahead. Can you believe that the size of the seeds from different genera range from 0.3mm to 2mm? Yet from these grow one of the world's most incredible flowers. Orchids produce more seed than any other flowering plants.

In the wild, the seeds tumble out of the orchid plants which live on the trees. They do *not* fall to the ground, contrary to logic, but they remain suspended in the mist, no lighter or heavier than mist itself, in Brownian Motion. They are carried in the next breeze to their distant destination. And with some of their symbiotic fungus, comes germination. Thus they carry on their new life cycle. Do we let God's word fall to the ground? It is not going to germinate that way. We should be the breeze.

We visited the orang utan sanctuary today as part of the Reaching Out For Christ (ROFC) programme. If we don't see ourselves as part of the society, the intrinsic system of the local culture, we are not missionaries. Hence the very word mission. We went further into the jungle again today, and we gave out food parcels to the villages and stationery to the children. Most of them have never seen a tin of Spam in their lives. So you can imagine their excitement. I got to practise speaking Penan. Sadly, we didn't see any orang utans. It's fruit season here, which means they don't descend from the tree canopy to be fed by humans at feeding times because they are picking their own fruits all day.

Kuching Prison is very interesting. I read the other day in *The Borneo Post* that the first RAAF operational flight of the DH98 Mosquito aircraft built by de Havilland was to Timor on 23rd March 1945; and the last, on the 11th August over Kuching Prison Camp, on detachment to Labuan, Borneo. In all it flew 21 missions over enemy targets on the Indonesian Archipelago and in the Borneo invasion. A bit of trivia for you, Margaret, as I know your Richard is very keen on his A52s. Sorry, I digress.

I was thinking when I went to the prisons last week, the bigger the crime, the bigger the cell. I can't name the convicts for obvious reasons, but those who have committed murders have their own 'studio apartments', with all mod cons. Sometimes even colour TVs. I'm not opposed to such worldly comforts but it does give them a 'glazed' impression of the world outside, so to speak. Those who steal wallets have to be stuck in severely overcrowded, hot, cells.

The serious criminals are like those rare orchids which get their own space, for instance, the exquisite *Masdevallia*, because they are so hard to understand. The minor criminals are like the common moth orchids, the *Phalaenopses*. They are everywhere and crammed in.

Education is the key. Some converts will be able to serve in the Ministry. They will naturally want to, as it is not easy for them to be re-absorbed into normal society and to get jobs. Education will steer them away from crime. We need to enlighten people as Christ enlightened us. It costs peanuts but it is worth it. Just look at the difference it has made to Boy-boy.

Hope that you and mum are well. If she asks again, just tell her that I don't miss Old Blighty but of course I miss you and her. You know I can't call her because she bursts into tears and tells me she misses me. I just can't bear it. Thanks for sending some PG Tips. Box arrived bashed but teabags still OK, undamaged. I can't get used to that Boh Tea they have here. Also thanks for the Father Ted episodes on DVD. Really enjoyed those.

I've got to go pack now. We're going further inland for five days with the group. I need tons of 'bug' ammunition. I'll be back in the weekend. Boy-boy is staying here with Wendy, who has made a start with the Christmas shopping.

May God Bless You.

Your loving brother,

B.

P.S. If you could just get me The League of Gentleman (2nd series). Thanks.

16

Minos

'Well, tonight we're going to talk about your Big Day,' say Pastor Bernard. Today he come een so late! After dinner-time! And I a little pist off that I miss episode of *Will & Grace* on TV. But I don't say nothing.

'You must be very excited,' Pastor smile. 'I'm going to be one of the first people to call you by your new name, Luke.'

I smile, but I look down. Check if Pastor wearing Caterpillar boots. And yes, he wearing them.

'I've just come back from the jungle, Luke,' Pastor continue, since I ain't sayin nothing much. 'I've been doing some work for Christ with educating children in longhouses. They are wonderful. The children I mean, not the longhouses. That's why I was delayed getting here.' He put his hand in his cloth bag and russell around for something. He find a peket of biskut. I look at the peket.

'Some biscuits for you and your mates,' Pastor say. 'Just to celebrate.'

To celebrate what? Ten years of time fucken wasted for nothing! I open it and take one biskut. Then I realise I forget something.

'Er, thank you!' I say, ashamed.

'No, no! It's quite alright!'

Pastor then give I a piece of paper. 'It's just in case I forget on your Big Day. It's the ADDRESS and PHONE NUMBER of the ministry. We want you to join our fellowship and continue in your growth in Christ. Don't let this Big Day put you off. We can pray for you such that wherever they put you, you can develop as a person and enjoy your work.'

'I gwanna be laying brick.'

'It's a fine job. After all, who is going to build new buildings? Young fit persons like yourself.'

Pastor also take a biskut.

'And I want you to know. Whatever it is that you need, if you are in trouble or anything, I'll help you.'

'What you sayin then. Trouble?'

'Don't take it too seriously. I mean, *just in case*. You never know, if you find yourself in any difficulty, maybe adjusting to your new life. I can't expect you to come to Sunday service because obviously we don't know where you'll be laying bricks. And as I understand they are putting you in a village that is far from where you came from originally. Isn't that right?'

'I dunno,' I shrug. I think so. This to prevent anybuddy to know that is me The Killer coming back. With new name, tattoo and new village, all will be OK.

'Minos, I mean *Luke*. I hope you will continue to worship God and to pray to him whenever you are in any difficulty. Read your bible every day. If you don't understand anything, ask me. If you are unhappy with your job, don't forget there are others. You can even work with the ministry. Because you won't need the parole officer then.'

Me ear suddenly fall open. No parole fellar?

'No parole fellar?'

'No,' Pastor say, 'if you are working closely with me, you would be more closely watched than if you were on parole. I can't promise anything. I will have to ask around the church elders and so on.'

Can't promise. Means no.

'There is some red tape involved, like the exemption from parole forms, lawyers' signatures and that kind of thing. I am not very *au fait* with every little detail of the legal aspect of the prison service. Sorry. But I can find out.'

What? What he mean? What is offay? I don't like sound of the red tape. Is painful?

'Yes,' I say, 'I want to work for God.'

'Very well, I will see what I can do,' say Pastor.

I look at Pastor diving watch, then at the TV which is off, black as the night sea. *Will & Grace* is over. So I may as well pray. That is what coming next. I just know.

'Let's pray for you then, Luke.'

LATE AFTERNOON, AND IS crazy hour again, cos so hot, some people actually tearing around, crying, all sweat and tears mix up. Vest and shorts soak through, everybuddy running around in field, in circle, circle after circle after circle. And nobuddy allow to stop or look back. Sometimes people collapse in field, cos they drink not enough water. If guard not looking, you can stop and look down, put hands on knees and pant, allow all the sweat and tears to drop on ground like rain, but if guard see, you will get whack.

I already think what I gwan do. First thing is get tattoo. Of course not by headman of any village, let alone my own village from ten year ago. No. Cos I have achief absolutely NOTHING in life. So no headman can possibly tattoo I. No. I will, I NEED, to get a REAL tattoo by tattoo artist in downtown Kuching. There is loadsa bars, nightclubs, neon light, et cetera. In basement of these kind of place you can get tattoo done. I gwan to get some pocket money on day of freedom. Like I say, I friend of the taxpayer. And I will use that money to get tattoo. This is first priority.

Priority is something that gonna get done before something else gonna get done. I am Iban. One of earliess, most fearless, civilisation in world. Even Pastor agree. So before I even go get bricklaying job, or whatever job they set I to do, I simply must get that tattoo. If not, even the bricklayers will laugh at I, cos they have achief so much more than I. Those fellars not gwan to see it from me point of view: and that is I AIN'T DONE NOBUDDY WRONG.

After the run around in circles, and a few buddies collapse, then hose down by guard, everybuddy go drink tap water from outside tap. Is so good. This water like being in heaven. And waiting in queue to drink it is like being in hell. So your buddy in front can make you wait long, long time.

And then, long, long, long, long, long, long, long long, long, long, long time. Again.

Until he satisfied.

Bastedd!

And in the queue, Watan is behind I. Is like voice of madman and cleverman all in one. Is Watan again, digging for info like some *gila* idiot.

'If you know where girl is, we find she.'

And I don't answer. I think first. Then I say:

'Is not very Christian. Everybuddy that done what they done to me, is up to me to forgiff. And I already forgiff them, like Pastor say to do. Only if we forgiff can we get on in life not feeling angry all time.'

'No shit.'

'What you sayin then.'

'What I saying is, why forgiff the girl? There is a better way. She can help *we*. I from St Josephs you know? You know how famous is St Josephs mishn school?'

So it's now 'we'.

My turn to drink. I go for it. Then I go 'way, leave Watan behind to drink. Cos I ain't entering this kind of gila talk. If I know that Watan is this kind of person, I won't have say so much to him in the first place. I won't have tell me story. Stories are to help people understand people, not to spoil things. People like him spoil everything, spoil plans, priority, everything.

And Watan call after I, his voice go up and up, and he don't care who listen:

'Lis'n to me! We make her pay for what she done, man!'

LAST DAY. IT'S TEN in the morning. It is Christmas Day. Is the best present! Many cons get released on Christmas Day cos is the day of forgiveness and love and freedom to remember what Jesus have done for us. Now is the hour that everybuddy and I have been waiting for. Already they have party last night. This morning, Watan cry. Is last breakfast with me, Luke, whatever. He say, 'Don't forget me. If you ever change mind about finding the girl, you know where I be. And I know where you be.' And we hug and I too feel all messed up inside. My head gwan round and round, like those days of running in the field in circles under hot sun.

I've got nothing. Just the clothes I come in with. Clothes from ten year ago. The prison warden feel sorry for I and say, 'Wait here.' He go and come back, with Parkson plastic bag. Don't tell anybuddy, he say. And in the plastic bag, I find normal modern clothes: there's Levi's jean, and t-shirt with only one word: the letters G, A and P. Not too many letters to read. And tennis shoes, as white as the Pastor. They very good quality, and not even old. I give a look to the warden, is to say, are you sure this

OK? Cos I dare not say out loud, in case not OK. In prison you get use to speaking only with your mind and your eyes. Cos otherwise you may get whack.

Mebbe some good-heart people donate clothes to charity. Sometimes, Pastor himself bring two or three suitcase full of clothes that people at the church give him to give away. A lot of the nicer clothes, like the type people go overseas and buy on holiday, they taken by the prison official fellars themselves. So only the lousy ones left for the crims. We crims deserve no better.

I look around, and nobuddy see I receif the good quality clothes from Levi's and so on. And the good-heart prison warden give I a nodding look, which says, *Go on, go on, just get changed, what you waiting for?* And I quickly get changed. When I come out, I already is new person. With clothes that come from a free world, where nothing is free, you smell like a baby plant: good, new, clean, *Luke*. A somebuddy. Not just anybuddy.

I TAKEN INTO A space which I never see before. A room where you can SMELL the outside world. A room where light is different, it ain't same as the prison. Cos it have more LIGHT. And if I have see this room before I don't remember. This place actually got wooden chairs, like a waiting area. And great big doors, they are as big as the side of a lorry. And they is double doors, make of metal, tons of buttons, locks, screws, chains, like a lorry that is going somewhere, a long, long journey. Doors which I know will be thrown open, and I will walk out FREE. A free man into a world which is not free.

With my Parkson bag containing money in envelop, one toot-brush and one toot-paste, New International Version Holy Bible and Ten Steps to Please God, and one of them sashays I use to pack. And the sashay contents can be see through the cellofane wrapper, which I myself have pack months ago, and at that time, I thinking: *Count one sugar, one salt, one pepper, one dairy creamer sashay, one stirring stick, one toothpick, one folded serviette, one refresher towel, then put in machine to seal up. What for?* And now I know: for my memory. For I not gwanna use and throw away. This thing help me remember me buddies.

And the wooden chairs NOT bolted to the floor. Cos where only the inmates hangout, there are only benches, and all them benches are bolted cos then is safe. Cos even chair is weapon. This mean that this waiting space is already AS GOOD AS outside world.

PASTOR WAITING FOR I. He already sitting on one of this wooden chair. And whenever I now see piece of furniture not connect to the floor, it mean I is free. It mean I can pick up chair. I can move it about. Which I now do. I lift up and put down chair, mebbe twice.

And Pastor laugh and say, 'What are you doing?'

And I say, shaking head, 'I see whether it work or not.' But I not laughing. Cos I not able to believe I is free man.

Pastor here to say goodbye, and to pray for I. And I at last sit down on a wooden chair. Don't seem right. Like I not use to it yet. Sittin on a chair that can be move to another place. And I get up and sit on another chair. Pastor already close eyes and praying, fingers connect, and he start his blah blah blah: 'Our heavenly father, today is Christmas Day, Luke's big day…'

I look down at Pastor shoes. Today he is wearing the tennis shoes again. Me own two foot look funny. Because I have no socks to wear with me new sport shoes. I look like somebuddy from the gila hospital. That is the look if you not wearin socks. Madman.

One of them officer fellars come out and give I city map of Kuching, and address of where I spose to be gwan to stay for *laybring* job. Also the bus numbers from the road outside. Cos if Pastor not seeing so many other inmates, he can give I lift, but Pastor not gwan just yet, so I have to take bus. And I don't wan lift anyway. I stare at map. I realise I don't wan leave. I wan stay here, with everybuddy, for all time. I can't cry. I can't do nothing. Me heart fly.

And Pastor ask, 'Is there anything I can do for you before you go, Luke?'

I think for a minute. Pastor is a spirit who grant wishes. And I is idiot if I don't take chance.

'Pastor, is OK if I have your socks?'

I WAIT FOR BUS. The smell of concrete, disinfectant, sweat, pis, food rottin in drains. Is all still strong, it come over those walls, no matter how high, and even them rolls of barb wire and broken glass on top of walls cannot suck the smell up. Cos is the smell of life inside.

The bus come. I find any seat. I find in this Parkson plastic bag one comb. Is come from somewhere, now I forget, is some inmate comb? Given to me long ago? Or something find in shower one day long time ago? I dunno. I gwan keep it for ever too, though the thing is broken. Cos only broken at one end. Other end still OK.

The very moment the bus drive off, is I travelling with spirit of wind, a strong wind, and all this awful smell of sweat, pis, concrete, disinfectant etc blow 'way.

Just like that.

17

Benjie

Ibrahim had taken time off last weekend. He was going back to his village in Kota Bahru for a couple of days. Talisa wanted to go to Kuala Lumpur, KL, for the day to hit the January sales. Chinese New Year would fall at the end of January this year and we would be too busy to go shopping then. In a few weeks, it would be the year of the Fire Dog. Fire meant that it was a Yang year. Yang was male, representing structure and form, whereas Yin being female represented substance. My mother said that when a strange dog followed you, it was considered a good omen. On our consultation with Mr Lim the fortune-teller, we were told that the home and the family were very important in the Dog year, hence structure. I humoured my mum by patiently listening to her translation of Mr Lim's tedious report.

Talisa mentioned getting some sheets for Wendall from Mothercare and browsing in Baby Gap too. We didn't have any big shops in Segamat. We wanted to see the spectacular display of lights and New Year decorations. There was a big golfing shop in KL that Ian wanted to go to, the kind that had a revolving golfer mascot outside and neon lights. He drove to our house, and parked his car in the shaded driveway. It was still only 8.03am on a Saturday morning according to the Seiko digital clock. I still often woke up forgetting that I sired a child and got married, imagining that everything had been a dream. Then I heard: 'We're going somewhere very exciting, Wendall,' my wife's voice. 'The big! The bad! The city!' I opened my eyes. I was still very groggy. I was on-call last night. I yawned a huge, ugly, animal yawn.

She picked him up and swung him in the air, which he loved. *Wee-eee-eee-eee!* He gurgled and laughed, looked around him, as though recognising the room at a higher level, a level above the door frames. 'Did you like that?' she said.

Little quilted blue bags of the boxy kind had appeared, with cows on them. Asuncion had already packed the baby's things. She was usually well-prepared, when we were travelling somewhere. She always packed early, light and terribly efficiently, like if she never came back it would be OK. As a family, we were now getting up early even on weekends. In the evenings, I went to bed early after watching pirate DVDs to catch up on the latest Hollywood films. You could pick them up for six ringgit at the local mall, you didn't have to go to KL for these.

'Less than a pound! Eighty p!' I remembered Ian barking. 'Bargain.' Despite being here these decades, he still could not stop converting prices to UK pounds. It gave him a great sense of satisfaction that everything was six times cheaper than in the UK. It was like being a child again, he said. He was of the older generation. People approved of his frugality. It made him seem Asian. I often thought he belonged here more than I did. Even his barking clipped Scottish voice could be likened to a Chinese dialect. The Cantonese sounded like they were having a heated argument even if they were discussing the weather.

I heard his sharp voice from downstairs. 'Driving licence,' said Ian. 'Don't forget!'

IT WAS DURIAN SEASON and the month of Ramadhan. Segamat went crazy this month. The other durian season was in July. Segamat was the town of durians. There was even a very kitsch homage to the King of Fruits: giant spiky testicles at the border. Welcome to Segamat. Home of the Durian.

The durian was a fruit as big as a football, covered with tough spiky skin. The pulp was pale yellow, with the shape and consistency of raw brains. The smell had been compared to rotting flesh, a rubbish tip, old gym socks, or sewage. Yet the taste had been called so exquisite that a European explorer of the 1700's claimed it was worth the journey to experience it and dubbed it "the King of fruits." I couldn't remember the name of the Dutch guy.

Many believed it aphrodisiac and hold durian-eating parties. Most hotels did not allow the beloved durian on the premises. The interesting fact about durians was that they cannot be plucked from the tree. You had to wait for them to drop. Well,

110

not exactly wait. It would be quite an injury. The durians themselves seemed to know this. They dropped at night.

Durian plantations in Segamat were often robbed. During the season, armed security guards often keep a vigil over their precious investments dropping at night. Last night I had to tend to two durian thieves: patients with bloody heads who, for stalking the plantations, had had their punishment, and no durians to speak of.

Talisa mentioned to me that Ibrahim had driven her in his silver Toyota Altis to buy durians directly from the plantations. You could sample them easily in shady makeshift huts put up just for the season, like marquees.

Now I knew how ang-mohs, like the white expats who played golf at the club, suffered when they had their first taste of durian. Foreigners had described the smell as a rubbish tip, old socks, or rotten animals. Ang-mohs hated it as much as Asians hated gorgonzola cheese. The local saying was that it smelled like hell and tasted like heaven. The closer you got to it, the less it smelled of rubbish and more like a pungent, sweet smell. The durian flesh was creamy and thick and very appropriately, it was a popular ice-cream flavour.

'Of course it's not easy to get to eat a durian,' said Ian, from the backseat. 'It's got to be opened with a parang. So for those who dare not give it a go, it's their loss.' Why was he telling me that? I was born here! A parang, or machete, was a standard tool in every Malaysian shed.

'They don't know what they're missing,' agreed Talisa.

'I'm sure they know,' I said blandly, though my mouth was watering just thinking about it.

We left Segamat on a highway and a couple of hours later, we were on Federal Highway with one of the best panoramic views of KL. We parked in some huge multi-storey carpark at Mid Valley megamall. Ian rushed off to the golf shop. 'I'm going to look at swimsuits later, Dah,' said Talisa, 'but I think we'll just wait for you first and have a coffee.'

I liked to go to European cafes in KL because there were none in Segamat. I found a table at my favourite place in Mid Valley City, a café called The Old Dutch. It was a rip-off of the one on the Kings Road. We both ordered durian ice-cream with a slice of warm crepe pancake.

I was just tucking in with my fork and spoon when I noticed that someone was standing next to the table. I thought it was Ian, so I just said, 'Want one?' without looking up. There was no reply, and when I looked up, I saw Talisa's iced reaction. It was a man in a police uniform. Behind him was a woman also in police uniform, whom I didn't notice earlier. Instinctively, Talisa reached out and grabbed Wendall. And the fork.

Ian rushed in to The Old Dutch from the golfing shop and grabbed his daughter's arm, showing the police officers her flower tattoo, her Iban branding. Ian explained that she was his daughter. I was so speechless that up to this point I did not jump in and say, 'she's my wife!' because I myself was amazed that I was related to her, that she was my wife. Talisa looked Malay and it was the month of Ramadhan, so she was supposed to be fasting because it was a Muslim country. Technically she could be apprehended and arrested by the police. But she was not Muslim, and therefore innocent.

'See? Same surname?'

Once Ian had explained that Talisa was Iban and not a Muslim, she was straightaway let go. They had a good look at her identity card which said she was Talisa MacFarlane. Having lived here for so long it was important to know the local adat or custom, which was that there was nothing more important than family. The officers offered profuse apologies. They were impressed with an ang-moh who spoke the native language fluently. The woman officer tickled Wendall under the chin and made clucking noises.

In the car journey home, Ian expressed his disappointment. I didn't stand up for my wife, he said. 'Why didn't you?' he demanded. 'Your family is the most important thing in the world, and even if they are wrong to other's eyes, to your eyes they are right.' I said nothing. There was nothing wrong with my right eye. He changed the subject. He thought that the woman officer's voice was not unlike a baby's. It was the most fascinating thing he ever said.

IT HAD BEEN A week since the police incident and my wife seemed to have taken ill as a direct result of it. She seemed distracted, and displayed symptoms of SVT, Supraventricular Tachycardia. Her heartbeat was 140 beats per minute, galloping like that of an unborn child. She had palpitations, dizziness, undue anxiety and shortness of breath, but frankly, and as a medical expert, I put it down to her general female neuroses and paranoia. At her insistence, I did an ECG as well as an Echocardiogram (ECHO), an ultrasound scan of the heart, blood tests to rule out thyroid problems and heart disease. Finally I ordered an angiography. All at my own cost since I had to send her away to a specialist in a private hospital.

The tests came back all fine, but she was nervous. She said to me in Mandarin that going out did not seem safe. She stayed at home watching Desperate Housewives on Astro and surfing the net.

'What is not safe?' I replied in English, irritably.

'Going out.' Her tears flowed across swollen cheeks, like those of an Oscar-winning actress. I wonder if she was actually upset. She wanted to say something. Her mouth open, I could see her bottom teeth.

Wendall had stopped kicking at the activity arch of his bouncy chair, from which colourful bears, balls and bunnies dangled. He looked up. Talisa leant forward, took his seat belt off and picked him up. She murmured to him in Iban, on purpose, presumably, so I couldn't understand what was going on. Her voice was a little sing-song, a little clipped, like a bird talking.

Now I was thinking back to the night when her eyes did not move when she read the poem, it was the exact same blank look. Her eyes were wide, staring, not like an animal, but like a tree with holes, shivering in a storm.

AT THE CLUB, MY dad was already there. He wanted to meet me here which was unusual as he was not keen on darts. A new sign had appeared at the entrance to the bar: (*We Love Them but) Absolutely Positively No Durians*. This was not a permanent sign. It only came out every January and July during the seasons.

Distant firecrackers drowned out the usual chirp of insects and birds. Bits of trailing plastic plum blossoms were draped over the chandelier chains and red twin calligraphy couplets were blu-tacked to the door ways. The Club's New Year decorations and lights seemed a bit abysmal compared to what we had seen in KL.

My dad was always early, unlike me. Since he retired from his job as a headmaster, he'd been catching up with his old friends – books. He tilted his head at a funny angle to read *The New Straits Times* on the horizontal wooden hangers near the bar. 'Dad,' I said, forcing a fake grin, 'why don't you take the paper off the hanger and read it properly?'

'Where's my grandson?'

'Talisa is not well.'

'Not pregnant again?'

'Oh Jesus. No, I don't think so.'

My dad chuckled.

'Come on, I'll buy you a drink, dad.'

'No! Come on! *I'll* buy you a drink.'

My dad bought me a bottle of Singha, and a Guinness for himself. We sat down in the comfy leather winged back armchairs. I loved these chairs for the fact that you couldn't see anyone and no one could see you unless he or she was in front of you directly. It was like being on a plane. If someone was approaching, you were warned: the tall parlour palms would rustle.

'Did y'all go to KL last week?' he said, popping peanuts into his mouth.

I sighed. Then I thought, sod it, I was going to just tell him. If I couldn't tell my dad, who could I tell? He listened and nodded without much interest.

'But why? And so what?' I asked him what I'd been asking my wife all week but to no avail.

'That I don't know, ' said Dad, sighing. 'In all my years of marriage to your mother, if you ask something like but-why-and-so-what, it will invariably lead to a blazing row.'

I laughed and drunk my beer.

'Don't you know anything?' said Dad. 'The correct thing to say is *yes, dear.* But I do know this: you mentioned them seeing her identity card?'

'Yes?' I put down my drink and became attentive.

'You see, she might have been worried about her date of birth being wrong.'

'Well I do know that already dad, remember I told you about the date of 5th May 1987 which she read off directly from the date the menu card was printed?'

'No, no, I mean the year.'

'The year? I don't understand, dad.'

'She wasn't born in 1987. Your mother told me when you met the fortune-teller that at first Talisa said she was a Dog but she turned out to be a Rabbit?'

'She did, but I assumed that because she's not Chinese, she didn't know her animal sign.'

'Impossible. Even the non-Chinese know their animal signs. It's like saying you don't know what year you were born. She has had Chinese schooling after all. For my own peace of mind, I had to find out if your mother paid the fortune-teller all that money for nothing. Accuracy, son.'

'I thought it was funny at the time.'

'Funny and forgotten about until now. Anyway, yesterday I casually asked the headmaster of the Chinese school she went to and I managed to ask him to look up the school records. I still have connections with schools you see.'

'Oh yes? And what did you find?'

'She is not a Fire Rabbit, my dear son. Her original answer was correct. She was a Water Dog.'

'Water Dog?'

'Born in 1982.'

'That means she's not eighteen. She's twenty-three. Dad, why did she fake the year for the identity card?'

'The headmaster said that when she arrived here with her Ebu she couldn't get into any primary schools because she was too old and her education in Sarawak had been minimal. Well, non-existent. When she arrived in this country she was already thirteen.'

'She passed as an eight-year-old when she was thirteen?' I asked, incredulous.

'Nobody said anything about her passing as eight years old. That was just the *age* at which she supposedly came to this country officially. She was privately tutored by the Scottish tutor for two years and she excelled. After that, the school took her into Standard Four as a ten-year-old when she was already fifteen.'

'She looked ten when she was fifteen? Do you think that's even actually possible?'

'She was tiny even then, said the headmaster. Have you ever seen a real Iban on those TV programmes? No, I didn't think you have. Malnourishment, Dr Lee. You know the headmaster turned a blind eye to the age issue because of Ian's authority? Because of the Scottish tutor that Ian hired? Rules are for little people, not people like him.' The old time entrepreneurial white landowners like Ian and their white subordinates, the tutor included, were exempt. I assumed some kind of 'gift' must have changed hands to grease the gears and tears of bureaucracy.

'Yes,' I agreed, 'I supposed it would be considered a privileged education. But dad, did the headmaster tell you why Ian stopped the private tuition?'

'She *had* to go to school. Ian did not believe in home schooling and only did it as a favour to Talisa's Ebu who was working for them. The moment the poor woman died, Ian pulled the plug on it. Saved money, of course. Now then, you know that you only apply for the identity card when you are twelve?'

I nodded.

'Well, she simply applied for her IC when she was supposedly aged twelve,' said my dad, 'all as per normal.'

I mentally calculated that in truth she was seventeen then.

'You know the orang asli are a law unto themselves? You did marry an orang asli, son.'

It was true – my wife was an indigenous person. I had this theory that people who lied about their age eventually believed it anyway. I would never have known. She certainly appeared as a petulant teenager. I decided not to confuse my dad with the fact that I suspected her of keeping a lover. He would probably have some great revelation which I didn't want to hear before I had a few more hard drinks.

'Why didn't you tell me this before, Dad?' I finally found my voice. 'We met the fortune-teller Mr Lim weeks ago!'

'We only found out yesterday ourselves from my dear headmaster friend! Why do you think I wanted to meet up with you here? As soon as I found out her real sign, your mother was on the phone to Mr Lim.' My dad sighed. 'He said, Sheep and Dog, a tiring union. Whereas before, my son, Sheep and Rabbit – mutual respect and understanding, a perfect match. So you see why I didn't want to give you the bad news?'

My dad shook his head and picked his drink up. 'So. Our friend is not a Rabbit but a Dog! Mr Lim said on the phone to your mum that Water Dogs had great foresight and were well-informed, which made them flexible and liberal. They were easygoing, but it made them spendthrift with money and less loyal. The Dog was generally being both a guardian and a scavenger.'

That sounded like my wife. 'Anything else?'

'He said Dogs liked to hold on to things and people. Your mum brought up her original comment to him that 'this girl no good luck', but Mr Lim said no, this was *her* year: Water Dog in a Fire Dog year, she would do well out of it even if others did not.'

I was sure by 'others' he meant me.

At that moment, I wanted to wring my dad's neck. 'He's a quack,' I said, after twiddling my fingers for a few minutes.

'A what?'

'Quack. You must know that, don't you, dad? Tell mum not to waste money on these bloody charlatans. I'm a doctor. I don't have to listen to this crap.'

I downed the rest of my Singha beer at one go. The rest of the conversation took place without referring to Talisa as anyone but 'she'. The Sheep was calm. I consoled myself that it was not too serious a deception. She could not get into any school and they were a desperate pair, she and her Ebu.

Women arrived at the bar in pairs or groups but men 'streamed' in, to make certain there was a clear view of who they were up against, who was in charge, who bought the rounds and cracked the jokes. That was what the club was about. Power. Why were there animal heads on the walls? To show everybody what men have achieved. And why heads? Because men were the original head hunters.

18

Minos

The needles they don't look sharp. Now I come this far, I must get it done. I must lie down, trust the old Chinese man of Jalan Wayang. Theatre Street. Lie on padded vinyl seat, with a few crack in it, so you can see the foam inside, like the meat of the seat. I have never see this man in my life, yet I let him put needle in me.

THIS MORNING, AFTER I get off the bus at the Malay kampungs, I walk cross tiny iron bridges, cos the Malay kampungs all standing on some kind swamp, yet is so near the city across Kuching River is big skyline, look so amazing, look so modern, like some kind of dream. This bridges, they are so small, and the bottom is see-through iron rod, so animal cannot cross. This bridges only as wide as you when you hold your arms out and apart. Is how wide. Pass the mosque. Is biggest building here. One two tourist, with map, camera, et cetera. How they even get here? How they find this place?

Plenty little wooden houses on legs, chickens follow by baby-chickens, follow by one two kitten. Everything is little, little. Everybuddy go a little, look a little, smile a little. Little mopeds, mebbe 25cc Hondas, buzz past me, so near, I can feel the cloth of the Malay ladies' sarong brush me. Schoolchildren suck on ice lolly. People look at me and I look at them. Is not how I imagine life to be, outside, the life of being free, free as those coconuts in the trees.

Then, at the timber jetty, I take the water taxi, nobuddy know me in the kampungs and I know nobuddy. I not a city boy anyway. It cost only 30sen. Is nothing of my money in my pocket. Is to cross the river to get to commercial part of city. I wan go find Chinatown, get my tattoo. I wan go to all places that normal people go to. I wan know, wha happened in all this ten year? I wan see it all.

The boatman wait for everybuddy to get in the boat. The boatman has bare feet, so I one step better than he, cos I got shoe and socks. The river is colour of milk tea, and look at the water I feel so thirsty, for first time, thirsty, like killing me sandpaper throat. And for first time in ten year, I touch the water that is not from tap. And put some on my face, cos is so hot now, and I waiting in the boat for boat to fill up. People on boat fanning themselves, cos is boiling, and the river it look like hot tea steaming. But when I put it on my face, is so cool.

When at last the boat almost fill up, the boatman start the motor. And the little boat then go, when the motor cough a bit. And there is a little breeze when the boat go, the smell of a breeze that suddenly make me swallow in my throat this smell.

And when I reach the modern city, Kuching, with all them 1950s buses and Chinese shophouses, I pass the waterfront, esplanade, is not a place I belong to, cos is not a jungle. All them tourist enjoying themselves in the sunshine, plenty plenty sunshine, tree, flower, park, cyclist, plenty shop, selling all them things that we have make in the jungle, all thing that tourist love, baskets, pots, t-shirts.

People are all out cos is Christmas Day, a public holiday. Ah. Girls everywhere. I never see any girl for so long I forgot there is such a thing as girl. There are old and young girls, in jeans, shorts, sarongs, girl in t-shirt, mobile phone, girl with friends, girl with mother, girl with child, girl on bus, girl walking, cycling, girl in bars, in shops. Fat and thin girl, small girl, big girl, ugly girl, pretty girl. Everywhere! Is like heaven. And then I think, any of this girls is THE one?

But now. I am a chile again. All these people in them bars, lunchtime, ordering, eating, drinking, smoking, coffeeshops, won ton noodles, fruit stalls, everything is shiny, shining, shine-shine bright as cut fruit. On the street, market stalls, everything got a price, just like everybuddy got a price. I have pay my price too. And I look at each and every girl and wonder if she the one? Is confuse! Is confuse! I think I have gwan crazy I don't know what to do what to do what to do have to eat where to eat what to eat where to sit what to do how to do how to eat where to go where is map?

I lose map!

I lose it on bus. Fuck. Shit. Idiot. Stupid stupid idiot Minos or Luke or whoever the shit I am. How the fuck can I find that brick-laying dump place that they help me get work? They gwan go berserk! They gwan put me away again! They will think I trying to escape parole fellar (and yes I gwan to, but they not to know that)! Look, look, look, all over Parkson plastic bag, it must have fall out mebbe on the little boat, if not on bus. Shit!

Not even in bible, first place I look. Pastor, pastor, I gwan pray, how I gwan pray when all I do is swear. All this people now looking at me and I looking at them but what I can do. My tum now starving I look for something to eat first then look again. Even the stupid brocken comb is still in the damn bag. Where is map. Where I can get another map? No tourist map will have this brick-laying dump on it. Is not even in town. Cos must take another two buses from Kuching bus terminus. I can't ask anybuddy. The tourist info only gwan laugh at me! 'What? Rehabiliation centre? On the map?' They gwan say.

Luckily have not lose money, if not how to pay for tattoo. But now I gwan have best meal ever and that is wan ton HANDMADE noodle that Kuching famous for. And I gwan sit down like a normal free man, like anybuddy else, on the wooden benches of the coffeeshop. And the table is marble, round, and is not chain to the floor. I order tea, big big glass milky tea, also made by hand, made on real fire not teabag or giant kettle like in prison.

I get this tattoo in Chinatown, dirty basement with sign outside saying they HIV safe and use new needle all time. Outside, in the monsoon drain, tons of needle, rubbish bag and even a chicken head, rotting. Is so yuck I am thinking no tourist will come here, unless they looking for girls. And just as I think it, an old tourist man come out of wooden shutter door, with young Chinese girl in ponytail. And is strong smell of incense coming from inside that dark terrace shophouse. They don't see me, like I not there.

I choose from book, dirty plastic file with see-through leaves contain designs. I know I wan Nabau, the serpent, around my shoulders, hugging me, like a mantle the Dutch mishnaries wear. For I will never have a Pua Kumbu around me. That is magic. Remember: the python skin. All sticky with beeswax.

IS PAINFUL. NOW I give the old man the money and almost no more money for sleep somewhere tonight. Mebbe enough for one meal, but I not too sure with the price increase after ten year. I don't know after where to go, until I look at Bible. Pastor say to look at Bible when you don't know where to go because God give direction. Bible is like map book of our life. If you ask God, He tell you where to go. So I am gwan to ask God. Yes.

When I take the bible out of the Parkson bag, that piece of paper fall out, which Pastor give me.

19

Bernard

Boxing Day

Dear Margaret,
I got a bit of a surprise. Luke has turned up. He seems to have lost his map to that construction apprentice centre, and when he prayed to ask for guidance, God spoke to him. That is why he is here. He took the bus from the city, and for someone who has not taken public transport for a long time, I am deeply impressed. Praise God.

Wendy is appalled. She's worried that we can't pay him. I tell her, Wendy, these people don't want money. Do you think that everyone is like people in England who only want money? These people want peace, tranquillity and a direction in life. It's what being a Christian is about.

I am finding it hard to give him a job straightaway. But that will come. He is full of initiative. We are starting a new project in another part of the jungle and he may be able to help us in that respect. God will find a way. For now he will have to help out with Boy-boy with daily tasks like the garden and maintaining odd jobs like the tiling in the church hall toilets. I speak to him in Iban and he to me in English. Boy-boy has no interest in learning any other languages. The boy from the prison however is very keen on developing other skills for church work. Already this morning he has been in the church library, repairing torn hymnals and prayer books. "Let him who stole steal no longer, but rather let him labour, working with his hands what is good." (Eph 4:28). All that work they did in prison doing bits of fiddly work obviously taught them patience. These repairs have been neglected, as no one thinks of them at all. We're ever so busy here.

The boy is sharing a room with Boy-boy until such a time as when we have a spare room. Boy-boy is obviously not happy about it but what can I do? I seem to have increased the number of staff against my wishes, but if it is God's will then I am fine with it. Boy-boy is, as one would delicately put it, a bit simple.

I am now using the spare room as my office. They will have to put up with each other for a while longer. Maybe we'll build an extension when we have more money. But for now, the funds are going to the new jungle project that we are anticipating to commence quite soon. And in that case, the boy will come into the jungle with me as he is and speaks Iban, and will be of use whereas Boy-boy has never and will never travel for God's work.

I've got a few letters to write, regarding exempting Luke from parole. He keeps going on about this parole officer lark. I suspect it's only a formality. And now that Luke is staying here I am happy to expect visits from the officer knowing full well that he will be able to see that Luke is settling in, and as well-behaved as he could ever be. In fact tomorrow he will be going on a trip of his own to explore the city and do a little shopping. I gave him some lunch money. He doesn't want me or Wendy to come along, and I think that's fine. It will be good for him to be independent.

May God Bless You.

Your loving brother,

B.

P.S. Internet has been playing up but it seems to be fine now. We've now got Astro TV. Boy-boy is so pleased. He never misses an episode of The Kumars at No 42.

20

Minos

Eternal Light Ministry Ltd, 'Orchid Villa'

So Pastor give me this letter, all seal up to show that he never open it. It arrive day after I arrive at Pastor house. I open it in Boy-boy room, which now I share. The quicker we go to jungle, the better. Pastor seem to want me to stay. He very happy to see me. I make sure I really busy. Cos I ain't going to lay brick when I can do easy God job. I read letter from Watan.:

Minos, *(Is in Bidayuh, Watan's mother language)*
    I hope you don't mind me writing to you. Very soon I will be out of here. How the damned hell are you? Life has not been the same here without you. Watch some DVDs and think of Watan, OK? I'll give Pastor this letter to give you. I know you will see him. How is your labouring/bricklaying job? Maybe I too will get that job where you are. See you soon.
    Your friend,
    Watan

I sigh, and I crush letter. I throw away.

IS SATURDAY. THE VERY word, Saturday. Is so nice. Is day of going out, doing nice thing. Everybuddy love Saturday. And I say to Pastor I wan go to city myself, just jalai-jalai, walk-walk, get to know place. But I prefer if Pastor or Wendy don't come. Cos I wan go alone. And just simply completely fully enjoy the city. And he seem happy with this.

    But I never go. Instead I go straight back to the village, where everything have happened that day ten year ago. To see if everything change or the same. I take bus to the start of jungle, at foot of hill, then do that long walk.

21

Bernard

2006

Now then, some paperwork. January was a great time to catch up. Recently it had been extremely hectic due to Christmas. I never understood when people used that hackneyed phrase 'first things first.' Of course they were first, or else why were they called first things? For me, it had been last things first. Where was I?

As I typed Talina Menduk's statement into a report at my own desk, it struck me that with the flying doctor's signature, Minos/Luke was now proven innocent. She said God gave her TB to punish her for harbouring the truth. 'God is omniscient,' I replied. 'He will forgive you. Each and everyone of us is a sinner.'

Talina protected her granddaughter, Talisa, but now she didn't want our good Christian God to turn her away at the pearl-encrusted gates. If she had been aware that I worked in prisons, she would not have confessed. I prayed with her at her bedside as she breathed scratchily like torn metal. 'God will most certainly welcome you into the Kingdom of Heaven. What you have done is brave and true,' I said. 'It is never too late for the truth.'

A lie. For Luke, it was too late. He had served his time in vain. Now then, perhaps he would leave us one day. He was not like Boy-boy. With the old lady's confession, I could technically apply for a State Pardon for him. I was going to, but I now had decided against it.

God needed him for ministry work. At first Luke would be over-joyed by the clearance. Then he would be totally crushed. He wouldn't let it down. A scapegoat was only tethered to the house of our Lord because he was meek. Were the meek not blessed? He was a scarred beast, captured a long time ago, when he was already a tau tepang cast out from society. A petty criminal. Attempted robbery. *Murder.* If he knew he was cleared, I would lose him. He would break free, raise his horns and charge for it.

Never tempt a wronged beast.

22

Minos

A nother letter come two day after first letter, which Pastor give me, when he come back from his prison visits. Also sealed up to show that it was never open. Is that idiot bastedd Watan again.

Minos, *(This time is in Inglish so that prison warden cannot read it.)*
I know you there cos Pastor tell me. What are you doing. Pastor say you are fine. You not lay brick. I got three week to go now. If you not lay brick I don't wan lay brick also. I also try to get off the parole fellar. Life is easy if just go and work for God. I am sure that is why Pastor doing it in first place. You mus be eating quite nice food by now.
Your friend,
Watan

Again, I toss letter in Boy-boy's bin.
Then I go back to do the book repair in the church library and put them back in correct places. The ones with missing pages to be put aside so I can get pages copied to paste back. And doing these things take all day. For lunch Boy-boy buy some Teochew porridge from takeaway. Is very nice, we eat with century egg and salty veg.
After *Friends* that night, Pastor and Wendy go play tennis. And is Boy-boy's turn to watch TV. He got some Cantonese soap from Hong Kong he been following. He lie down on sofa since Pastor and Wendy out. I sit at Pastor desk. Under the desk is a box with the words *12 x pairs Tai Sing rubber sandals (free size) 100% recyclable product Made in Malaysia.* Inside it, is people's *surat-surat.* Letters.
I pick up any pen from his mug of plenty pen and pencil. The pen is called: **Sheraton** *Hotels & Resorts* and is black, is the

spring type you press and the pen tip come out. Press again and the pen tip go in. This I play with for a while. Click-click, click-click. Just thinking about what to write. Click-click, click-click. With the paper that got the Eternal Light address at top of page, I start to write in Iban. Is not bad considering I don't write, even though I am not from St Josephs, which Watan always talk about like anybuddy care.

Watan, *(I also write in Inglish so that prison warden cannot read it.)*
     I got your two letter. Why you write to me. All is OK. I got tattoo now. Is very nice. God is kind. Pastor and Wendy go play tennis at the Club. Is very posh club. I know you like to talk posh things. Is call Sarawak Club. You know? The club is very old. Pastor say build in 1832. Or something. For white men to go play. Drink. Swim. Smoke c-gar. Beautiful place say Pastor. Olimpic-size swimming pool. But I have never see this place.
     I have go to the village. Saturday. Take me all day to get there. Longhouse that the evil headhunter Peliris live in, still there. But nobuddy in it. Is ruin. No roof. Is like never happen. Is like dream. Bad dream. I am now grow so old from being lock-up. Defnitely not a boy now. You understand.
     I share room with Boy-boy. Is not like you. He don't like share room. Chinese boy. He do all the donkey work here. Cos that wha the Chinese do. I help him a bit. He don't talk much. Pastor and Wendy work him to every bone. He cook every meal for them and even wash Wendy bra panty. Without him they are finis. And without them he is finis. He got no place to go. This place his home.
     Friends is finis now. Pastor and Wendy back soon. Now I gwan on internet for some surfin. Something I just learn. Very fun.
     Your friend,
     Minos/Luke

Better not say about what food is I am eating, like the Teochew porridge, cos that will only make Watan sad. After I write, I throw letter away. Wha's point of writing to he.

23

Bernard

I t was market day today. I had no chance to email Margaret for a few days. I went to Satok Market with Luke to get some vegetables for tonight. Wendy and I were going to have a little dinner party get-together for a few friends from the church.

We'd received the funds from England, another reason why I hadn't emailed Margaret. I'd done my grovelling and got my scraps. We usually used the Malayan Bank for general day-to-day local withdrawals, but for international telegraphic transfers we used the HSBC. I went to the HSBC today and checked that the electronic transfer worked. I didn't ever trust the system anywhere, in UK or here. This meant that we could at last initiate the jungle project. I'd got lots of proposals, we'd see what the villagers say. I didn't think we had quite enough to build a small dam for electricity. We'd work on education and medicals, such as vaccinations, for now.

There were lots of nice fruit and veg at the market. Mum would have enjoyed it. Wendy was attending a class today at the Museum, a one-off for enthusiasts of natural history. Probably attended by bored housewives of the Sarawak Club. Wendy excluded, of course. The Sarawak Museum of Ethnography was the best museum in South East Asia, but not my sort of thing, stuffed animals.

Saw lots of paper lanterns, bird's eggs, socks in packs of three, at the market stalls. It was heaving. Hot. The smell of banana fritters and tapioca fritters drifting, dwelling, formed a dense air of grease and humidity. Many stalls were selling the local snake oils, various viagra copycats, and of course the general cure-all, the Sarawak gambier. Apparently it was good for headaches, stomachaches and toothaches too, and... heh heh, kama sutra type applications. People believed anything. The bomohs and the dukuns, witch doctors, still had a strong hold on the ignorant and uneducated (or both). Charlatanism was shamanism's best friend.

Luke had not been adorned with any tattoos until now. A tattooless Iban was someone of incredibly low status. He did not even have the basic eggplant flower tattoo, the Bunga Terung, because of his family circumstances and his early involvement with petty crime. This was a stylised and circular coming-of-age tattoo, with a spiral called the Tali Nyawa meaning the rope of life. It was awarded to a good brave boy who upon reaching puberty had learnt some rudimentary skills like woodcarving and spearfishing, a badge which undoubtedly attracted the girls.

Luke didn't seem too bothered, for he seemed to have now gotten himself a gigantic serpent cape tattoo around his neck and shoulders. He didn't tell me he had it done, but then it was his choice and he does not need my permission. What on earth was he thinking? A shaman had not done this. It was a machine job from Chinatown. I had been around here long enough to know that. He looked like a leaf insect. Women were giving him the quizzical eye. They were probably wondering the same thing as I was. He hadn't seen women for so long, he stared back at them a little too obviously. Now that there wasn't a parole officer, it was my job to keep him in check. A sharp tap on the shoulder did the job.

A twinge of guilt pricked me. I couldn't afford to have him leave me. I couldn't allow nayap. Iban courtship was complicated and would involve the boy carving a pair of rudings, or mouth harps, one for the girl and one for himself so that they could play each other tunes every night until they decided they liked each other. Luke couldn't carve, I remembered with relief.

My thoughts were interrupted when I saw some quails' eggs at a stall, which Boy-boy adored. It was handy to have Luke doing the bartering in Iban. To my mind, this whole process would make the eggs taste even better. Boy-boy would be so proud of me when I told him how much I paid for them, not realising that a certain local did the haggling! We got a pack of socks for Luke, which he seemed to think very necessary for his well-being.

Last week, we went to the district post office. It was a fair drive away, probably 20 minutes, to pick up the mail for the village in which we will be administering the ministry's work. I had been doing it for a while, and since I visited the village regularly, I didn't mind picking up their mail. Junk mail, job offer letters, bank statements, that kind of thing (if they even have bank accounts.) Who could say? And really, I only picked up their letters whenever I could. Only medication was urgent, all other mail could wait.

Three days ago, we went into the jungle, and I introduced Luke to everyone. We didn't get to Peliris' longhouse as we did not have time. Luke'd now seen how the mail was picked up and delivered, so he could do it without me the next time. The undeliverables were taken back to *chez moi*, Orchid Villa, and placed in a box under my desk until Wendy had the time to sort them through. If they were not collected and not delivered, they were just dumped. I had to check for return addresses if any, decide whether they were important or not, sort out in piles those to be re-delivered, dumped or returned as no one would be able to do that here.

I was the only whitey here, so they knew me as the bloke from the church who picked up mail. Now they would have to recognise and remember Luke, the small, well-built Iban church assistant. On Monday, before the prison visit, I would take Luke and their mail with me. They might as well get used to him. They wouldn't know who he really was. Firstly, his appearance had changed tremendously. Secondly, he was originally from a village miles away.

Now back to nayap. If Luke courted a girl and they got married, he had to live with his wife for two years in their bilek before going on his bejalai, journey. He had to travel for an extended period of time to seek his fortunes. In the good old days, it meant coming back with heads and other treasures. Today, it was money and valuables. What would happen to Eternal Light should Luke go on his bejalai?

If Luke could carve, he would not be a tau tepang, a pariah who ruined everything. I was happy for him to be feeding on the Eternal Light rice bowl. I was relieved. We did not need a pair of grotesquely naked agoms to protect our pantry – we had our Lord.

24

Minos

The quicker we go to jungle, the better.

Cos all this girls I see at the market, they are not The One. If Watan ask me how I know, I just know. Like you know someone in you family. Now, with Nabau the serpent on my shoulders, I should start new life, marry Iban girl, have children. But I can't. Watan words no lehme alone. I am twenty-eight and I have no dreams. I am not a good Iban boy who learn to carve from the time he is five years old, first some toys and then musical instruments. My father went for his bejalai and never come back, so nobuddy to show me how. I wonder if he die. I cannot nayap, because I cannot carve the ruding for myself or for the girl.

Every boy should look to marry a girl who is top class at weaving. After you married, the carving don't stop. Oh no. You have to carve your wife a bamboo box to put her weaving things in. You have to carve all the weapon for hunting. You have to carve new weaving equipment so that she don't have to use her mother's anymore. Boys want girls who are good at weaving because it is a tough tough life in the jungle. The girls they weave to make clothes for war and for every day. They weave pua, and the blankets help you dream well. In Iban, dreams are the most important gifts from the gods.

I come from that tough tough life, but with no pua, no dreams. But at least I'm not Boy-boy. He know of nothing outside this house, outside church. I not surprise if he never even been in jungle. Pastor tell me somebuddy, girl, (always is girl, why is it, dammit), many years ago, not marry, give born to him and don't wan him. And leave he at steps of church. And he cry and cry for mebbe one...two day, and that is why he grow up here and only know of this world. He never cry again after them two days, cos he tears all finis dry up.

When I was eighteen that time, I full of life, laugh and joke with girls at the river, river that go so fast you head spin. With other boys we meet girls at the border town before we go logging. Usually no air, no wind, in the jungle, but the river so fast you get breeze just over water. You got to be fast-fast too, or you flow away, you come back no more, even the lizard spirit flying over you head cannot protect you. Is so hard doing logging and when you see girls, you heart just bursting. They don't know I cannot carve a ruding, let alone play them any songs. Is a miracle if any girl marry me. She have to marry me for true love, cos I have nothing. I am a nobuddy.

Logging to me nowadays just means logging on to Pastor computer. Is not so exciting, but I cannot complain if I compare me with Boy-boy.

IS NIGHT-TIME NOW. Pastor and Wendy having party. Don't know if from church or from Club. Is all same to me. Of course I not invited. How I am part of all this? I just worker for Church, for Pastor, for Wendy.

ER is finis, *Friends* is finis. Boy-boy is in room, cut toe nail. In the dining verandah, we hang paper lanterns early early on. Which I have see in the Market, but Pastor didn't buy from there. He already got, from trip to Malacca las year. And we got to eat pork chop that Wendy make. Is rubbish. No way as good as Boy-boy make. And I know how lucky I am, be look after by Boy-boy.

I can hear they laughing, eating and drinking. And through the window shutter I can see candlelight, and light from the paper lanterns and people laughing, eating and drinking. Two woman and one man are orang asli people like Watan and me, two (a couple) are Chinese like Boy-boy, and one white woman.

I go back to Boy-boy room. I sit on bed opposite he. He still cutting toe nail. The toe nail clipping all drop onto open page of Chinese comic book. He like comic. We eat sepritly from the posh guest people, Pastor and Wendy. We of course meaning Boy-boy and me. Even if they invite I won't go. Cos what I can say to them? "Oh yesss, sir, life inside ver tough, ver ver tough. And I been there too long time, what bout you. You ever been lock up?"

And is strange to think this place as home. Cos if you can't sit at dinner table then you not at home. That is what something Boy-boy must have accept. 'Do you ever think of looking for your family, your mother?' I ask, in Malay. He never answer. 'You like da quail egg?' I ask he, in Inglish, this time, just to check if he alive or not. Also no answer. But I know he like very much quail egg.

I sit on bed thinking to mysel, since Boy-boy not talking. I been in the jungle two time now. And nobuddy know me and I know nobuddy. The girl is gone. The mother is gone. And that is all I know. And on my next trip mebbe I find more. But IS THE JUNGLE. Is thick as mud. Even the air don't move. Nobuddy see, hear, do anything. If the spirit of the animal don't come to you, you ain't got nothing in the hand. Is more important to know and friend the spirits than real people. Cos real people ain't gwan protect you when thing go wrong.

Las week, I got to collect all this mail. No address, cos everybuddy got the same address, which is the village, becos the village is so small. Some time Pastor go sometime he don't. So is always, a lot of mail. And I go to village to give out everybuddy letters. But there is one letter that is for the name Talina. No return address. Postmark is Johor, Malaysia. Johor is on the peninsula. Everybuddy in village say that she is dead.

I bring the letter back to Pastor. And he say: 'Oh! Yeah, that's right, she's an old lady who died a few months ago. Wendy will open them later and get the sender's address. Don't worry. That's not your job. You just leave it in here.' He take out this cardbox from under he desk, and he open it. The box say: *12x pairs Tai Sing sandals (free size) 100% recycled rubber Made in Malaysia.* And inside, there are a few more letters with same name! All not open yet.

I say nothing more.

But he take the box away from me. He not put it back under he desk. So where he takin it? I not ask the question, but he seem to reply: 'Just going to give it to Wendy,' he smile. 'She'll write to them to let them know not to send anymore letters to this lady.'

And then he take the box and go away to get ready for the party. From Pastor desk, I get pen, paper. Now is time to report to headquarters:

Watan *(I write in Inglish, which is getting better every day now)*
    Threes day ago, I go back to village. Pastor introduce me to everybuddy. Of cos they don't know me now. I look like old man. I cut my hair like girl. And I got tattoo. Wan see? Ver nice. I know you very soon out of this place. I got some DVD for you see-see. Is from Satok Market. Buy four, one free. I got action one from Thailand but is shit. Quality.
    Your friend,
    Luke/Minos
    P/s no sorry I just check, is buy 5 get one free. My mistake, is not buy 4, one free....

Haven't finis yet. But Boy-boy looking over shoulder. He don't wan talk to me so why I must let he see what I doing. I seal up envelope, fas-fas, so he cannot look. Why he so kaypoh? Cos he usually not so nosey. Mebbe he think I write about he! Hahaha! No way. I not so stupid, write about someone who in the room. He read Inglish a bit, my standard or even better. He seem deaf when I talk to him but not so blind.
    This letter for Pastor to take to Watan on next trip. Probably Monday. I use lick and the envelope flap stick. I put under the pillow and try to get to sleep. Now that Pastor got the money, we be gwan into the jungle to do new project. Mebbe even Monday. And can say bye-bye to Boy-boy.

VERY LATE, I MUST have sleeping some time. Look at clock, and is almos midnight. Sound of plate and glass and knife fork from kitchen. Scrape, splash, tap running. Wha that sound? They still here? Pastor got to do morning service, got to wake up early, all we have to wake up early. Wendy too. So all these people still here? I get up in dark and go to kitchen.
    But no, they not here. Is Boy-boy. He doing washing up. Alone. Like a mug. One plate by one plate. Through and through. I can see he thinking even if I see back of he head. He thinking: *do it now so don't have to do it tomorrow, before going for service.*

25

Bernard

Margaret,
    I was glad to hear that Mother, your Richard and your two boys, are all well. You hardly ever email, but I do understand you are very busy. Thanks for attaching the pic of the Wickes conservatory. I'm sure that Mother is over the stress by now. From the sound of the builder that you selected, I was beginning to worry that she would need more Valium.

"... all things work together for good to those who love God." (Romans 8:28). We have been very busy working on the longhouse. We would like to get it ready for the school term. It is seriously run down even before the old lady died, for she was too ill to take care of the place, and it is falling apart. We have had to put new boards down for the tanju, it is so rotten from being exposed to the elements. When we took the boards off, a cloud of variegated brown leaves appeared to hop away. They were actually a family of leaf frogs escaping from their shelter.

The nipah roof has crumbled to dust in several places. We've disturbed the bedroom of a shy sleepy pangolin, a toothless anteater, coiled up like an articulated tin cat in the warm loft. The rice grain store in the loft has been raided, the rice tempurungs shattered, all the terracotta pieces scattered. Who had broken in, animals or the tau tepang, we don't know. The carved pair of agom grotesques supposedly safeguarding the tempurungs must have been on holiday when this happened!

Yet God has blessed us. For about half a mile along the track to the longhouse, clusters of *Nepenthes ampullaria*: short and squat, flask-shaped pitcher plants (*ampullaria* is Latin for "flask") are amply growing. I know you would be interested in this Margaret. I'm told by Mother you have all the new TV cookbooks. The "lids" are very narrow and small compared with the pitcher openings, and when compared with the large, showy lids of *Nepenthes rafflesiana.*

Now then, this may not be known to Delia and Nigella: *Nepenthes ampullaria* are known locally as "monkey pots" (periok kera). They are generally bright green, or bright red but occasionally they are green speckled with red. Ours are speckled. The Ibans use them as little containers in which to steam or cook rice. The *Nepenthes* stems are strong enough to be used as rope. One of my predecessors from the late 19th century, an Italian botanist by the name of Odoardo Beccari, lived in a temporary wooden bungalow at Matang on the other side of Kuching from Bako National Park. He said the locals used pitcher-plant stems as rope to secure the beams and planks of his hut.

It is a good idea going to Eden Project in Cornwall this year. I heard that there is a "rainforest" section there. Please do look out for a longhouse, albeit reconstructed and if you are lucky and they are being authentic, some "monkey-pots"! I understand you are taking Mother along. Is it a self-catering cottage?

B.

Bernard,

It is a self-catering cottage that Richard found from some website. Speaking of which, (I know it's not the same, but…) the derelict longhouse you mentioned sounds ideal for conversion for a general office, meeting room and school. What about running water? Will Luke take care of that?

Rice cooked in a pot plant? Think I'll pass. What about the soil? Does it not get into the rice? Anyway, I couldn't get used to using an outside loo with all the creepy-crawlies. What is all this business with rice gods being worshipped? I'm glad the jars broke. People should know by now that only Jesus will save them, not the devil's dolls.

It sounds like you have pressed on this week. Wonderful. There is no need to waste time. You've had the permission from the Sarawak government for a month already. What will Wendy be doing? She must be so brave. Don't you think she should be staying back in the city with Boy-boy?

I'm glad the funds have arrived safely in your account. Luke can lead the way in the jungle and be your Iban guide.

Remember, our prayers have really been answered. Everyone at church has asked how you are. When you went on the missions to Penang and Ipoh eight years ago, how brave you were. Some of the church members have had their fair share of politicking. They've been moaning that you were spending too much money. Sarawak must seem like a challenge. The cost of living is so much lower as it is undeveloped, I understand. Most people here in Brighton have not heard of the place until you went.

Anyway, we are praying for you. We have had a lot of successful prison ministries. One ex-prisoner, DeLancey ("Jon-Z") Jonston is now a successful journalist. He attends our fellowship and we are very impressed with the touching column ('Life Inside Out') he writes for Brighton This Month. Can you not tell from his name? He is black, you know.

You've been there all these years and we've never come out to see you. It's difficult with mum being old and if Richard and I take the boys it will simply cost too much. Besides I don't know what we'll eat. Richard will have a fit. Is it true that you have to eat live bugs? Or even cooked ones? That's what the celebs had to eat on *I'm a Celebrity Get Me Out of Here*, filmed in the Queensland jungle. Do you get this programme on Astro?

After the longhouse conversion, you must let us know when you need more funds. We don't want the children to be without medicine, stationery or books.

When you were bitten by a river snake last year and the shaman came to your assistance, don't forget it is through God's blessings that the shaman administered the right treatment, and you were relieved and cured of the snake bite. You have one of them on your side now. Make sure you know what Luke is up to. Be careful.

"Seek ye first the kingdom of God, and his righteousness..." (Matt 6:33). Don't swim in the river if you can help it, especially if you can't see through that thick mud.

Love,
Margaret
P.S. I posted you another box of PG Tips for your morning tea in the jungle. Can you let me know when you receive them?

26

Minos

Is so dark today.

No light in this part of jungle, hard to see night or day. Sometime when the leaves move, a bit of light come down like a string. One second later, no light again. Today no electricity. Cos generator not working. We cutting down all the lantana and the circle weeds by hand, that is, without chain saw, cos no electricity. Is very painful. Wendy never come. Sick or shopping or something. Just me, three other Iban boys plus Pastor. And if Ingland wan pay for it, we gwan get solar power. Means need to fix solar panels to top of tree canopy. Plus fix all wiring needed.

But first thing, is to find some periok kera. Cos it take a few hours to cook the rice ready for lunch. We make a new rice store in the loft. Pastor have to get new tempurungs cos the old ones all smashed up. We need to get somebuddy to carve the agom. Every house must have agom to stop thief from stealing all the rice.

We also need somebuddy to carve the wood over the front door with naga the dragon and of course, my friend, Nabau the serpent. Cos the bad spirits enter from the front door. At night, we need pua to sleep. But we don't carve and no girls here to weave blanket for us.

All round the longhouse is the area that we working in. The thorns sharper than needles. The parang blunt after four or five hack, that is how thick the weed. The girls make some new floor mat, from woven attap. Cos no flooring in the longhouse.

Everybuddy covered in cuts and bruises. When the sweat go in to the cuts, pain, akh! Not hard work compare with logging. Even yesterday when I swim in river to wash mud off, no sign of turtle. And I think back to days doing logging. How hard work. How many friends lose fingers from the chain saw. Blood and mud, mud and blood. Also somebuddy once get sting by river wasp on the eye. Now is blind. And snake bites – countless time. That is what happen to people.

NOON. THE RICE READY. Now we make fire, put some water in pot to boil, to make tea. Pastor give a letter to me:

Minos, *(Is in Inglish again, so that the prison warden won't be able to read it..)* You bastedd, you never write long time, how are you. I so enjoy get your letter. Improve my Inglish. I fed up of waiting. So I write again. Tomorrow I out of this place man. Tonight party. You comin to get me tomorrow? Pastor coming to say prayer. Then he off to jungle. And I got set up with your bloody job, at that brick-laying place. The job you don't wan. You think I wan take job you don't wan?

So how is life as Luke. That house you staying in sure sound nice even if you share with your friendly room-mate Boy-boy. Not everybuddy nice like Watan, you know. Anybuddy recognise you yet?

Can't wait to see you. I gwan see all my old contacts when I come out. No kaki no jalan. No contacts, no contracts. Then I gwan look for you straightaway. Cos I ain't havin no parole fellar at my arse.

Now I repeat to you! I out tomorrow!

Your friend,

Watan

No point replyin since he out tomorrow. I don't have time to write now, I'm busy doing this site clearing work. And praying. Of course. But already I have find out more.

People who have disappear include one old man. He gone mad. So spirits take him away. And he walk away into the jungle. Smaller and smaller until he just a dot, in the black, and then nothing. Nobuddy ever see him again. Another time, another fellar went to city. He also never come back. Someone say he got job in rubber factory, make nipple for baby bottle. But somebuddy say no he didn't. He got job in city in hotel. Opening and closing car door. Wear monkey suit with gold buttons, covered in traffic smoke all day.

And of course, the other people who disappear is this girl – Talisa – and her Ebu. This I find out from the tattoo lady, who with her own hand, tattoo the girl. The tattoo lady is only a young woman herself. The tattoo lady is only five years old when she first learn how to tattoo, and maybe only thirteen when she tattoo Talisa. Girls must tattoo girls, so that the trade will never die. Now she trying to remember design. When she remember she gwan tell me. She say the very next day the mother and daughter leave. And before the sun come out. Nobuddy known that they were gwan to leave. If they known, they would not have tattoo the girl.

People can only disappear by land or by river. But there is no way out of jungle by land so if people really, really want to leave, they will leave by river. I find the boatman. He tell me he cannot remember anything. He take people to the jetty at end of river every day. The boatman don't know where they go. He don't know what is beyond the jetty. And leave it to the spirits to take good care of travellers.

Tomorrow expecting to see Watan. He sure ain't doing that brick-laying job. Only thing is Pastor must agree that he not gwan to do that job. And sign all those papers again.

So that Watan can be comin to the jungle and help with this project. Means he and me stay in the longhouse. Together again. Is gwan to be fun. This huge longhouse, the jungle's new church, Peliris old home, is gwan to be home. And Boy-boy got no worry he got even more room-mates. Cos now he get to cut his toe nails in peace.

But only prob is no TV here, cos no aerial. How me and Watan gwan to watch Friends? We need internet, TV and TV aerial, we tell Pastor. Cos if none, how to communicate with Ingland? How to learn children education video? Pastor not gwan to be happy. Cos it means must ask more money from Shivering Cold Place. Land of dreams. Land of plenty. Plentymoney.

I remember it good: the day Peliris fall, the day I almost fall. Remember: the python skin. All sticky with beeswax. Serpent spirit, Nabau, you look after me. Now I look after you back, cos I got Peliris' home.

27

Bernard

My dear Bernard,
Solar power? Absolutely not. Mother hasn't even got central heating here. Do you know how long it takes to get the landlord's attention? She's seventy-nine and she hasn't got central heating. We can't provide solar power, instant hot water and instant electric light to your longhouse. The church will go ballistic.

And what about this other ex-con turning up? I thought one is bad enough but I was prepared to accept it based on the fact that he seems reformed enough, going by your description. But now two? Bernard, it's another mouth to feed. Are they all going to turn up at the church to avoid the parole officer?

We're not made of money you know. We're not a charity.
M.

Margaret,
As a matter of fact, we *are* a registered charity.

May I remind you: "... Knowledge puffeth up, but charity edifieth." (1 Cor 8:1)

And what's happened to 1 Cor 13:13? " ...faith, hope, charity... the greatest of these is charity." Why should they not get running water and electric light? Are you trying to say that people with UPVC double-glazing in the UK deserve it but not people who live in the jungle? Richard's paid enough tax, for God's sake get the council to provide Mother with a boiler!

Are we not "... God's fellow workers"? "You are God's field, you are God's building." (I Cor 3:9). The boys have put in an immense amount of work, without running water or electricity, to rebuild this longhouse and convert it into a school room. They dug out a well so we can have drinking water. Do you know it took ten days without stopping, just to dig this hole?

They do all the building work, all the wiring, by the light of three tilly-lamps!

The boys are even doing the postman job for me, so I can just get on with the ministry. Margaret, you've never even been here, how would you know the daily hardships that we have to go through?

I don't think you understand. Instead of being a financial burden, they've contributed more than I imagined. They never come back to the city even in the weekends, unless they want to use the internet. They are skilled hunter-gatherers. They gather ferns for soup and mushrooms for protein when there is no meat, which is often. If there is, they have to make it last. They hunt bearded pigs using poison in their blowdarts made from the sap of the labau tree (*Vitex pubescens*), which paralyses the pigs. The labau is thought to be a magic tree. Do you know the bark is made into a potion given to women after childbirth to ease the pain of the uterus contracting back to its original size? Tell that to the NHS midwives.

There is no B&Q here. Everything is made on the premises. They fish using spears whose handles are made out of the dilleh tree trunk (*Polyalthia* glauca) and tips are made from the nibong palm (*Oncosperma tigillaria*). They know the vicious spines from the nibong trunk are as sharp as needles, and therefore used to make natural weapons like blow-pipe darts and fish-spear tips. The boys have incredible eyesight. They are able to hunt and gather night and day, in 98% humidity. They can catch the common ikan semah, Sarawak's state fish, which is no bigger than a 50p coin.

The boys have applied waterproofing to our longhouse and our sampan boats by melting down the oily resin from the keruing tree (*Dipterocarpus borneensis*). From the species name, you can tell the keruing is native to here. Have we used a penny from the mission or acquired an IKEA storecard?

Their kind of existence is something we could never aspire to. A few thousand quid will get them solar panels so they can watch telly in the evenings rather than just swat mosquitoes. Jesus said 'I am the Light'. Hence, solar panels. Even this little basic requirement you've chosen to deny them.

We'll just have to raise the funds here ourselves, with help from Jesus. "I will lift up my eyes to the hills – from whence

143

comes my help? My help comes from the Lord." (Psalm 121: 1-2). The church members here have already donated a couple of old laptops, with modems, which we will be able to use with battery power. The Malaysians don't need central heating so perhaps they'll be more charitable.

    B.

28

Minos

So no TV. Ingland say no. If land of plentymoney says no, it means no. But Pastor say yes. Somebody in church donate a little TV. It only as big as a chicken. And it got re-chaggable battery power. Watan and me put up massive aerial. We watch TV until battery conk out. On alternative days, cos the next day Pastor take battery back to he house to re-chag, and then next day he bring back. And then we watch it until battery conk out again. And next day give it to Pastor again to re-chag.

So all working quite well. Except one day, when Pastor forget to re-chag battery. We go mad in our heart, cos it mean TWO WHOLE NIGHT without TV! But we can't get angry at Pastor, cos already he kind enough to give us chicken-size TV. And on alternative evenings, when got no TV, we go out and see who-who around, if can get a meal or not. If cannot get meal, alamak! Is a real drag! We pick up some mushrooms, some ginger to steam for food, together with rice already steamed from morning. Mushrooms – if rotten, covered in worms, means OK to eat. If all complete and untouched, means poisonous.

Always, every night, we make fire in the big hearth, in the central hall of the longhouse, and we cook and eat by kerosene lamp light.

There is much staring at the fire when you make food this slow way. A lot of time to stare and to think. Sometime I think of Boy-boy. What he would do if he come to jungle and have to cook without his gas stove. Make me laugh. Watan it seem have already forget about this girl. He more worried that parole fellar after his arse. But I say, not to worry Watan, they got more important crims to run after. And he feel better, for a few minute.

Cos he also run away from the brick-laying place. Means that they must be short of two bricklayer by now. But do we care? Now the longhouse is good as new. Even have all sort blanket and quilt, mattress that people in other longhouse donate to the church.

But once or twice, we see tattoo lady in the evening. She always around. She live with her husband and children in another longhouse with twenty other families. Her husband already gone on his bejalai, maybe he come back next year with tons of presents and money for everyone like some kind of Father Christmas. So one night, Watan ask her to come by. She leave her children with her husband parents. We have catch a big mountain pig. Is staggering half-paralyse into stream, and we finis him off with the nibong spear. We gwan roast him tonight! Take about four hour slow roast. Plus some jungle melon. Is very nice. Big feast. Some leftover for Pastor tomorrow. We got no fridge so we must tie up tight and put in a hole of a big rock, where it is colder than normal air temprature. 'Slong as ain't no snake in the hole. Then OK.

And so tattoo lady come by, to eat the mountain pig as well. Nobuddy invite her long time since her husband gone on his bejalai. She's all high and her teeth all rotten and red from chewing on betel nut, the nut from the areca palm tree. Addicted, though she only a young woman. Watan already interested in what the tattoo lady have to say. He seem quite comfy in speaking in Iban now, is still not as easy as his mother-tongue, Bidayuh.

'So, tattoo lady,' he say in Iban, 'you told my friend here that you did the tattoos for the mother and daughter who ran away. Why?'

'The girl's great achievement was to have cured her mother of bruises, aches and pains. You know she is a manang?'

'Is that right?' I ask in Iban.

'Yes that's right. Her mother, Surya, is a gifted weaver blessed by the gods. Her pua kumbu is very special. It has magical properties.'

'How?' I ask.

'You know, in Iban stories, the cloth helps ordinary humans to fly and to visit mythical heavenly lands. Very bad things will happen to those who try to do them harm.'

Watan and I think for a bit.

'If I had known they were leaving,' the lady continue, 'I would not have tattooed her. I was only a girl of thirteen myself. Even her Nenek was devastated.'

'Nenek?' say Watan, in Iban, 'There was a grandmother?'

'There was. The girl's grandmother. Talina. But she's been dead for over a year now.'

I remember the name, Talina. Where have I hear this name?

'Where did the grandmother live?' I ask, just to check-check.

'Why,' say tattoo lady, 'right here of course!'

'Right here? In this longhouse?'

'Where else?' She laughed. 'You have so many bilek here, enough for eight families! We were waiting for developers to demolish the whole place. Our prayers to Jesus and the tree gods have been answered. You've done a great job here. You are wonderful builders.'

She's a Christian, too? I am thinking to myself.

'Thank you,' Watan smile. Fat lazy Bidayuh arse. Dayak from the Land! It is I and the good Iban boys and girls who have done all the hard work.

'Before she died, it was already going to ruin,' she say. 'After she died, the white man, came and asked the tuai rumah whether they could use it as a school.'

Of course, the headman will say OK to Pastor. The village in need of food, books, medicine from the church. Why will they say no?

'Did the Nenek know that the woman and her daughter were planning on leaving?' ask Watan.

'No,' she say in Iban. 'She said to me that she didn't know until they had left the next day.'

'But why did they leave?'

'The pua gives them the ability to escape,' the tattoo lady shrug her big shoulders, heavy cos of tin and copper medallions, sewn onto her kelambi, her woven bird jacket. 'Have you heard the story?'

'What story?' asked Watan.

'The story of Landu. He was sleeping inside the covered dais when a grey spotted hawk invited him to fly. He said he couldn't fly because he had no wings. The hawk told him to use the pua. As soon as he put it around his shoulders, a wind came and blew him away. Landu and the hawk flew towards the halo of the moon and the mountain tops. Finally, the hawk perched on a tree and Landu fell onto a great rock. Here he was consecrated as a manang by Grandma Inee, who is a Brahminy kite. Manangs have fish hooks in their shoulders, you see, to which are attached the pua.'

Many times I have seen the very sky high Brahminy kite but I never knew she is Grandma Inee. She never gwan to stop and talk to someone like me. I am not Landu and I have no pua.

'The girl is a manang, my friends. The spirits must have told them to go away,' she whisper, as though the spirits are listnin.

IS A BIG, BIG longhouse that Peliris once rule, and now is rule by myself, Watan, the serpent Nabau and the church. And after she go, and Watan and me put away the leftover, we look again over the whole longhouse, look, look, look, is anything of the Nenek left? No, the whole place already been blitzed. Nothing that we can say is not Pastor's or ours. And slowly by slowly, the light from the kerosene lamp going more faint and more faint, until is like seeing light through mud and then very sudden, light is gone and we in complete black.

'I wan give up this search Watan,' I say, in the dark. I know he not asleep yet. 'I tell you many time', I say straight in his earhole, to bypass the listnin spirits. 'I DON'T WAN look for this girl no more.'

'Are you mad? Why give up now? You rebuild this longhouse for nothing?'

'Is for God, Watan. You forgot already? Why we come into jungle in first place?'

'To get the parole fellars off our arse.'

'No. To start life new. To begin. To be. To forgive and to forget.'

'Bullshit. I ain't doing that,' he say.

I grab he neck and I squeeze like hell until he sound like a wild duck on the last day of sacrifice week.

'What you fucken get me into? Hah? You and your bullshit. St Joseph reject!'

His hands pluck at me but I know I much stronger cos he is just a fat arse.

'Shit! Uh! Uh!' He scream. 'Lehwe go, you stupid bastedd!'

In the dead dead night, a wood-owl answer back.

I let go. Then silence for a while. Then Watan say in creaky voice:

'I never bust my arse for this longhouse, work like shit, just to forgive and to forget. I can easily do that on my own. We gwan make her pay.'

AND NEXT DAY, BEFORE Pastor even arrive, cos he got to do the prisons first, Watan already go play postman for the village. He go to the collection point in the jungle. Is like a resting station for mountain trekkers and tourists. Is about one hour walking through the jungle. Watan, like myself, now know every branch, every fallen tree, every little stream. We jungle boys know every smell. Smells that are salty, bitter and strong are no good. Means predator near. Salty smell is actually sweat and saliva. If you can imagine, is a bit like smell of coffee and cash mixed up. If too sweet a smell, means is very late. Means night flowers have all open up, and you must get home quick. If too rotten a smell, all safe because something is dead. Means the predator have eat already, and is gone away.

The collection point is just a hut with water, electricity, air-con, maps, seating, a few woven souvenir for tourist to buy. Vending machine just outside the hut, with Fanta, Coke, Sprite, Milo, tea, coffee. Sometime, in the slot where the drink come out, you can check-check, cos sometime snake sleep in there. Or big jungle rat. Or frilly-neck iguana.

Watan know the rules. He just get the mail. He try to chat up the girl at the counter. But is all pointless. He impress her with his Inglish, but she answer back in Bidayuh cos she can tell straightaway his accent. No one can fool this girl. Her hair is long and shiny, in a ponytail. She look very pretty in her Iban outfit, the woven stole, the wraparound skirt, the headgear of gold stars and flowers. She got a plastic name tag. *Rachel. Sarawak Tourism Information Centre.* Is Christian name. Maybe she already been convert by Pastor. And he can see she got a flower tattoo on the wrist. Means she got achiefments, like weaving or languages.

Rachel give him the village mail.

And he turn around to walk out the door, sad to leave the air-con space.

She say, 'wait!'

He stop.

'There are still a few letters for Talina Menduk,' say *Rachel*, in Bidayuh. 'Again!' She roll her eyes like she tired of saying it.

'Who that?' Watan say, pretend to be innocent.

'She died over a year ago. But we keep getting her letters. I've already told Pastor and I think he's returned the other letters.'

'OK.' He smile. 'Hey, you know where we are, right? Why don't you come round for lunch? We've got a nice barbequed mountain pig.'

'No, thanks,' say the girl called *Rachel*. 'I have my own lunch here.'

AN HOUR LATER, WHEN Watan get back to the longhouse, Pastor still not arrive yet. Is still very dark and overcast because it look like it gonna rain. Means Pastor will be delay.

'I pick up mail for village and church,' say Watan.

But I suspect something, from he voice. Watan tell me about the letters for Mrs Menduk. 'You know who dat?' He say. 'Is the girl's Nenek!' The tattoo lady mention her name before and I have see the name on the letters. But I say nothing. I am stirring the firewood and getting the fire going. The box under Pastor's desk is full of letters for this dead woman. The box he take away and say he gwan give to Wendy to sort out.

'So?' I say.

'So nothing,' say Watan, smiling. BIG SMILE.

29

Benjie

When I got home after work on a Friday in May, I brought the teak garden furniture further into the shade of our wide verandahs with Asuncion's help, so that they wouldn't get prematurely aged. Talisa's dislike for antiques was hypocritical – did she not lie about her age? 'You can talk,' I said. She had turned twenty-four.

Since I found out her real age, I anticipated more worms crawling out from the woodwork of our marriage every now and then. It was immaterial that she was twenty-three when she married me and not eighteen. The fact was that I had been deceived, even if she and her mother were victims. Why could she not, before, during or after our wedding, at least have informed me about her identity card being false? That would have been more seemly. She asked what difference did it make to me. Her answer appeased me temporarily. She wanted her age to remain official as per her IC.

Asuncion fed Wendall his fruity yoghurt snack, after which she strapped him into his car seat. He was six months old and was weaned onto semi-solids. He had four teeth, two top incisors and two bottom. Talisa came downstairs after she had put her make-up on. We headed off. Even at 6.30pm, the air-con and the ceiling fans at the Club were on full blast. All the shutters had been kept shut to keep the heat out. A girl in a mini skirt was playing pool at the Club bar. I thought she was very nice. When women said *nice*, they meant understanding, compassionate, friendly. When men said *nice*, they meant *hot*. She concentrated on her shot, her mouth slightly open and wet, and her eyes were so fixed on the tip of her cue that she looked slightly cross-eyed.

The girl playing pool was probably older than my wife's real age. Her father was probably some rubber tycoon type. She would be under no pressure to get married or have children. She was probably on her term holidays from her university in

England. I thought about her as Wendall was playing with my car keys. The fact that I didn't know anything about her did not stop me looking at her lustfully, and only a day after my wedding anniversary.

After giving her best shot, she blew the end of her cue with blue dust.

I heard a squeal, maybe an eck or ugh. My daydream broken, I pushed Wendall back to his mum.

WE HAD NOT CELEBRATED our first wedding anniversary, although I did remember the date as it approached. It was the date of my incarceration. At least it was a true date. I also remembered her so-called birthday on 5th May, but I ignored it on purpose and she didn't hint or bring it up either. We understood: in our household, there were to be no birthday celebrations except for Wendall's.

Wendall still woke Asuncion up at 5am for milk. I was sleeping in the guest room, so my wife and I didn't exchange dreams anymore. We now communicated through Asuncion about Wendall, and then it was only about bowel movements, sleeping and feeding.

My father encouraged me to take Talisa out for our anniversary. At least we made it through a year. Since she was called up by the police in KL four months ago, she had been feeling crap and acting up. My dad said she needed cheering up. What had it to do with him? If he wanted to cheer *me* up, he should not have told me the truth about my wife's age and her sign. Things had improved with the medication, since I had become her silent drug-dealer. I tried the tricyclic type such as Lentizol but she had bad side effects of tiredness. I decided to go for selective serotonin re-uptake inhibitors, such as Fluoxetine. In other words, Prozac.

I was hesitant in referring her to a psychiatrist, such as Dr Velloo or Dr Wong Choy Sum. The latter was named after a vegetable and must have been the butt of jokes all his life which I was certain had made him want to become a shrink. The former had the reputation of being a casual alcoholic, depending on the performance of his stocks and shares. 'One shrinks, the other drinks,' was the local joke.

152

My status would go down the monsoon drain if the medical profession in Segamat, and the entire state of Johor, found out that my wife was mentally unwell. It would have to remain a family secret. I had already suffered one humiliation by having to marry her, and now possibly a second or third humiliation. I didn't trust her after she kept her true age from me. I worried that she had been unfaithful. She displayed the symptoms of keeping a lover – secretiveness, bad-temperedness, anxiety. I didn't want to look through her mobile phone address book or itemised phone bills.

With a reticent sense of duty, I obliged my father. As it was Asuncion's time off, I even organised to drop Wendall off at Ian's. He was delighted. Someone like him couldn't just be OK or fine with something. He had to be *delighted* or *appalled*. I got home early from work. There were two cases of severe food poisoning of the workers, one 26 years old and the other 33 years old, both female, from the semiconductor factory – they had to be hospitalised. Canteen food.

A few routine check-ups for the elderly and one forty-eight-year-old Tamil lady, a tapper, who was brought in by neighbours. She tried to kill herself on Paraquat. It happened in these estates. The man usually gambled or drank it all away and the wife took weedkiller. I dared not bring it up when I dropped Wendall off. But I knew that this couple worked on *Delighted* or A*ppalled*'s estate.

My wife said she really was not hungry as she had been grazing all day. I pictured her ruminating in front of the lawn sprinklers. 'The ang ku kueh seller wasn't round today, was he?' I said, referring to the door-to-door peddlar who came by bicycle selling the glutinous red rice-flour cake with bean-paste or peanut-paste fillings, laid on a banana leaf. It was her favourite Chinese dessert snack but it made her lose her appetite for meals.

'He was,' Talisa gave her slow awful smile. The sound of the bicycle horn toot of the ang ku kueh seller cheered her up. He came twice a week to our street. He was an elderly Chinese man but looked more like a walking corpse in rags, pushing his bicycle along, one hand holding a battered black umbrella for shade, the other guiding the handle bars. He wore a battered torn hat with a sewn-on badge saying *Disneyland, Tokyo*. A glass wooden container displaying his cakes was strapped to his pillion seat. The heat slowed him down. His eyes were always fixed on the tar road under his feet, as though he was afraid to tread on his own shadow.

We had a simple subdued meal in a hotel bar. She had not got me a gift and I had nothing for her. The girl-woman who was my wife. A stranger.

30

Minos

A nd Watan ain't stop smiling. He already open the letter. Read it a million times. It is from Talisa to her grandma Talina Menduk. But there is no return address. Is in Iban. The girl write like a little girl. There is a heart instead of the dot of the 'i' in her name. It just says hello. There is nothing important. Watan ain't gwan give it to Pastor or Wendy. Already he has open it.

On Sunday, after church service, everybuddy go back to Pastor house for lunch and for going on internet. Boy-boy make lunch for Wendy, Boy-boy, Pastor or course, Watan and me. While waiting for lunch to be serve, Wendy sit around on verandah, fan-fan herself, cos is so hot. Blow air out of mouth every now and then.

But what is Watan smiling about? That he find the letter? We have no evidence. The court case is over. Long time ago. My word is of no value. The girl is still innocent, and I am guilty as charged and I have serve my time. Watan is too stupid to know this. I can explain to him, but he won't understand.

Boy-boy he make clear Chinese soup with wonton and chye sim for lunch. So civilise! Five thousand year old history given us wonton! Wendy is very old-fashioned, must have soup with every meal, even tho she not Cantonese or even old, she act like some old granny.

After lunch, I go on the internet to check-check email, do MSN Chat, Skype, Facebook, Myspace. Improve my Inglish, make new friend, is all. Now I got many internet friends, all from church connections. I love networking. Guanxi. That is Chinese for 'connection'. Literary it mean, 'anything to do with it'. No connection, no nothing to do with it. Watan use the Malay word, kaki. Foot. Means the same thing. Foot in the door. Contacts. Friends that email me come from everywhere. Some in USA, some in Ingland, one in Hong Kong, some in Malaysia on the peninsula itself. I already cover the Pacific rim. Is like I am some sort of VIP biznessman myself. Haha, but of cos I am not. I just Minos, Luke, whatever, who live in a longhouse.

This is my new life. Life outside. Five rules, say Watan about doing this filem bizness is that ONE: must rely on regular clientele. Find them and keep them. Them are filem buffs. Without them, no bizness. TWO: Is no demand for new music. So for CDs, only need to make the classic rock stuff to sell. Old farts still buy. All them new bands – nobuddy gwan buy CD when they can download. THREE: Watan and I filem new releases ourself at cinema. But they are, of course, not clear. Whereas DVD releases copied from originals, are as good as original. Only slightly compress to make file smaller, but that's all. So Watan and I gwan charge less for new releases (filems that are still in cinema). And charge more for DVD releases. FOUR: You must pay your local snakehead! Without he, police come for you! He help you keep everything going. He pay the police every few weeks pocket money to drink coffee! FIVE: never step on another DVD gang's regulars. Them are like you – DVD gang trying to stay alive.

And after lunch, Pastor read until fall asleep, and Wendy do a bit channel surfing or she also read The Sunday Times until fall asleep. I don't like to read. Ever since I got given that Ten Steps book, which is very boring. I know is gwan to take me some time to better my written Inglish if I don't read, but that is OK. My spoken Inglish is already ten times better than before, says Pastor.

Boy-boy clear table, wash up. He like to listen to Chinese station on radio when he wash up. All this songs with funny up and down sound, and it make him look sad.

Watan's turn to check email and surf. Which we enjoy so much. Of course cannot looking at anything naughty. We got proxy server. We look at nice things, like mountain bikes or movie review, or news. We like news. Cos I think I'm gwan need 'years to get back into the swing of things', as Pastor says. I been inside so long is like dream. And to wake up from this dream, or nightmare, is gwan need more than strong Sarawak arabica coffee. Is gwan need time on TV and internet.

Watan is waiting for Pastor and Wendy to go out. He is surfing to be killing time. Boy-boy is always in. Either we wait for he to fall asleep, or I get he to help me in the garden to tie back Pastor's orchids.

At about 5pm, Pastor and Wendy getting ready to go to Sarawak Club to play tennis. At this time of day, is not so hot. I get Boy-boy to help me in garden, and he say yes.

So this is his chance. Watan is looking for that cardbox, the one with words *12 x pairs Tai Sing rubber sandals (free size) 100% recyclable product Made in Malaysia*. All the *surat-surat* that we collect, that could not be deliver. Letters that have come for Mrs Menduk. A dead woman. One who get more letter than anybuddy alive. Ha. Wendy you clever cat. Where you hide this box? Is not much time, but Watan is neat and methodical, his hands small. Is come from DVD experience, handling clean, small equipment.

I am outside in the garden. I look into Pastor and Wendy's bedroom window. I can see Watan. Must be careful, first I make Boy-boy go into the potting shed. He need to get the orchid fertiliser tritment. So he will take some time. I keep one eye on Boy-boy and one eye on Watan.

Now Watan find it. Is on top of Wendy's wardrobe in a big Parkson's plastic bag. Not well hidden. She is lazy, the white woman. Doesn't even bother return them letters. Pastor give her the box so many weeks ago, and yes, everything still here. Is because she never think why we will want this box, and Pastor have never tell her why. Maybe he donno why himself.

So Watan open them letters and is reading and reading. Yep he like to read other people letter cos he always so *kaypoh*. Nosey. He like to show fucken off that he so well-read, so clever, so St Josephs. Which nobuddy care about.

Hey! I whisper. Ssst! Ssst!

He just ignore me. He wave me away. And he is reading and reading, with the bladdy box on his lap, Watan got a smile on his face. And is shivering from the excitement. And sometimes, he look up and me and I just shake my head. Every now and then, he say, The Lord above so good to us, the sweet Lord above.

He take all them letters out, put the empty envelopes back into the cardbox! And he put back the cardbox in the plastic bag on top of Wendy wardrobe.

'What the fuck you doin,' I say. Trying to whisper.

'Tell you later,' he whisper back. Then he leave the bedroom.

Later, Boy-boy is making dinner and Pastor and Wendy on verandah having drinks. Now! This is the time. We go into Boy-boy's room and lock the door.

'See this?' Say Watan, quietly.

I take from him and see properly. Is photo. Girl with baby. Is Talisa and her baby!

'LUKE. Look at the flower and bamboo shoot tattoo.'

'Yes I know who it is!'

I look again. I cannot believe it. I am shaking head. Yes, is true. I keep thinking of the young girl. But of course she be about twenty-plus years by now. And now she got baby. But the mother not in photo with she. I would have definitely recognise the mother!

'You don remember? We go to tattoo lady and invite her eat our snake curry and then she draw on the ground this design?'

'Of course I remember.'

'I thought you too stupid to remember.'

'Fuck off. I remember.'

'OK then. Is the exact design, LUKE! See photo again.'

I think for a bit. Then I say:

'Watan, just forget it. Is too late.'

'You so stupid. People who dono anything, never go anywhere, and never do anything. People who wan know all answer to all question, they success. Ask anybuddy that question. All your dumb internet friends'

'Enuff, enuff.'

'No enuff. Look at all them letters. I already look through. Not just the photo. The girl's ADDRESS is here. LOOK: *5, Jalan Merbuk, 85000 Segamat, Johor*, from her first letter to her grandma, when the girl and her husband the doctor fellar have just moved to they new house. She been writing to her granny, sending photos, sending money. Since the old lady dead, the girl have already send something like three thousand ringgit. LOOK. Cash. Look Minos. Minos. Look. Minos.'

'Fuck sake. I'm lookin. I'm lookin.'

'Good. BUT. This money not our money. We give Pastor. We put into offering bag. Duzzen matter how we give it. We give it all away, to church. Cos Pastor he good to us. And mebbe if I feel sweet, I may even think about givin to Boy-boy but he don care about money. Anyway that is all by the by. Not important to us right now. Minos I have never take money that I don earn myself. All that money I make from the DVD, I make myself. I got learn it when I pick up that stupid pillow case that the robber drop. If is not your money, YOU DON TAKE. We gwan get money. Ourself.'

'From where? For what?'

'One question at a time, Minos. Steady on. Is like you only just come to your senses. First question, we earn it, from the girl. Second question, for travel to whole world. Buy all kind of thing. Start DVD bizness. You always say you wan travel. And if somebuddy say to me go tomorrow, I go. I say we now go find answer. Actually Minos I know your whole story. I can very very easily carry out whole operation myself. So I ask again. Are you with I? You wan stay in jungle rest of life? You wan stay with Pastor and depend on church members to give you money? Boy-boy to feed you, like you charity case? You wan say that ten year not enuff of SHAME? Is time you think for yourself man. So I ask you again, are you with or not with I?'

I sigh.

'Minos, are you with or not with I?'

'OK, OK! Fuck sake. I go with you. May God forgive you your evil attitude.'

'Donworry about that. He already forgive me cos I believe. If not why He die on cross? And why all this spirit in the jungle still protect you and protect I? So that is great news. All round. Feel we should cell-brate!'

'Nothing to cell-brate,' I say. 'You gwan do some evil to somebuddy.'

'Only much less than somebuddy do you evil. Come on, you miserable sod, as Wendy like to say, haha. Minos, lehwe go get some money and lehwe go party on.'

While I stay out on verandah to chat to Pastor and Wendy to distrack them while they having drinks, Watan tiptoe back into they bedroom. He put all the letters back in the cardbox inside the plastic bag, on top of the wardrobe. Boy-boy serving dinner. Can hear the sound of the plates and bowls. Tomorrow we go back to jungle, there is no chance that anyone will find out. Oh oh oh.

In the evening after dinner, Watan go on internet. He got all kind of contacts, guanxi, kaki, connections, whatever, from his DVD days, that he keep in touch with. Remember Rule FIVE: never step on another gang's regular customers. Or else the snakehead come for you big time. Idea is to keep tight to our own DVD contacts and my gang, Watan and me. And sometime Watan print out his email on the laser printer, using Pastor's posh A4 paper for writing to important people only. I say use the rough paper, or paper which have been use on one side. But he don care.

And he is sure happy tonight, happy like some kind of buddha crazy rich biznessman.

'There is one thing,' I say.

'What?'

'We have no evidence. You can't just go and get money from someone. They just gwan report to the police. They just gwan say you kacau them. Then you'll kena tangkap again. Then what you gwan do when you inside again? Make new friends?'

He say nothing. Cos he know I am right. Where is evidence that I am innocent? If we ain't have evidence then, we don't have it now. It's all fantasy.

31

Bernard

Sunday

Margaret,

God certainly moves in mysterious ways. I knelt down and thanked the Lord today. Two weeks ago, a very kind and God-fearing member of the congregation donated three thousand ringgit in cash. I can still barely believe it.

Wendy has found it in the offering bag when we were counting up today. They must want to remain anonymous because the whole amount is in an envelope, unmarked. We certainly do not need that money now from England. I thought I should at least let you know. I would be amazed if it would be this quick for the council to get Mother her central heating!

I hope you will forgive me for being peeved in our last correspondence. Things are getting a little tense and we are worried about the solar panels. People have already donated laptops and modems, as I told you before. We are still short of money to get solar power fitted. Even with the government grants, we need the right infrastructure rigged up. Still we are more than grateful to God that we can set up a new fund. The boys will have aerials, internet, whatever and yes, even a telly and DVD to show Christian instructional and inspirational videos to the village.

Just when I thought that the miracle is over, another wondrous thing has happened. Another two thousand ringgit has come in today. I will make an announcement during the service next week. Whoever they are they should be proud and assured that their faith is intact. They've reserved the best for God. Together with donations that others have put in, we have about ten thousand ringgit. That means solar power is now a reality. We are even going to be able to have a microwave oven for meetings! All these miracles in the space of two weeks.

How thrilled the villagers would be when we are able to 'microwave' their deretang soup made from the bird's nest fern! Hot food has been taken for granted for so long in the West. Imagine what it's like to be foraging for days to gather some overripe mangosteen, a few different gingers and kulat si'ang, the red mushrooms which grow on the riverbank meadows under the purple rhododendron shrubs. The boys need time for prayer, edification and communion with God. Hunting fish and animals equals hot food, and hot food eats time. We can stop using the periok kera and start cooking rice in the microwave to save time.

"The Lord is my strength and song... I will prepare him an habitation; my father's God, and I will exalt him." (Exo 15:2) When I quote from the Scriptures to illustrate my point, I am not leaning on God's word as a drunk leans on a lamppost. The Scriptures should *be* the lamp-post, casting the light which illuminates our way, not a prop for our support.

Just like people come to Borneo to see the legendary Flying Rhino, they believe it when they see it. The rhinoceros hornbill is a most magnificent creature. Margaret, I hope that you are strengthened by my story. Do not underestimate the power of prayer. Everything is now a reality. Praise God for all these blessings. If we believe, everything is possible. Praise God!

Your loving brother,
Bernard

32

Benjie

someone who was foreign and remained foreign. My wife. I always had a thing for foreign girls. The whole point was that you didn't really understand them. They would always be an enigma. In London, there was lovely, slim Urszula. It was during my final year. We nearly moved in together, we were that serious. I think I could have even got around the neurotic racism of my traditionalist Chinese parents. They were racist and classist. Urszula was training to be a doctor too. She was a terrible cook. If food was a priority, I would have gone out with an Italian or Chinese girl. French girls probably had good taste, but they'd be too proud to cook for me. I loved racial stereotypes: 'I'm not a racist but my sense of humour is.' I enjoyed Seinfeld, My Name is Earl, Curb Your Enthusiasm and so on.

This was what I got for marrying a foreign girl. My guard was down. Even doctors made mistakes. What had I done? The right thing when I saw my own progeny. Wendall was now seven months old. He could sit up for a few minutes but he toppled easily. He amused himself by kissing his own feet. He was fascinated with them. He could make the sounds Da Di Ma Mi which could make any of my rotten days at work melt away when I saw him. I cared little for material things nowadays. I was content watching Wendall play with stacking cups and occasionally looking up as if to say 'Dad, look.'

Talisa bought a Louis Vuitton bag today. She said it was for our anniversary because she didn't get me anything. 'I don't want one,' I said. She said, 'have it.' We never went on holiday last year and she said she wanted to this year, 'somewhere fantastic, like Maldives or Thailand. A paradise,' she read out from the travel section of Vogue. 'Let's escape this place,' she said, but it was Asuncion who had escaped. I could sense her disappearance into the shadows again. Like mice, how fast they sniffed tension, how hastily they made themselves scarce.

Wendall put his cups down and picked up an empty cereal box. His favourite objects were indeed not toys but packaging. He put it down and picked up a rag book. He flipped it through, pressing various buttons which released synthesised animal sounds and matched the animal illustrations to their sounds. How fortuitous these books existed – real animals were dying out fast in the wild. The demand from the Chinese for traditional Chinese medicine was killing animals like the rare and shy Sumatran rhino, and the demand from the West for hardwood and granite was killing natural habitats. Both East and West were responsible for the devastation of the planet.

'You keep it,' I said to Talisa, not wishing to sound negative. I'd grown quite afraid of upsetting my wife due to her mental state and my suspicion of her keeping a lover. If I freaked out over expenses, she would simply gravitate towards and seek comfort from *him*.

A terrible thought came to me: could it be Ibrahim? No, that would be ridiculous. Ibrahim was penniless and *only* a driver. I shivered at the thought of Ibrahim in my Italian emperor-size bed. Yet why not? What about when they were out gallivanting? Oh my God! Had I been blind? He was a tall, devastatingly fit-looking forty-year-old Malay from the northern state of Kelantan, with intense eyes and one earring. On the souped-up stereo in his Toyota Altis, he played old school funk continuously, while I was still stuck on learning Chinese CDs.

Since I refrained from touching her, maybe she was using Ibrahim? I felt sick. He probably bopped groovily as well. This was worse than two bloody bags. I missed what Talisa was saying. She was shaking my arm and I was shaking my head.

'No, no, it's for you darling,' she said, her voice oozing with lollipop sweetness. 'Did you hear what I was saying? You have no luggage. We will need it for holidays this year. It's already June and I want to escape this heat. I've got another one for myself. A matching one, darling.'

Another? I thought I kept my cool long enough. I knew how much these damned bags cost. They were rich enough, Vuitton and his compadres, and I was not! Ever since I was a student I neglected checking my statements. Now I married this woman, child, whatever, I'd suffered from a kind of slow financial hæmorrhage. I wished I could have a row in Chinese. It had no irony.

'What?' I snapped. 'You are going to spend another five thousand ringgit? Are you absofuckinglutely insane?' I looked at the bag, that brown leather with the initials of someone else all over it, the gold zip. I felt nauseous. Wendall dropped the rag book and was looking for Asuncion, who had conveniently vanished like a magician.

If I was thinking like Ian, I would be thinking that it was seventeen or eighteen hundred pounds, on two fucking bags for weekends away.

'I think you should stop doing this, spending money in a crazy way, if you don't mind me saying. We could have used the money to go on holiday instead!'

Wendall couldn't see Asuncion and started fussing. He could only sit up on his quilted playmat. He could not crawl to her room though he was still looking at her door. He whined louder. I shouted at him. He yelled. I felt awful straightaway and wondered where I got that kind of voice from.

Talisa wept. She picked up the bag. I bent down and swept Wendall up. 'Daddy's sorry,' I said into his ear but he couldn't hear me because he was still screaming. She shouted over his screams and said that a doctor's wife should carry original designer bags, not fakes.

I distracted Wendall quickly. I locked the keypad on my mobile phone and gave it to him. He knew he was usually not allowed to play with it and therefore this was a very special treat. I put Wendall down and sat on the floor with him. After a few minutes, Wendall calmed down as he sniffled and snuffled. I wiped his snot with a tissue from my pocket and he ignored me as he jabbed the tear-drenched key pad. I looked at Talisa from the corner of my eye and she was still holding onto the blasted bag.

'I've never asked for it,' I said to Talisa in a kinder tone without looking at her. 'We haven't got this kind of money.'

She didn't answer. She dropped the bag on the floor.

'I'm sorry,' I said, 'actually you can just take it back as it's from Louis Vuitton, a proper reputable shop. You can easily get the money back.'

She froze. 'I can't get th... I don't want to take it back. We've got two now. They are a pair. I want us to go away.'

'Well, *I* don't want to go away.'

She was indifferent to me yet she had lavished a designer bag on me, and not her lover, if there was one. Unless the second one was for her lover? I did not actually see the second one. No, that would be too obvious. Ibrahim would have to take it back to Kota Bahru with him so that I never actually saw the second bag, if it *was* Ibrahim. I was confused. I couldn't believe we were having a row about a fucking bag.

'I can take it back if you want,' I suggested in a fake helpful voice. 'I can get a refund. I'll drive to KL this weekend myself. Don't worry.'

'Please don't.' Her voice was hard and cold. I hadn't seen those concrete eyes since she read me Tang poetry a long time ago.

'I don't want the bag and it's my money,' I said.

'If you take it back, we are finished,' she said.

'Why?' I said.

'Because I want us to have matching bags when we go away. Because I'm a doctor's wife. And I want people to see us with the bags. Because because because. Why can't you just be cool?'

I laughed. I was not cool because that would just be too funny. I couldn't stop laughing and she was speechless. Her rage made her back off. Wendall looked up from my mobile phone momentarily but it was too precious a treat to him to be distracted by his mum, so he went back to his random pressing of buttons. His mother ran up the stairs and slammed the door. I could hear her weeping like a windstorm over an ancient mountain.

A COUPLE OF HOURS LATER, I put Wendall to bed. In the glow of his panda nightlight, he rubbed his eyes and looked for Asuncion, who usually put him to bed. I looked for his *In the Night Garden* pyjamas which he liked but I could not find them and Asuncion was not around to ask. He grumbled when I put him in a t-shirt and pair of shorts. Eventually he settled. Talisa came downstairs for a sandwich. I was watching ER. She sat next to me on the sofa and munched away, her eyes silent and swollen. 'Don't worry,' I said quietly, 'just keep the bags.'

Talisa gave her awful smile packed with deceit and she squeezed my arm with gratitude.

I heard Asuncion's door click shut. She was going to bed and it irked me. There was always a shadow or a clink or a cough, as though this house was possessed, haunted by staff.

I didn't have any receipts, documentation, anything about these bags. If I wanted to return them, I would need all that. I couldn't possibly walk into the shop otherwise, yet I didn't dare to ask Talisa for them. I just *wanted* to trust her.

All those Italian girls, Chinese girls, Polish girls –now all that was finished, gone from my life forever. I could barely think about old girlfriends, girls on the beach, girls at bus stops, girls who play pool at the club in miniskirts. Those thoughts were faint, disconnected and distant, like dreams. For a married man, memories were all you had. Plus a huge house, a crazy wife, a sleeping baby, and quite literally, baggage.

33

Bernard

After I had whooped with joy and thanked the Lord on my
knees, it appeared that it was too good to be true. Wendy
discovered that someone had broken into the box of
letters to Talina Menduk. I remembered from her confession that
her grandaughter was Talisa, and all the letters were from this
Talisa. I could not read them without a dictionary since they
were in Iban.

Wendy was just about open them individually (in case they
were all from different senders) and send them back, but she
realised they had all been opened and read! I knew it was the
boys. Who else could it have been? They were the postmen!
They had seen and carried the letters to Orchid Villa. Boy-boy
would do no such thing. In the first place he couldn't read Iban.
Even if he could, he had no interest in anything. I wondered if
the anonymous donation was a coincidence? My instinct told me
the money had come from the letters.

I went to visit the boys in the longhouse. Upon
confrontation, the boys admitted that they opened the letters.
They said they had to because letters for the dead harboured evil
spirits which had to be freed. 'There are no spirits in the letters,'
I said. But they also admitted that they took the money they
found and donated it to the Church.

Their kindness and generosity to God made me forgive
them, though I knew we had both done wrong. They stole
money. I spent the stolen money. *Mea culpa.* Yet we simply
could not go back. The money had been absorbed and spent
already on the Church, and there was no way of retrieving it.
What would the Church accountant think if the money
mysteriously disappeared after it mysteriously appeared?

Dear Lord! I would have to keep their secret and they mine.
Wendy must not know. She would make my life hell by getting
me to retrieve the money no matter what, despite the fact that it

was due to her slackness in the first place that we were in this predicament. If only she had done what she was meant to do here in the missionaries – her work, and if only she returned the letters as and when we received them!

Margaret must not know either. That would be a complete disaster. Wendy would just be told that the boys opened the letters to free these damned evil spirits. No mention would be made of the money. As far as she was concerned, there was no connection between the anonymous donations and the letters on her wardrobe. I'd tell her I'd taken care of informing the sender, so she didn't have to do it now.

How could we blame the boys for what they did? They gave the money away! They had no greed! I prayed that our dear Lord Jesus would forgive us. All of us. I was sure some dread punishment will follow. But if we never wrote back or returned those letters to the sender? More money might arrive. Or the sender herself, Talisa, might arrive. But indeed there was no way that they could trace the letters. They could have all got lost in the post. The notes were large. She posted cash – what did she expect?

Jesus I was in trouble. Tonight I slept badly in the bilek, hearing only the deafening hoots and howls of animals. A moon moth fluttered in front of my eyes at dawn, and woke me up. The ominously *aaaaargh!* sound of a black hornbill's call sounded like someone being repeatedly sick and it alarmed me. The boys were making me eggs for breakfast on the timber deck. They were toasting slices of white bread on the fire they have just lit. Rice was already steaming in the red speckled periok kera, for our lunch. Morning Pastor, they each recited, like schoolchildren.

'Luke, I need to talk to you, my boy.'

169

34

Benjie

It had been the hottest June on record. Temperatures and tempers soared. By a very wet October, everyone was ill. Snake bites, bee stings, flu, miscarriages, rabies, migraines, dengue fever, allergies. Fever fever fever. It was a crazy time. Patients did go mad from febrile inflictions if untreated. It was late and I was dog tired. I'd been to see two extremely ill patients at Ian's, who had lymphatic filariaris (LF).

Beware the Big Foot, went the local whisper.

According to popular legend, the unseen monster called Big Foot roamed the jungle. No one had seen him, but they had seen the footprints. It was now believed in the medical profession, less romantically, that the footprints might be of those who suffering from elephantiasis, one of the consequences of LF, which made the limbs swollen with dramatically thickened, hard, rough and fissured skin, like an elephant's legs.

LF was a devastating parasitic infection spread by mosquitoes, and caused by thread-like parasitic worms that damaged the human lymphatic system. If untreated, there were nasty consequences, particularly the lymphœdema, elephantiasis and hydroceles. It seemed to affect the Indians, hence the tappers, very poor people who were exposed to mosquitoes all the time. Filariasis was spread from an infected human – someone with worms living in his/her bloodstream and lymphatic vessels, to an uninfected human, by mosquitoes.

I had to charge Ian more because I would be performing blood tests at midnight. It sounded very Count Dracula but the parasites had a "nocturnal periodicity" that restricted their appearance in the blood to only the hours around midnight when the worms were most active. Therefore, it was necessary to diagnose LF based on the lab tests of blood extracted between 10pm and 2am. Fortunately, the disease was treatable. In a rural town like Segamat, where I was treating Indian patients working long hard hours in the deep, dark estates, the infection was not unusual. Malaysia was one of the forty countries in the world that currently had elimination programmes set up, where the government contributed substantially to mass drug administration treatment because it was extremely cost effective – typically about three ringgit per person per year, the cost of a cup of coffee.

At sundown today, I had a personal call. The family of the patient, a coffee planter, could not get hold of other doctors and they had my mobile number. It was an emergency. He was a neighbour from when I lived behind the coffee plantation. Memories of my free and easy days in my peasant cottage days of waking up and smelling the coffee returned to me. He had had a stroke, which has resulted in some paralysis of his right side.

The suffering of these grotesque patients helped me forget about Louis Vuitton bags, Talisa's stilettos and credit cards for a while. It was not schadenfreude: I did not need the grim hopelessness of these people's lives to remind me how lucky I was. It was the constant amazement of how bizarre the medical profession was, how dirty you were prepared to get your hands, how late you would get your hands dirty in this slow, sleepy agrarian world and how both patients and Ian MacFarlane so depended on you.

A bloody circus.

NIGHT. THE BREEZE WAS slow, the air stifling. I was going home to have a bite of Asuncion's boiled pig stew. Yeah. On second thoughts, I should probably have dinner at the Club instead followed by a slug of strong Segamat robusta arabica blend coffee. (Wa-hey!) If Ian was there, I'd make sure he knew about the bill that was coming.

I had been working late for more than a month. It was claustrophobic as the plantations themselves. On my way to the Club, I drove past the Segamat River, crossed a new bridge and I spotted some rabid river dogs foam at the mouth and howl in the moonlight. Water rats scuttled and gleamed like tins.

I reached the familiar uphill road, and went slow for snakes. I remembered that clinical years as a medical student were rather disappointing. An administrative preoccupation with filling in logbooks tested everyone's ability to lie to the utmost. I felt this urge to lie. Most of our first pre-clins was spent doing complicated algebra because one of our dear physiology lecturers was obsessed with correct dosages.

Was I correctly prescribing my wife's medication? Her addiction to spending had increased. I had written off those bags. I just didn't have the time to drive to KL to return them. I'd been so busy with all these ill people that I'd neglected my wife and baby. She didn't complain. When we did speak, we ended up rowing about money. I consoled myself that one would expect all married couples to behave this way and have similar rows.

At the Club, I tried to get some money out at the Maybank ATM in the entrance lobby. I pushed my card in and keyed in my pin number. I requested the amount of fifty ringgit, which I thought should be enough for buying a round for the girl who was playing pool and her father if he was there glowering at me. It said that the bank had denied the transaction. On my second attempt it was the same message. Insufficient funds! I didn't understand. I knew that Talisa'd signed up for some course or other. She went on and on and I said yes. There should be something like two grand. How could it be we hadn't even fifty ringgit? Eight pounds! It was probably some genuine mistake that the bloody bank had made. Or maybe there was some credit card scam from all that internet shopping that Talisa'd been doing.

They were all useless. Banks, post offices, the town council, phone companies, controlled parking. Moan, moan, moan. I sounded English. I used another card. Malayan Bank Visa. No luck. I used yet another card and tried the ATM next to it, HSBC, and it was the same response again on a different screen.

I carried on straight to the bar. I would take a chance with the barman and put it on my membership tab. When you were married to someone, you trusted them completely. Otherwise what was the point? I hardly had time to eat let alone do a bit of light reading of bank statements before bedtime. I did try every month but it was complicated and there were now all these credit cards. Some of them were in her name and I could not read every thing on them. Hell, she might not even show me the statements.

'Transaction denied due to insufficient funds. Contact your bank'. Why? Why contact them? It would only prove to them further the state of my idiocy. Worse still, what if the bank manager was my patient? No. He probably had posh private specialist healthcare. I didn't welcome him laughing his head off that a doctor hadn't got fifty ringgit after working ten hours a day six days a week.

It was a quiet night and the DJ's voice was crackling from the security guard's tinny transistor. A fast, night shower arrived, from the dense thuds on the verandah roof. It brought with it the grassy metallic stench of the tropical ground, baked all day in the sun. A brush-tailed porcupine crossed my path on his way to the kitchen looking for food scraps from the kitchen. Lucky him. It seemed so long ago that I ran in the monsoon mud in order to be floored by Ian. Now I was in the monsoon of my life. All my money had drained away.

I sat in one of the winged armchairs so that no one could see me. Of course, Ian caught sight of me straightaway. His reflection was on the large French windows: his large hawk eyes scanned the whole room, looking for people to beat up and/or insult. Even the camouflaging tapered leaves of the giant parlour palm couldn't save me now. Perhaps he would buy me a drink as I had none in front of me. He was behind my armchair, barking, before I'd even turned around. 'What have we here? Fucksake? What you doin here? What's going on? Aye? Aye?' That awful voice. When I did turn around, I realise that he was not even talking to me. He was snapping at the barman.

Ian was a real man who never carried an umbrella. He shook himself like he's a dog or something. 'What have we here?' *Now* he was talking to me.

'I've got no money,' I said.

'I got some,' he said, taking his jacket off and hanging it on the back of a chair. 'Buy you a drink.'

'No. I mean it. I got no money.'

'We'll sort it out later,' he said, patting my shoulder. 'Hey what's the matter with you, mate? You look just mental. You seen a ghost or something?'

I didn't just 'luke' it. I *was* mental. 'We've spent all our money. I'm serious.'

'What? Explain, young man.'

'There is no money in my account. It's all gone!' I almost cried.

'How did you do that?' He frowned, as though I was responsible for it.

'I don't know. I think Talisa's spent it. I have been so busy working, I definitely have not spent a cent.'

'You fool!' He sighed. 'Do you always blame it on others? Don't blame it on others, my man! You are supposed to take care of her and the lad! Do you ever use your head?'

'What? What do you mean? It's not *my* fault the money is gone,' I added, perplexed, 'is it?'

'Yes. It. Is.'

'No!'

'Yes. It. Is.' He leant towards me, his breath rabid and hot. 'You can't expect your wife who is a full-time mother to know what is happening to your finances?'

'Maybe it's a bank mistake or a credit card scam.' I changed my tune, too hopefully.

'You're insured, ain't you.'

'Yeah.'

'Fucken relax.'

'OK.'

'It may all be fine tomorrow. You can buy the rounds next time.'

I said nothing, then: 'I've got to work again later tonight.' A *non sequitur*.

'Fucken buy you a steak and chips? Or a pie-type thing?'

'OK.'

This was the last person on earth I wanted to see. I couldn't believe he was 'hir'. I just wanted to sit here on my own, in the winged chair, under the canopy of the parlour palm foliage, twiddling my thumbs until midnight. I checked my mobile phone. No calls. I wanted to see if it was cut off. I'd better not bring up the fact that I was going to bill him for the LF patients' blood tests later on tonight.

'Well which do you bloody want?'

'Um, the pie-type thing. With chips.'

'Ooch ay. Drink?'

'Whisky,' I said, like I was stoned. 'Make it a double. Cheers.'

'Chirrrs!' He shouted from the Bar, with a wink and a side twitch of his head, raising his own glass, a Tiger, which the waiter had poured for him first, to be getting on with.

The night was as black as the seeds of the duku fruit. A deep sweet scent from the night-blooming *nymphæa* near the riverine swamps drifted into the car via the air-conditioning ducts. I soothed myself with the scent of these water lilies on the journey towards the estates again. It was nearly midnight. I had to get back to the clinic to leave the blood so that Shue Ling could send the samples off first thing.

I was sure I would find the receipts. I had to return the two Louis Vuitton bags. Otherwise, how could I pay Ibrahim and Asuncion at the end of the month? I'd say nothing to my wife. I could not lay the staff off yet. Their wages would be delayed while I got my act together. They were hired to prevent Talisa from hassling me. One took her out (well that'd better be all that he did) and the other took care of us all. Talisa wouldn't and couldn't.

She was asleep when I got home at about 1 a.m. I crept around like a thief. Drawers? Cupboards? What the hell were in those besides shoes and clothes? I wanted to go through the receipts (the bag receipts, the guarantees), statements, letters, whatever. What about that course she was on about? Yes, I knew men didn't listen, but I really didn't pay any attention. It was something mad and insignificant, maybe interior colour schemes or koi garden design, a course that specialised in fleecing desperate housewives. I was certain that it wasn't astrophysics, or I would have sat up.

I didn't know where she kept things like documents and things she didn't want me to see. How did women do it? They were so good at hiding, oops I meant, tidying things. I was so, so tired. Sleep came agreeably but I woke up a few times, dreamt a few times.

In the last dream, elephants were kicking me and stamping me with their monstrous feet, with gold LV initials on their nails.

THE NEXT MORNING, BEFORE Talisa or Wendall were awake, I took off. I stopped by at the Petronas station to use the ATM and test the cards again. They were still not working. The moment I got to my surgery, I nearly boxed Shue Ling out of the way. It was not even twenty past eight. She was probably wondering why I was an hour earlier than normal. 'Don't just stand there,' I shrieked. 'Send those bloods off, pronto!'

Think think think. If my maths was right, ten thousand ringgit had gone on two designer bags. When I left London, I had nothing, probably because I worked at the NHS. Since then, in addition to my own wages, my mum and dad put money into my account every now and then to help the bad boy. After all, I was building up my practice. Three years on and I had thirty thousand ringgit, not a bad sum for a non-saver. It was five thousand pounds! I needed to change the names of the signatories. My account was 'safe' because it needed two signatures, my wife's and mine, before any money could be taken out.

Right now, I had to bite the end of my pen and put up with Vivaldi's Spring from Four bloody Seasons punctuated by 'Your call is important to us blah blah blah' every ten seconds.

35

Minos

'What is it Pastor?' I say. I leave Watan as he cooking eggs for Pastor breakfast. We must stay in his 'good books'. Pastor and I go outside and go down the log ladder.

'Luke,' Pastor say, 'I saw the old lady before she died. She confessed to me that she saw what happened. So what it means is... what I am trying to say is...'

'What you sayin then, Pastor.'

'What I'm saying is she saw everything. We have the proof that Talisa killed her stepfather.'

I can see from corner of eye that Watan is listening in. He was leaning over the edge of the tanju, the very deck that Peliris he fall from.

'What do you think of all this, Luke?'

'Dono what to think.'

'It means that you didn't have to open those letters and release the evil spirits. The old lady was already a Christian. There are no evil spirits. You should have left her letters alone. What you did was wrong. Do you understand?'

I feel a sharp pain like a kite just flown into my stomach.

'Pastor.'

'Yes.'

'The old lady died last October. Now is June. Eleven twelve one two three four five six.' I count with my fingers. 'Eight months! All this time you knowing that I am innocent?'

Pastor looks at me as tho he never seen me before.

'You are not officially cleared. As far as the Home Office is concerned, you pleaded guilty, remember.' He is slightly angry, like is my fault that I am not cleared.

'Can I see the confession?'

'Yes. The next time we are back at Orchid Villa, I'll get the files.'

'Is it all OK? Legal-legal?'

'It could be.'

'How?'

'We...e...ell, um, we have to report it and get the State to pardon you. Then you will be officially cleared.'

'Why you didn't get me the Pardon when you already know the truth?'

'There was no need to. At the time.'

Whose need he's talking about? From now on, I don't have to follow everything that Pastor says, or promise him anything, cos *there is no need to.*

'Can you please make it legal-legal please.'

'What are you saying, Luke?'

'Pastor, what you did also wrong. Better all this forgotten about.'

I can see Pastor is uncomfortable. Cos he cannot possibly return the girl's money to her nenek when it's already spent. He sighs.

'Can you apply please Pastor?'

'OK. But I don't want any hassle, Luke. You promise me? We cannot possibly return the money soon to Talisa, and therefore I do not want to take her to court. You cannot take this document to the State and prosecute her. Or else, everything to do with money will be out, the Church, the school and the mission will be shut down. It will be end of Eternal Light.'

'OK. But what if she send more money from now?'

'We return it. We send the money back to her.'

'No, Pastor, we cannot.'

'No?'

'No, Pastor, the Church need it. If you see what I mean.'

'No, I don't. What do you mean?'

'Firstly, you already used up the money from before. You cannot return that now. But if you have no more money coming in, you gwan back to Inglan.'

Pastor look at me for the first time with look of pure hate and sadness. Then he quickly look away cos he cannot look me in the eye no more.

THE MOMENT I GOT to see the confession that Talina Menduk dictate to Pastor, I quickly remove the original from the *Tai Sing*

178

box. When the State Pardon arrives, I also take it and keep it. Watan, I was always unsure about this, but I now I have heard what Pastor have to say, and how long he have kept the truth from me, I say, let's go for it. This is the start!

We write to the girl. In Iban. So she know that we know. No sender name or signature. The first letter, we ask for NO money:

Hey Tattoo Girl, *(we write in Iban)* nice house, nice baby. We know your secret. We know what happened to Peliris.

THE SECOND LETTER WE ask for five thousand ringgit.

Hey Tattoo Girl, your secret is safe. See the post office box address at the top? If you want to keep your nice house and baby, you will send five thousand ringgit cash in five notes. Make sure it's packaged beautifully. If it goes missing or is lost, it's the same as us not receiving it. Who do you trust? Us or the postal service?

THE MONEY COME. OF the five thousand that our friend courier to us, we give two thousand of it to the church on Sunday. Pastor did not ask any question.

Means we already GIVE seven thousand to the church. We gwan stop there. Is good. We proud. Cos at least we get benefit too. We gwan get solar power in jungle. And long after Watan and I gone, travellin the world, et cetera, the village and the church can still use it. No wonder he keep his mouth shut. How can Pastor complain? Pastor is silent partner, he is in this now with Watan and me, there is no going back.

So with this three thousand leftover from the second letter, we planning what to do. Watan already take the money to buy equipment. And this week we gwan buy equipment. We gwan go to some big computer camera electrical electronic type warehouse, we buy camera, printer, CD blanks, everything. Even tripod. Cos he keep tellin me. How do you think DVDs are make? This is the way to make. He know where the warehouse be. We go on weekday, early-early. In some huge industrial estate, everything at wholesale price. Is near Indonesia border. Near where I use to do logging. A place called Back of Bayonet. Pirates hang out there, like sharks. And really hang out. Checking everyone out. And is like a big headquarters of everybuddy and anybuddy who is a snake head. And everything very competitive there. If go late enough, everything is auction off in a big lelong sale. And we buy, buy, buy.

We take all this equipment and we set up in the longhouse. In one of the eight bilek, cos they are just empty rooms. Everything is set up, rig up to the solar electrical supply, to the lighting and the only thing we do not have it phone. Just internet line but no mobile or actual phone. Pastor use walkie-talkie with we.

I use to think Watan make fake DVD cos of money. But now I know. Is not cos of money or sell to people or whatever, but he really love filem. Every filem, you just name it, he have see before. Even terrible four hour foreign filem, like Turkish or Kazakhstani filem, or ten-minute student filem about nothing, filems with no money to do edit, he have see all of them.

Fac is I trust him because he have see so much. Even if through the eyes of some filem maker or director or whatever they be called. I just blind. And I let Watan lead me. I have learn so much from Watan already. Is not just the money. Even if got no money involve and no girl to hunt down, still there much to see from his eyes.

There is no need, Pastor's voice keep repeating in my head. Everybuddy need to tell somebuddy something. If not be telled, we gwan explode. The girl keepin her secret must wan to explode. How can Pastor keep it from Wendy even? I am sure she does not know, because if she know the whole world will know. The white woman has no idea of anything, and if she even be careful about her job, Pastor will not be in this situation today. How can Pastor know for so long and not explode? I know now. Because he love me and don't want to lose me.

But he love money more and don't want to lose it. I help fill up the Eternal Light rice bowl. The fire in Pastor eyes has died. Pastor when he used to come to prison and talk to us et cetera, he love to chat and pray cos praying another excuse to keep talking. Now we can never talk about what has happened between us. It is a like the river baya, the crocodile. It just lies silently, waiting in the water.

Now I am doing DVD with Watan, in Pastor's very own longhouse, use as a church on Sundays in the jungle! Is of course illegal, is secret. But Pastor won't have to know. Cos *there is no need.* Watan and me do this DVD thing on the side. When we get enough money, we wan leave this place.

When a boy at St Josephs, Watan go every day to cinema. Sometime he even miss school to go cinema. He gwan make us rich. We make our own DVDs, we watch them and we sell to tourists. He says we can make A LOT. Very quick. Once you buy all the equipment, and pay small fee to the boy in the projection room, there is no more cost. It is the easiest and most fun job in world. What is better than going to cinema all the time and fileming filems that you can watch over and over again?

Now we have solar power to do it. Watan and myself do all the wiring. Takes a whole week. Pastor come and go, just like before. And we do everything in the locked bilek. *There is no need* for Pastor to go in there. But we need him to do all the documentation for the solar power, the forms, grant, whatever. Make all them phonecalls to important people. He doesn't like paperwork. Yes, we know that now. Then solar installers come in.

Everything starts from there.

I learn to make the DVDs quickly because of saving the solar energy. If not, we cannot watch TV or DVDs at night. In the day, we work with daylight. At night, we use the energy supply. Is not like in the city, people waste electricity cos it's unlimited.

I do DVD cover, scan, or get from internet. I know what is low and high resolution. Resolution. Is so nice word. I have hear Pastor use it before. It means so many thing to so many people.

Watan learn me all tricks and ways of making something that is nothing look nice. He call it presentation. Nowadays he say you cannot sell crap cos people very choosy. They are customers. They wan everything neat and nice and perfect and cheap, like a day on the beach or something.

Now I am Minos, Luke, whatever, and I am on high resolution. I learn in two weeks how to edit filem, photo, how to use scalpel blade, steel rule, cutting mat. Everything happen so, so quick. It make me sad why the ten years I spent in prison go so slow. And why it eat up so much of me, so I feel hungry all time, and only then, I feel so ANGRY.

I need Pastor more than Pastor need me, so I can only say, I have to ignore the *baya* that swim in the river silently, the river

181

that is between us. Why, I am even holding a scalpel chopping up pieces of colour printer paper. I feel mad, and when I pick up scalpel one day, I stab it so hard it go into the bamboo table that Watan and I have make, the blade snap off.

I call out to Lang Singalang Burong, god of war: I am sorry! Now we must ask again for money! From HER! Letter number three. We gwan get another five thousand ringgit!

The blade break, then it fly. It fly into dark space beyond longhouse. Just like Peliris done. And I don know where it go but I see the light shining on it as it fly.

WE WRITE TO THE girl. Third time.

So easy to make money. Especially if they are fraid of you. And if they concern for their gran. This time the money is for us to put aside, go for holiday somewhere. Apply for passport. To travel. That is Watan's dream. Plus all this money we have make on the DVDs. He sells to tourists at a slightly higher price than if they is locals.

We write to the girl. Fourth time. No reply. No sign of Brahminy kite across the sky. Lang Singalang Burong, god of war, what news you bring us? We wait, days, maybe one week and two days. And no reply still…

And…

36

Benjie

After I'd waited for twenty minutes on the phone and got Shue Ling to courier the LF bloods to the lab, a patient arrived. I asked her to re-schedule him, I was still holding on. I was drenched in sweat and the air-conditioning repairmen had failed to turn up. We were relying on minuscule desk fans.

Finally, I got through. The bank told me that 'Madam Talisa' had already come in the day before to try to withdraw from *my* time deposit savings account. The bloody nerve. What was going on? Luckily, she could not, because she was too thick to realise that two signatures meant two signatures. The teller thought nothing suspicious because my wife was just told to come back with me another day. Fat chance.

My mother had said to me before we got married: 'this girl no good luck.' The girl was a thief, a pirate, a Sea Dayak through and through. I said to the teller to email me my current statement since I never read them or have ever checked them. It seemed that RM10,600 had been withdrawn, not RM10,000. What was the six hundred for? Maybe that was immaterial. The possibilities were that a) the bags were actually RM5,300 each, b) the RM600 was just for my wife's lunches and yoga lessons or c) for her lover. Loose change.

Now that course. What was it again? Fashion management? Designing koi ponds? But had she already paid the fees? Maybe she needed more money to pay for the course. That would make sense. I couldn't think about it now, I hadn't done any work yet and it was already 11.06am. There was a queue of sick people outside. I washed my hands. Shue Ling must be wondering if something was wrong. No matter.

I might be a sucker for women but I was sharp as a leech's hook when it came to shattering my wife's spending rampage.

The monster had awakened!

I HAD TO WAIT until my wife was out for at least two hours, visiting Ian or the gym or the beautician. It was late Monday afternoon when I discovered Ibrahim was taking Talisa, Wendall and Asuncion to Ian's.

I could not find the medication I prescribed her, in the kitchen nor the three bathrooms. Not a single tablet. I doubted very much that she would carry them in her damned Prada handbag. How would she fit them in? Her handbag was only as big as a spectacle case, slung over her shoulder and pressed down to keep it under her arm. I could scarcely remember that once she wore a kangaroo pouch money belt.

I did not buy her a car when she badgered me. By hiring a driver, she'd turned my middle class sensibilities around. She flaunted them. She made herself appear pampered. Whereas I had been the master of understatement: the BMW being my only concession to brand allegiance. Now that Talisa and her entourage were off, the house was eerily quiet.

I was an intruder in my own house, an outlaw. Something took over me – instinct, in layspeak. I had this compulsion to open all the drawers in the dresser. I slid open the Italian mirrored wardrobe doors of the spare bedroom, having found nothing in the master bedroom. I found myself liking the very political incorrectness of *master*. It would only take me a second. I knew this from having heard of burglars who 'did' the whole house in five minutes. I was only 'doing' two pieces of furniture.

I flung open the drawers. I found *stuff*: Talisa's knickers and lycra items, chunky Bulgari and Tiffany trinkets still in their original boxes, about 28 bottles of nail polish, fifteen vials of lip gloss and other miniature tubes of unidentifiable cream, three different sized tweezers and what I though was a pair of nail pliers. It was like a lab minus the small animals.

I kept going, my fingers agile as if washing vegetables. There were photos of Talisa and her classmates at her Chinese high school, and a photo of a woman holding the baby Greg and the toddler Melita, a woman who looked incredibly like she could be Talisa's Ebu, Surya.

My heart skipped when I found a bundle of letters. It was a wad of four letters, only perhaps 5 mm thick all up. It was secured with a shiny purple elastic band, the hair kind, the type that was wrapped so as not to hurt when one was tying or untying a ponytail. The elastic was so strong and tight that the letters were curled up into a roll, like a certificate. All the envelopes were brown and the same, and were addressed to my son Wendall. The postmark was recent, and from Sarawak, Borneo. The last one was postmarked only a week ago.

I opened the first two of the four. They had all been opened, and presumably read. I didn't recognise the handwriting. All the letters, I noted with disappointment, were in Iban, therefore I was not able to read them, not straightaway anyway. Quickly, I pulled off the purple elastic band and put that back in the drawer. I stuffed the letters into my jeans' back pocket.

In the garage, I found the second bag and documentation for those damn bags. Guarantees. Serial numbers. For the first time, I examined the bags carefully, like they were patients. I could not tell whether or not they were genuine. I had heard that there were very good copies these days, made in proper 'fakes' factories in South China, so good that you couldn't tell. The label said Made in France and every detail to do with documentation, the inscription on the zip and the tags, was replicated.

I got back to the kitchen, where all the mail and bills were stacked in the filing tray. I said I was not going to do this, but I was actually looking through her itemised mobile phone bill. I called the mobile phone number most called, and last called, in the past month. I carried the cordless into my office downstairs and shut the door.

It was a Chinese woman's voice, common and with a harsh accent, the sort who said, 'harlow', rather than 'hellow'.

'Harlow Talisa!' she said. I still had no idea who I was calling.

'Er, it's not Talisa, I'm her friend.'

Silence.

'What you wan.' She sounded like the Wing On Chinese Takeaway and Fish and Chips shop woman in Leytonstone whom I used to laugh at on the phone when my housemates and I would ring up to place an order.

'What's your name?' I asked.

'Mei. Who are you?'

The person most called, and last called, was *Mei*. I had never heard this name. Talisa had no friends. Women she knew were either other mums (i.e. compatriots in motherhood) or subordinates (i.e. people paid for services). I'd heard many other female names being mentioned, mums of Wendall's friends, hairdressers, babysitters, nail artists, dressmakers, fashion 'consultants' (more bullshitters), but never *Mei*.

Uh-oh. Was my wife from the island of Lesbos? This was very hard to take.

Shit! I heard the sound of keys in the door. She was back! If I knew her, Talisa would be switching on the telly staightaway, which incidentally provided quite good sound insulation from what I was doing.

'Can I see you tonight?' I whispered into the phone receiver, knowing full well I was pushing it. Mei didn't even know who I was. It therefore surprised me when she responded.

'What's your name?' she asked.

'Um.' Quick, think, think. I look down at my brown leather Kenneth Cole sandals. 'Kenneth!'

She said OK. 'Ask for Mei. Everybody know who is Mei,' she said in English, somewhat impressively.

'Where?' I urged, hastily.

I scribbled down the words 'Ah Hock Hotel' on a *Zantac – Fastest Relief from Gastritis* notepad, one of many message pads dotted around the house, compliments of the various pharmaceutical companies. Ah Hock Hotel sounded vaguely familiar. It was in the seedy part of Old Town. My mother would rather eat her own flip flops than go to that area of town.

'Talisa?' I called out, grabbing my keys. 'I need to go out now. Someone has had a stroke on the coffee plantation. Back in half an hour.'

'OK,' she said.

'I'm locking all the doors and putting on the alarm downstairs,'

'OK.'

I goose-stepped my way across the gravel to my BMW.

AS SOON I LEFT the house, I went to the local 7-11 newsagent and bought a phone card. I crossed the road to a phone booth and rung the Louis Vuitton shop in KL, in Starhill Gallery, an exclusive European designer label mall. The great thing about mobile phones was that no one used public phones anymore. Even vandals had their own phones. The first phone that I found actually worked.

I decided to speak in a false but clear BBC accent. 'Yah, I'm terribly sorry to bother you,' I said, 'but my wife came in and bought these lovely bags. With all due respect, she has lost the receipt. I wonder if we could we possibly have another sent by post or email? We would be utterly grateful,' I sounded like a conman. 'We're on holiday, so if you could send it pronto, that would be lovely. The serial numbers are...' I read out the serial numbers on the phone.

The man tapped away at some computer keyboard and said that the bags with those serial numbers were still in the shop! He said something about it being illegal buying them in the first place, and they definitely did not come from the LV shop in KL or an authorised dealer. Before he could rant on any further and report me to the authorities, I hung up.

If they were fake, where had the money gone? *To her lover.* All I needed was another piece of evidence. I didn't want to hire a Private Investigator yet. I would ring my mate from Uni, James Selvarajan, a top divorce lawyer in KL. He could do things for me "on account". At last I would be free of my sham marriage.

AH HOCK'S LODGING HOUSE was, as I suspected, the kind of establishment that had rooms by the hour, a hostelry of sorts. It dawned on me why Mei did not hesitate agreeing to meet me. What was my wife doing with the likes of this woman? For a second, when I drove past it, I was already changing my mind about coming here, just by the sight of the building. It was a guano-splattered three storey concrete crate, probably circa 1968. Dirty curtains on the windows were so torn they looked like cobwebs. I could just drive off. I cheered myself up with my review of the cackytecture: a Mondrian structure with the Pollock-influenced guano. This building would not look out of place, in parts of, say, Catford. I found a space to park in the next street. These hundred-year-old lanes were impossible to park in.

It was not hard to find Mei. Around the lobby area, there were four women, all tarted up and loitering with intent. They all looked at me as though they were housewives in a market examining a slab of meat (how easily roles were reversed). Only one of them said, Kenny. She said it a few times, because I was not used to having a pseudonym. At first I was not aware that I was being called.

'Oh yes! That's me!' I said, startled.

'Come on upstairs!' she said in English with a grin. 'Don't waste Mei's time.' She referred to herself as Mei, like she was a third person. Maybe it was not her real name anyway. Mei. It meant something to everyone. It could mean beautiful or sister or blossom. Whatever. A name that you'd remember and you'd forget. A name that men would not find offensive or bold or naggy. A name that no one's wife had.

I climbed the three flights of gloomy stairs with short-breathed disgust. I glimpsed the bathroom at the end of the corridor. It was tiled in mosaic on all six sides of the room, the ceilings were filthy grey, the basin streaked with rust. Many tiles were missing, like teeth on an old woman.

I entered her room without being invited in. There was only a bare light bulb, but I could see her clearly. She was actually not young, but not old either, probably late forties if I had to make a guess. It was all in the eyes and the neck. She was wearing jeans shorts, cut like someone had ripped them off with a saw, a mango green bikini top and high-heeled silver sandals. Sweat had formed a glistening film over her chest where her cleavage should be, but she was flat-chested. An attractive woman, despite her bruised legs and crows' feet.

'What can I do for you, sir?' she said. 'You sit?' She pointed at the bed. I sat on the bed, wondering what this girl could do for me in an instantaneous fantasy, because I remembered then why I was there.

She did not sit down on her own bed. She was cautious. She leant against the light switch near the door like she was a film star, her legs crossed like scissors.

'You like speak English or Mandarin?' A choice!

'Er… English,' I replied, deciding that my Mandarin was not good enough to sustain a possibly complicated conversation. 'Can I pay you to talk to you?'

'Oh, you are one of those,' she said, nodding understandingly, maternally. 'What you want talk about?'

'Do you know a lady called Talisa?'

She folded her arms. The Chinese had a marvellous propensity to make their faces go utterly blank, like they'd drawn a curtain.

'I need to talk to you about Talisa,' I added.

'I don't know this person.'

'I think you know her. She called you.'

'Are you police?'

'No,' I laughed. 'You can check.' I emptied out my pockets. 'I need your help,' I said.

'Why? Are you sure you not police?' she grinned.

I grinned back. She relaxed.

'I know Talisa,' she said in Mandarin, nodding. 'She and her mother Surya used to live here when they first came from Borneo. They had a room on this floor before Surya got a job at a rich ang moh's household and moved out. More than ten years ago now. Twelve. What was his name? Let me think... Ewan MacSomething....'

'Do you still see Talisa?' I asked, ignoring the info about Ian.

'Not really. Not much now.'

'Not much?'

'Only when she wants something.' She pointed to something in the corner of her room: a row of those repulsive Louis Vuitton bags next to her battered wardrobe. They were neatly wrapped, each in its own cellophane condom, and more bags too of various sizes and designs: Chanel, Prada. I recognised some that my dear Talisa had worn on her arm before, all those iconic burdens, candies fit for the tattooed arm of a doctor's wife.

'Nothing wrong with them. They are made in a huge Shenzhen factory which makes the originals as well. The top ones go to the originals shop, the middle ones to here, and the rubbish ones end up in street markets. I'm an agent,' she smiled modestly, pausing to let the word take effect on me. 'When I say middle ones – they are classed as Triple A. They are as good as original, but not original, you know?'

'How much are they?' I asked. I didn't actually care about the bags, just the price tags.

'The little ones start at a hundred. It goes up from there.'

'What about this one?' I pointed to one that was identical to the contemptuous LV Weekender bag with the gold zip.

'Oh that's completely made of genuine leather. Four hundred for normal punters. But since you know Talisa, you'll pay what she pays. She bought two of those recently. I only charged her six hundred for the pair. Do you know that they can pass for the real thing?'

'Really?' I said to humour her.

'Yes, the real thing costs five thousand. Customers buy them for their wife. No one can tell. It's got all the documents inside. And look at this, it's really fun: a till receipt! Ha ha. From the LV shop in Petronas Towers KLCC. Even the dust bag has the logo.'

'What's a dust bag?'

'It's the bag for the bag.' She smiled and shook her head as if to say, *you stupid men!*

'Oh I see.' I thought about it for a minute.

'Have a look-look. See anything you like, I'll give you a good price.'

'What about this one?' I pointed to a cute pink Prada coin purse. A gift for my mum, I thought.

'You can have it for a hundred,' she said, but seeing me demur, she added in a hushed voice, 'as you have come all this way and you are Talisa's friend, I've given you a really good price. I have to pay the snakehead you know, before I get the agent's cut!'

I pictured a Gucci skinhead stomping around Ah Hock's and pounding on her door. 'Pay the snakehead? For what?' I asked.

'Protection from the gangs. The designer bag gangs. You can't just pitch up and start selling. You have to pay them to be a seller. They pay the cops and everyone is happy. It's like a membership subscription. Look.' She showed me a catalogue in a see-through folder. She flipped the pages. Every page had a grid of images of bags, bags, bags by every top designer of the Western world, counterfeits to choose from, though of course, the photos were of the originals. 'All these lovely designs, new, this season's. You can order any design and we can deliver it.'

I took out my wallet, teeth gritted: she had given me the proof that I needed: Talisa deceived me by passing off two fakes worth a total of RM600 as genuine bags worth RM10,000. QED. I suddenly did not want to part with my last one hundred ringgit.

'You think about it,' she spat. 'I give you good price already!'

I fled without a second thought. I could hear her screaming in Mandarin down the corridor, 'Hey! You said you were going to pay me to talk, you impotent prick!'

IT WAS ABOUT SIX o'clock when I left Mei's. Near the markets in Old Town, I walked into a local bookstore cum newsagents cum roti paratha snack café stall, Mohideen's, run by Indian Muslims. Newspapers and magazines dangled on cables, outside the shop along the verandah, held by clothes pegs to the cables. I brushed through the curtain of publications and entered the cool, dark interior of the shop. I purchased a dictionary of Borneo dialects, after I'd checked that those did include Iban. On my way out, I picked up a takeaway of nasi biryani and a packet of muruku as well from the café side of the business. Very enterprising, these Indian Muslims.

Back home, I heard the clatter of fridge door bottles, Asuncion's laughter and Wendall chatting to the TV. I locked myself in my gigantic den with its safety blanket of floor to ceiling hardwood shelving and wall to wall seagrass flooring. I ate the biryani first, in order not to leave oily fingerprints on the letters. After I washed my hands, I opened the Iban letters. I wantd to have a go at translating them tonight itself. Only four, and how short they were. How hard could it be? I'd memorised entire tomes for my medical exams before. This should be easy peasy and achievable with my eyes closed.

As it turned out, my eyes *were* closed. I had not even started on my amateur translation exercise. I was so tired I fell asleep at my desk. My wife called out to me but I didn't answer. She said she was going to the supermarket and taking Wendall. I heard Ibrahim start his Toyota engine. He revved it too much and my teeth grated. Thank God he couldn't touch my BMW. Later I heard the front door click, and then the automatic gates whistling as they swung open on their tracks. I dreamt of my son. He was in my subconscious. I missed him even if he was away for a few minutes, a few hours. What if I never saw him again? I was his father. He was my little boy. Men had no words for missing their offspring. Miss was somehow the wrong word. It was more like 'fear of losing'. How fortunate women were, so be so vocal, pliant and reactionary, so *allowed* to do so, I love you, miss you, thinking about you, blah blah blah.

Perhaps it had to do with giving birth. Surrounded by strangers, who opened you up, took a living thing out of you, sewed you up. What was there left to hide away from the world, your friends and family? Women were born to be exposed, born to give life. Your entire genitalia, your thoughts, your breasts, your past and present aspirations, your own childhood before you grew up and had children yourself, your fanciful and fantastic career, your appearance without make-up, earrings, shoes or any dignity, were exposed, talked about, read about, thought about, written about. Stitches, the Great Leveller.

Men's level of so-called participation was being allowed to *watch* childbirth. Life. Proudly brought to you by Woman, our official sponsors for millenia. No wonder men did not have words for it. No slogan. No hip hip hooray. No send off, no penalty shoot outs. No one said 'well done' to a father.

Not a night went by when I did not think of the night my son was conceived. I remembered every detail. The wayward bougainvilleas tumbled over Ian's porch columns, their thorny limbs arched, creating a cave-like mouth to Ian's entrance door, their papery-orange flowers see-through in the glare of my headlights. High above, a pungent musky scent floated down, of tree moss and wet orchid roots, clinging to the banyan tree. All around, it was dark, the only illumination came from my car. The headlights in my own head had been turned off.

A gecko clucked. When I woke up, the lights were still on, it seemed to be 2.51am, the 'clever' hour, and why I was having these extraneous tenets in the twilight zone of who-am-I bullshiterrania. I went over the summary of my findings so far.

Assiduously, I got up from my desk, sat down on my leather sofa and translated the letters, word by word. For the man who had no words, it was hard work.

The first letter had no meaning to me, yet it was still menacing: *Hey Tattoo Girl, nice house, nice baby. We know your secret. We know what happened to Peliris.*

Who was Peliris? The second and third letters each asked for five thousand ringgit. A blunt ache entered my chest, and I felt dizzy.

The fourth letter, the most recent, simply said *Where is the money?* That was clear in whichever language.

I took a sheet from the *Zantac – Fastest for Relief from Gastritis* notepad and scribble some notes in bullet points to aid my ageing brain. I sprawled myself across the large leather sofa in my study. Talisa'd paid them my RM10,000, used the bags to deceive me, and now they wanted more. She had been blackmailed by these scoundrels! But for what dark secret?

At dawn, I dreamt more dreams. I tried to remember them the second I woke up, but it was impossible. Even as I slept I was conscious that I wanted to write them down. One by one the dreams left the scene until there was a complete blank when I woke up, an empty stage. I must have been waving the proverbial fist, for my fists were clenched when I opened my eyes.

Tuesday. An overcast morning. I crept into the master bedroom. Talisa was asleep. Wendall was awake, being dressed in his own room by Asuncion. At eleven months, had just started nursery so that he could socialise with other babies and toddlers. He could stand and walk unsteadily, a few steps at a time. When he saw me, he pointed at his new Thomas the Tank Engine socks. 'Oh wow!' I replied with hammy enthusiasm. 'That's very nice, where did you get them from?'

Wendall couldn't speak yet. He just kept pointing and looking at me. 'From grandpa,' said Asuncion.

Unfortunately, Asuncion was around and Ibrahim was waiting to take Wendall to nursery, because what I really wanted to do was confront Talisa, wake her up and shake her to pieces, just to say: 'I know you are being blackmailed! I know you have a secret! Tell me!' Instead I found myself smiling calmly and congenially at my son while sweat gleamed at my temples. 'Say bye-bye to Daddy,' said Asuncion. Wendall gave me a sad little wave.

With a heavy feeling, I went back to my study. The PC was still on. I shut it down. Somewhere in the neighbourhood a horrid child was practising Grade One piano scales. I ate some stale bread spread with kaya for my breakfast. I took the four letters and the Iban dictionary to work to keep them safe with me.

IT WAS ALREADY TOO late when I got to the clinic, red-eyed and extremely tired. The till had been broken into. In shock, and guilt, I straightaway thought of Talisa. I must be crazy. How could I think my wife had done this? I was shaking. I quickly glanced at the still locked glass medicine cabinets. Shue Ling said nothing, but she knew. Women knew these things. She said matter-of-factly that the burglars did not force entry. Look at the front door, she said. I suppose they could have carefully picked the locks, she added. Then to shame me further, Shue Ling said, shall we report it? I said no. She looked away, perturbed, but said no more.

'Go out and get me a real coffee please,' I said in a deathly tone. 'None of that Starbucks shit.'

'But, Doctor, the patients are...'

'Do it.' I snarled, my voice still trembling and weak.

'You look...' Shue Ling started to say. She couldn't say it. I looked like death. She took her coin purse and walked out. Even her heavy eyeliner did not disguise her contempt. I knew that my wife had robbed the till, so desperate was she. I would not ring Ibrahim on his mobile to ask him if he took her and Wendall to the clinic the night before. No. That wouldn't be necessary. I would ask Talisa first. If she denied it, then only would I ask Ibrahim. He might lie for her. They all would and had already done so, though it was I who filled their rice-bowls.

My wife still had the keys to the clinic from when she worked here. She never gave anything back. She must have sold all the Prozac that I'd given her. That was why I hadn't found it yesterday during my house search. Now she had taken the one thousand ringgit I kept in the till, which was the sweetener for the junkies who might break in. My wife displayed the behaviour of a junkie. Unsound, frantic, hopeless.

A whole day passed at work, during which I dulled my senses by reminding myself that I needed to stay open to earn more money. I needed to earn more money because I had none. Time passed quickly and through sheer need, like urine.

37

Minos

We gwan pay the girl a visit, say Watan. Get a whole lot more out of them if we are there. I don know anything about Segamat. But Watan say, don get hopes up. Look on internet first. There ain't nothing but the blues there. Just plantations, estates, logging, that kind of thing. No beach even. Quite boring then, I say.

Well, say Watan, you can't have everything. We gwan there for work!

Pastor always say, save for a rainy day. Actually that is what they say in the Shivering Cold Place Inglan, but it rain here every day, just for a few minute. So when is it actually a rainy day to use the money? On a rainy day, nobuddy feel like spending money. People stay at home and eat and drink watch telly surf internet do laundry. It should really be called saving for a sunny day. Because only on a sunny day you want to party.

Is straightforward to apply for passport. We can do online these days.

I got a new name, which is Luke, anyway. Minos now officially gone. Watan is just Watan. We got no birth certificate so we just apply from scratch. Three hundred ringgit for a passport. I have seen Pastor's Inglish passport in his drawer. It looks like the Holy Bible. Is red leather cover with gold lettering cut into the leather. Is it because Holy Bible is passport to heaven?

I very interested in design these days, since I am now making DVDs. I look at everything that have got a cover. Books, CDs, DVDs, passports. The passport we get is very flat, the lettering not cut in. And is not even leather. Pah.

I think is like vinyl or something. But anyway. It qualify us travel to Malaysia for our 'working' holiday. I tell Pastor we gwan away for maybe four day. He say, fine, send us a postcard. He wan give us spending money. He say don't tell Wendy. But I

195

say, no thank you Pastor, already you very kind to we and we don't need money. And Watan say, we need money, and he take like a couple hundred ringgit from Pastor. Later on, Watan say, if we don take he money Pastor will get suspicious. He will wonder where we get money from.

Before we leave the jungle, we pack something important – the black glue from the labah tree. We will need this. We put it in empty Pepsi bottle with screw cap. That way it look like Pepsi.

We gwan fly from Kuching International to Senai International Airport in Johor Baru. We book on internet some place is called the Ah Hock Hotel. We gwan share room and they say no prob, they can put two beds in the room if they move the cupboard out. Work out at something like thirty ringgit a night before tax. Is the cheapess place in town so as to make our money last. There is a Old Market nearby.

No way we gwan on ship. It's expensive and wastes time. Nowadays everybuddy who is anybuddy can fly. We get the Air Asia flight. Twenty-five ringgit one-way. And domestic flights they don't check bottles and make you drink it. Or else we'll be dead if we drink the labah glue in the Pepsi bottle. You can book online or you just buy the ticket and get on. Even Pastor swear when he hear how cheap. He say, 'That's like three pounds! It's basically Ryanair or Easyjet,' he says to Wendy who says, 'You won't catch me on a flight like that.'

It's a morning flight. It's like 5am. So we travel from longhouse day before and we stay at Orchid Villa overnight. We sleep on sofa cos Boy-boy sure as hell don't wan Watan and me share his room. Is bad enough when I share his room and look at him cut toe nails.

Cos we need go to Kuching International Airport and is nearer to Pastor house than the jungle. And so have to waste money on taxi. Boy-boy wake we up early and give we breakfast of half-boiled eggs, and kaya on toast. We sit at round dinner table, on the verandah. After we have coffee, luckily Pastor awake. And he offer lift to airport.

And he pray with everybuddy, Boy-boy, Watan and me at table, and like always, I keep my eyes open, and look around when Pastor praying. Wendy still asleep in bedroom so not at table. Even Watan eyes shut. For long time we have not pray like this, like we are in prison again. How hard Pastor have pray for us, time and time again. I wouldn't do that for anybuddy.

I look at Pastor fingers, lock together, on table, his hands look like a little basket. His nails clean, and his fingers loose-loose. I see all the breadcrumbs, what a mess, and egg shells lying around the table like baby chicks have hatch.

38

Benjie

But there was a fifth letter, when I got to work.

They'd sent the letter to my clinic. They must know that she was not in control of the money anymore. They did not get paid when they sent the fourth letter to my home address. Damn! I wondered if they did break into the till last night?

'Three patients are here, doctor. Waiting to see you,' said Shue Ling in a monotone. She must have seen me somehow drumming my fingers, staring into space and waiting for her to leave.

That dreaded familiar handwritten envelope. Shue Ling brought in some patient cards and my cup of strong coffee. I hid the envelope from her view by putting it on my lap. When she left the room, I opened it carefully, not destroying the envelope. I stopped, got up and locked the door. I stepped away from her view of me through the glass vision panel where she could check what I needed and whether to send the next patient in. I grabbed the Iban dictionary again, sighing as I began to translate word for word again. But first, a shot of whisky might aid concentration. I poured it into the coffee.

Inside the envelope was a postcard with the photo of the giant durian mascot that we had on the traffic island in town. My translation was not complete or good, so I'd managed to do it with a few missing words:

Dear Tattoo Girl,

We are enjoying Segamat's durians and coffee.

We know you killed your stepfather Peliris. Your gran Mrs Menduk told us. She's a lovely old lady. What a naughty girl you are. They even gave you a tattoo!

But now I have official clearance from the Home Office, thanks to your gran. Sadly I have already gone to prison for ten years for your crime. Let's try to forgive and forget. (Something something) our last letter, the five thousand ringgit you never paid up. You will give us 200,000 ringgit to clear the debt once and for all. We are not greedy. We worked it out quite fairly: ten years' lost earnings. Courier cash only to this postal box address.

You've got three days. If we don't hear from you, you will say bye-bye to your big house, your husband and your son. Your only view will be the four walls of your cell, for a long, long time.

My blood iced over. The postcard had been placed into an envelope first and the postmark was Segamat, yesterday. The postal box address was also in Segamat, presumably to make sure that the postman could not read it.

Despite my shaking hands, I studied the postcard and the handwriting. The bastards wanted more money. They were in town. My wife was a murderer. They wrote in 'we' and 'us' and 'our'. The person who had served time to pay for Talisa's crime had now been officially cleared of all charges. There was now sufficient evidence to press charges against Talisa. I gasped. I didn't want her to go to jail. Ian would never forgive me. He would stop sending me his tappers and fellow old time colonials and I would have no patients. I would be cut off from my own community and my practice would close down. Wendall would not have a mum.

I shut the clinic at lunchtime and rushed home. Irritatingly, only Asuncion was in, who caught me in the foulest mood. Ibrahim, Talisa and Wendall were out. I was still shaking with fury, especially as I saw all these things in my own home, which were all mine, the plasma screen TV, the DVD player, the stacks of children's educational DVDs, the wedding photos on the shelves, a large framed black and white photo of our baby at six months, my paperbacks and my medical textbooks on display, the frosted wall lights we chose together. All these things now meant nothing to me. She deceived me, again and again. I sat and waited at the door like a crazed assassin.

The silver Toyota Altis pulled into my brick driveway. Perfect timing. The buggy was lowered. Wife and child alighted and approached the house. I waited for Ibrahim to bugger off after that jaunty wave. Keys in the door. Talisa had her sunglasses on her head.

'Hi, darling!' she said with false cheerfulness. 'We went swimming and Wenda...'

'What, with *Ibrahim*? Did he *swim* as well then? What does he do besides drive and *swim*?' I didn't wait for Asuncion's shadow to melt away into the wings: it always seemed to do at the right moment.

'No, he didn't swim,' she answered in a serious tone. 'What's wrong?'

'Well, guess what, darling?' I cut her short. 'I read your letters. I know everything. The bags, the till.'

A long silence.

'Yes,' I continued. 'And we're broke!'

'But it's only four days to the end of October. And you get paid then don't you?' Her breathing quickened.

'By who?' I smiled benignly, and folded my arms.

'Um, by patients?' She looked quizzical, like she had never thought about the question before.

'Why did you not tell me any of this?' I pointed at the damned letters.

'I was afraid of losing you, our son. I wanted...I wanted only to protect my family. If I gave them money, I was hoping and hoping they'd just leave me alone.'

'Well they haven't, have they?'

'Just don't. I just can't. I'm not.' No verbs. She waved her hand like I'd pestered her with questions an interminably curious child would ask. I grabbed her hand firmly.

'Why did you kill your stepfather?' I demanded.

'He was a bastard! He beat up both me and my mum! Oh God, please don't be angry!'

'I'm not angry!' I yelled.

'He was cruel and drunk. I saved my mother and me. We ran away.'

'Someone, this- this person who went to prison? Who is he?'

'He...he is someone who came by to ask about a job. Ebu told the court he tried to rob us. She said that my stepfather tried to stop him, that...that there was a...a fight, which ended when this man pushed my stepfather to his death from our longhouse.'

'Your mother covered up for you.'

'Yes,' she shook her head pleadingly. 'I was thirteen.'

'What actually happened?'

'*I* was the one pushed my stepfather down. It's about a twenty-foot fall onto the nibong fencing which is as sharp as glass, slicing him like a cheesegrater...'

'OK, enough. Got it.' I knew the Ibans used nibong palisades to keep animals and intruders out, but I was rather surprised to see that she had let out the Iban in her – the fearlessness and thirst for violence. It was the first time I had seen her invisible mask come off.

'The man...the man who came by about a job simply...he ran away,' she continued, 'not knowing what had happened. Nenek must have seen the whole thing. But she would never have told this...this man, she would do no such thing. I mean, she helped us escape! Why would she tell him anything?'

'Is there no way you can get hold of your Nenek?' I ask.

'No,' she said. 'She has no phone and I can't write to her because there is no time left.'

I bit my nails, thinking hard what to do next.

'I think we should go to the police. You're being blackmailed.'

'NO. No way, Benjie. Are you kidding? NO. There's more than one of them. They will kill us.'

'Any idea who the others are?'

'I have no idea. They've tracked me down these years, not the other way round!'

'We have to stop them, then, my dear. Do you know that I have no money left? How long do we have to keep paying them for? And also, by the way, I'm making Ibrahim and Asuncion redundant.'

That got her attention.

'What?'

'You've asked for it. We can't afford them.'

'I'm sorry,' she pleaded. 'I need them!'

'No, you don't.' I said.

She appeared quite dispirited. 'My own father died and abandoned me and my mother,' she sighed. 'My stepfather beat us. *That*'s the real crime.'

She had had three fathers. They were all interchangeable as far as she was concerned. For a minute, I felt sorry for her. It's not her fault her mother married an abusive man, and had to lie and cheat through life. Her escape story was quite remarkable in fact and I was oddly touched.

'You need Ian,' I said.

'You mean?'

'If we're not going to the police, let's get Ian.'

'What?'

'Is he not your closest relative?'

'No, you are.'

'Don't patronise me.'

'Well,' she exhaled a solid, compact sigh. 'He's...'

'Oh for fuckssakes. What is more important? They're in town!'

39

Bernard

L ast night, I stayed behind with some of the Iban teenage helpers at the longhouse, unloading some medical supplies – toothpaste, toilet rolls, medication, first aid stuff, babies' food and so on – which have arrived three days late by river transport. Giving a tube of toothpaste worth 30p to someone here is like giving someone in the UK a Harvey Nicks gift hamper.

Fireflies glowed through the screwpine palms of the mangrove swamps like fairy lights. The river was a liquid blackness made evident only by the stirring of the boatman's oars. Only the cracked appearance of the moon's reflection in the water provided low level lighting. Half a dozen Malaysian night herons descended like ghosts in anticipation of a free supper. They flapped their wings loudly and took off when they quickly recognised that the supplies were of no interest to them. The boatman stood stick-like in the longboat, not moving anything but his arms, and the sound of the oars was like crocodiles gliding by. The sulphurous odour in my nostrils was comforting. I would lose my sense of smell if that odour disappeared. It never did, it kept morphing into other smells: it was not of rotten eggs but of boiled eggs now.

While unpacking the supplies, I discovered I was short of space and I needed to unlock the padlock to one of the many bilek in the longhouse. I could not find the key, the boys must have taken it with them to Segamat. I had to break the door down. I found that the bilek was filled to the ceiling with pirate CDs and DVDs, computers, printers, cases, print paper. Thankfully, none of the DVDs were porn. I didn't know why I thought that was in itself a consolation. Perhaps because if indeed they were found by children, it would be a crime and not just a sin – no, the other way round – it would be a sin and not just a crime.

At first, I was disappointed at myself for not being more angry or more censorious. I sat down, rifled through and found some stuff which brought back my youth. All these bands from the past sixty years to the present. I couldn't believe the boys had the entire world of Western music in this longhouse. I switched on the computer and put on a massive pair of expensive-looking headphones with leather ear cushions. I forgot what brand they were. I was not an audiophile. I found and listened to Led Zeppelin's first, with my eyes closed. I shoved it into CD drive.

I listened until the end and put another in. And another. I sank down onto the attap matting, and sat there cross-legged. They were my favourite albums before someone said that rock music was the work of Satan, and, when listened backwards, had satanic lyrics.

I was a boy once, a youth. I had no idea. I believed it. I sang along to Pink Floyd's *Comfortably Numb*.

I had never listened to rock music backwards. Who did that? I wondered. The records I had as a youth included a *Home-taping is Killing Music* sticker. More than thirty years had passed and there was now more music than ever. Music was alive, even in the darkest, deepest Bornean jungle. With my super headphones, I couldn't even hear the Dayak fruit bat's mocking cackle. Home-taping did not kill music, it gave us more music.

When I opened my eyes, after I didn't know how long, I realised my face was wet with tears. I, a religious man, a Pastor, leader of the people, had enjoyed stolen wealth! I had sinned. I was weeping not for my sins, but because a door had been opened.

I asked myself: was I *ashamed*? Would that not be hypocritical? After all I had brought with me liberal thinking to the developing world along with newspapers, burgers, infant formula and syringes. When I saw the film titles and the music range, something in my heart dissolved like poison in a drink. I put some of the more interesting DVDs aside, in my ministerial briefcase: *The Painted Veil*, *The White Countess*, *Apocalypto*, *Borat*. Perhaps when I had more time, I could luxuriate with other classics like *The Usual Suspects*, the *Star Wars* trilogy. What a rich and varied life these boys were enjoying, and all on solar energy. To think that all this time Margaret had been posting me the original DVDs of Father Ted, the Kumars at No.

42, the League of Gentleman second series. I would be alone with my secret history forever, without the knowledge of Margaret, Wendy, Boy-boy, or any of the church elders.

DAWN HAD COME QUICKLY. The last calls of the night cicadas gradually faded like the ending of a song. Siamangs howled their morning alarm. A buffy fish-owl whooped from the mangroves a couple of times to signal its bedtime. I almost forgot I was here to unpack and store the medical and stationery supplies. Quickly, I shoved them into stacks and shelves, not bothering with unboxing them. In the early morning light, I drove hurriedly and guiltily back from the jungle to Orchid Villa. My breathing was uneven and my heart heavy.

I was young again. How exciting! Yet it pained me that I was in fact breaking the law, 'stealing', infringing copyright. This was the developing world's revenge on the West. What a dilemma. Then questions. How much money were the boys making? What were they doing with their money? They didn't look like they have anything or wear anything ostentatious. Then a more distressing thought: were they giving any or all of their money to the church?

I drove fast, faster than the church van has ever done, which was not very fast. A pair of brahminy kites soared across the greeny grey sky. In the distance, across the bay, the Gunung Santubong mountain appeared to blur like a large ink blot.

I passed the Bako National Park ranger's office and noticed a grove of mango trees, heavy with the heart-shaped fruit. They reminded me of my artist friend Vi Simmonds. She once told me that the vivid watercolour pigment 'Indian yellow' came from the mango tree via cows' pee. Vi specialised in batik art and had lived here as long as I had in order to learn it. She said that in 19th Century India, there was a practice of feeding cattle mango leaves. The cattle then produced a bright yellow urine, which was collected and dried to extract the pigment. The cattle's kidneys were eventually destroyed, their death slow and painful. 'Now then, Bernard,' she said to me, 'what the white man needed, he had already taken – the piss.'

'Yeah. Out of art,' I chuckled. Vi laughed, though in embarrassed realisation that her *local* Asian art was made for the Western world. The brown man turned our insatiable appetite for consumer items, whether it was film or art or music, into commodity. There were cities in Asia specialising in copying European masters – Van Gogh, Monet, Renoir and so on. It was their revenge.

I'd left the jungle path. I was on the highway now. Christmas was round the corner, but you wouldn't know because there were no malls, no painful shopping and no ear-bashing Christmas songs. What we needed to give to each other had already been given, the love of our Lord Jesus Christ.

I became aware, as the highway sun blazed down on me on the driver's side of the window, the boys were doing their illegal business in broad daylight, albeit inside a locked room. Other than the boys and myself, no one went into the longhouse except during school or medical hours.

My own stealthy nature had soaked in like the eggy smell of the river. My findings last night had urged me to travel to Segamat to find Luke and Watan. It was too urgent a matter to wait for their return. I needed to speak to them and they were not calling or emailing me. A pressing sense of dismay overwhelmed me. No one must know of this piracy business.

Margaret,

You ask what Wendy would like. Wendy has indicated to me her selection from the Whistles online catalogue. I'll email you the reference, Margaret, when I find it. A hand-knitted scarf from Boden is going to be of no use in the tropical climate, so it is best she chooses her own presents to save on unnecessary waste (although, arguably, all gifts are unnecessary waste unless they are essentials like toiletries and food).

I am vaguely uncomfortable with your comment that you are thinking of withdrawing support for Eternal Life Borneo. What will happen to Wendy and Boy-boy? Do you want to take us all back to England when our lives are all here now? I wish you would stop talking to Mother and fantasising. The day I leave the damp thick air of the jungle and stop hearing the crimson-winged woodpecker's incessant tap or the casual tune of the mangrove whistler, will be a sad day.

We are competing with older religions. Buddhist and Hindu stone sculptures from the eighth century have been found on the other side of the Gunung Santubong mountain, brought here by Indianised Javanese settlers in Sarawak who also brought with them the assam (mango) tree. Hence its latin name *Mangifera indica*.

If you shut Eternal Light down over here, firstly you are allowing them to continue their tribal life. The people here are still afraid of their ancestral spirits, their antu nulong, or spirits of animals and plants no longer alive. How can a man serve two masters? By freelancing. They will never leave their tribal life behind. It will take decades of deculturisation.

Secondly, evangelism is related to social responsibility. Jesus came to teach, preach, heal and look after the poor. Margaret, we have to face up to the fact that mission work is always going to challenge social and political structure. Maybe you find this hard to understand: our culture is to do with doing well for yourself. Even the board games are about doing well for yourself. Risk, Monopoly. The primitive cultures are at Risk of Monopoly. They are losing their habitat fast. We need to get to them, pronto. To them we are not only bringing the salvation of the soul, but the gospel of modernisation: through education, healthcare, agricultural techniques, technology.

Thirdly, we are central and well-connected to expand into the rest of Borneo and into Indonesia. Eternal Light did not start in Sarawak in order to be shut down. In Kuching itself, the congregation has grown so much we have split into the morning service (English) and afternoon service (in Iban). We have prayer meetings in six other languages (Kayan, Penan, Bidayuh, Chinese Mandarin, Chinese Hokkien and Chinese Hakka). We run a Children's Hour both in Kuching and in the jungle longhouses, where we bring toys and books and supervise playtime and storytelling. We have plans to go further and further into the interior of Borneo island, including Brunei and Kalimantan, Indonesia. The jungles are disappearing, Margaret!

Lastly, have you thought that I have not completed the work that He has started? I've answered His invitation to come out here. Our Lord will speak to me when this work is done. Margaret, "...if ye have faith as a grain of mustard seed, ye shall say unto this mountain, Remove hence to yonder place; and it shall remove; and nothing shall be impossible unto you." (Matt 17:20). Faith does not appear in one's fridge like a jar of ready-made food, it takes years of practice, it is a God-given skill, an art.

I hope you will stop saying that I may lose my head. I may lose my mind first. How many times have I heard Mother say "Just a little off the top, please."? What kind of image is being portrayed to our brothers and sisters?

The last head was taken in the 'sixties. He was a poisoner, a Communist rebel hiding in the jungle manufacturing propaganda leaflets. The second last head was a Japanese soldier's. My European predecessors did not lose their heads. It's a myth. James Brooke, the British "White Rajah" who introduced written records to Sarawak, was granted control of the area in 1841 as a reward for helping to crush a local revolt. He lived happily ever after. There are even butterflies named after him. The Brooke family held feudal power until the Japs came in WWII, hence the poor Jap chap who lost his head.

Well I must go now, all this talk of heads have got my head in a muddle. I have some work to do before my prison visit. I wish you a nice time with your Christmas shopping, you must be ever so busy now. We are praying for you. Wendy and Boy-boy send their love.

Yours, in Christ's name,
B.

P.S. Please carry on saving the Sudoku clippings for me. They are not for me, I have no time for puzzles, life is puzzling enough, but it is for the children. I photocopy them at the Orchid Villas office and bring them with me to the jungle. They love games and puzzles. Some of the members of the church have donated games like Scrabble.

40

Benjie

At Ian's, the TV was loud. A red-spotted katydid buzzed and crash landed over the car windscreen as we got out. Barbets rapped their percussive songs, engaging in curious question-answer repartee with the plantation dogs. A forest rooster crowed but it was still night.

From the window I could see Mrs MacF watching America's Top bloody Model on Astro TV. Greg and Melissa must be in bed. We left Wendall with Asuncion at home. It was past all their bedtimes.

I parked on the gravel, on which a couple of dragonflies glimmered momentarily. Talisa got out and crushed one with her Jimmy Choo without even realising it. Mrs MacF was too engrossed with the TV to even budge, so she stayed in the family room. Ian descended the stairs at a stallion's speed.

'What are you doing here?'

'We need to see you.'

'Come into my study, then.'

My teeth were gritted like a feral dog's. The TV was deafening from the family room, so Ian shut the study door. I tossed onto his giant oak desk the five letters and the bundle of four other letters. 'What's this?' he said.

'Do you know about these?'

'Well obviously not!' said Ian, or 'I wouldn't be asking you 'what's this', will I?!'

'Talisa is being blackmailed.'

'Aye?'

I explained to Ian how an innocent man had been incarcerated for Talisa's crime – killing her stepfather. 'He ended up in prison,' I concluded, 'and now they have the evidence required to put Talisa away. She,' I pointed to Talisa like she was a dangerous beast. 'spent all my money paying them. She told me nothing about it, and now they are here. They ate me up and they want the crumbs. Two hundred thousand. You've got that haven't you?'

'They're here.' He mused. 'What is the evidence?'

'They *say* that Talisa's grandmother saw the murder,' I said, looking over at Talisa, who buried her face in her hands in silence. 'She must have been willing to testify. Anyway, they're here. In Segamat. As we speak.'

Ian rubbed his moustache like it was Aladdin's lamp or something. No genie appeared despite brisk stroking. 'The letters say 'we' and 'us',' he said like he was some genius. Genie-arse. 'There is more than one.'

Talisa bit her lip, looking down. Obviously, Talisa had no money of hers, or mine for that matter, and I was no longer interested in the past now I'd heard it.

'Well, *I* can't pay them,' Ian said.

'What?' she said with disbelief.

'I can't,' Ian said. 'What if they want more? And more? And more? What are we going to do then?'

'Please, Dah!' she lamented pitifully. 'I don't want to go to jail!' I was not sure if she was genuinely pleading or if she was raging inside.

'Noo,' Ian shook his head. 'Sorry.' He looked down, unable to make eye contact with Talisa or myself.

'Dah,' said Talisa, 'don't make me do this.'

'Do what?

She sighed. 'I know what happened between you and Ebu. My mother.'

Ian looked up, but his moustache did not even twitch. Only his eyes gave away his surprise.

'Fuckssakes. What you trying to say? I adopted you!'

'Noo. I was thirteen. Where else could I go? You asked Ebu to work and live here. And you had to take me in too.'

'Did I not put you through school, bought you clothes and food?'

'I knew what was going on even if Mrs MacF didn't, cos she was about to give birth to Greg!'

'Keep your voice down, you hear?'

'Er, I think that the TV is quite loud,' I offered some distracting info to thaw the Scottish conversation, if you could call it conversation, 'so Mrs...um...MacF won't be able to...'

210

Ian and Talisa both ignored me. I didn't like confrontations. I felt like leaving the room. She put her hands on her hips, displayed her decorated arm as if she was a ruffled bird.

'Ebu was pregnant when she died.'

'Noo.' He said quietly, still shaking his head. Beads of perspiration surged from his temples, where his vein pulsed like a vine. His fists were clenched.

'You killed her,' Talisa's fingers suddenly lunged at his neck with a ferocity that I had not known. 'And your own baby!'

'I didn't,' he unclenched his fists and grabbed her tiny wrists to restrain her. 'She died of TB! You fucken liar.'

'What? She could have lived! You never wanted to pay for her medication,' she kicked his shins hard, 'until it was too late.'

'Ugh! Ugh!' He shouted out in pain, still wrestling with her. 'What do you fucken want?'

'Dah, for Wendall's sake, so that he will have his mum, stick your hands in your pocket and give me...'

'Noo. Are you out of you fucken mind?'

'Do you want me to tell Mrs MacF about Ebu?'

What was it about the Scots? They really loved a brawl. Ian probably lived on fights and chips.

'Tell me what? What's going on?' Ian's stout Teochew wife, Mrs MacF, Pam or Teo Bee Lian, whatever she called herself these days, had not bothered to knock. She opened the door and entered the study, looking alarmed. 'I heard all these voices! Tell me what?'

'Pam, can you please leave us alone,' Ian said, panting, letting go of Talisa's wrists. 'We're just discussing-'

'Hello Pam,' I greeted her politely. 'We were going to tell you, er, when we know- what- we're- doing. We're planning a... surprise...for um...my mum...for her birthday...'

'Oh! Is everyone OK?' Mrs MacF said, looking a little lost. 'Everyone seems a bit...'

'We're fine. We can't decide on the venue, heh heh. And... the...budget. Which I think is quite sizeable!' I winked at her, with as much charm as I could bring to the room. Talisa and Ian were still glowering at each other.

'OK,' she said, 'I'll get back to my show. You want to drink anything?'

'No,' I said, 'we're off very soon.'

'Are you sure? The ads are on,' said Mrs MacF. 'Very long ads, on Astro TV.'

'Of course,' I said. She left the room a little reticently, leaving the door open, in case she missed out on further conversation. She must have sensed something was not right, but she couldn't press on, since I fobbed her off.

'We should go, Ian,' I said, glancing at the grandfather's clock in the hall, before walking to the study door and shutting it. 'What do you suggest?'

'I'll take care of it.'

'What?' I said.

'I'll take care of it,' he repeated, having calmed down.

It was my turn to chew my lip, like I was playing chess. I was relieved. He barked but didn't bite this time. After all that sermonising about family life, I was glad he was going to help us at last.

'I suggest that you go home and have a good rest,' said Ian. 'Let me think about it tonight. I'll call you tomorrow morning. I need a plan to work to. Can't think right now.'

'So what are you saying? Just forget it for now?' I asked.

'Just forget it for now. Tomorrow morning first thing I will let you know the plan. Lock your doors and windows. I'll get a security guard send out straightaway from the estates. He'll be outside your gates just after you get in and set the alarm. Tonight itself.'

'Thanks so much, Dah!'

He didn't reply.

ALTHOUGH IT WAS IMPRESSIVE, her row with Ian only managed to confirm to me what sort of person she was: always with cards up her tattooed sleeve. She herself was a virtuoso at blackmailing, compared to these anonymous letter-writers. This had nothing to do with her deceased Ebu. Her Ebu was only dragged up for the purposes of blackmail. Perhaps it was the Iban way. She never was straight with me from the start. She was twenty-three when she married me, not eighteen, and even now she was only twenty-four. I should commend her for saving her Ebu and herself from her violent stepfather, but being deceived for so long had left me lukewarm – no, cold. Her past crime aside, I did not deserve being used as an open wallet. I had never laid a hand on her or my son. I was in such a predicament – I wanted so much to forgive her, and to love her. I was duped into marriage, and duped into designer bags. She had made a mockery of me.

'You *did* rob my till?' I turned and asked Talisa in the car.

'Oh God. Yes I did. Please forgive me. I needed to get ready the next instalment, you see?'

'I was just checking.' Suddenly it was I who felt guilty, like I was a sun bear foraging a National Park bin or something. Only a few hours to go and it would be light. Not much sleep at all for me, never enough.

Of course, she successfully got the money out of Ian. She was as strong as a viper and would not hesitate to strike and harm. She also managed to make me feel guilty, though I had not done anyone wrong. The fact that she always got what she wanted through her insidiousness was unenviable, yet I envied her. I fantasised suffocating my wife with the goosedown Habitat duvet she bought online.

When the sun was up, so was my member. I found her attractive and repulsive again. The familiar oily, sweet and salty scent that came from her clavicle turned me on. I breathed in her weighty serpentine odour. She smiled but her eyes were still closed. Why was she smiling and baring her fangs at me with that detestable coy overbite? I made love to her roughly and quickly. I went downstairs. I needed coffee.

I was sick. I vomited into the cleaner's basin near all her magnificent shoe cupboards, thinking if Ian was going to phone and if not, could I make it through the day? Luckily, there was no longer Asuncion watching derisively from the wings. Like a barn swallow, she used to flee so swiftly.

How easily you ended up relying on domestic help. One day, you did everything on your own, and another day, you didn't know a thing about yourself. You didn't even know what was in the fridge or your wardrobe, because *they* knew everything. The Chinese saying went: those who washed your underpants knew you better than you did yourself. There was no escape from their eyes and ears. What were they thinking? Did Ibrahim pity me? Did Asuncion laugh at me? Did she not care because she was a science teacher from Manila who couldn't make any money except as a servant in this country?

The house was strangely quiet. I listened for the hiss of the plants being watered outside by the invisible serving force but there was none. Even the driveway looked empty without the sight of Ibrahim polishing his car. The chirps and twitters of the Filipina voice when Asuncion sang to Wendall had been replaced with CDs playing bland children's songs. I was stuck with a murderess and our offspring for company.

It didn't seem real that my wife had killed a man. Murderess. The sound of the word sighed with the dawn breeze, barely moving, like a pair of heavily-lined damask curtains.

Then my mobile, in my pajama pocket, rang. I looked at the microwave clock. It was 6.47am. 'So what's the plan?'

'The plan is this: listen carefully,' said Ian. 'You will reply to the letter, postcard, whatever, saying that you agree, you have the money, and you want to meet them in daylight, at a public place, of course. This is for their own safety and ours. It cannot be couriered to the post office box because it will get lost. What if it is stolen by the post office staff? You put this in your own words. So. Tell them that you will meet them. Make no mention of me, whatsoever. Just say that only you will be there, to meet him. Since you are the last person that he wrote to, having addressed the letter to you.'

'OK.'

'Then arrange to meet him at this children's playground, at the water lily pond. Where the pavilion is. I'll email you the map. Print it out and put it in the letter.'

'Well you won't get your money back then, that's for sure. There will be people around.'

'Wait for it,' he said. 'What they don't know is, when they get there, there will be a letter stuck to the pavilion asking them to meet in another place. And because they will be so mad and desperate by the treasure hunt, they *will* proceed to the second meeting point.'

'Why are we asking them to go to two places?' I asked. 'Why not just one?'

'You make my blood boil!'

'I'm stupid,' I said, shrugging my shoulders and waving my hands, even though he couldn't see me. 'So tell me.'

'The first meeting place is a red herring. It's a public place to put them at ease. If you ask them to go to the *actual* meeting point, they will case the joint every day. That will blow our cover. Do you know what I mean by case the joint?'

'Yes. That much I understand.'

'Good. The idea is to catch them off guard. So they never actually get to reccy the second meeting point. It's for our protection.'

Interesting, I thought. 'Go on. About the second meeting point.'

'The address will look like it's in the Old Town, so they will just assume that it's another public place. But they would be wrong! It's an old house, in the middle of an old estate, mine of course, and what's brilliant is, it's in the middle of town!'

'What house?' I asked.

'An old disused estate manager's house. Don't worry about that for now. It's basically in the jungle.'

'How can that be?'

'There's nothing on the site! It's just a piece of land, 160 hectares. Nature reserve, call it anything. No one even thinks about it as they drive past. Bought it æons ago. I have it marked on the map which I am emailing you right now.'

I didn't answer.

'It will be remote, very private,' he continued in his gritty tone.

'I don't feel very comfortable about all this.'

'Shut up. Listen. What's comfort got to do with anything?'

'I just think I...'

'We will train you up beforehand obviously.'

'Uh huh.' I didn't like the sound of his army general voice.

'Say to them in the letter that you have the money. You will pay them when you meet. What's today? Thursday. Post the letter today. Tell them to meet on Tuesday next week at the children's playground. Put your phone number in. Say that if you don't hear from them, it means they concur with the meeting time and place.'

'And when they go to the second place, this derelict *house* in the jungle you mentioned, how do we get your money back?'

'Well, for a start, *you'll* meet him, not *we*.'

'Me?'

'Sure. They want you and your wife, not me. Your job is just to meet them, get the evidence from them, hand them the money and ask them to go. They will have to go through the jungle to get back to the road, but that's where I will be waiting for them.'

'What if there is only one of them?'

'Then it's even easier. I'll get him first and I'll get the others next.'

I said nothing. 'What do you mean 'get'?' I asked meekly.

'I have a gun.' Ian grunted. 'And so will you. Just in case he tries anything funny, we'll train you up. Tomorrow.' He was trying to be macho. I detested his sperm count already.

Sensing my demurral, he added, 'You'd better get used to it. You get your tight-arsed small brain around it.'

After we hung up, I rushed off to get changed for work. I would check my email and print the map out when I got to the office. I reminded myself that he was providing the payment, and that I was going through all this because when I married her, I married the entire family. I feared Ian so much that I didn't want her to go to jail. I didn't want my mother or Ian to care for Wendall, which was what would happen if Talisa went to jail. Talisa had to be right here, in my house, not for me, but for Wendall until he grew up. That would be the right thing. It was the Hour of the Earth Sheep: intuitive and sure-footed.

THE NEXT AFTERNOON, WE visited the 'house' and began my training. We went to Ian's and dropped off Wendall with Pam. Ian took Talisa and I in the mud-covered Land Rover. We had to get back for Friday evening back at the Club for the usual piss-up. I was in no mood, but Ian seemed to be in high spirits. His eyes scanned around, hawk-like, spotting the killer lallang weed that competed with rubber trees.

We turned off the tarmac main road about four miles from his mansion, and we were on an unmarked dirt road within one of his plantations. After a while in dim lighting, I lost track of time and the space, with endless tree after tree in exact intervals. We probably passed thousands, maybe tens of thousands.

'You know,' he began, and I was already thinking: today's lecture. 'I've put all my money into all this,' he gestured, 'and I never take out the dividends. You know why? The dividends are the food for the growth of the company. That's why when I see that dreaded lallang, my heart bleeds. Why do I pay the lallang gang? Those guys are supposed to make sure every blade of that damned weed is pulled out.'

'Dah, please,' said Talisa, in a strained voice. Since her revelation about her Ebu, she'd kept away from 'Dah'. Ian continued to display his false sense of gung-ho cheeriness, seemingly denying the newly-discovered information that he had had an unborn illegitimate child. If it affected him at all, he showed nothing. His view of infant mortality must have been swayed by the grim 'old days' when 'life was so tough, ye'd eat yir own boots' during his arduous life as a planter. 'Well! One fewer bastard in the world.' I imagined that was what he would say.

'And you know, I remember a time when I joined my first estate. It was up north, aye, you wouldn't know where, near Kota Bahru. We lived rough in those days. There was a well from which we got water. But for lighting, all I had was my tilly-lamp. At night, I would go from one room to the next, and there were only two rooms, it was more like a shed than a bungalow, I tell you! Where was I? Oh yes, the tilly-lamp would follow me from room to room, like it was a dog. That was how I lived. None of the extravagance of electricity all wired in. And of course until today I always switch off the light if there is no one in the room. If I am home alone, one light in the whole house is enough.'

As his hard voice crunched on, he sounded more and more like part of the snapping and grating twig sounds around us. 'Sometimes, I sit in the dark,' he said. 'Light is a luxury.'

Weirdo. The dirt road narrowed and narrowed, until we get to a sort of intersection of dirt paths, a clearing. We crossed the junction and the dirt road was so narrow that it was now just a dirt path, no wider than the vehicle's wheel axle. From here on, we were in thick jungle, with raised tree roots, fallen trunks, dense undergrowth, ponds where the rainwater cannot drain quickly enough. The air was almost liquid. Only tiny shafts of light in straight lines pierced through the tree canopy every now and then. Insects and animals buzzed around us like tinnitus. A barbet chatted percussively and a monkey yelled, intermittently breaking the sepulchral hum in the air, loud as a room full of machines.

A gloomy afternoon like this did not stop him from noticing obstacles like broken trunks. About halfway through the jungle,

Ian switched on the headlights because it was as dim as night. As hard to believe as it was, we were on Ian's so-called *land* in the middle of town.

And then I see it.

41

Minos

ROOM NUMBER: 4F, AH HOCK'S LODGING HOUSE, JALAN
KEKWA, SEGAMAT, JOHOR
PROPRIETOR: MR T.C. WONG (TOPCAT)
OPEN SEVEN DAYS A WEEK AND ALSO ON WEEKENDS. NO
TRESPASSERS WITHOUT PERMISSION.
PLEASE RING BELL FOR ATTENTION, IF ANY. MANAGER MAY
BE NOT AT DESK.
RECOMMENDED BY: MR TOPCAT WONG, WONG'S KWALITY
MOTORCYCLES, PARTS, REPAIRS, 2ND MILESTONE, SEGAMAT.

I read the sign outside our hotel. We have just parked up our new motorbike. Secondhand. Is only Honda 25 c.c. But is ver easy to park outside Ah Hock's cos is free for motorbikes. Lots of bikes outside the hotel. Here we hang out with the other guys on way to prostitute or to work.

But after the last letter, we getting somewhere man. Cos of final demand for payment. They write back so quick. Today is Friday and we got they letter. Is in Iban, so I think must be written by the girl. She writes that her husband will meet me. The doctor fellar will meet me in the children's playground on Tuesday. There is a map and everything. I must bring all the original evidence. They say they got the money in cash. When the doctor fellar get the evidence, he will hand over the 200,000 ringgits. In our room, lying on the bed, I start dreaming about what I'm gwan do with all that money.

'Why, Watan,' I say, 'this money can really set us up for life.'

'You know, Minos, YOU have to go and meet him.'

'What do you mean?'

'Means you go alone. They don't know about me. If something happen to you, I can come get you...'

'What? I...I...NO! We in this together,' I say.

'No. You the wan who did nothing, have no evidence, no idea of how to make all this money until I help you. I only your helper.'

'I don't wan go, Watan. I got no good feeling about it. Cos what if they don't have the money?'

'Then don't give them the evidence. You check the money is there. You count it. Then you leave the documents behind. That's it!'

'OK. But I'm scared.'

'Don't be scared.'

'OK.'

So we write up all this condition in a note to say, OK, we meet on Tuesday, 4pm, children's playground. That is the plan.

Happy. We gwan eat Chinese food again tonight. But in my heart, I am scared. What if this what if that? What if there is no money, and they kill us anyway? Yes is good that Watan is looking after me. He must hide when I meet the doctor fellar. If anything happen to me, he will jump out. Anyway, there be lots of mums and Indonesia and Filipina maids at the playground, and of course, lots of kids. Nothing can go wrong.

Tonight maybe if we see Mei, we gwan buy her a drink. But tonight she probably with her clients and dwan we to disturb her. It is a waste: Mei's long legs, long fingers, wasted on short ugly men. She a bit old. Sometimes I think she already fifty. Very hard to tell, cos she wear so much make-up and so little clothes. I still think she is lovely girl.

We gwan go cybercafé first. Write to Pastor, Wendy and Boy-boy to say how are we. Then any bar in town, see if anyone selling DVD, find out who is snakehead. We gwan try sell some DVDs tonight to him wholesale. We bring over so many that we make in the longhouse in Borneo. Now sadly we cannot take order for DVD tonight. If the snakehead ask if we can get such-and-such, we tell them we can only sell what we have bring with us across South China Sea. This is the last time we have to work so hard for the money. I jus keep reminding myself, 200,000 ringgit! That is no joke! All them years in prison all them wasted years. Now I get paid for it. A part of me feel bad that Pastor don't know what we up to. But that part is slowly becoming far away, like Borneo, and the life we have leave behind.

42

Benjie

The dishevelled mansion stood on a hill. We got out and walked the last hundred metres because the weeds and growth came up to almost two metres high. Ian attacked these with his parang in great swoops as though he was playing golf. I got out of his way, lest inaccurate motions caused accidental amputation.

On close inspection, the mansion was not just dishevelled, it must have been disused for a long time, a ghost of its previous fabulous self. It looked like one of those gigantic black-and-white 1920s or 30s timber detached houses. Some parts of the house did not even have a roof. A hammering tick-tock drill noise was coming from the house at regular intervals. The demolition was being carried out by a green and maroon woodpecker with a yellow mohican who was hard at work on one of the columns. If you liked woodpeckers, you'd like Malaysia, went the saying. Indeed they were everywhere.

Trees had fallen on the derelict building for years and on those trees, more trees and more wild plants had grown. At the end of the path which Ian had hacked out, I noticed a pair of rusted, partially fallen iron gates. Next to the brick piers holding the gates was an *amherstia nobilia* tree with pale purple leaves and heavy with flowers like chandeliers. We carried on to the house itself.

Most of the structure of this ruin was intact. The main part of the house still had its roof. The parts with the missing roofs are of no concern to me, said Ian. They were the amahs' quarters and the lean-to bedroom of the syce ('sigh-chair', which is Hokkien for 'drive car'). A long breezy corridor led from the front door to the living room, where open windows faced east and would let in the morning sun. Very high curtains hung like shreds of rags. Moon moths and lacewings flew out from them. On the grand merbau staircase, solid brass bars, tarnished to a brown verdigris, held down what must have been the red carpet, which was now mouldy and rotten in parts. Great beetles and moths had feasted on the carpet for decades. A giant tree shrew, or perhaps a great squirrel, scurried across the rotten floor.

A large ancient rain-tree grew next to the long corridor, throwing its gentle generous shade on the tall windows and casting a shadow on the corridor floor. Looking back down on the stair well and landing, I got an overwhelming sense of the parties that used to take place here. An estate manager's house, this was a house for partying in, until the troops burst through those heavy doors. Those weighty thirty-lamp lead crystal chandeliers, probably imported from the old Czechoslovakia, probably would not even sway a millimetre during serious tropical thunderstorms. I imagined big band music from a Gramophone and war bulletins from the Art Deco radiogram.

We followed this corridor until we got to the bedroom, which was over the car porch overlooking the driveway. Ian had bought many parcels of land since he arrived, including the one we were standing on, and it just so happened to include the house. 'Oh yes,' he droned on, 'many estate managers, planters, have come and gone. We had a fairly jolly time here!'

He used the word *bungalow* to describe this house. In England, a bungalow referred to a single storey building, but in the colonies, a bungalow was the ultimate sign of wealth and arrival: it was a massive detached house on more than one storey, surrounded by verandahs. The word bungalow was from the Hindi *bengali*, in the Bengal style.

In what seemed to be the master bedroom, the sloping ceilings were possibly fifteen feet high, with exposed rafters and a ceiling fan attached to the ridge beam. Cobwebs clung to every rafter as if we were under clouds. A gigantic timber wardrobe, with carved gables, probably Dutch, sat against the wall. The mirror was damaged, and looked like someone had split tea all over it. I saw myself and I was confounded by how aged, worn down and exhausted I appeared. A ghost, just like this house.

I looked out over the path beyond the driveway and beyond to the dirt road. You could definitely see a faint almost illusory demarcation of where the driveway and road used to be, despite being completely overgrown.

The two bedrooms at the back overlooked the steps which descended to the amahs' quarters. Rambutan and durian trees grew in the kitchen garden. Further on was a fish pond over which the flowers of the cassia fistula bent, shedding a few gold petals.

The sun was setting. I heard the flapping wings of a pair of milky storks taking a sip at the pond. It was easy to daydream when you were in Eden, surrounded by birdsong and the chirrup of insects, but my mind quickly got clogged with concerns about the dastardly deeds we had to get on with.

'Wait, before I forget.'

Ian pulled out from somewhere behind him, a *gun*. I might know all my Chardonnays and my pastas but I had never seen a *gun* in my life, except in the cinemas of Leicester Square. What did I even do with it?

'Don't worry, it's very easy, even illiterate criminals can use it,' Ian growled. 'There are all sorts of wild animals here at this twilight time. Ever find yourself with an *unwelcome* guest of sorts...'

My hair stood. 'Like? Such as?'

'Oh, all sorts, cobras, pythons, kraits,' said Ian, chuckling. 'You're lucky tigers are practically extinct.'

I swallowed. Suddenly the urge to look around my feet was strong. 'Just remember,' he said, 'If someone says don't move, you don't move.'

I agreed.

'Like I say, don't worry,' he said. *R...ight.* 'Let me show you how to use it. Pay attention, too, Talisa...'

'Dah,' said Talisa, 'I don't need to. I've put a wounded dog out of its misery before.'

That'd be me in a day or two.

'Well, I'm delighted, love.' Ian said. He avoided all eye contact with her, and continued explaining it to me: 'This is better than the .38 Colt. This is a .45. Feel how light and easy it is. Much more accurate than the .38, I tell you. You've ever gone hunting?'

'Nup.'

'I prefer a shotgun myself, Dah,' Talisa said without sarcasm. Since their spat, they spoke only when necessity dictated, and only indirectly, each trying to outdo the other.

'Well, that's a shame,' I muttered, 'because you haven't got one, have you?'

Ian cocked one eye and pointed it at some imaginary target, as if taking aim. 'Beautiful. I brought it back from Scotland in the days before terrorism. The design is over a hundred years old but the .45 still has a wide range of uses. Very versatile. Not as effective as the Magnum for long range hunting. Know why? '

I stifled a yawn but shook my head silently.

'Because of the steep trajectory. So! The answer? Shoot at close range. Make sure you practise, there's blanks in this jiffy bag.' He hands me a small white padded bag from his pocket. 'Loading a .410 shotgun shell into this baby here makes it a "gambler gun", based on the story that such a combination was sometimes used to shoot someone from under the table for cheating in a card game.' He laughed. 'Let me show you how to load it. Just normal hollow point 200 grain bullets.' This time there was no jiffy bag. He produced five slugs from his pocket, each half the size of an AA alkaline battery, yet so much more fatal. Now I knew why he had so many pockets. He really *was* in combat gear.

'Always keep it loaded, understand! Practise every day.'

It was getting dark. We were sweating profusely from the walk and the excitement by the time we left.

THE NEXT DAY, I returned and explored the compound with Talisa. We dropped Wendall off at my parents'. She said I needed her to teach me 'the art of gun', as she called it, and reminded me I was here to practise. I hoped I didn't need to use the gun. It was only there to be used if the thugs themselves were armed. She did not touch me or the gun once. She had become my Shi Fu and I her Tu Di. I learned. She trained. No way would I ever see her as my partner much less my accomplice. Nevertheless, it was now both our responsibility to see that I was qualified.

A tropical bungalow almost always sat in its own vast compound. The word *compound* was a colonial corruption of the Malay word kampung, or village. *Compound* basically meant grounds, gardens, orchard, driveway and all the trimmings and trappings of the good life in the Empire. I could imagine the Ians of this world and their spouses during the golden days, having

Sunday curries, sundowners on the verandahs, a Hainanese chef, a Malay syce, an Indian gardener, a Cantonese amah or two, who lurked in the shadowy compound. Normal local people like my parents and grandparents would never have access to this secret world, this life of great mystery.

My mind had instantly gone into holiday mode, neutral gear, until I found a four foot high, two feet thick castellated brick wall. The wall completely surrounded the compound of the house. In this battlemented wall, the crenels were overgrown with pink and white periwinkles and ferns. I would say that the wall was for defence for constables who guarded the house and its occupants during emergency in the Japanese Occupation. The sight of this wall brought my holiday mind to a halt.

'You can practise here,' she said. I remembered the *gun*. Where was it? Oh yes, I was so used to it now I couldn't feel it against my back. I loaded while Talisa supervised. She had smothered us in jungle-strength mosquito repellant. I practised a couple of rounds. The mosquitoes were wild. The itch and the heat made it quite hard to think straight let alone shoot straight. At the height of the itching, I could feel myself slipping into delirium.

That was the end of the practice for now. Next time, I would come on my own. After all, on the day of the 'exam' I would be alone. We got home fast. Talisa gave me a shot of whisky. 'Where did that come from?' I asked. 'From the house,' she said. 'I found it in the kitchen while you were practising and I put it in my bag. You're very lucky, there is very good, very old whisky here,' she said.

I was not sure 'lucky' was the word I would use. I gulped down the shot of Laphroaig, realising how the colonialists survived here in the tropics. Covering yourself in salt and being drunk made you smell awful to humans, unappetising to the mozzies, but attractive to butterflies.

EVERY EVENING, I RETURNED here alone to practise, when the light was low. Ian said that I needed to get used to the light levels, in case on the day we met the blackmailers, it was overcast. I even came to enjoy the place. I retreated into myself and I felt like one of those sullen cowboys who sat in his unlaced

225

boots polishing guns while the lady scrubbed laundry in the courtyard with a baby strapped to her breast.

In the evenings, the verandah was a good place to sit at and look at the garden. The libation-ready colonials used to call the cicada the 'cocktail bug' or the '6 o'clock bug' because their calls are loudest at early evening. Twice I saw a pair of golden orioles who flew in pairs in search of the papaya trees. Talisa tied hessian bags around the papayas to protect them. She'd kept her green fingers up her sleeve until now. I should not be surprised, knowing her primordial origins. Why would she not know about protecting our assets? The fruits were for us, not the birds, she said. She knew who our enemies were.

43

Bernard

Dear Bernard,
I'm very interested to read the summary of your sermon last week which I'll be including in our Eternal Light newsletter this month. What kind of work exactly are you doing there, if you say the boys still think rice has a soul? You must soon remove these silly superstitions, now that they are committed to the Christian God. I seem to remember you saying that animism and Christianity have to go hand in hand in Borneo, otherwise there would be no Christians. But surely they cannot go on praying for the soul of rice? It comes from Tesco's.
M.

MOHD ABD KASEEM LICENSED CYBER CAFÉ
155, JALAN GENUANG (BEHIND TAXI STAND), SEGAMAT, JOHOR.
DVDS, VIDEOS, TAPES, LAPTOP AND COMPUTER REPAIRS, INTERNATIONAL PHONE CARDS AND TOP UPS. HIGH SPEED BROADBAND, IRC, ICQ, NETWORK GAMES.
(INCORPORATED WITH LEE'S QUICK PHOTO DEVELOPING, PASSPORT AND I.C. PHOTOS, AND MOBILE PHONE SIM CARDS)
WIFE – YES, WIFI – NO.

Saturday
Margaret,
Rice does not come from Tesco's. It comes from Asia.
Each family has a field. In June, rice is sown in a nursery. Buffaloes, which are like a food processor, are driven through the fields to acquire the right consistency. In July, it is re-planted into the fields, after the buffaloes have done their 'mixing'. In December and January, the rice is hand-harvested and stored in barns. They are then dried in the sun and milled to remove the

husk. To steam it every morning, they put it in the 'monkey pots' over floor level chimneyless wood fires. And that is where rice comes from.

Anyway, I am writing to you from a cybercafé in Segamat, so I'd better keep it brief. I am staying at the Mercure Hotel in Segamat. I have decided to make a quick trip here for the weekend. I have not heard much from the boys and they are supposed to be under supervision by me. I am liable if anything goes wrong. That will teach me! Give them an inch...

I only arrived this afternoon, and they were not at their hotel room. Hope they're not being treated like dirt here. As you know, the orang asli or indigenous people have the lowest status amongst all the races. There is a queue building up now behind me so I'd better log off.

Your loving brother,

B.

44

Benjie

Ian had to free up his money by selling some land he would not even notice was missing. I didn't care as long as it kept the thugs at bay and didn't cost me a cent more than it had already. He sold it to a cash-rich mate so we could have the money straightaway, and their paperwork could be done later on. Otherwise, buying and selling land would take months. If he was doing all this in order to prevent his Mrs from finding out about Surya, then I admired his passion. He loved Mrs MacF. Time and again I remembered Ming Jen. I used to think stringing her along must have meant that I loved her. No, it was not love, it was fear of love.

On Monday night, my pulse raced as I waited for the mud-covered Land Rover. My throat was dry with stage fright. The Nepalese gurkha security guard stood at the gates at the end of my driveway, and had been briefed to look out for Ian's imminent arrival.

Ian turned up at my house with a large white nylon Adidas sports bag, containing the money and all five of the letters. 'Guess how much this weighs?' He said. 'It's like going to the airport! I got them in big notes, so that it makes it easy for them to count it.'

'What if they refuse to go to the second meeting point?'

'What are you, bonkers? Of course they'll go to the second meeting point! They want the money, don't they?'

'No, what I mean is, what if they give up?'

'Listen you carefully, I'm not saying it again: here's the plan,' he sighed. 'We do what they say, *at first*. You meet the wee fucker and you put the bag down. He hands you the envelope containing the evidence. Go through it. You are supposed to make sure it's all there, while he is counting the money. I worked out, it will take him, if he has half a brain, about 4 to 5 minutes, at the rate of 1 second per note, if he is doing it properly and slowly. So make sure you can read all the evidence in four to five minutes. If you can't, say so now, and I will change the notes to smaller denominations.

'We're not going on holiday, Dah,' said Talisa. When she was mild, she was cold as an Iban dawn blood pudding.

'Four minutes is fine,' I replied. 'I... I... read... fast... when I have to.'

After Ian went, Talisa disappeared again to check on the baby in his cot. I unzipped the bag and looked in. There were plenty of five hundred ringgit notes. I counted up the money. It was correct. I timed myself, not quite believing it took only two minutes and a half.

Talisa returned. 'Wendall is fine,' she said with a smile.

45

Minos

Monday morning early-early we gwan to Old Market. We buy some feathers, a peket of sewing needle and two sheet of children's gift wrapping paper from market stall selling all kind craft, sewing and knitting stuff. Since we ain't have the nibong plant to get the sharp needle. A big thick wooden stick and four-foot long bamboo pole from the plants and flower man on Jalan Kekwa. He sell wood and bamboo as support for plants. And 2-in-1 Araldite glue from the hardware stall man.

At the same time we buy some lunch from market to eat back in our room. While we eating lunch, I look through the Ten Steps to Please God book which I have bring with me.

'Minos, don't look at that now, what you doin that for.'

'Watan, I just got a very good idea from this book. Ten steps.'

That afternoon, we go about making the sumpit and three dart. Each dart to have three needle. Very careful! We wan make sure enough poison for blowpipe to finish off the doctor. Watan, since he from St Josefs and so smart, he calculate the amount poison we mix. He say, the doctor ain't no mountain pig, so he need a lotta lotta poison.

We dip all them needle in the poison from the labau tree, which we have bring over in the Pepsi bottle. In jungle we have the tree glue to use, but here, we have to use the 2-in-1 Araldite. Is to form like a base for the labau poison. Now is taking one day to dry. Very careful!

ON TUESDAY, GET READY evidence in envelope and the big wooden stick, wrap up in children's wrapping paper, to make it look like present for a chile, since we are going to children's playground. Watan bring the darts in his pocket, and the blowpipe wrap up nicely also in children's paper. It remind me of time in prison, when we wrap up all kind plastic cutlery and paper napkin and toothpick. Ah! Those days – how I suffer, how I think they never over. We wearing our sunglasses and long sleeve. I don't want them to see my tattoo or to know Watan have no tattoo.

Now in park pavillion, we looking over the water lily pond. Four ducks and many, many carp fish. Is one Indian man, retired maybe, walking his small dog. Two Filipina maid chatting and pushing the swing, and there is two Chinese chiles on them swing. Three other chiles playing on sand. Two mothers looking at them and chatting. Reason why I know they are mothers: they don't look Filipino. Two chiles on seesaw, one Malay woman looking.

Nowhere, ain't no Chinese doctor. One hour we waiting and waiting, going round and round the pavillion like we are those crazy horses in children's merry go round. Then Watan find a big envelope, is tape very high, to the pavilion pillar, and is say, in Iban:

To Those Meeting Doctor at 4pm

Watan and me open, read the letter and the address they give inside.

'I think we better not go, Watan.'

'Why?'

'Cos they wan trick us, Watan. Can't you tell?'

'No. They say that they cannot be here cos they have to be in town to pick up the money to meet us. The bank about to shut. Is now 4.50pm 'ccording to my watch, Minos. They bank is in town.'

'And you believe them?'

'Why they stick this letter on pavillion? We come all this way already. I just wan get the money.'

'Watan. Be serious. As Pastor say, 'read between the lines'.'

'I am serious. The address is in town, Minos. Wha's wrong with that. Same as here.'

'Suit yourself. Is a trick, I tell you. You go yourself.'

'No. Why should I? Is your tattoo girl, not mine. Look at this address, this map. Will be people there, no problem.'

'Watan, my tattooless friend, we can forget this right here. Go back to Sarawak now.'

'No. We in this together. You can become snakehead yourself after today! What about our filem business? You wan owe the snakehead forever? Share the room with Boy-boy forever? Minos?'

'No.'

With heavy heart, I think about all them filems we have watch and make. Once we get the money, I swear I gwan have nothing more to do with the girl. I am doing this so Watan and I, future snakeheads, can make and watch filem over and over again, travel to Hollywood and Cannes, see originals at film festivals, and never rely on anybuddy in the world again. If not, what money is for?

And so we pick up the sumpit and get on the Honda 25 c.c. We gwan to the town.

'Minos. I got a little surprise for you.'

'What?'

'I already book our ticket.'

'Ticket to where.'

'Two economy. Japan Airlines. Stopover in Tokyo.'

'Watan! Ticket to where.'

'LA.'

I kickstart the engine and turn the bike around. Watan sit pillion, holding the sumpit, the stick and the envelope.

46

Benjie

It was Tuesday. I did not sleep last night at all. It might as well have been an extension of Monday. It could either be a clean end to the rest of my life, or a clean new beginning. A beginning was an end, an end was a beginning, and all that bullshit. All day I muttered delirious comments as though I was a junkie. A locum had been organised for two days at the clinic. Perhaps it should be more, if this 'holiday' ended with my funeral.

The mud-covered Land Rover arrived at about three o'clock. I was planning to get there in plenty of time. Talisa was to stay at home with Wendall, but she demurred. She said she felt awful and didn't want to be alone, in case of something happening to me. My heart melted just a little at its ragged edges. Did she really think about my safety? How could she get us into such trouble in the first place? I softened but I thought of nothing to say.

Ian said that he and I would drop Talisa and Wendall off at my parents'. She would have some company then, albeit my mum's. Talisa then dashed upstairs and she took down the Pua Kumbu from the wall over our bed. She rolled it up and put it in Wendall's nappy bag.

'I'm ready,' she said.

'What's that for?' I ask.

'Wendall needs it to nap at your mum's,' she said. 'The air-con is a little too chilly in her bedroom.'

It reminded me that I had to make some terrible excuse to my mum about where I was going. I never usually took Wendall to my mum's as Ian always jumped at babysitting so readily. As predicted, my mother was suspicious. 'It's a school reunion, mum,' I said, 'I absolutely have to go.'

'Alone?' came her statutory reply in Mandarin. 'What about your wife?'

My mum never called Talisa by her name. 'Mum, partners are not invited.'

'No, we're not,' said Talisa, backing me up. She shook her head, like she was saying goodbye to me forever.

'But you don't look dressed!' my mum said, more perplexed than ever. I looked a mess and I must have stank like fermented prawns. I couldn't explain it to her now or ever. I didn't know where to start. My mother who was from Bau, gold mining town in Sarawak, where Talisa was born and brought up, would never have thought in a million years that if one didn't go to the jungle, the jungle came to one, in the form of a Tattoo Girl.

In the mud-covered Land Rover, Ian and I travelled to his jungle in town. It was so apt, considering he was in camouflage make-up and gear. We parked some distance away from the road entrance. He jumped out and said he would wait in the bushes. He needed to make sure that there was no one with the 'wee fucker'. I trudged up to the house with a heavy bag and a heavier heart.

I sat on the cane verandah bench, gripping my hands tight to stop them from shaking. They were as cold as a corpse's. It was November in the land where there was no winter but I felt a chill that was alien to me. Even during my own wedding speech, I had one milligramme more life in me. I looked down at my feet, pressing them against the Adidas bag. I felt the weight of the RM200,000 inside. It had been a long time since I used an Adidas golf umbrella to shield the new girl from the monsoon downpour.

Sweat poured from my head and neck like icy rain. The gun was on my back, I let Ian know earlier, just to make him happy, a *gun*, *your* gun, I thought. I didn't care about his money. I had lost money too.

At 5:30 p.m., I heard a rustle from beyond, from down the hill. They were an hour and a half late, presumably because they went to the playground. I jumped off the verandah and waited in the front garden, under the frangipanni tree whose creamy white flowers smelt like perfume at this time of the late afternoon. Talisa went upstairs to the long corridor above the verandah, as agreed, hiding behind the French windows.

I breathed slowly and steadily.

This was the moment.

A little man, thin and muscular as a boy, jumped over the four foot walls, my battlement. With a thud, he was in my compound. He was carrying a large brown envelope and what appeared to be a long stick-like present for a child, wrapped colourfully. Here was the man who had blackmailed my wife for so long and depleted my funds. He was in disguise, like a ninja, with a black bandanna around half his face, cut-off shorts, a baseball hat which said 'Atari' and sunglasses. It made him appear much meaner without a face. He wore long sleeves and a high collar, perhaps hiding a tattoo, like I would know anything anyway. Seeing my potential nemesis made me calmer. I was in pieces before, but they say 'it is a wait worse than death'.

He threw the envelope down which hit the dirt ground with a thwack.

'Leave the money,' he growled in English, 'walk Ten Steps away from me.'

Perspiration ran down my face and neck and I wiped it away. The 'ten steps' was not in the original plan! I put the bag of cash down. I hesitated, wanting to draw my gun, but I couldn't. Think, think!

Ian would go ape shit. I was not getting a chance to check the documents. The thug asked me again to turn around and walk away. He said again in English, 'Turn around and walk away.' His voice was shaky and unreal too. He was as nervous or more nervous than me. I was still frozen, but it gave me hope. He sharply repeated his instruction, and his hand grabbed the stick. He asked me not to turn around. He waited with his colourful stick poised, until I complete my ten steps.

My feet dragged as I positioned myself like a puppet with a few broken strings. Nothing seemed connected, and in this stupefaction I made my way back to the verandah as instructed by him. I heard him throwing the stick down on the dirt ground.

On the verandah, still facing away from him, my ears strained to hear him unzip the bag. Like a child opening Christmas presents, he was preoccupied for a second. I heard him counting the notes.

The bugger was fast too. He'd run away already. I turned around. I could just see a shadowy figure leaping over the crenellated walls with the Adidas bag.

I heard a gunshot.

'Bugger!' I heard Ian shouting, so he must have missed. I ran to the wall and jumped over it, running after him. Ian was giving chase too.

'The fuck were you doin?' He shrieked. 'How long did you need?'

'I... I...' I replied, gasping. My voice was shaking with a tremolo I had never ever heard before. 'He...he asked me to take ten steps away from him!'

'And did you?'

'Yes,' I puffed, running fast.

'Why?' He screamed. 'Why didn't you fire a shot then?'

'Because he had a stick or crowbar or whatever it was! If he had seen me drawing the gun from my back, he would have whacked me first!'

'Well I wish he did! I grabbed his leg,' said Ian, in between breaths, running. 'But the bastard has covered himself with oil! Like the Orang Minyak! So I had to pull the trigger!'

Orang Minyak was literally Oil Man, a legendary local streaker and fantasy naked rapist who roamed the jungle, covered in palm oil. He supposedly jumped in through windows and molested women, before running away. No one could ever catch him because he was greased up. The only sign of his visit was oil-stained clothing and sheets.

Ian fired another shot, but it must have scared the Oil Man. He suddenly threw the bag, to somewhere in the distance. That confused Ian and myself even more. Did he not want the money? Where did he throw it to?

I ran and tried to keep up with Ian, between the broken tree roots, the banana groves. I kept running. I couldn't see straight. All the trees were tight as slum-dwellers, not letting me through. It was getting late. I knew this place better than him. This was my compound. I'd find him. My legs were bruised and cut from the thorns and weeds but I kept on jumping over hoops of branches and spiky plants.

Ian was cursing. We had lost him. He had become more and more like a shadow, and then finally a dot in the distant trees on the estate. We had lost him! Shit! Now we needed to look for the bag.

'Fuck!' screamed Ian. 'Where the fuck is it?'

'Um.' I wished he would stop swearing. The sound of his voice was worse than gunfire. Ian was not a sharp-shooter at all. He was full of bullshit just as I thought.

'Where's the fucken bag?' He said every two seconds. 'This is all your bloody fault. You should have just shot the bastard.'

We heard a blast. 'The fuck was that?' said Ian. Another gun shot? I looked around.

'Our friend is armed, mate,' said Ian. Cautiously, we slowed our search right down, craning our necks to listen hard. Despite the amount of undergrowth around, the shot sounded dampened yet amplified: we could not pinpoint where it originated from. The plantation was alive with bedlam and noise: the cacophony of the 'cocktail bug', the cicadas, whose volume control was cranked to maximum at the hour when day became night, the song list from a thousand birds and the full reverb from about a million bushcrickets. If you were not attuned to the sounds of nature, as I, you could not separate the wavelengths into distance. 'About a hundred and fifty yards away, I'd say,' assessed Ian, reading my mind.

'Do you think he's telling us to piss off and not follow him?' I said.

'Damn right,' said Ian, 'but I'm not going to stop looking for my bloody dough.'

It was dark and quite hard to see in front of us. We heard feeble voices in an exchange. We stopped. They stopped too.

We must have spent a good fifteen minutes. We didn't know where we were looking in the thick undergrowth, and it all happened so fast – where did he fling the bag? We looked everywhere in the thickets of fern, fallen logs, mossy branches and parasites. Nothing. Ian chose white because he thought it would stand out. We were almost at the semi-collapsed high iron gates of the estate already. I could hear faint traffic sounds from the road. He definitely threw the bag into the bushes, but it was impossible to find it now. Ian was shaking his head hysterically. I walked with a slow stiff shuffle like I was on medication or something. My knees felt weak and uncontrolled. Every step felt like a long time. I wanted to suggest to him that we looked for the bag again tomorrow, when it was light, but...

Then I saw him. He was fallen just behind the gate.

But he was not the guy.

This one was a slightly overweight, short bloke, not the one who came to get the money, but who was wearing an identical outfit, cut-off shorts, black bandanna. Yet... he had the bag! Did he find it or did the skinny thug throw it at him? He was obviously preparing to run for it...

I couldn't think. His lungs had been shot. There was blood everywhere. He was lying in a puddle of blood, sticky blood dripped from the branches of the undergrowth and the trees. I looked beyond the gate. The street lights had just come on from a distance, and I could make just make out the cloudy glow. But who was this...who shot...?

My mind spun. I scanned the iron gates, the driveway, the tree with chandelier flowers, the corpse already buzzing with flies, the front garden, up the steps to the verandah...

Talisa crept out from behind the ferns. She stood in front of me.

She held a long rifle, I thought, since I knew nothing about guns.

'What are you...? Where did you...?' I couldn't think. She had a gun?

She looked stern at first, only because she had seen my face, whatever it looked like now. Then her lips slowly parted into a smile, like a tiny curved leaf.

'What's this!' I asked, meaning I couldn't believe you shot the guy, but she misunderstood my exclamation.

'It's a shotgun,' she replied. 'For hunting. I'm quite good at medium range.'

'I mean, how did you get here?'

'Since you sacked Ibrahim, how do I get anywhere?' She came towards me slowly, goose-stepping through the long weeds and undergrowth. 'By cab.'

'But what about Wendall?'

'He's still at your mum's.'

'You left him there?'

'Why can't I? She *is* your mum, isn't she?'

'No, I mean, where...what did you tell her?'

'That I was gutted. You didn't invite me to your school reunion when in fact partners *were* invited, and I really wanted to go.'

'And she said fine?'

'Like, yeah?' She said in that American Pie tone that normally grated on me but was mildly amusing to me now.

'And you came.' I was dazed. 'Well, I...you...saved me. Us,' I said in a confused way. Ian rolled his eyes. 'Oh, *please*,' he yelped.

'But where did you get that...that gun...from?' I pointed.

'It was here,' she said, trying to kiss me. I was filthy and I recoiled from her at once. She did not react with surprise or animosity, seemingly intent on her explanation on finding the rifle. 'It has always been here. All those people who lived in this house – did you really think they didn't need self-defence?'

I never thought about it to be honest. 'Bollocks,' said Ian. 'If self-defence ever worked, they'd still be living in this house.'

'No one knows I've got this gun,' she said. 'Not even you, Dah,' she faced Ian. 'The guy had a sumpit,' she said. 'Blowpipe. The silent killer. So I had to shoot. Thank God you are OK!' She cried, putting her hands on my shoulder. 'Look at these!' She turned round and picked up from the ground what looked like a four-foot long bamboo pole, also strangely wrapped up in cartoon wrapping paper. She threw it down, as though reviled, and then she showed me a dart made of chicken feathers and very sharp needle-like tips. There were two more scattered on the ground. Ian put his hand in front of the man's nose to check that he was actually dead. He pounced on the bag and unzipped it open.

'I can't be sure,' Ian said solemnly, 'but I think it's all there. I'll have to check in the light. Did you see the other guy?'

'Oh yeah, the skinny guy.' Talisa said. 'Well, I asked him to go away and never to come back.'

'Let me guess,' I said. 'He said fine.'

'He...' Talisa replied. 'He just ran for it.'

'Let's deal with Fattie first,' said Ian. 'We can't leave him here.'

Talisa looked around. The brick piers and the gates were covered in blood. 'Don't worry,' she said, like a practical housewife, 'the rain will wash off the crap.' It was only at this point did I even notice that she wore the Pua Kumbu tied as a sling bag over one shoulder, into which she placed the shotgun. How casual her gesture, yet I wonder how could she have...? I was supposed to be the hitman, but my wife had made me redundant.

I took Talisa home and instructed her to set the alarm. The security guard alone was not enough. While I was still filthy, and bleeding from the thorns and insect bites, I might as well go back to the body and bury him with Ian, who would wait on site, on guard, armed, to make sure that the skinny guy did not return.

From the dilapidated gardener's shed in the back of the compound, Ian and I found a couple of tilly-lamps and rusty shovels. Lit only by the tilly-lamps, we dug a grave in the jungle, a proper grave, at least four feet deep, and round with a tree planted in the middle, to make it look less grave-like. Moths swarmed around us like snow swirling, attracted to the lanterns. We dragged the body to the hole in the ground. It took us several hours of surreal hard work, using the rusty shovels we found in the gardeners' shed at the back of the compound.

'What if we get arrested?' I said, with genuine concern. 'I mean, Talisa *has* killed a man.'

'Don't be silly, my man, we won't get arrested.'

'Why?'

'Cos these guys are immigrants, for fuckssakes. They come and go all the time. Do you know how many Indonesians we have buried on the estate?'

I gasped. 'Indonesians? What do you mean?'

'Indonesians, Sri Lankans, Laotians. They drink paraquat, they hang themselves, they are illegal workers, what do you do when they kill themselves? If they are illegal you can't report them, cos it's like admitting that you hired illegals. So they get buried here.'

'But how many?'

'Oh, only six. So far. It's very rare. Six in all the time that I've run the estates.'

More chilling stories of the MacFarlane proportion. So. It was not the first time. I pictured myself digging my own grave. Right now I didn't have any way of escaping. I seemed to be digging deeper by the day.

When I got back to the compound, the envelope of evidence was still on the dirt ground where it was flung down with a thwack. Ian shoved at me a vial of TCP and a wad of ancient yellowing bandages (probably WWII in origin) that he found in the disused estate manager's house. I said we definitely had no dressing kit at home. Funny how a doctor's house had no first aid kit. When I was searching for that missing Prozac, I realised that we only had a couple of paracetamol. I was not keen on antique wound dressing but I accepted them anyway. We were both too tired to say goodbye to the other. I sat in his mud-covered Land Rover in silence.

I ARRIVED HOME IN the early hours. The sky was midnight blue. The Nepalese gurkha nodded and waved to me as I went through the gates in my BMW. He asked no questions.

Talisa had been awake all this time.

'Do you have the envelope?' She asked me.

'Yes, madam. Here.' I placed it gently on the kitchen worktop. 'Can you help me with my minor injuries first, please?' I said, slightly annoyed that she did not seem to notice my arms, hands and feet were bleeding with tiny cuts, and stinging from mud and thorns.

'Don't snap at me,' she said. 'You wouldn't be alive if not for me.'

I said nothing. She hurriedly bathed and dressed my wounds with the antique TCP and gauze. Unable to put it off any longer, she ripped open the envelope and read the contents, which were only four sheets of paper.

'Well?' I said, 'what does it say?'

She dropped the pieces of paper. There were tears in her eyes.

'She's dead,' my wife said quietly. 'I knew it. Nenek would never tell on me.'

I snatched the documents from her. I read them myself. Her nenek, in her conversion to Christianity, had revealed to a clergyman and a flying doctor what she saw the day Peliris died. Her Nenek died more than a year ago.

It was almost dawn. I hugged Talisa tightly for what seemed like a long time. Our eyes were closed. We were both so, so tired.

'Why did you not–' I searched for the word, unable to even think it, let alone say it, 'kill...him – the other guy – as well?' I whispered finally.

'Because for him,' she said without hesitation, 'it is much worse to live.'

'Why?'

'Because he has nothing to live for now.'

I glimpsed the true nature of my wife's assassin instinct. It was not a random impulse. She was not a psychopathic serial killer. The 'art of gun' summed up her survival tactics. She was a hunter.

'Did you sell the Prozac?' I asked.

'Yes.'

'To who?'

'Unhappy people.'

'Like who?' I asked but she decided to ignore me.

Talisa smiled and shook her head. She pulled away from me and retreated into the master bedroom while as usual, I went into my chamber, the guest room. My sleep would be light from now. I shuddered at the thought of the revenge coming on like a gigantic typhoon. Would the skinny guy not avenge his mate? Typhoon, from the Cantonese, tai fung – Great Wind.

I tiptoed into the master bedroom to check on Talisa without waking her. My wife slumbered on. In her grief, she managed to look so peaceful. In fact, she looked like an angel, her guilt-free, worry-free face illuminated by the moon. What was she dreaming of? We hadn't exchanged dreams for a long time. Perhaps she didn't dream anymore. The pua had not been replaced on the wall over the bedhead.

In my chamber, I turned over and tried to sleep, but already a rooster was crowing in the distance.

47

Minos

Akh! I must have been dead, and either Nabau the serpent spirit which saved me the first time and saved me again or the good christian god above me, have saved me. I am alive! But Watan, I have not been able to accept it, he is dead.

I am bleeding and cut and torn, but the spirit of the jungle keeps me safe from the hunter. I jump back on to the motorbike and race back to town. I need to be bandaged.

God has punish both me and Watan, because of our greed. My tears fly as I ride down the motorway. Fuck if God he kills me now, in some traffic accident, I deserve it man, I deserve it. Cos I ran away. And I did not even want the bag of money, because that money cannot bring Watan back. More I think of it, the more I hate Watan. He brought me into this trouble. If I got discharged from the prison and ended up laybring and lay brick, none of this shit would have happen. So blame him for it. What's the point. What's the use. He's gone. And I have left the bag behind.

WHEN I GET BACK to Ah Hock's, is already late, maybe half past six, is Saturday night. All these drinkers, diners, enjoying themselves. The motorcycles gang downstairs, the butterflies of the night hanging around, children selling drinks and fireworks. Everyone is so happy – how can they see my sadness and fear? What is going to happen to me now? Will they catch me again and lock me up again? And then in the neon light shadow of the arches of Ah Hock's, I see a familiar figure: Mei. Smoking a cigarette. Thank God! I need to see somebuddy I know, a buddy, anybuddy!

'Mei, Mei!'

'Luke! What are you doing? You're bleeding!' She say in Malay.

'I'm fine. Only small cuts on my foots.'

I used to be so good and quick in jungle, barefoot, leaping over all them trees, without one cut. But now, my foots have injury. Cos I have got used to wearing socks all the time. Tho that is not the reason why I'm weeping. Mei immediately wipes my tears with her tissues that she digs out of her sparkly handbag.

'Let's just get you some help,' she say, in Malay.

Then she takes me to one of those 24-hour polyclinics in Old Town near the market area. She tells them that I been involved in rockclimbing accident, that I am on holiday.

'I need to go back to work, Luke. Where's your friend?'

I just cannot reply, I am so, so sad, ashamed and in shock.

'I go back myself later on, Mei. You go without me. See you back at the hotel.'

'See you.'

She presses two hundred ringgit in my hand to pay for the medical bill. I just got no strength to say no to her.

'Pay me back later, Luke! No problem!'

I see her long legs run out into the hot, humid night. There is a powerful smell of rain coming. I wait so, so long, in the clinic to be treated. I thought this is private, and is quicker! But it seems that I can jolly well wait along with all this people who have had work accidents. All the sick and injured people of Segamat. I am as good as anybuddy.

I see somebuddy! Outside the clinic!

Man! I can't fucken believe it, is Pastor! Man! Is Pastor. He's outside looking in, checking whether I am here.

'Pastor, Pastor!'

Pastor comes in to the clinic, and all this sick people look at him, like he is Jesus or something.

'Minos, I mean, Luke! I have been waiting and waiting for you in Ah Hock's lobby. Did you not see me? I just bumped into a lady called Mei, she said you're here! What's happened to you? You're bleeding!'

'Nothing is wrong with me,' I cry. 'God save me.'

'He did. And where is Watan?'

'I'm so sorry, Pastor, I'm sorry, please don't report me! I ain't going in again.'

The receptionist nurse then asks whether Pastor related to I. And he says that yes, he is my buddy, and I am from his church,

I work for the church. I then say that we been rockclimbing, and Pastor say nothing for a second, but after that he agree that I am injured from rockclimbing accident.

I know that Pastor don't like to, but he told a Little White Lie cos Pastor is white and they will believe him. I am not white. They will not believe me.

He says to me, God will forgive you, if you just say sorry to God. While we waiting to be treated, Pastor closes his eyes and he prays. Silently. My tears just fall free, and I don't close my eyes as usual, but this time I am looking at the floor and it is agony. I'm praying for Watan's soul but I cannot tell Pastor that now – I say I don't want to talk about wha happen. Cos all these people are here and listening and looking at my bleeding foots.

'After this, Luke, let's eat something and have a drink and you can tell me what happened.'

He treat me like I am a chile. And you know, I am like a chile. I don't seem able to stay out of trouble. No stitching, just bandages. Pastor is given spares of dressing to change me in a day. Pastor say I got to take the antibiotic as well. He pays the bill: something like one hundred and eighty ringgit. Medicine is extra. I tell him that Mei give me money, and Pastor say, 'Well, just give it back to her later then! Oh bless her!'

So we eat and drink in Old Town but I really cannot eat. I feel sick actually. I cannot stop thinking of Watan. Then Pastor he take me back to Ah Hock's. He is staying in another hotel, but he wan see me back in my room first. Climbing the stairs nearly kill me, every part of me weeps.

In my room, I take from my money to pay Pastor back. I unzip my shorts pockets. Five bundles. We open them and count them. TWENTY THOUSAND RINGGIT. Akh! I have twenty thousand ringgit on me, on my body, and yet Pastor pay my medical bill!

'Oh!' say Pastor. I can see he well shocked and he don't know what to say. Actually I am not sure how I am going to explain all this.

'Um? Is that money?'

'Uh. Yes, is money. I's gwan give you back for doctor's bill... '

'Luke. This is serious. Do you want to tell me where this money came from?'

I just cannot answer. I have no words to say to him. I have never see him get mad before. But his voice become hard olafsudden.

'TELL ME. Where did this money come from? Luke. Look at me. I know about all the DVDs and CDs that you're selling! I found everything in the locked bilek. You'd better explain, Luke! Look at me.'

I can't look at him. I just keep shaking my head, sighing, I can't think, I can't think, I look down.

'Something bad happen, Pastor,' I finally say.

'Why didn't you ring me, for goodness' sake?'

'Cos phone run out of credit, Pastor!'

'And you didn't email.'

'Is not so easy, you seen the queues in the cybercafé? Also Watan and me really wan get a job first, so that we got money to get more credit and to email you...'

'I'm very concerned. You know you are still under my supervision?'

'No... yes.'

'TELL ME WHERE DID YOU GET THE MONEY FROM?'

Oh shit.

'Yes! Pastor. Is from the DVD and CDs that me and Watan selling. You know already! You have find everything in the bilek which I lock up! We go to some shutdown factory to meet the local snakehead. Long time we never pay. So they kill Watan and I run away with the money.'

'Luke. Do you think you're the only person selling DVDs in the whole of Sarawak? The truth. Please.'

I sigh. But where to begin?

'Luke. You tell me and we'll go back to my hotel. The Mercure next door. It's much safer than this...this, er... establishment. Since we have so much cash on us. We have air-con, shower, breakfast, Astro TV. And tomorrow, we'll fly back to Kuching. Now then, Luke, I'm listening.'

I smile a little though there is no place in my heart for Astro TV cos it reminds me of Watan.

AFTER I GOT THE bag of money, I run for it. I run to where I know Watan is hiding. I hear first shot, and I know the doctor trying to get me. I run faster. I hear second shot, and I thought that Watan is shot. I look around. No one. I stop running, open the bag. Is so heavy. I take as much money as I can put in my zip up pockets. I throw the bag away so they won't kill me. But I hear the third shot, and I see her at last after all these years, in the plantation. It is the third shot that kill Watan. In his hand he has the sumpit and... the bag! He found the bag that I throw away. He is trying to blow the darts at the doctor fellar to save us.

The manang girl is wearing the Pua Kumbu around her shoulders. Under this sacred cloth, the wide mouth of her rifle is pointing through. It is too dark to see the patterns on the cloth, the mark of the weaver. Cloth and bird wings are the same meaning in Iban stories. She wears the cloth to say that the antu of the forests have given her their protection.

I charge towards her screaming, like a wounded bearded pig. I knock the gun out of her hand. Akh! She fall down to the ground. I reach out and grab the gun. It is dark so I must be quick. I fumble with it – how do you use this? I am going to shoot her back, I swear to Nabau my serpent friend. I hear her voice. She calls out, 'stop right there', in Iban but where she is calling me from? I look up, point the gun to where the voice coming from, anywhere. 'Come out wherever you are!' I shout. I cannot see her anywhere, I just hold the gun like I am a watering can swinging my spout. Where is she?

I cry out! The last thing I see is darkness. I see nothing. A thick blanket cloth has been put over my head, tight, pulled back as though is my ponytail. Akh! Must be the Pua. I drop the gun in order to free my hand. I pull the sacred cloth off my face, but is too late. I hear clack-clack. She has pick up the rifle and she poke it against the back of my head. I spin around in case it is not a rifle I am feeling but a tree branch or something. No. The manang girl is pointing the rifle at me. Straight at my face. Am I dreaming it? I see it. My blood drains from me, leaving me cold. The spirit catcher's tattoo! She whisper, 'If you ever dare to come back, I will blow your head off, just like I did your friend.' I turn around and I flee.

I have travel all this way to be an idiot. Watan have sacrifice own life. It is not worth it, 'cept that I got twenty thousand ringgit out of it. If I have not suffer so many cuts and bruises, if I have not panic, I would have taken the whole bag and not tossed it. Akh! I am also stupid, like Watan, like all us boys from the jungle. No wonder we are good only for hunting and living in prison. What is the use of praying? Ain't done us no good. We're just nobuddies. We ain't never get rich.

Talisa, my old friend, the person I write to all this time, I used to wonder if she pretty, or fat. Is tall or short, dark or fair. Many years I have think about her, the little girl all grow up. She got her own baby now. Does the baby know his mummy have kill someone? No, more than one. A skinny girl with big black eyes. And of course, song irang tattoo. When I see it, I know, to be afraid. Oh how fast I run that day!

For Watan sake I wan go back and squeeze her neck like a chicken at katang festival, but she gwan blas my head off. She ain't no messin bout with the sumpit. Why she needs blowpipe when she got gun? She have already move on from the jungle. She probably live like filem star in her big air-con house. Whereas, I am just Minos, under the new name Luke. All this time I have achieve nothing but a nabau tattoo and some computer equipment. Even all my clothes have been given to me by Pastor.

But at the very least, I have kill no one. Maybe inside I am still a good chile. The Nabau serpent save my life. But poor Watan only have Christian God, he ain't got no Nabau serpent and that's why he no make it.

For Watan sake, I carry on making filems and songs for everybuddy. Doing Myspace, Facebook. I remember Watan's Five Rules. Rule number one: regular clientele. Find them and keep them. I got guanxi, my contacts, from Watan before. We got whole longhouse running on solar. I got outsourcing and distributors and street vendors all waiting for my DVD and CDs. Can sell them and make more than one thousand a month.

Not a day go by when I don't think of Watan and the funny things he have say. The filems he like to watch. Korean gangster one. Brazilian slum one. Iranian gay one. All kind interesting filem, cos he have never travel, and he so much want to travel. That's what Talisa's money was for....

But always, always, I remember them filems we have watch over and over, Get Shorty. Be Cool. Pulp Fiction. Reservoir Dogs. We especially like Quentin Tarantino....

The tattoo lady say the song irang is the bamboo shoot tattoo. Cos bamboo grows and grows. Is never end. Clever one. I am finis with the jungle. Is like praying, it ain't done me no good. All them names of animals and fruits that I know, useless info. Names of filem directors – even more useless info. Talisa move into some town, she got rich, doing no work. Tha's the real skill. Tha's where world is gwan....

Me, stuck in jungle forever, in the dark-darkness of Eternal Light. Me, good at gathering a few ferns and wild snails. Kill a deer or two. Repair a few hundred hymnbooks. Make a few thousand CDs and DVDs. None of that ain't gwan make me rich. For all I know, every night she's watching DVDs and listening to music CDs that I made....

Sssst! Like a snake in the bamboo, she got away again.

48

Bernard

I took Luke back to my three star hotel and checked him into a single room. I removed the money from him, to keep it in my hotel room safe. If I left him the twenty grand, I might never see him again. I didn't quite trust him now.

Luke wanted to give the RM20,000, to the church. He did not want a cent of it. Actually I believed he said, if I understood his English correctly, he never wanted a cent of it. Praise God. *Praise God.* The church was so short on funds for the extension and renovations. All our money had been pouring into the jungle mission. The roof was almost caving in. Eternal Light Brighton would not budge. Margaret avoided our cry for help. She did not even write to me anymore. All I got from her was a vapid Christmas card. I didn't want another card. This money could not have arrived at a better time.

Luke might hate Watan with all his heart, but God would heal that hatred. Never underestimate the power of God's love. I would carry out a service to mourn his loss. I knew he wasn't a good influence on Luke, but he was still one of God's children. I would like to collect his body and do a proper memorial service, but in the scope of recent events, that might not be possible. It was too dangerous. It would involve returning to the scene of the gunshot and they would have removed his body by now.

The next day, the cab I booked arrived to take us to Senai International Airport. Soon we would be re-united with Wendy and Boy-boy. I could not wait to get back to Orchid Villa. Home. Before we left, I went over to the esteemed establishment of Ah Hock's Lodging House, to say thank you, to Mei. She might not be up yet, so I would have to wake her up. Luke had written a letter to say goodbye to her, using our Orchid Villa letterhead. In the letter to Mei, I'd also put in the two hundred ringgit she shelled out for Luke' medical bill. It was only right that we returned it to her. "...Her sins, which are many, are forgiven; for she loved much: but to whom little is forgiven, the same loveth little." (Luke 7:47)

I sealed the envelope and knocked on the door until she opened it.

A STRONG SENSE OF forbearance overcame me, both for Luke and Mei. When we touched down in Kuching a couple of hours later, Wendy was here to meet us in the church van. It seemed that there was much dust flying about the road, but as we approached the dust storm, it was in fact hordes of butterflies including the dramatic Rajah Brooke's birdwing (*Troides brookiana*) welcoming me home. They were attracted to the salt seepage along roadsides.

We drove past the avenue of huge pong-bong trees on the sandy road home. I had authority from my good friend in Myanmar, Pastor Richard Stephens, the Burmese made oil from the pong-bong seeds for rubbing through the hair to kill lice! Richard was a very accomplished and devoted servant of God. He had a gift for languages. He was working in a team translating the Word of God and scripture material from English and Chinese into Kayin, Falam Chin, Lai Chin, Lau and Siyin Chin – the languages used by the ethnic minorities in Myanmar. Richard was a friend of mine way back from when we were botanists working in Kingston, as in Kingston, Jamaica, not Kingston-upon-Hull.

One of my predecessors, if I could call him that, was Rumphius, a 17th century botanist working for the Dutch East India Company. He wrote that a local home-made laxative was a drink made from the pong-bong bark grated into coconut milk and vinegar, but it was not to be *home-made* unless you knew the proportions! Oh, how Wendy suffered.

I looked over to Wendy, who was driving silently with a steady frown. She had endured much suffering on the Lord's account. Mosquitoes, bad roads, thunderstorms, unendurable heat, sauna room humidity, me. Rows and rows of the pong-bong, *Cerbera odallam*, these magnificent shady trees, with smooth, grapefruit-sized green fruit greeted me as we approached Orchid Villa. Children and visitors both had to be warned of the inedible pong-bong.

Like Borneo, the fruit was attractive and innocent on the outside, but filled with danger on the inside. The seeds, which the locals used as rat killer, contained a very potent poison, *cerebine*, from *Cerberus*, the three-headed hell-hound which guarded the entrance to Hades.

Wendy, I found, often wanted to say that we had come to hell. She was almost on the brink of saying it, yet she didn't say it: Borneo was hell. She restrained herself, but I sometimes wished she would say it. I clasped my hand over my Bible in prayer. Luke's eyes were shut. I prayed silently for our safety.

Lucifer, the Shining One, Morning Star. Luke, *Luke*, the angel, had fallen. The boys had been poisoned by the fruit, "... but God is faithful, who will not suffer you to be tempted above that ye are able; but will with the temptation also make a way to escape..." (I Cor 10:13)

We passed the riverine swamps and the lowland mixed forests of dipterocarps, mainly kawi trees with their enormous canopies. The roadside was littered with the pong-bong fruit, the Cerberus of Borneo, fallen from the trees. Sunlight glittered on their green skin. Indeed God had made a way. We were going home.

WHEN MEI VISITED, WE showed her around the extension to Orchid Villas which had taken four months, spanning over Christmas. Luke no longer shared Boy-boy's room. We took her to see a longhouse, which she had never been to. She insisted she always paid her way and she stayed at a local motel in Kuching. She gave myself and Luke a black Prada laptop bag each. Of course I assumed they were fake. Still we were moved by her kindness.

We now needed to clear some space at the original Orchid Villa. We had more children attending the jungle school and administrative space there was limited. It seemed ironic that after the extension one seemed to end up with less space. Hence, some light filing, since no one else cared about this place. "No one" meaning Wendy. I chanced upon the *12 x pairs Tai Sing rubber sandals (free size)* box. Surat-surat. Ah, Mrs Menduk's old letters, her unclaimed mail, which our boys opened because Wendy had been remiss.

I found Talisa's photo, with her baby. I covered the bottom half of the photo with my fingers. This was how the Sarawakians did it. The subject was first viewed without the tattoo, and then with.

Without her tattoo, she was just an ordinary dark-skinned Iban girl. Her large cowering eyes resembled the hollows of the benuah (*Macaranga pruinose*) which ants crawled into. The tree's low-growing leaves were very tasty to forest browsers like tapir and rhinoceros. Her thin dry lips were slightly damp as sap from a twig and her crash helmet cheekbones had the ghoulish radiance of a long-tailed broadbill. They gave her the appearance of supplication, someone in camouflage. I sensed the primordial blankness of an animal in fight or flight, a prey.

It stung me that the boys were capable of betraying me, without so much as a consideration for Jesus. Satan had come in the night, barefoot and creeping, and taken away the boys' hearts and souls.

CICADAS SANG THEIR DEAFENING electronic beeps to the beat of barbets. It was night when I arrived at the longhouse. I drove the church van like Satan himself in order to drop off last minute supplies for the children attending school the next day.

One day I will be judged by Thee, O Lord our Saviour, and I pray that You will show me mercy too. We ask for your forgiveness and guidance, Lord. In the name of our precious Heavenly Father, amen.

I thought of the innocent GP who had lost twenty thousand ringgit. I agonised over this matter, practically staying awake all night on the uncomfortable nipah matting in one of the bilek, the one which Luke used for his 'filem and music business'. I was shoved in a corner, next to an impressive skyline consisting of towers of jewel cases, arrays of sleeve notes, columns of blank discs, CDs or DVDs, who knew. Sleep didn't come.

At dawn I prayed hard again. I stared in an exhausted daze at the amount of equipment and paraphernalia he had accumulated in his 'business suite'. An idea occurred to me. But right now, I was heading back to Orchid Villa.

In the morning, before the children arrived, I said to Luke that we had to return the money to the 'doctor fellar'. Luke said that Watan had *given his life* to the church for this money. Of course he did, I sighed.

'We still have to return it, Luke,' I said.

'Pastor,' he asked, 'why did you spend it then? You spent it fast-fast.'

'We *had* to, Luke. The roof was caving in.' I said nothing of the fact that Margaret had been ignoring me. Money would always be tight when you worked for God. Luke once reminded me: if it got tighter, I had to go back to the 'Shivering Cold Place'. Then Eternal Light would close. He knew full well if we shut down, he and Boy-boy would be out on the streets.

The children had arrived to do the activities that Luke set out. I said goodbye to him. As I was driving back to Kuching in the church van, I thought: the only way I knew if Luke was telling the truth this time, if he was indeed a savage made noble by our Lord, was to make him prove it. I had a delicious idea. There was no better way to prove it, than to make him pay back the twenty grand himself.

After my initial discovery of Luke's 'business suite', I left it intact. I made no attempt to clear it out or change anything. Not that I condone piracy, but Luke made about a thousand a month, he told me, from his 'filem and music business', totally illegal. Finger-wagging educated westerners were often too quick to condemn the piracy trade in these parts of the third world.

Was I to judge? "For with what judgement ye judge, ye shall be judged: and with what measure ye mete, it shall be measured to you again". (Matt 6:15) People only did it out of desperation and need. He an unskilled ex-con. Yet he had distributors and vendors waiting for all the latest releases. Luke made the whole package ready for sale, even the artwork.

Like most people, I saw digital downloads as valueless deletable bits and bytes. The record companies were only keen on CDs because they were lower quality and cheaper to produce than vinyls and sleeves. I realised this as soon as I sat down on the floor cross-legged and eyes shut that night when I discovered the 'business suite', listening to Pink Floyd.

A CD was not a piece of art, a flower or a book. One couldn't be fascinated with a plastic disc and definitely not a download. Anyway, the most pirated CDs were those of top selling artistes, who wouldn't even know they were being pirated. Their managers and agents were too busy snorting cocaine in their twenty-room mansions. They wouldn't be affected by piracy.

Who were the pirates? They were the Watans and Lukes of this world, skint individuals. Our Lord was the first pirate. It was the reason why the symbol of Christianity was the fish. Jesus turned "seven loaves" and "a few little fish" into food for four thousand, in the same way a few little originals became fodder for the "multitudes" of consumers.

Would piracy halt the film business? How could it? There would always be new films, whether or not they got pirated, because films were made by and for people who watched films.

The money must be paid back to the GP, at the expense of Luke's 'filem and music business' which was in turn at the expense of the film and music industry. Films and music would become folklore: they belonged to no one and everyone. Was piracy stealing? Yes. Did we steal from someone? *Yes.*

Therefore, I say, Luke – go forth and multiply. You will come back with the twenty thousand ringgit from your 'business' to be returned to the good man, the doctor. And bloody pronto. Not two years. Six months or fewer preferably.You will do it as fast as your fingers can trim those colour-printed sleeve notes. Otherwise, Eternal Light bids you farewell. There is no room at the inn.

SINCE LUKE STARTED HIS Theology course, he seemed a lot happier. The beautiful Psalm of Praise, Psalm 103, reassured me of God's continuing kindness: "the Lord is merciful and gracious, slow to anger and abounding in mercy." Luke wanted to commit himself fully to working for the church. If he didn't, he would be destitute. Occasionally, to those in our prayer group, I innocently cited the verse from Jer 45:5: "Do you seek great things for yourself? Do not seek them", though it was quietly intended for Luke, and he knew it.

We all had our ways of staying afloat. Luke and I seemed to have reached a symbiotic level in our relationship at last, like the birds which rode on the crocodile's back, eating the lice trapped in its scales.

The GP fund was building nicely. Luke didn't mind hard work. In fact, he had drily commented that the doctor was his new snakehead, due to the noteworthy sum being paid to him.

I WAS AT MY desk, looking up the online medical directory for the GP's clinic address. My fingers dipped into the *Tai Sing* box and I fished out her photo again. Until now, hardly did we think about the lovely Talisa, for whom men had run up considerable bills. How strange that this vulgar, lowly-educated girl, had created waves of iniquity rippling through the placid currents of our rural life.

I covered the top half of the photo, her face and shoulders, exposing just her tattooed forearm, the living batik sheath of bamboo shoots, the song irang. Early explorers mistook women's tattoos as silk gloves, so delicate was the appearance. It was stencilled onto her brown skin in black, beast-like, like sunlight on the skin of a deer.

I uncovered my hand to view the entire photo again. Seeing Talisa, her tattoo and her baby together – was the magic. When I first saw this photo, I sensed the primordial blankness of an animal in fight or flight, a prey. Seeing it again, she was in fact a predator, not a prey. Hadn't she claimed the life of at least two men?

There was something in all of us that wants to be wild. That was why Luke got his tattoo in Chinatown even before he had a hot meal. He wanted to be like her, to be her, but he was also fearful of her. A tattoo was about escaping the boundaries of civilised society. To be wild was to be free, like nature itself. I once wanted to be free too. Of England, Margaret, WHSmith, curry houses. God sent me to Sarawak.

I ALSO HAVE A tattoo myself. But that is another story for another evening.

49

Minos

'Watan, is that you?'
        'Is me.'
                'It's so dark. Is it really you?'
'Yes. Is me. Sorry, I wake up you.'
'What you doing here?'
'Visit you, bro.'
'Are you alive?'
'No, I'm gone, Minos. Just came back to say bye-bye.'
'Don't go! Watan! Please don't go! Why you leaving me here like this? What happened that day?'
'You gwan enjoy filems. You already speak so good now. When you speak the perfect Inglish with Pastor, maybe one day you make you own filem! You promise me.'
'Promise what? I am not going back to the girl.'
'No. Don't go back. The girl is finis. Promise me you gwan keep watching and making filems. Make many, many filems and make people happy.'
'Watan, where you going.'
'I gwan now. Go back to sleep, Minos.'
'Watan, don't go!'
'Go back to sleep, Minos! I gwan see you again some other time. I promise.'

50

Benjie

2007

A secret shared was halved. We were a team now, the Dog and the Sheep, each our own guardian. Talisa was not interested in the evidence, now that Nenek was gone. By 'taking care' of Peliris, Talisa, a child of thirteen then, had done her family a favour.

Re-reading the documents, I concluded that Surya was the real culprit and she was dead. Though it was now only four pieces of paper, it was my trophy. I'd lock them in the prescription drugs cupboard until I wrote my memoirs. I changed the combination.

TALISA STARTED READING. I saw stacks of recent Vogue and Marie Claire journals in my waiting room. They were all she ever read, but now they had been relegated to my clinic. Shue Ling said that my wife asked Ian to drop them off.

Just last night, after I repeatedly badgered her about where my keys were, she reluctantly looked up at me from *To Kill a Mockingbird* with an immense frown. The thought that I disturbed her was very exciting to me – soon, I would be able to have dinner parties! I would be able to take her to the Club bar and not be embarrassed in front of fellow professionals previously alarmed by her ignorance and shallowness.

She had no maid and no money to shop for designer rubbish now. Talisa had to do all the housework and cooking. We were both exhausted, like any normal parents. We now felt quite *normal*. When we had staff, the order divided us and now that we lived in chaos, the disorder united us. We knew where everything was. Talisa and I both had to change nappies, with the dreaded potty training to look forward to. I admitted that the house was a tip, but indeed I was cooking my favourite pastas with white wine sauces. I pureed my son's food and I put him to bed. I washed my own car. Before I was overrun by staff, I used to do all the cooking in my bachelor 'peasant cottage' and I thoroughly enjoyed it.

Segamat sucked me back in, familiar as a river leech on a schoolboy's shin. I used to be the town's most eligible bachelor. UCL, MBBS, BMW, HSBC were the abbreviations of my status. Then, I fell. Even Shue Ling practically threw my cup of coffee at me. She made terrible coffee anyway.

It was Chinese New Year again before some part of my brain triggered the memory off. I ignored the astrological report that my mother was so keen on. For months I had deliberately not thought about the return of the surviving blackmailer. Like the striae of a complicated tattoo, my crime was permanent and could never be washed away by the river.

The Fire Pig trotted in. Pig years, said my mum after her usual consultation with Mr Lim, were known for their respite from strife, patience and passivity, but also for indulgence, sensuality and fleshly delights. As the last sign of the zodiac, he said the Pig represented *resignation*, accepting human nature as it was – content to live and let live.

I had not been able to speak to Ian, who each time tried to accuse me of nicking the twenty thousand. Did the money drop out of the bag when the skinny bloke flung it into the bushes? More likely, he grabbed it before flinging the bag, but why did he not take the entire bag and contents? Ian and I had been back to the disused estate and we looked hard for the missing money. Nothing. While on the estate, I had at least managed to harvest the ripened papayas that my wife wrapped in hessian bags to protect them from the orioles.

SHUE LING POPPED IN to tell me that a white man was here to see me. 'The English Patient', I joked to myself. Shue Ling thought he was a Uni friend from England and let him into the surgery. I had never seen him before in my life, and I was experiencing a mixture of intrigue and fear. He said he was not ill. He had a kind but troubled appearance, and he was wearing white shorts and Caterpillar boots. Was he a tourist? He looked a bit old and too clean for a backpacker.

He handed over a jiffy bag. He asked me to look inside. I saw the bundles of money and I went into a mild spasm, wondering if this had anything to do with what happened.

'Who are you?' I asked.

'Don't worry who I am. I'm just the courier.'

'What's this for?'

'The surviving man is under my care. We are returning your money.'

'Why?'

'Because it's yours.'

Well technically that most recent amount was Ian's, but I said nothing. I had myself lost so much money on the wretched Louis Vuitton weekend bags!

'But...' I started to say, when the corpse I buried flashed into my mind. Talisa might have killed him, but she was my accomplice and I had to protect my accomplice and myself.

'In return,' he said, 'I would like the envelope of evidence, please.'

'I don't understand.'

'You do still have it, don't you? The evidence, please.' He stretched out his hand.

'Ugh..' I stammered, not knowing what to do. 'Do you...do you not have copies?'

'The Home Office Letter of Pardon is on special paper that cannot be copied. We know you killed our man. So I'll say this: keep the money and give me the evidence.'

'Um...'

'So what you're saying is, you don't want your money back?' He set the jiffy bag heavily on my desk which landed with an alarming thud. With a hefty sigh, I picked the jiffy bag up, went over to the prescription drugs cupboard and open the combination lock. I took the papers out and I shoved the jiffy bag in.

After he left as mysteriously as he arrived, I opened the cupboard again to check that I had not dreamt it. I changed the combination on the lock, hoping never to see 'The English Patient' again.

VARIOUS REGULARS WERE PERCHED at the bar like crows. Cricket was showing on the plasma screen. Talisa and Wendall were at home. I was looking through the bar menu. Occasionally I looked over my shoulder.

'He won't be back,' Ian admonished quietly, as if reading my mind. Why did he say that? Did he know I received the money today? I decided to test him.

'Who?' I said, shifting on my leather bar stool uncomfortably.

'He won't be back. He ran away from his mate and the bag of money,' he snapped. 'Are ye a fucken moron? Twenty is a helluva lotta money to them.'

Ah. Clearly he did not know about the jiffy bag. My grilled fish and green salad, no dressing, ordered from the pool bar arrived. 'And besides,' he paused, waving his hand to me to start first without him: 'The amount seems like a reasonable price to relieve me of Talisa. From now on, she's all yours, mate.'

'What are you talking about?'

'I took her into my home only for her mother's sake. I got her a job interview at your clinic. I thought if you married her, I am no longer responsible for her.'

'Why?' I believed I was set up, but I was too surprised to even say it.

'Because I'll have one fewer mouth to feed. To save me money, my man. Have you been listening at all? Pregnant, tattooed and single, she did not and still does not belong here. Who'd marry her? Look around you, what sort of place is this?'

Small-minded, scorching, mosquito-infestedville of carpenters, rubber tappers, durian planters and pineapple farmers. I gave her a job because she was pretty. She was a door that was open. I wanted so much to escape my safe dull life and be part of that which I did not know – the arcane world of spirits and secrets.

Ian wrote the money off. To someone like him, it was a silly amount not worth losing sleep over. It was the value he had placed on Talisa, the price for her to keep his unborn child from Mrs MacF's knowledge.

'Though, she does have an eye for style...' he said slyly.

'You mean...' I said. My mind drifted to the damned bags again.

'I've been thinking. You know that house and plot of land? It's totally wasted, Doctor. It's been ramshackle for thirty-six years. I've been toying with the idea of developing it into a boutique hotel. Beautiful spa. Rainforest walks. Organic food. Eco bullshit. The works. What do you think if I put Talisa in charge? Interior design?'

Talisa would be thrilled. I could already see the koi pond design handbook arriving on our doormat. 'I don't...I mean...I don't know what to say.'

'You never do,' he shook his head. 'She could do the whole jobby-job. When the building work's done, she could run the place too! Like Mrs Fawlty. You know she'd love to. It would be *just fan-dabi-dozi*, in her own words.'

I guffawed momentarily, startled at the unexpected sound of *her* word coming from someone else. I saw that Ian had not meant it as a joke. 'Talisa would be honoured,' I said.

'She'll get a wage, and you can have a profit share if you want,' he said. 'We can talk numbers later. Something to think about anyway.'

I thought of the last time I invested in Ian's rubber and how it failed me.

'You know she would die for beauty,' he grunted.

'I know.'

'What I don't know is where the hell my burger is,' Ian growled, rubbing his hands and unfolding his napkin.

I ignored him and unfolded my own napkin. I fell silent, careful not to let my inner smile seep through.

I DIDN'T STAY TO the end of the darts game. I said a crisp farewell to Ian. Without turning around, he muttered 'fucken grand' under his breath just so that it was audible to me, and no one else. I didn't hear if the 'fucken grand' was preceded by the word 'twenty'. He concentrated on his throws, each dart smooth and exact. He said things the ugly way because he did not know beauty. He had not been a papaya wrapped in hessian and watered every day. His first wife's illness had first eaten her away then him.

Never mind those wretched Louis Vuitton bags. I traded the evidence and got money back! My hands would never be clean again, you'd be glad to know, Ming Jen! The black-and-white tiled verandah hummed with the throng of barbets and bushcrickets. I gave my keys to the friendly Indian concierge in a batik shirt who retrieved my car from the back car park. I listened to the rat-tat-tat of Chinese firecrackers in the distance, let off by boys who still had some of their New Year ang pao money to burn. Moths stuck to the bulbs of the English-style lanterns, the ashes from their cremation floating away into the shadows, the night. Moth suicide was a built-in malfunction in its navigational system. Moths and butterflies, night and day.

My butterfly was asleep when I got home. Her bedside lamp was still on. She was very loosely holding *Moby Dick*, which lay on the duvet, open, spine up, page down. I recognised it as my copy from a secondhand bookshop in World's End, Chelsea. I gently removed it from her. She did not stir. I read the page:

"And this tattooing had been the work of a departed prophet and seer of his island, who, by those hieroglyphic marks, had written out on his body a complete theory of the heavens and the earth, and a mystical treatise on the art of attaining truth; so that Queequeg in his own proper person was a riddle to unfold; a wondrous work in one volume; but whose mysteries not even himself could read, though his own live heart beat against them; and these mysteries were therefore destined in the end to moulder away with the living parchment whereon they were inscribed, and so be unsolved to the last."

I held the page close to myself for a few seconds, feeling the warmth of the cover where her hand lay on it.

TALISA WAS REMOVING SOMETHING from the oven in the morning. The papayas I saved from the orioles were in the fruitbowl on our marble worktop. They now looked ripe. 'We can eat those tonight,' I said.

'You have them, I'm fine. We've been busy,' she said, turning around to rest the oven tray on a wire stand over the island unit. 'He was up at half past five, as usual. Asuncion used to wake with him and we had no idea.' Wendall laughed as he picked up a little green car, tottered towards me to give it to me. I dared say it was the first time our Smeg stainless steel double range oven had been used. She was wearing oven gloves which my mother brought back from her holiday in Taiwan. There was an aroma of baking.

'Miracle if this turns out!' she said in her Scottish lilt. On the tray were 24 little golden brown crescents of curry puffs for Wendall's snack when he got back from nursery in a few hours. I picked up a curry puff from the tray. It was so hot that I nearly dropped it. I bit into it. I didn't sound too earnest. 'Not too spicy for Wendall. How did you do it?'

'Magic.'

'Your own recipe?'

'Of course,' she grinned.

Wendall shook his head as if he understood what was being said. He pointed to the tray and his mother picked a curry puff for him from a cooled earlier batch. He bit into it so enthusiastically it made me laugh. Before he had chewed the first bite, he stuffed the rest whole into his mouth. He had eight teeth, all incisors, but he hadn't figured out how to use them yet. I used to be one of those people who hated children. They were boring, annoying and they cried and demanded all the time. Now I realised how foolish, trite and… *childish* I sound. Where did I think adults come from? Children were the future.

I never wanted to get attached to Wendall in case his mother and I split up and I never saw him again. If such a thing happened, it still would not change the fact that he was my son. He had my eyebrows, forehead and mouth. He had his mother's large deer-like eyes and mousey nose. He started from a seed and now he was a boy.

'I'll pick him up at twelve as usual,' she said. 'I have to do another batch now,'

I left quickly. Could this be a murderess speaking? I shuddered, picking Wendall's bag carrying his nappies, sippy cup, rusks and a change of outfit. Even a one-year-old had luggage. I was his porter. He waved to his mum. I felt a little niggle of guilt, just a tiny one. She had to pick Wendall up in a taxi since we had no driver now, but she was not the one complaining. She might have once seen me as the gravy train but she didn't expect the train to arrive punctually.

After I dropped Wendall off, I carried on to the clinic. I saw flooded roads, the colour of tea, people running for cover. The thunder claps sounded like someone was demolishing your house while you were in it, each roll booming like felled timber. I considered giving Talisa driving lessons and a car. If public transport was reliable, there would have been no ride, no Wendall, no grave-digging. All this would have been monsoon rainwater under the bridge.

At twenty to twelve, I opened the cupboard and removed the jiffy bag. I put it in my raincoat's inner pocket. I told Shue Ling to shut the clinic for a short while – I had to dash.

THE VIEW OF THE green Pulai mountains was shrouded by the rain. I passed the farms, inhaled the acrid whiff from the coffee plantations. Acres and acres of oil palm estates around me were replacing more virgin jungle for biofuel. When Wendall grew up, it would be gone. Our jungles, which were millions of years old, were being fed into our petrol tanks.

I listened to the slish-slash of the windscreen wipers. Lightning split the dark sky, so bright it was a momentary beam of searchlight on the car. I counted the seconds in between the lightning and the thunder roll, one... two... three... every second represented a mile.

I drove past my old school again, the basketball courts outside as wet as a lake. Traffic was slow. Broken down cars, their hazard lights flashing, hogged the roadside like swamp logs. Black clouds of mosquitoes over the windscreen were swept by the rain and wind, like out-of-control bin bags. Stray dogs, limping and mangy, hovered under angsana trees. Broken umbrellas, plastic bags, takeaway cartons, polystyrene cups flew like winged creatures. This was what our planet was being turned into – rubbish.

I passed the timber mills, Coffin Lane and the car workshop garages. Dead animals floated down the Segamat river. Everything I was so familiar with was everywhere. This was home, even if I didn't feel at home. Did I want to leave all this? Should I take my family and escape like beasts?

No. Everything I hate is here.

TALISA SAT ON our porch bench, waiting with her folded umbrella. She looked serene. Had I been the one in this marriage who was always choleric, while she, who had come from wilderness, was eternally unruffled? After my conversation with

Ian, I concluded that maybe I was the only man who had ever found her beautiful. Beauty was a lonely place. When she saw my car pull up, a big frown came over her. She jumped up. I pressed the remote which opened the gate. I drove onto the driveway.

'I've called the taxi!' she mouthed to me, with her hand on her chin, making the universal telephone gesture.

'Cancel it!' I shouted.

'What?' She mouthed. I beckoned her to get in the car. 'We're going to get Wendall from nursery,' I said loudly, but she didn't hear because she had started walking over to the passenger side. It had been a long time since I asked a girl with a money belt to get in the car. I leant over and opened her door. She got in and as she did before, put on her seatbelt automatically, expecting to be driven off straightaway. But I didn't drive off straightaway.

'How would you like to pack those fake Louis Vuitton bags?' I mused.

'Where are we going?' She looked at me, surprised. A slow smile.

I didn't know the answer myself. She undid her seatbelt. It slithered back into its hollow. She bent towards me, like a flower, and kissed me. My heart pounded in surprise at the unclouded memory of our first kiss. Tender and new, like a shoot, but how it grew wild. I got entangled. She put her hand on my face, her forearm resting on my shoulder. Her tattoo. *Her* story. History.

The sky had transformed into a kind of sea. Each drop of rain a miracle, each melting into another, until at last, the distant mountains seemed to vanish.

GLOSSARY

Word/phrase	Language	Meaning
agom	Iban	carved figures on sticks on the road to the rice farm and the longhouse loft to guard the stored padi
alamak	Malay	*(exclam.)* oh dear
amah	Cantonese (Chinese)/Hokkien (Chinese)	traditional bondmaid servant
ang ku kueh	Hokkien (Chinese)	A red tortoise cake is a small round or oval shaped Chinese pastry with soft sticky glutinous rice flour skin wrapped around a sweet green mung bean filling in the centre.
ang moh	Hokkien (Chinese)	*(Sl.)* white person (lit. "red-haired")
ang pao	Hokkien (Chinese)	red packet (auspicious cash gift)
angmoh gwee	Hokkien (Chinese)	*(Sl.) (Derog.)* white person (lit. "red-haired devil")
antu	Iban	spirit
antu nulong	Iban	ancestral spirit
attap	Iban/Malay	thatch made of palm fronds of the *Nypa fruticans* or Nipa palm
baya	Iban	crocodile
bejalai	Iban	a journey or expedition undertaken by men with the intent of acquiring material profit or social prestige, a type of coming-of-age customary wandering
bilek	Iban	room
bomoh	Malay	witch doctor
bunga terung	Iban	eggplant flower tattoo, basic achievement tattoo
compound	Malay-English	estate or land surrounding house

diam	Malay	*(impolite)* shut up
dukun	Malay	witch doctor
Gawai Antu	Iban	Festival of the Departed Souls
gereja	Iban/Malay	church (from the Dutch *kerk*)
gila	Malay	insane, mad
guanxi	Mandarin (Chinese)	connections, contacts
gwailo	Cantonese (Chinese)	*(Sl.) (Derog.)* devil bloke
jalai-jalai	Iban	leisurely walk, stroll
jalan	Malay	way, road, path, walk
kacau	Malay	annoy
kaki	Malay	connections, contacts
kampung	Iban/Malay	village
kawi	Iban/Malay	monkey orange tree or *Strychnos innocua*
kaya	Hokkien (Chinese)/Malay	coconut and pandan jam (made with leaves of *Pandanus amaryllifolius* or the screwpine plant*)*
kaypoh	Hokkien (Chinese)	*(Sl). (Derog.)* Busybody
kek wa	Hokkien (Chinese)/Malay	chrysanthemum flowers
kena tangkap	Malay	get caught, got caught
kenyalang	Iban	rhinoceros hornbill
kopi	Iban/Malay	coffee
kulat si'ang	Iban	edible red mushrooms
labi-labi	Iban/Malay	river turtle
lallang	Malay	blade of grass, a weed
lelong	Iban/Malay	auction
lesong	Iban	long pestle to grind rice
manang	Iban	shaman
naga	Iban	dragon of the underworld
nayap	Iban	courtship
ngajat	Iban	a traditional dance
orang asli	Iban/Malay	indigenous people
Orang Minyak	Malay	*(lit.)* "Oil Man", fabled, legendary well-greased streaker
padi	Malay	rice grain
parang	Malay	machete
pasar malam	Malay	night market

periok kera	Iban/Malay	*(lit.)* "monkey pot" ie.pitcher plant for cooking rice in *(Nepenthes rajah)*
pua	Iban	wings, blanket
pua kumbu	Iban	magic or sacred wings or blanket
roti bakar	Iban/Malay	toast
ruai	Iban	reception lounge, living room, hall
ruding	Iban	mouth harp
semangat	Iban	gusto
siamang	Malay	native arboreal tailless black-furred gibbon *(Symphalangus symdactylus)*
song irang	Iban	traditional bamboo shoot tattoo symbolising connection between plant life and fertility
sumpit	Iban/Malay	blowpipe
surat-surat	Iban/Malay	letters
syce	Hokkien (Chinese)	*(lit.)* "drive car", driver, chauffeur
tai fung	Cantonese (Chinese)	*(lit.)* "big wind", typhoon
Tali Nyawa	Iban/Malay	*(lit.)* Rope of life, stylised and circular coming-of-age tattoo
tanju	Iban/Malay	verandah or deck
tau tepang	Iban	*(lit.)* "person with the evil eye who ruins everything and anything he looks at", pariah, outcast of society, nuisance.
tempurung	Iban/Malay	large terracotta rice urn
tuai rumah	Iban	headman, head of household or longhouse
tuak	Iban	homebrewed traditional rice wine or liquor
yang	Mandarin (Chinese)	as in yin yang, yang being positive, masculine, bright cosmic force, yin being negative, feminine, dark cosmic force

ADVANCE COMMENTARIES

(We suggest you read these after you have read the book to avoid learning the plot.)

After twenty-four years in Hong Kong, I now live in Johor Bahru, Malaysia. I think I can state that it is not exactly a centre of literary activity and judging by the number of half-finished housing projects scattered about this rambling semi-urban landscape, not exactly what one would consider a hive of frantic energy of any kind. So a novel written by someone who can claim to be "Bangsa Johor" (Johor Citizen) is quite an event. One would imagine that Johor would put out some flags somewhere, but perhaps not. Malaysian friends repeatedly tell me things like "Malays don't like to read", despite them having bookshops with a surprisingly wide range of choice. Though given that a fair number of the Malay language books seem concerned with Islam and various conspiracy theories, perhaps it is just the "novel" that they do not like to read, or write. Which does make *Cry of the Flying Rhino* worth a look.

Another reason is to discover what a Flying Rhino is, so I will not spoil it by telling you. Building up suspense and tension is what the whole plot edifice is about. Even though things are never about what you might think they are about even if they are about them! I'm sure Father Ted must have said something like that about a book? If he didn't, he should have. And I am sure, given the novel's number of references to Father Ted and other TV shows and films, it would have been mentioned.

Most people interested in this region, apart from Malaysians, will have read Anthony Burgess's three expat novels par-excellence, The Malay Trilogy. It was banned in Malaysia for reasons that are far from apparent when one reads the book. It is a warmly told tale of the end of British rule and the various cultural confusions among the Brits and the locals that ensue. Its narrative, one assumes, must have contradicted the newly formed Malaysian federation's preferred narrative of what it means to be a Malay.

Cry of the Flying Rhino is interestingly more "Bangsa Johor" than "Malay", which I suppose also contradicts the preferred narrative. The main characters are Iban and Dayak, Chinese and Scottish, which at the same time reminds one that the bumiputra (Sons of the Soil) are not all Malay, and suggests that the colonial heritage – as we Brits call the imperial shake down of the natives – is still working its way through the cultural movements of the country. Ethnic and cultural purity for any modern state seems impossible and only desired by those who have no issue with slow Internet connections. This wider concept of Malaysia's cultural landscape beyond the idea of Malaysia for the Malays, fits in nicely with the cultural nuances of Johor Bahru, which has a Sultanate that has been promoting a concept of citizenship that is multi-cultural since the 1920s, though not necessarily a particularly democratic one.

This might make the Flying Rhino's cry into a political statement of some sort, but the novel is a tale of accidental murder and half-baked blackmail schemes, which might sound like typical S.E. Asian politics, but instead the story told is a sort of tropical "Fargo" with characters who go along to get along in the depths of provincial Segamat and up-river Sarawak, where an Iban longhouse houses a pirate DVD factory rather than the trophy heads collected by one's grandparents. There is an amiable incompetence that afflicts everyone, and perhaps a lesson that one does not take a blowpipe to a gunfight.

The gentle satire of the story feels very much in line with the ironical shrug and sigh that Malaysians often display when talking about their country. It is a rich land with a slow tropical pace that the newly air-conditioned urban population is beginning to find just too slow. Even so, the world of designer bags and shoes that grips the main female character is perhaps not quite as exciting to her as the Iban world of snake spirits and magical tattoos that mean a lot more than just decoration! And at the end of the novel, one is left suspecting that the Doctor's new wife with her shotgun skills and ever-present call of the jungle still has a few more surprises left for him.

Tell a Singaporean that you live in Johor Bahru and they will always commiserate and warn you to be careful. It is seen as the badlands of the tough neighbourhood that Singapore's Lee Kwan Yew once said Singaporeans lived in. The inhabitants of Johor Bahru will poopoo this as nonsense, then delight in telling you of some outrageous house break-in or car-jacking. *Cry of the Flying Rhino* revels in this attitude and takes subtle pride in the cultural incoherence, blind-eyedness, and joie de indolence that everyone lives in. Given that the bodies in Malaysia seem to stay buried in the novel's rubber plantations of pistol-packing Scottish colonial throw-backs, a certain amount of give and take in one's relationships is required for the sake of harmony. This is the message of the book. Or perhaps the message is that tattoos are only cool if hammered into your arm by a less than hygienic shaman giving you a permanent record of your achievements in life. Either way, it is definitely worth riding along with Dr Benjie's car crash of a life along some of the lesser travelled pot-holed roads and rivers that the Malaysian Tourist Board does not include in their brochures.

Lawrence Gray,
author of the novels, *Adam's Franchise* and *Cop Show Heaven* and the short story collection, *Odds and Sods*

*

Ivy Ngeow's first novel, *Cry of the Flying Rhino,* is written in a lyrical style infused with Borneo folklore, Iban dreams, and peppered with startling fresh similes and metaphors both illuminating and culturally apt. She has an eye for rich telling detail and a deft ear for dialogue, with added ability to use local dialect that feels not only authentic but easy to read.

Told from three viewpoints, Ngeow has created a colourful cast of characters for a her plot-driven novel: Benjie Lee, a clueless, spoiled Chinese General Practitioner pummelled into marrying his part-time assistant, after a misguided tryst that led to her pregnancy; Talisa, a status conscious, tattooed Sarawakian beauty with a dark, mysterious past, fully capable of committing murder to save the ones she loves; Ian, Talisa's combative and crass adopted father, a tight-fisted, Scottish plantation owner used to doing things his way, using violence if necessary; Bernard, an underfunded, misunderstood, botanist-cum-missionary who takes under his wings a pair of ex-cons; Watan, a pirate-DVD film maker with an ambitious plan to finance his travels; and Minos, trying to make sense of the ten years that he lost after being falsely accused of murder by Talisa's mother.

From the Borneo jungle to Segamat, Johor, their lives clash in a climatic blackmail scheme that was doomed to fail, yet, ironically, succeeded to make Benjie finally appreciate his wife and her hidden talents and their loveless child. It also gave Bernard the much-needed funds for his longhouse school in the middle of the jungle....Funds that Minos had to pay back – with Bernard's blessing – from his pirated CDs and DVDs.

With all of their debts and obligations seemingly wiped clean by salvation and a bit of fortuitous luck, Bernard and Minos and Benjie and Talisa can continue on with their lives, doing more good than harm, in their separate worlds in both East and West Malaysia.

Robert Raymer
Sarawak, Malaysia,
author of *Lovers and Strangers Revisited*

*

With *Cry of the Flying Rhino*, the multi-talented Ivy Ngeow has accomplished several feats all at once. Sure, she has written a well-paced and well-oiled thriller which keeps a reader smoothly glued to the pages. Indeed, she has crafted a clever plot-line, yet it is replete with multifarious extra social and cultural brain teasers, which cause a reader to pause and reflect on issues of colonisation and cultural usurping, while at the same time being impelled and compelled to keep reading. More, for me, she has also viscerally captured so well the ambience of living in Malaysia and its neighbouring countries, in Borneo especially. When reading this vivid and vibrant novel, I am immediately thrust back into the jungles, the small towns, the sweaty heat, the barrage of animal noises, the pungent smells and tropical odours, Ngeow has so well depicted throughout.

Vaughan Rapatahana, poet, literary critic, essayist and novelist, spent several years in Brunei Darussalam and has extensively toured much of Borneo, as well as peninsula Malaysia

~~~

*

THE INTERNATIONAL PROVERSE PRIZE

The Proverse Prize, an annual international competition for an unpublished single-author book-length work of fiction, non-fiction, or poetry, the original work of the entrant, submitted in English (translations are welcome) was established in January 2008. It is open to all who are at least eighteen on the date they sign the entry form and without restriction of nationality, residence or citizenship.

Founded by Gillian and Verner Bickley, the objectives of the prize are: to encourage excellence and / or excellence and usefulness in publishable written work in the English Language, which can, in varying degrees, "delight and instruct". Entries are invited from anywhere in the world.

PREVIOUS WINNERS OF THE PROVERSE PRIZE

Rebecca Tomasis, "Mishpacha – Family" (novel)
Laura Solomon, "Instant Messages" (young adult novella)
Gillian Jones, "A Misted Mirror" (novel)
David Diskin, "The Village in the Mountains" (novel)
Peter Gregoire, "Article 109" (novel)
Sophronia Liu, "A Shimmering Sea" (sketches)
Birgit Linder, "Shadows in Deferment" (poetry collection)
James McCarthy, "The Diplomat of Kashgar" (biography)
Philip Chatting, "The Snow Bridge and Other Stories"
Celia Claase, "The Layers Between" (essay / poetry collection)
Lawrence Gray, "Adam's Franchise" (novel)
Gustav Preller, "Curveball: Life never comes at you straight"
(novel)

Victor E. Apps, "The Perilous Passage of Princess Petunia Peasant" (young adult novella)
Rupert Kwan Yun Chan, "Chocolate's Brown Study in the Bag" (autobiography)
Sally Dellow, "Wonder, Lust & Itchy Feet" (poetry collection)
Patricia Glinton-Meicholas, "Chasing Light" (poetry collection)
Lawrence Gray, "Odds and Sods" (short story collection)
Patricia W. Grey, "Death has a Thousand Doors" (novel)
Emily Ho, "Memoirs of an Ice-Cream Lady"
Henrik Hoeg, "Irreverent Poems for Pretentious People"
L.W. Illsley, "Astra and Sebastian" (young adult epic poem)
Akin Jeje, "Smoked Pearl: Poems of Hong Kong and Beyond"
Lelawattee Manoo-Rahming,
"Immortelle and Bhandaaraa Poems"
James Norcliffe, "Shadow Play"(poetry collection)
Jan Pearson, "Red Bird Summer" (novel)
Jan Pearson, "Tiger Autumn" (novel)
Jan Pearson, "Black Tortoise Winter" (novel)
Jason S Polley, "refrain" (poetry collection)
Jason S Polley, "cemetery miss you"
Shahilla Shariff, "Life-Lines" (poetry collection)
Laura Solomon, "University Days" (young adult novella)
Laura Solomon, "Hilary and David" (novel)
James Tam, "Man's Last Song" (novel)
Dennis Wong, "Revenge From Beyond" (novel)

THE PROVERSE POETRY PRIZE (SINGLE POEMS)
This international prize was founded in 2016.
An inaugural anthology of selected entries, "Mingled Voices",
was published in 2017.

FIND OUT MORE ABOUT OUR AUTHORS, BOOKS, EVENTS AND LITERARY PRIZES

Visit our website: www.proversepublishing.com

Visit our distributor's website: https://www.chineseupress.com

Follow us on Twitter
Follow news and conversation: twitter.com/Proversebooks>
OR
Copy and paste the following to your browser window and follow the instructions: https://twitter.com/#!/ProverseBooks

"Like" us on www.facebook.com/ProversePress

Request our free E-Newsletter
Send your request to info@proversepublishing.com.

Availability
Most titles are available in Hong Kong and world-wide from our Hong Kong based Distributor, The Chinese University of Hong Kong Press, The Chinese University of Hong Kong, Shatin, NT, Hong Kong SAR, China.
Email: cup-bus@cuhk.edu.hk
Website: <www.chineseupress.com>.

All titles are available from Proverse Hong Kong, http://www.proversepublishing.com
and the Proverse Hong Kong UK-based Distributor.

Stock-holding retailers
Hong Kong (Growhouse, Bookazine)
Singapore (Select Books),
Canada (Elizabeth Campbell Books),
Andorra (Llibreria La Puça, La Llibreria).

Orders from bookshops in the UK and elsewhere.

Ebooks
Many of our titles are available also as Ebooks.

www.ingramcontent.com/pod-product-compliance
Lightning Source LLC
Chambersburg PA
CBHW051336020726
47501CB00007B/2109